In memory of Colin Moore Ewan,

my wonderful dad

27 June 1942–19 August 2018

A WINDOW BREAKS

C. M. EWAN

PAN BOOKS

First published 2019 by Pan Books

This paperback edition published 2022 by Pan Books
an imprint of Pan Macmillan
The Smithson, 6 Briset Street, London EC1M 5NR
EU representative: Macmillan Publishers Ireland Ltd, 1st Floor,
The Liffey Trust Centre, 117–126 Sheriff Street Upper,
Dublin 1, D01 YC43
Associated companies throughout the world
www.panmacmillan.com

ISBN 978-1-0350-0235-1

1 3 5 7 9 8 6 4 2

A CIP catalogue record for this book is available from the British Library.

Typeset in Celeste by Palimpsest Book Production Limited, Falkirk, Stirlingshire
Printed and bound by CPI Group (UK) Ltd, Croydon, CR0 4YY

Sparkles in the dark. They're the last thing Michael remembers. The glitter-dazzle of tiny beads of windscreen glass flying towards him, stinging his face.

And before that, a weightless sensation. Like he's an astronaut tumbling through space. Like he's somewhere – anywhere – other than this place. This reality.

Then the jerk and bite of the seat belt. The savage, wrenching pull.

Michael can feel himself pivoting forwards into the airbag – the insides of him still accelerating – as the belt strains to pull him back, impossibly, against the forces of gravity. Back, out of this moment. Back, to the world Michael knows with absolute certainty he is leaving. Back, to a place in which nobody goes this fast, or stops this abruptly, without everything stopping with them.

1

Driving scares me. I get nervous. Edgy. Itchy with guilt.

It didn't used to be this way. I can remember singing along, carefree, to classic rock tracks on the car stereo. Holding Rachel's hand on romantic trips away. Or my weekend Dad Taxi Service, transporting the kids in happy chaos from soft plays to birthday parties, then later to the local cinema and teenage discos.

But things change, and today, our family Volvo felt like a cage filled with my worst thoughts and fears. Thoughts about Michael. About Rachel and Holly. About what had happened to us in London and what lay ahead.

The wipers beat side to side in the drizzle. Scotland was wild and blurred. The only noise was the whine of the engine and the hiss of tyres on wet asphalt. Silence crept out of the vents like a toxin.

I squeezed the steering wheel in my hands and glanced again at Holly – that's my thirteen-year-old daughter – in the rear-view mirror. A scorching hot needle pierced my heart. Four days since the attack and Holly looked like a grenade had gone off in her face.

Her nose was swollen and discoloured, the bridge badly bruised beneath the strips of white sticking plaster that criss-crossed it, her nostrils rimed with dried blood. The puffy skin beneath her eyes was a deep mulberry colour, fading to yellowish gooseberry at the sides.

Holly locked on to my gaze and held it with eyes like shattered marbles – trying to reassure me, I guessed – and something inside me ripped and came loose.

My daughter has gymnastics training twice a week. She plays hockey on Saturday mornings. To watch her sprint across a field of AstroTurf is to see a warrior princess intent on scalping a sworn enemy. I'd always thought of her as fearless, but here she was, staring back at me, trying to appear strong when she was so clearly hurt and upset.

My throat burned. It stung me to see Holly like this but it stung even more when she tried on a brave smile that didn't fit her quite right, then immediately winced with pain.

I blinked and my mind flashed on the alley.

Hearing Holly's fractured scream. Seeing the man in the hoodie lash out. Watching Holly fall backwards, knowing I couldn't get to her in time.

My lungs cramped. My eyes felt hot and scrubbed. My fingers knotted into fists on the wheel. In all the things I do know (not a lot) and don't know (so much) about fatherhood, one thing I can tell you is that seeing your child in danger is about as horrendous as it gets. I had no way of knowing if Holly would ever fully get over the trauma, but I already knew it was something I would never forget.

Next to me, Rachel stared forwards with a far-off expression – the one that told me she was really looking deep inside herself. She must have felt my eyes on her because she turned to me with a vague, distracted smile.

My wife is beautiful. Always will be. But she'd lost too much weight over the past eight months and now, in the dreary, early afternoon light, she looked pale and drained, her normally lush brown hair limp and mussed. I could have kidded myself it was the 6 a.m. start, or the hours of driving the previous day, but I knew it was much more than that.

'Did you say something?' she asked me.

'No. Just looking at you.'

In the past, Rachel might have played along, flirted back, but now her brittle smile only emphasized how thin and hollowed out her face had become. 'You always were easily distracted.'

'It helps to have something worth being distracted by.'

'Tom.' She shook her head, sighed. 'Don't, OK?'

'Too much?'

She jutted her chin towards the world outside the windscreen. 'I don't like these conditions a whole lot.'

'Early June in the Highlands. Just as well I packed my sunscreen.'

Yeah, so I was trying too hard and we both knew it. But I needed to. With the way things had gone between us lately, it was better than not trying at all.

'Do you want me to drive?' Rachel asked. 'Are you tired?'

Rachel knows how I feel about driving. I know she feels the same way. So it meant a lot to me that she offered, even as I understood how relieved she was when I shook my head no.

And yes, I was tired. Tired of asking myself questions I couldn't answer. Tired of wondering for the hundredth time what Rachel was thinking and if it had been a mistake to come all this way.

'We could take a break?' My wife used to be the decisive one in our relationship. Or – to get a little colloquial here – she wore the trousers in our marriage. I was always fine with that. Now, though, I couldn't help noticing how many of her statements were framed as questions, or how often she deferred to me or Holly. 'Holly, would you like that?'

'Mum, I'm fine. Really.'

'Are you sure? I can give you more codeine?'

'When we get there, maybe. It's not too bad at the moment.'

Rachel hummed, unconvinced, and looked off into the spiralling drizzle. She touched a finger to her neck, tracing loops over her skin.

Another flash on the alley.

The hooded man yanking hard on Rachel's hair. The knife blade at her throat. And that disabling look Rachel had given me. Pleading. Scared. Lost.

Hot sweat broke across my shoulders and back. My hands almost slipped from the wheel. And I found myself – not for the first time – wishing I had the power or the strength of will to scrub disturbing images from my mind.

A road sign blipped by. Our turning for the unnamed road towards Loch Lurgainn was coming up. I hit the indicator and negotiated the turn. The satnav predicted a journey time of thirty-nine minutes until we reached our destination on the west coast.

I rolled my shoulders, cracked my neck. Normally Rachel hates it when I do that, but today she didn't say anything and the quiet between us pressed out against the windows of the car like an expanding gas. I felt a pang as I thought about reaching out to her with the words she needed to hear.

But it had been too long now since I'd known what those words were. For weeks, Rachel had been telling me we needed to talk, bugging me to make the time. I'd been dodging and evading her, feeling too weak and too scared to hear what she had to say. And now, maybe, it was too late.

Behind us, Holly pulled some slack into her seat belt and leaned down to nestle her head on Buster, our chocolate Labrador. Buster is big and soppy, with a thick, lush coat and dopey brown eyes it's impossible to resist. We brought him home from a rescue centre when the kids were small and there are still times when he acts like he's afraid we'll send him back. Maybe that's why he's the most loyal dog I've ever known.

A white van hummed by, flinging spray across the windscreen. In the distance, jagged peaks cut into the gloomy sky like some dystopian terrain. We passed tan and green fields scattered with sheep, swathes of dewy woodland, remote coastal lochs.

I was just reaching for the radio – anything to fill the silence – when the speakers buzzed and crackled as my mobile phone began chirping over the hands-free system. The number was unrecognized.

I pressed a button on the steering wheel, waited for the call to connect.

'Mr Sullivan? Constable Baker. I wanted to update you on some developments.'

My heart lurched and I traded a worried look with Rachel. *Should we do this on speaker?*

'It's OK, Dad.' Holly sat up and leaned forwards between our seats. 'I keep telling you both I'm OK.'

Rachel hitched her shoulders and gave me a cautious, yes-no tilt of her head, like she didn't know what was best for sure, but maybe on balance it wouldn't be such a bad thing for Holly to hear.

I waited. The Volvo droned onwards. Finally, I cleared my throat. 'Have you found the man who mugged us?'

'Not yet. We've had some luck with CCTV. We have footage of a man who matches the description you gave us running away from the area. He's seen carrying what could be your briefcase.'

My phone buzzed and the audio cut out for an instant. A text message had come in, but I didn't check it right now.

'Can you track him?'

'We lose sight of him near Leicester Square.'

A cold stab of disappointment. I let the information sink in. It was odd picturing the man in the hoodie in such a public area. In my mind he was a figure from the shadows.

'How is that possible?'

'It's not like on TV, Mr Sullivan. Footage doesn't always link up. Some cameras we don't have access to.'

Rachel sighed and shook her head, arching an eyebrow with a cynical look that seemed to ask me, *What did you expect?*

Truth is, I hadn't expected much. Perhaps not even this call. As a family, we haven't had the best of experiences with the police in the past – hence Rachel's attitude. And I knew the Met were busy. I knew they had countless new incidents to deal with each day.

An idea I'd had before nagged at me again. Maybe I should ask my boss, Lionel, to pull some strings with his contacts on the force. But what were the chances of anyone catching the mugger? Maybe it would be better to put it all behind us.

I was still thinking it through when Baker resumed talking.

'There is one thing we should have discussed, Mr Sullivan. You told me you didn't recognize the man who attacked you.'

That wasn't what I'd said. Not exactly. I'd told him I couldn't see the man clearly because of his hooded top and the pair of tan tights he'd been wearing over his face. But it was close enough.

'Well, what I didn't ask was if there could be anyone you know who might want to harm you or your family.'

'You don't think this was random?'

'I'm asking, do you have any enemies at all, Mr Sullivan? Does your wife?'

This was crazy. 'No. No enemies. There's nobody I can think of who might want to hurt me or my family. I'm just a lawyer. My wife's a GP.'

'Forgive me, Mr Sullivan. But there is the matter of your son.'

Suddenly, an oncoming delivery truck seemed to hurtle towards us too fast.

I veered into the side of the road. Stamped on the brakes.

My heart slammed into my throat.

'I understand he was killed in a road traffic incident,' Baker pressed.

The truck hammered by. I watched it wobble away in my side mirror. Our Volvo was stationary now and I didn't make any effort to drive on.

Silence again.

Rachel gave my hand a quick squeeze and reached past me to flick on the hazard lights. The indicators flashed and clicked. She smiled weakly and leaned towards the speaker. When she spoke, I could hear the strain in her voice.

'What does that have to do with anything?' she asked.

'There was another victim, Mrs Sullivan. A young woman.'

Without Holly in the car, I might have slumped forwards and banged my head against the steering wheel.

That cage I mentioned? This was the one memory in particular I'd been trying *not* to think about.

Eight months ago, our son, Michael, was killed driving my Audi in a wooded area several miles from our home. He was only sixteen. Not old enough to drive legally yet. He took my car joyriding. It was a wet night. The road was greasy. Michael went too fast, slewed off on a tight corner and hit a tree.

The post-mortem revealed that he died instantly. So did Fiona Connor, his girlfriend. They'd been going out just over a year.

There are still dark moments – many times each day – when the horror of what Michael did washes over me and tugs me down, like being pinned by a black wave. It was bad enough that he took my car without permission. That he drove without a licence. That he was reckless with his own life and the lives of the other motorists on the road that night.

But to kill Fiona too. To snuff out the life of a fifteen-year-old girl with a loving family and her whole future ahead of her was much worse than that. It was unforgivable.

This was where Rachel and I differed. This was the jagged

fault line that ran beneath our marriage. Whenever I thought of Michael now, it was hard for me to do so without my memories being eclipsed by an overwhelming sense of shame.

Rachel, though, refused to acknowledge the bad in our son. She remained convinced that Michael had simply been unlucky when his one, singular act of teenage rebellion resulted in such total devastation. It was a view that, in my mind, went beyond maternal loyalty to an act of wilful self-delusion.

'Mr and Mrs Sullivan?' Baker prompted.

Somehow, I recovered the ability to speak. 'That's a totally separate matter. Fiona's family know how sorry we are.'

This time, my mind flashed on Fiona's memorial service. I remembered how Fiona's father had spun in his pew at the front of the church when we'd tried to slip in the back. How he'd stood, red-faced and stupefied, then shouted and raged, storming down the aisle to chase us out. Rachel and I had run back to our car and locked ourselves in. Rachel hadn't stopped shaking for hours.

Did that make him an enemy? I didn't think so. He was just someone else who'd been wrecked by that night.

'I'm sorry to have brought it up,' Baker said. 'I hope you can understand. It's just—'

'What else?'

'We've submitted the knife for forensic analysis. With any luck, we'll get something from that.'

Unlikely. Our attacker had been wearing gloves. The tights he'd had on over his head would have prevented him from shedding any hairs.

I supposed there were other things I should be asking Baker but I couldn't think what those things might be. And I didn't want to cause Rachel or Holly any more distress.

I thanked him for the update and ended the connection.

Rachel turned to peer out her window, too late to hide the tears in her eyes. Holly laid down on Buster again and hugged him tight.

The hazard lights flashed. The wipers thumped.

In a daze, I picked up my phone and glanced at the screen. The text message was from Lionel.

Don't let your ego get in the way of fixing things with Rachel, Tom. Listen to what she has to say to you. Your marriage is too important. Take it from someone who knows.

2

We almost missed the turn-off for the lodge. Rachel was the one who spotted it. She pointed it out to me, then flattened her hand on the dash as I braked and the Volvo shimmied on loose dirt and damp.

The entrance was mundane. Just a ragged gap in a knotted hedgerow opening on to a steep rock and gravel driveway. A bleached wooden sign read: WEBSTER. PRIVATE ROAD.

I gunned the engine. The tyres slipped against the sudden loose gradient, then bit and clawed forwards, spitting soaked gravel out the back like it had been fed through a wood chipper.

At the top, we caught a glimpse of torn grey ocean beneath low grey rain clouds, then the track dipped towards a tall, ugly gate set in a shallow compression.

The gate was a surprise. It was formed of two slabs of green metal sheeting that had to be at least ten feet high. Extending from either side of it was a metal fence constructed from bevelled, green metal uprights. Lethal barbs ran along the top of the gate and the fence, splayed outwards and inwards. On the inner side of the fence, thick woodland trees pressed up against the perimeter. If I didn't know better, I could have believed we'd arrived at a remote army barracks.

Weird.

I slowed the Volvo next to a compact video camera and an intercom fitted to a short metal pole. The forest silence had that hear-a-pin-drop clarity to it as I buzzed down my window and leaned out to talk, but before I could speak I heard a low electric buzzing, followed by a metallic *clunk* as the gates trembled and separated and began to swing outwards on two tight arcs.

I tried to quell a small judder of surprise. Before we'd left London the previous morning, Lionel had asked me to text him our number plate. I guess now I knew why.

Rachel frowned at me, Holly looked up from her smartphone and Buster scrambled to his feet to take a peek at where we were. I switched off the wiper blades. The drizzle was light now. Barely even a mist.

'So . . .' Holly said. 'You think Lionel needs therapy, much?'

'Holly!'

'What, Dad? I'm just saying, after what happened to his wife . . .'

She left the rest unsaid but we were all thinking it. The gate and the fence were clearly excessive for such a remote location but, now that my own family had come under threat, I could easily understand why Lionel would prioritize his security.

I eased off on the brake and the Volvo started forwards, then gathered momentum as the drive fell away sharply. Behind us, the gate mechanism started up again, whirring and grinding, and Rachel glanced back over her shoulder to watch as the gates shuffled closed.

'OK?' I asked her.

Was that a shiver? 'I guess.'

Funny thing. Rachel was the one who'd pushed for us to come here but now I sensed some disquiet. Perhaps she was only now beginning to realize what had already occurred to me. Out here we would truly be on our own. There could be no more hiding from whatever we had to say to each other – or the awkward truths we might reveal.

The woodland trees pressed in on us, high limbs stretching out across the driveway and intertwining to partially blot out the sky. We splashed through muddy potholes and drainage gunnels. Then the slope flattened out and the track opened up into a wide gravel circle carved out between a towering ring of spruce, larch and pines.

'Dad? Is this really it?'

Lionel had called his place a lodge and in my mind I'd pictured something rustic and modest but nicely appointed. A kind of logger's cabin with rough-hewn planking and an open porch out front, or maybe a whitewashed croft with a thatched roof.

I couldn't have been more wrong.

On a spit of rocky land jutting out from the coast, in a tight clearing between the pines, was one of the most stunning properties I'd ever set eyes on.

It was tall and thin with an asymmetrical pitched roof, a fieldstone base and an elaborate timber and glass structure between. The timber was arched and vaulted, curved and bent, forming a complex latticework for the tinted glazing to fill. High up at the rear, a balcony ran across most of the upper floor. I could see patio furniture up there. A gas heater under a nylon cover.

The place had the appearance of a luxury ski lodge and if it had been situated on the slopes of Val d'Isère or Gstaad it would have been seriously impressive. Out here, hidden from view and alone in the Scottish wilderness, it was jaw-dropping.

'Holly, what do you think?'

'Pretty cool, Dad.'

'Rachel?'

'Breathtaking.'

We opened our doors and stepped out onto a carpet of crushed gravel and fallen pine needles. Fragments of rain scattered on the air. The wet woodland smell was intense.

I turned a full circle, drinking it in. The trees that surrounded us were densely packed, their trunks spearing upwards like telephone poles. Beneath the lush green canopy, a carpet of mulch and lichen undulated in humps and ridges, dissolving into impenetrable black. Somewhere close by I could hear the rustle of waves striking the shore.

'Buster!' Holly called. 'Come on!'

My heart contracted as I watched Buster bound out of the car and follow Holly towards the treeline. Take it from me, if anyone ever tells you dogs don't grieve, that person is lying. Buster continued to sleep on the bottom of Michael's bed for three months straight following his death. Rachel tells me she sometimes still finds him noodling around in there late at night, nudging the duvet as if searching for our son.

It's no exaggeration to say that having Buster around is the main reason Holly's been able to cope with Michael's death. She hugs him all the time. I've overheard her confiding in him. And Buster, in turn, has grown ever more protective of Holly. He follows her from room to room at home. He pines for her when she's at school. A psychologist would probably tell you that Holly leans on Buster in the way she does because she can no longer lean on Michael. I don't know if that's true but I do know the two of them share an unbreakable bond.

Footsteps on gravel.

A burly man was striding towards us from the front of the lodge. Buster turned and growled, then barked twice in rapid warning as Holly looked quickly down at the ground, hiding her face.

'Hello there, Sullivans.' His Scottish accent was as warm and smoky as good whisky. 'I'm Brodie.'

He was big and tall with wide shoulders and large hands. His brown hair was tightly curled, his face dominated by a bushy hipster beard. The plaid shirt he had on over beat-up jeans and hiking boots was pulled tight across his over-developed pecs and biceps. It wasn't the first time I'd set eyes on him, though we'd never spoken before.

'Hey, dog, how are you?' Brodie patted his thighs and beckoned to Buster, but it was only when Holly gave Buster a nudge with her foot and told him it was OK that he jogged over to sniff Brodie and be patted and fussed. 'Did you find the place easily enough?'

I told him we had and he straightened to lean forwards over Buster and shake my hand. His grip was fierce, his palms rough and abrasive, and I had to fight not to wince as he nearly crushed my fingers. His tough-guy act softened when he shook hands with Rachel. I noticed him give her a quick, appraising look and then glance down, as if shy. It was hardly the first time I'd seen Rachel have that kind of impact on a man, though lately it had been bothering me more than I wanted it to.

'Hello, missy.'

Brodie waved to Holly over by the trees. She was twisted at the waist, her shoulders rounded, like she was trying to blend in with the woods. Brodie made no comment about her injuries. He didn't stare. My guess was Lionel must have briefed him ahead of time and I was glad of it.

'That's Holly,' I explained. 'I'm Tom. My wife is Rachel.'

'Aye, it's good to meet you all. Holly, welcome to the most beautiful spot in all of Scotland. Help you with your bags there, Tom?'

'That's OK. We can manage.'

'It's not a problem. What I'm here for. And trust me, Lionel will check up with you on that. He hates it when I slack off.'

I knew the feeling.

Brodie snuck another quick look at Rachel, then strolled past me to open the Volvo's boot. He tucked Holly's holdall beneath his massive upper arm and reached in for Rachel's suitcase, lifting it out of the car like it was filled with nothing but air.

'You ready to see the place, Holly?'

My daughter – normally so talkative – shrugged without speaking. I felt a hollow sensation open up in my chest.

'You're going to love it. I promise. Want to walk with me?'

At first Holly didn't respond. I was pretty sure she was going to shake her head no. But then she glimpsed Buster, his jaws parted in a blissed-out smile, his tail beating enthusiastically against Brodie's leg.

'OK,' she said quietly.

'Excellent. Tom, you'll want to move your car over there.' Brodie used the hand holding Rachel's suitcase to point out a timber carport with a vaulted ceiling. 'That'll keep the pine needles and sap off it.'

The carport had spaces for two vehicles. A mud-splattered Toyota Land Cruiser was occupying the left-hand berth.

'That's my ride,' Brodie explained. 'But don't worry, I'll be out of here before you know it. I'm based near Lochinver.' He turned to Rachel. 'Ready?'

She nodded, smiling in warm encouragement, and I watched Brodie stride off with my wife, daughter and dog for company, then lunged into the boot for my own suitcase, still struggling to wrap my head around the idea of being here with my family, so far away from London. There were plenty of reasons for that, of course, but also . . . Lionel's *lodge*. Until four days ago, I hadn't known this place even existed.

The first I'd heard of it was at a glitzy charity function in a Mayfair hotel. The fundraiser was being held in aid of Justice For All, a foundation that seeks to educate and rehabilitate repeat offenders. Lionel hadn't just hosted and bankrolled the gala; he's also the founder and chairman of JFA. There are those who think Lionel only started JFA to burnish his political ambitions. As the CEO and owner of Webster Ventures – the UK's leading investor in tech start-ups and specialist engineering firms – he's a fabulously wealthy and influential man, and there's long been talk of him one day running for mayor. I know for a fact he has several Cabinet members on speed dial. But, call me naive, I happen to believe Lionel when he tells me he started the charity because of what happened to his wife.

I never met Jennifer. She was killed nine years ago, before I knew Lionel, in a horrific attack in their main residence, close to Regent's Park. Lionel was in Hong Kong on business at the time and the police theory was that Jennifer had disturbed a burglar. That theory was given credence when an original Degas – a bronze statue of a young ballerina – was discovered to be missing from Lionel's study on his return from Hong Kong. The police also had a suspect. A man called Tony Bryant had served time previously for aggravated burglary. He'd been released from prison just months before the crime and his fingerprints had been discovered at the scene.

But despite this credible lead, the case against Bryant had gone nowhere fast because the police had failed to locate him or recover the missing Degas. There were rumours Bryant had escaped to Spain. Lionel's belief – and, yes, maybe he's a little naive too – was that if Bryant had received the right kind of support and guidance after his first conviction, then Jennifer – the great love of Lionel's life – would still be alive today. Lionel had once told me that if Justice For All could help save just one person the heartache he himself had experienced, then it would all be worth it.

The truth? Much as I like and respect Lionel, I hadn't wanted to be at the gala. Not because JFA isn't a noble cause – it is – but because after what Michael had done . . . Well, let's just say that being there made me uncomfortable. The only reason I *did* go was to support Rachel. Lionel had asked her to help organize the event. She was giving a speech and I was pretty sure she'd be nervous about it.

But still, when I'd got there, Rachel had barely looked at me. I'd spent the first five minutes lurking by the buffet table, watching from across the room as a handsome young guy in a tux flirted with my wife, touching her arm, making her smile. Rachel, of course, looked extra crush-my-heart stunning in an elegant black dinner dress. Her chestnut-brown hair was up. I always loved it when she wore it that way. I watched her throw back her head and laugh at something the man said, and it wounded me to think that I couldn't remember the last time I'd made her laugh that way.

'Just a small point,' Lionel whispered as he sidled up to me, 'but I hear scientists now believe it's almost impossible to make a man's head explode simply by glaring at him.'

As well as being my boss, Lionel's also my friend and, it's fair to say, my mentor. I've been his head of legal affairs for six years now.

'Look at that guy,' I said. 'Do you think he even cares that she's married?'

'Do you?'

Lionel arched an eyebrow. Like the rest of him, it was immaculately groomed. His steel-grey hair was gelled into a severe side-parting, his dinner jacket expensively tailored. The banquet hall was filled with the great and good of London society, but in this crowd Lionel drew more spotlight than a movie star, and I was aware of several partygoers circling closer, trying to grab a few precious minutes with him.

'Hey. Low blow, Lionel.' I folded my arms and went back to glaring. 'Who is he?'

'You don't want to know.'

'Rich?'

'Now *that* you really don't want to know.'

I stared some more at Rachel and Mr Probably-A-Dot-Com-Millionaire. Uniformed waiting staff flitted to and fro with silver platters bearing champagne. A string quartet played in one corner. Another time, I might have been impressed by it all, but tonight I had other concerns.

'Look, Tom, why don't you ask Rachel to go away with you for the weekend, just the two of you together? I have a lodge, in Scotland. You could use it.'

I reared back and frowned. A Scottish lodge. It didn't sound very Lionel. A chic apartment in Paris, maybe. A brownstone in New York . . .

He smiled, as if he could read my mind. 'Only very few people know about it. It's where I go to recharge. Get off the grid. It's . . . well, remote isn't really the word. See that guy over there?'

Lionel pointed across the room to where a big man with a bushy beard and an ill-fitting tuxedo was standing awkward and alone, clutching too many canapés in one hand and tugging his shirt collar away from his throat with the other.

'His name's Brodie,' Lionel explained. 'He looks after the lodge for me. Until tonight, I'm not sure I've ever seen him without an axe in his hand. Why don't you do me a favour and go and ask him about the place? He could use someone to talk with and I really think it could be good for you and Rachel to spend some time there together.'

'It's kind of you, Lionel. But . . .' I shrugged. Nodded at my wife. 'I think we both know it's not going to happen. Besides, it's still too soon to leave Holly.'

'Is it?'

'You know it is.'

'Well, perhaps we should ask her about that . . .' He seized me by the arm and dragged me through the crowds in the direction of the bar.

'*Holly?*'

'Hey, Dad. Mum's sitter cancelled. And Lionel's been bugging me for, like, forever to come to this thing.'

At the mention of Rachel, I had to fight the urge to look round and find her again. Holly was perched on a stool, her bright pink smartphone in her hand. She was dressed in her school uniform – blue blazer, grey skirt, dark tights – and her frizzy brown hair was pulled into a ponytail. Like always, the smile she gave me pretty much melted my heart.

'How's the party?'

'I guess it's not *totally* lame.'

'This is what I love about your kid, Tom.' Lionel poked Holly in the side. 'She always brings the sunshine.'

'I suppose that's why you've been hanging around our house so much lately.' Holly rolled her eyes. 'Seriously, Dad. Your boss is actually kind of sweet. He's been making sure Mum and me are OK.'

'Has he now?'

It was hard to know what to do with that information. I knew Lionel was fond of my family. There were times when

I felt like he viewed us as a surrogate for the family he'd never had. And I'd lost count of the number of times he'd told me to get over myself and mend my relationship with Rachel. But still, it irritated me to think that he'd been dropping in on my wife and daughter without telling me. And I didn't exactly appreciate Holly's not-so-subtle reminder about how I'd let her and her mum down.

Lionel – clearly aware of how awkward this had suddenly become – began peering around the room for a distraction.

'How is Mum?' I asked Holly. 'Is she stressed about her speech?'

'Dad. Not cool.'

I held up my hands. Holly was right. One thing Rachel and I had both agreed on after I'd moved out of home was that our trial separation had to be as painless as possible for Holly. And that meant not putting her in the middle of things.

I was about to ask her about her school day instead when Lionel lunged out to grab someone standing behind me, pulling them forwards. He clapped a hand on my shoulder and spun me to face two police officers in full dress uniform.

'Tom Sullivan,' Lionel said. 'Meet Assistant Commissioner Richard Weeks. And you'll have heard of DCI Kate Ryan.'

I had. DCI Ryan had been all over the news recently, identified as the off-duty hero cop who'd stepped in when two moped thugs had almost pulled a pregnant woman under a bus as they tried to snatch her handbag. Footage of the incident had gone viral. Ryan had been lauded by celebrities and politicians alike. It was a good news story for the Met and a bunch of profile pieces had followed. Maybe I'm a cynic, but I don't think it hurt that Ryan was statuesque, fit and toned, with very short brown hair and sharp features. I could remember that her father had been a police officer, that she enjoyed outdoor pursuits, including sailing and climbing, that she'd suffered a bad fall while rock climbing the previous year but had swiftly returned to duty and, oh yeah, that she was currently single.

Assistant Commissioner Weeks seemed keenly aware of that last factoid. He was a good fifteen years older than Ryan with a severe buzz cut, a chiselled jawline and a no-nonsense demeanour, but from the way his hand had slipped off her lower back as we were introduced I sensed there was something more than strictly professional about their relationship.

'Mr Sullivan.' Weeks nodded, without a great deal of interest.

'Tom is my primary legal brain,' Lionel explained.

'For JFA?'

I glanced away a moment. Rachel must have moved because I couldn't see her or the man she'd been talking with. I wasn't sure whether to feel relieved or concerned about that.

'I pitch in where I can,' I mumbled.

'Well, it's a fine cause, Tom.' He pumped my hand. 'You should know that we at the Met appreciate everything JFA accomplishes.'

'And not simply because it makes our job easier,' Ryan added, with a wink.

She waited for the assistant commissioner to say something more, but before he could pick up on his cue the tinkling of a champagne glass cut through the noise in the room. Rachel was up on a dais. Next to her was a large colour portrait of Jennifer. For a fleeting moment our eyes locked, and Rachel gave me a fractured, almost apologetic smile. Then she hooked a strand of hair behind her ear and leaned towards a microphone.

'Ladies and gentlemen, many of you here tonight may know that my son, Michael, was killed on the second of October last year.'

A sympathetic murmur passed through the crowd. I swallowed hard and reached out for Holly's hand as Lionel clenched my shoulder. Far off to the side, I could see Brodie glancing over at us. I guessed Lionel had already primed him to come and talk to me about the lodge in case I didn't follow up on his suggestion.

'As you can imagine,' Rachel continued, 'Michael's death has been overwhelming for us as a family. And as his mum, it would be all too easy for me to believe his death was the only event of any real consequence that night. But I want to talk to you about . . .'

I tuned out. Not because I wasn't interested, but because my wife is first and foremost a doctor and it was no surprise to me that her speech leaned heavily on statistics. Mostly they were about how many crimes had been committed on the night of Michael's death by offenders with previous convictions. Which was sad, I knew, but in all honesty I was too busy marvelling at the way Rachel was able to keep it together while I was struggling to breathe. Michael's death had hit her so hard. There'd been days when the grief and depression had been so bad she could barely get out of bed. And now. Well. Suffice it to say my heart swelled with a mixture of sadness and pride as she neared the end of her speech.

'. . . There is just one final statistic I would like to tell you about,' she said, her eyes misting up as she found me in the crowd again. 'My wonderful son wasn't the only one to die that October night. A young man called James Finch, a two-time former offender, took his own life on the same evening. He was twenty-eight years old. He left behind his six-year-old daughter, Phoebe, and his partner of eight years, Janine. Justice For All couldn't help James, but with your kind generosity tonight we aim to guide other former offenders just like him towards a better life, a different future. And, speaking from the heart, I'd like to thank each and every one of you for your support.'

I wish I could tell you the story of that night ended there, on a bittersweet moment backed by the swell of applause as Rachel made her way through the crowds towards us – as we hugged and I kissed her cheek and we looked at one another for a beat too long. But instead Rachel had smiled warmly at Lionel, then reached over to Holly, teasing a strand of her hair between her fingers.

'Big speech is over, sweetheart. And it's a school night. Are you ready to head home now?'

Holly frowned. 'I thought you said it wouldn't look good for you to be the first to leave?'

'She did.' Lionel patted Rachel's arm and I felt a small jolt. I don't know what surprised me more. The casual intimacy that seemed to have grown up between my wife and Lionel, or the fact I hadn't seen it coming. 'And then *I* explained that it wouldn't look like anything because I've arranged for my car to be waiting for you in the alley behind the kitchen. You can sneak out that way. No one has to know.'

At first, Holly brightened. Then a flicker of doubt crossed her face. 'What about Dad?'

Rachel turned to me and tipped her head to one side. I could see the hurt and trepidation in her eyes. 'What do you say, Tom? Can we give you a lift to your new place? Maybe we could even fix a time to finally have that conversation?'

Perhaps it was wanting to get Rachel away from Lionel or the guy in the tux who'd been flirting with her. Maybe it was the hopeful look on Holly's face, or hearing Rachel talk about Michael. Whatever the reason, I said yes, fetched our coats and joined Rachel and Holly outside in the alley.

And then had come the mugging. The dizzying rush of breathless, desperate terror. As bad as it had been, it could have been so much worse if one of the kitchen staff hadn't stepped out through the swing door into the alley to smoke a cigarette. If they hadn't shouted for help until more staff emerged and the mugger ran away.

Strange how life works. Because standing there now in the woodland clearing, looking at Rachel and Holly, I couldn't help but wonder: what would have happened if I'd said no to going with them? How might things have been different for us? Would the mugger never have attacked? Held a knife to Rachel's throat or punched Holly's face? And – most crucial of all – would we be together at Lionel's lodge?

3

After I'd reversed our Volvo into the carport, I walked back to pick up my suitcase.

'Tom?' Rachel called to me. 'Wait until you see this.'

I lugged my suitcase over to join them and looked. And honestly? It was incredible.

Extending from the front of the lodge was a wooden deck that stretched way over the shallows of the coastal waters, framing a view out to sea that somehow tricked the eye into believing you were standing on the prow of an exclusive ocean liner.

A plastic leaf rake was propped against a railing to the far left. Judging by the mounds of fallen pine needles, twigs and other woodland debris close by, it looked as if Brodie had used it to clean the deck before our arrival. A flight of steps led directly into the water behind where the rake was resting.

I gently squeezed Holly's shoulder – her muscles were tight as guitar strings – and together we tracked the view along the coast. The treeline hugged the water's edge for as far as the eye could see, fringed by boulders and slivers of beach, interrupted every so often by rocky ridges and concealed inlets. The sea was an oily, mirrored grey that reflected the rain clouds overhead in much the same way as the giant wall of glass at the front of the lodge.

'How much of this is Lionel's land?' Rachel asked.

'Pretty much everything you can see and more,' Brodie told us. 'Nearest house is over two miles that way.' He pointed north. 'Nearest settlement approaching anything like a village is four miles beyond that. But save some of that view for later. The inside of this place isn't too shabby, either.'

He moved back and slid aside a door in the glass wall with a flourish, leading us into a vast living space that extended right up to the very apex of the roof and was flooded with light. There was a double-height mezzanine at the back of the room. The floating timber staircase that connected to it was set flush against the far wall and a huge modern art canvas was hanging above it. The opposite wall was dressed in grey slate and dominated by a futuristic log burner that was suspended from the ceiling and hovered over the oak timber flooring and the cow hide rug that had been laid in front.

Either side of the log burner were two L-shaped couches with blankets draped over them. Set back a little way was a wire-framed recliner covered in animal fur that was pointed towards the view. There was a telescope, and behind that a glass dining table with seating for more than a dozen guests. Back the other way and running along beneath the high mezzanine was a top-spec kitchen with white granite countertops and brushed aluminium appliances.

'Gee, I don't know, Brodie.' Rachel turned slowly. 'I suppose this will have to do!'

I should have been happy Rachel was sounding more like

herself. Since the attack on Holly she'd withdrawn from me again, to the point where it made me nervous. I knew that was why I'd been trying to force things in the car, and I couldn't help cringing at how my attempts at humour must have come over. Perhaps Lionel was right. Perhaps what Rachel needed was some space, a change of scenery. It was a reminder that our being here wasn't solely about Holly and the attack. Lionel had offered the lodge to me before that had happened for a reason.

I love my family. They mean everything to me. Moving out of home was the most difficult decision I'd ever made. And yes, it was selfish. I knew that. But I didn't do it because I wanted out of my marriage. I did it because I wanted Rachel to let me back *in.* I don't know. I guess I thought that by leaving I might jolt her into fighting for whatever was left of us. But now, perhaps, the mugging had jolted us both.

'Is that by somebody we should have heard of?' I pointed to the massive art canvas above the floating staircase. It featured a bright and colourful sphere made up of lots of multicoloured dots.

'Damien Hirst. You'll see some other stuff around too. Holly, want me to show you to your room?'

My daughter bit her lip and clenched her hands, looking to Rachel for help. Again, seeing her act so nervous and shy made it feel like there was a tiny chip of ice in my heart.

'I think Holly might prefer it if you just pointed it out to her for now,' Rachel said.

'You could come too?'

'I think I'm going to take a look around downstairs.'

'Aye, no problem. Holly, I'll carry these bags up and you can explore for yourself. Sound good?'

Holly nodded, still a little reluctantly, then lowered her hand to Buster. 'You wait here,' she whispered. 'I'll be back in a minute and we'll explore.'

Buster didn't like it. He watched Holly climb all the way up the stairs after Brodie, then collapsed in a heap with a grumping noise.

'Holly, you're just along on the right here.' Brodie set her holdall down by her feet. 'Door is on your left. Your parents are going to be down here at the other end of the mezzanine. Did you see the big balcony when you were pulling up?'

Holly gazed at him without speaking.

'It connects with one of the rooms down this way. I'm going to put your mum's suitcase in there. Your dad'll be just across the hall.'

Huh. So Brodie hadn't just been briefed about Holly's injuries. He also knew something about the situation between Rachel and me. I wondered how exactly Lionel had explained it. I wasn't sure that I could.

I looked at Rachel – she had her back to me – and felt my throat begin to constrict. Our bedroom arrangements were no real surprise, especially since we'd taken separate rooms at a Travelodge near Penrith the night before, but I still wondered if she felt the same ache of regret.

Above us, Brodie walked off, leaving Holly to grip hold of the polished metal railings fronting the lofty mezzanine and look out at the view. The vaulted space seemed to swallow her.

'Do you want me to come up with you?' I called to her.

'No, it's OK.'

'Wait until you see the swimming pool and spa,' Brodie shouted, from somewhere out of sight on the mezzanine. 'You'll love it.'

That word 'spa' seemed to hover in the air between Rachel and me like a note struck on a tuning fork. I studied my wife in the silence that followed, aware of a tingling heat spreading up my arms. I saw no sudden tensing of her neck, back or hands. No abrupt or agitated movements. She watched Holly duck and carry her bag away along the corridor, then turned to me with a smile that was willing, if a little wistful.

'Swimming pool?' she asked me.

It took me a moment to gather my voice. 'First I've heard of it.'

'Isn't this place amazing, Tom? I feel like I've stepped inside the pages of a glossy magazine.'

'It is pretty plush.'

'*Plush.* Come on, don't you feel it?' She reached out and brushed my hand with her fingers. Her eyes darted from side to side as she studied me. 'I think this is just what Holly needed. Us too. Don't you?'

Maybe. Maybe not. I really wished I could believe it. You have no idea how badly I wanted to tell Rachel what she wanted to hear. But right then all I could do was force a smile and nod robotically as my mind looped again on everything that had come between us and all that had led us here.

4

'Beer, Tom?'

Brodie was kneeling by the steps at the side of the deck with his shirtsleeves rolled up past his elbows, tugging on a length of fishing line knotted around a mooring post. A six-pack of ales bobbed to the surface. Brodie grabbed them and set them on the deck.

'Beats the fridge,' he told me. 'These are from a local brewery. You think Rachel would like one?'

'Later, probably. I think she just wants to spend time with Holly right now.'

And more to the point, I didn't want him going in search of Rachel again. I'd already caught him hanging around her on too many of my trips in from the car with the rest of our gear and groceries. Rachel had been polite but firm in deflecting most of his attempts at conversation. My guess was she didn't want me getting the hump about the attention he was paying her. I was doing my best to take it easy, but my patience was beginning to wear thin. If he didn't leave soon, I was going to have to say something.

I caught the can of beer he tossed my way and popped the lid. Icy suds frothed over my hand and wrist. Out towards the far horizon, rainwater twisted above the turbulent sea.

I couldn't see any ships out there, which was probably a good thing. The waves were so jagged they looked like something out of one of the picture books about pirates I used to read to Michael as a kid. He'd really loved those books, though probably not as much as I'd loved reading them to him.

'Won't be long until that lot hits,' Brodie said, indicating the rain clouds.

I nodded, listening to the waves gushing in under the deck and rattling back out over an unseen gravel shore. I pulled my mobile out of my pocket to check for messages and saw that I didn't have any.

'No signal?' I asked Brodie.

'Sorry, Tom. You'll need to drive two, three miles that way.' He pointed with his beer back the way we'd driven in. 'But there's Wi-Fi if you need to check emails. Code's by the fridge. Lionel couldn't stream movies to his home theatre without it now, could he?'

I had no idea there was a home theatre, let alone where I'd find it. I hadn't had time yet for the tour Brodie had given Rachel and Holly.

'How often does Lionel come up here?' I asked, slipping my phone away.

Brodie raised his beer can to his lips, monitoring me over the rim. 'Often enough to keep me occupied.'

'And when he's not here?'

He drank, swallowed, wiped the suds from his beard. 'I manage the estate, take care of the grounds and the lodge.'

'And the fence?'

'Aye, that too.'

'How far does it go on for?'

'Like I said, Lionel has a lot of land.'

'And it's all fenced?'

Brodie nodded vaguely and swirled the beer in his can, glancing out to sea without saying anything more. I suppose I shouldn't have been surprised. Lionel has a knack for encouraging discretion in his employees. And, like Holly had said, Jennifer's murder had made Lionel acutely aware of his own personal safety. I knew, for instance, that he hired close protection experts from time to time, especially if he was heading away on a foreign trip. He'd also put protocols in place that meant I needed two forms of ID just to get into my office.

'Holly's a great kid, by the way.' Brodie toasted me with his can and swigged more beer. 'Hope you don't mind my saying, but I heard about what happened to you after that party in London.'

'I guessed that you had.'

'Holly mentioned it to me just now as well. I think she wanted to explain about, you know.'

He circled his hand in front of his face and I rocked back as a vision of Holly being punched filled my head like a vibrant red slash of paint. Her nose had been broken. After we'd arrived at the nearest hospital in a blur of blood, shouts and panic, the A&E doctor had told us it would have to be reset. I could still hear the awful crunch and Holly's gargled scream; the thrashing of her body against the mattress. The memory made me feel ill.

'What did she say?' I asked Brodie, trying to keep my voice neutral.

'That some creep tried to mug you. That he hit her before you could do anything to stop him.'

'I guess that's one way of looking at it.'

'Is there another way?'

'No, probably not.'

But it was still a difficult thing for me to accept. When you stripped everything else away – the suddenness and speed of the attack, the fact the mugger had been armed with a knife and I hadn't been – I was still a father who'd failed to protect his daughter when it counted. Simple as that.

Brodie tapped a nail against his can of beer. 'When I was fourteen, there was a fair near my house.' He looked at me cagily. 'Came every year. Nothing special, but it seemed it to me. I kept on at my parents. When could I go and join my friends, you know?'

I nodded. I knew.

'It took most of the day but I broke them down. They finally said I could go. But I had to take my little sister, Ailish, with me. Ailish was ten. I wasn't allowed to let her out of my sight. And guess what?'

I shrugged. 'You were fourteen.'

'Right. I went off with my friends. Lost track of time. Must have been an hour went by before I realized Ailish was missing. We found her an hour after that. She wouldn't say where she'd been, or what had happened to her. But she was scared. And she was never the same again.'

I let that sink in for a moment. 'You blame yourself.'

'No.' He shook his head vehemently. 'That's the point. I used to blame myself. But then I realized. I was just a kid.

So was Ailish. The only person to blame for what happened is whoever got to her when I wasn't there. Whatever they did.' He shook his head, exhaling long and hard.

I nodded awkwardly. I was sorry for what had happened to Brodie's sister and I got what he was trying to say to me, but I didn't know if I could view the mugging like that. I wasn't sure Rachel could, either.

'Were you scared?' she'd whispered to me, once the A&E doctor had finally gone and the pain meds and the shock had tugged Holly away into sleep. I'd told her I'd been terrified. That – for those seemingly endless seconds as the man attacked us – I feared I'd lost them both.

Rachel had nodded and blinked back tears, and I'd looked up along the hospital bed, from where Rachel's knuckles had whitened around Holly's hand to my daughter's ruined face. It felt like someone was cutting me on the inside, over and over. The cuts got deeper as I thought about Michael. I hadn't protected him either, had I? And suddenly, I'd needed out of that cubicle. Needed air. I told Rachel I was going in search of a coffee machine, and that's when I pushed aside the cubicle curtains, staggered along the hushed night-time ward and ran into Constable Baker for the first time.

He was standing outside the triage room. Square-jawed, clean shaven, pushing six foot three with a muscular physique beneath the Kevlar stab vest and police uniform he had on. In his hand was a clear plastic bag with a Stanley knife inside it.

I stared at the bag. Felt myself sway.

'Mr Sullivan? Why don't we sit over here?' He guided me towards some plastic chairs set against a scuffed beige wall.

'You recognize this knife? One of the kitchen staff saw the man who attacked you drop it at the end of the alley.'

I nodded, hunched up, my leg jiggling with nerves, then gave him my statement, telling him about the alley, the darkness, the flashes of memory I had from after the man had appeared. Baker scribbled notes, nodding all the while. I didn't mention how terrified I'd been. I didn't say that the fear and adrenaline were still fizzing in my veins like battery acid.

When we'd finished, we both stood and I gave him my contact details, but then I lingered, wanting to ask him something, unsure if I should. He was fully a head taller than me. Probably weighed more than fourteen stone.

'What would you have done differently?' I blurted out. 'If you'd been in that alley instead of me, I mean?'

Baker frowned. 'Nothing. Look, maybe you don't want to hear this, but you were unlucky, Mr Sullivan. You gave that man your things as soon as he asked for them. I wouldn't have done anything differently at all.'

I didn't know whether he meant it or if he was simply telling me what I wanted to hear, and I was still wrestling with that conundrum when I returned to Holly's cubicle to find Lionel talking with Rachel in hushed tones.

They stopped speaking when I entered. Lionel's collar and bow tie were undone. One shirt tail was untucked. Standing there, looking rumpled, he seemed strangely reduced. Oddly mortal.

'Tom.' He embraced me – scents of sandalwood and cigars – then pushed me back to scan my face. His eyes were red-rimmed, the skin around them deeply lined, and I realized

– with a start – that he'd been crying. 'I hate that this happened to your family. I hate that I sent you into that alley.'

I told him that was nonsense. There was no way he could possibly have known what would happen. And I meant it too, because if Michael's death had taught me anything, it was that life can throw the worst, most random experiences at you out of nowhere, for no reason whatsoever. I was pretty sure Jennifer's death had taught him the same thing.

I went over to Holly. She was trembling in her sleep. I laid one hand on her hip, another on the crown of her head. It's something I've done a lot over the years. As an infant, it had soothed her.

And that's when Lionel started talking again about the restorative powers of his Scottish lodge. He waxed lyrical about getting back to basics, connecting with the landscape. I could tell he'd already mentioned it to Rachel. His voice grew husky as he spoke about the trauma we'd been through as a family during the past year and how, as a doctor, Rachel would understand that the best way of getting over a trauma is to rest. He said he was insisting that I took time off work. He wanted me to take Rachel and Holly away from London, to a safer place where we could heal. That his lodge would be perfect for us because—

I raised my hand and cut him off. I told him how much we appreciated his offer but that right now . . . And then my own words faded into silence as Rachel reached out to grip my hand, her face a mess of tears.

'Please, Tom,' she whispered. 'I want us to try it. Please. For Holly, if not for me.'

And so now here we were. Together. Sort of.

I swirled my beer and glanced away from Brodie into the lodge. Buster was lying with his head hanging off the end of one of the modular couches, watching us. There was no sign of Rachel and Holly. The last time I'd seen them, Holly had been bugging Rachel to change into her swimsuit so they could try the pool. I guessed they must have shut Buster out. Otherwise, he would have been splashing around with them in there.

'See this, Tom?'

Brodie stamped his heel on a puddled area of decking, then squatted, hooked his finger through an inset steel ring and heaved a concealed hatch out of the way with a fine spray of rainwater.

'Fire pit. Already laid. The wood is good and dry. If you get a chance, you should come out and light it with Rachel and Holly. It can really be something at night.'

I nodded absently. 'Thanks. We might just do that.'

'If you take my advice you'll get to it this evening. It might be a touch wet but the forecast is set to get worse the rest of the week. Out here, the storms can be wild, believe me.' He dropped the hatch back into position and wiped his hand on the seat of his jeans. 'Well, that's everything, I think. I should probably get out of here, Tom. Leave you to your family time.'

Those words 'family' and 'time'. These days they fitted together about as well as two shattered Lego bricks.

'I'll just go and say goodbye to Rachel and Holly then, shall I?'

'No,' I told him, a little too sharply. 'I mean, there's really no need. I can do it for you.'

He looked a bit offended, and I suppose he had every right to be, especially after he'd tried to connect with me about his sister, but I didn't back down.

'Aye, OK.' He toed the ground with his foot. 'Well, if there's anything you need, Tom, my number is programmed into the landline phone in the kitchen. Just hit hash one. I'm based about a half-hour drive away. But if I don't hear from you, I'll be back on Saturday to see you off.'

I nodded and we shook hands again, then I watched as he strode off quickly around the side of the lodge and disappeared from view. I waited until I heard the crunch and grind of his Land Cruiser starting up and pulling away. Then I exhaled and turned to the wall of tinted glass in front of me, staring at my reflection, alone by the sea.

5

The pool room was in a glassed-in side extension to the main lodge. I walked across the deck to it and peeked inside. The interior was done out like a spa in a boutique hotel. In the middle of the space was a long, thin lap pool, surrounded by sleek tiling, Scandi-style wooden recliners, piles of fluffy white towels and plastic shower clogs. To the right of the room I could see two doors with glass portholes. One was marked SAUNA. The other read STEAM ROOM. A door on the left connected, I guessed, with the rest of the lodge.

Rachel was swimming lengths, the water frothing and churning around her, swamping the drains at the sides. Holly waved to me from the other side of the glass. She was lying on a recliner, her legs bent at the knee, watching something on her mobile. A white cotton towel was wrapped around her torso, over her swimsuit. Her hair hung about her in wet curls.

The moment she saw me, I clapped my hand to my heart and staggered backwards, feigning shock and surprise. Holly shook her head and mouthed the word 'Dork' to me, but she was smiling as she returned her attention to her phone and I felt a small buzz of warmth spread through my chest.

It faded when I studied her face. Rachel had warned me

the swelling would get worse before it got better but right now I was scared to think how much worse it could get.

My heart sank. I wanted to cradle Holly in my arms like I had when she was a little girl but instead here I was, standing outside and separated from my daughter and my wife by a sheet of double glazing. I supposed it was the kind of image a marriage therapist would get a lot of mileage out of, but recognizing that didn't make me feel anything except cheap and sad.

There was a swell of water to my right and I watched as Rachel completed a length and hooked her arm over the side. She saw me and puffed out an exaggerated breath, then swept her hair back from her face, pushed out of the pool, grabbed a towel and padded towards me. Her swimsuit was cut high around her thighs, water sluicing off her trim shoulders and over her breasts.

And there it was again. That old familiar desire; the hormonal stirring that just a glimpse of Rachel's body could trigger in me. Even if I wanted to deny it to myself, there would be no point. I'd loved Rachel too hard over too many years.

Ask me when I fell in love with Rachel and I can pinpoint the precise second. It was two weeks after we'd met, dawn light leaking in through the window of my university dorm room. I'd been leaning on my elbow, watching Rachel sleep, and then – eyes still closed – she'd smiled at me, called me a 'perv' and pulled me in for a kiss. And *bam*. That was it. I knew right then that this was the woman I wanted to spend the rest of my life with. Corny, I know, but absolutely true.

But ask me to tell you when things fell apart and that's where things get hazy. Was it the night of Michael's accident? The gruelling months that came afterwards? Was it when we started arguing? When we stopped? Was it six weeks ago, when I packed a bag and moved out of our family home? Or was it four days ago, when I failed to prevent a stranger from attacking our daughter?

She looked at me now, dabbing her face with the towel and pressing it to her chest, then she leaned forwards and exhaled against the glass, tracing her finger through the condensation, scrawling the word 'Hi'.

I raised my hand, fingers spread, feeling awkward and uncertain. Rachel contemplated me with a slight, serious frown.

And I wondered: What did she see in me?

What could I see in her?

There are things I know for certain about my wife. Intimate things I've learned over the years about how she feels, how she thinks. Confidences she's shared. And then there are the things I'm afraid to know.

Like the spa hotel. Three weeks ago now.

It had been my weekend looking after Holly and Rachel had told me that she'd booked herself a spa break with some girlfriends. On the Sunday morning, I'd needed to speak to Rachel about what time I could bring Holly home so that I could get into the office for a work matter I had to clear from my desk before Monday morning, but Rachel didn't respond to my texts and when I dialled her phone it was switched off. I tried the hotel instead and the woman I spoke with on reception said she had no record of Rachel staying with them. I asked the woman to check for the names of Rachel's friends and, again, I hit a blank.

And OK, I knew it was possible that her plans had changed, but then a new, more dizzying thought had struck me. Maybe she was with another man.

I didn't know if that was the case or not because I hadn't tackled Rachel on it. I hadn't wanted to come across as paranoid or make things worse for Holly. And I hadn't – truth be told – wanted to confront the fallout if my suspicions turned out to be right.

You could call it cowardice. Or denial. Either way, it was a combination that had worked pretty well for me until Brodie had mentioned the spa here – until that word had hung in the air between us, and I'd felt my breath snag in my throat as I'd looked at Rachel for a tell.

But there'd been nothing. No hint of guilt or awkwardness. Just my own toxic, lingering suspicions and maybe a phoney story about a weekend away with the girls, and who knew what other secrets besides?

I blinked. Rachel was wafting her hand slowly in front of me, mouthing my name, snapping me out of my daze. Once she had my attention, she pointed from me to the pool, then mimed swimming breaststroke as her face framed a question.

'Later,' I mouthed.

I wasn't going to tell her I'd forgotten to pack my trunks. It was the kind of detail Rachel used to remind me of.

She made a performance out of stroking her chin and staring at me with a deep, contemplative frown. Then she glanced towards the woods and her face brightened with an idea. She carried out another mime, this time taking the fingers of one hand for a walk along her palm and then pointing to all three of us.

I shrugged, *Sure. Why not?* And Rachel turned to tell Holly what was happening. I saw Holly throw back her head in exaggerated despair and start to whinge, but by then I was already backing away across the deck to wait for them at the edge of the woods to the south.

It was so quiet here. So green and eerily still. The only noise was the faint breeze through the pines, the chatter of birdsong, the hush of waves against the shore.

Michael had died in a place not too unlike this. A wooded strip of land bordering a quiet back road. I'd seen photographs of the crash taken by the road traffic collision unit. All kinds of angles. Unforgiving shots. They'd been projected on a television screen during the coroner's hearing. I'd seen how my Audi had deformed and crumpled in the middle; how the windscreen glass had shattered and imploded; how the tree Michael had hit had been half felled by the force of the impact.

Confession time: I don't just blame Michael. I also blame myself.

Why? Well, for starters, I was the one who'd taken Michael for occasional Sunday driving lessons in an old disused car park close to our home, beginning almost a year before he could learn legally, circling round and round in my car.

I was the one who'd encouraged his relationship with Fiona, even though Rachel had wanted me to talk to Michael about how maybe they should cool it until after his exams were over.

I was the one who'd come home late from work on days when Michael had been sullen and rude to Rachel, when he'd bickered with Holly, when he'd gone out with his free-running friends to local rec grounds and car parks after we'd told him not to. The one who said I'd talk to him in the morning. The one who rarely did.

I'd given Michael a whole lot of latitude. Too much for a reckless sixteen-year-old to handle. Too much to take back now.

All the signs had been there. I just hadn't wanted to see them.

He'd stolen my car. He'd driven it fast. Trying to impress Fiona. Thumbing his nose at laws and rules and common sense.

It had cost him his life. Robbed Fiona of hers. It had ruined his reputation. Exposed me and Rachel as bad parents. Blown our marriage apart.

And even still, Rachel couldn't accept the truth for what it was. She wanted there to be a bigger reason for Michael's death. A deeper explanation that could somehow make sense of what he'd done. A cause for the effect.

There'd been times after the crash when I'd found her in Michael's room, searching through his things. As if a random scribble in the margins of a book, or a scrap of paper folded in the pocket of a coat, might somehow help her to understand Michael's actions.

But, of course, she never found anything.

Sometimes terrible things just . . . happen. A stranger breaks into your house and brutally slays your wife. Your daughter gets hurt during a mugging. Your son is killed in a car crash.

These things happen all the time, all over the world. You know that and you hope it'll never happen to you.

And sometimes it still does.

A few weeks before I'd left home, sleepless in the dead of night, Rachel had stirred and whispered something to me, out of nowhere, in the dark.

'I still can't believe he did it. It wasn't like him. He just wouldn't, Tom.'

But he had.

The tree looms in Michael's vision. It is enormously tall and the trunk is many metres wide. Like one of the giant redwoods he's studied in geography class. An epic tree. Mythic.

The bark, starkly lit by the brilliant glare of the headlamps, is as gnarled and tough as stone.

Michael has mere seconds until he hits it. Less than seconds. Time enough, maybe, to turn the steering wheel.

But turning the wheel would be futile now.

The car vaults forwards. Thumping over a drainage gully. Airborne.

Michael is sitting in the driving seat but he knows he's nothing more than a passenger. The car is locked on course to the tree, just as Michael is locked on to the tree.

Fiona's hand reaches over and grips his arm. Her fingers clenching and tugging. The tree speeding towards them. Fiona's scream in his ears.

6

The noise of paws scrabbling on timber snapped me out of my thoughts and then Buster streaked by me in a haze of woodland debris. A stick was on the ground between us and Buster nudged it closer to me. I picked it up and threw it away between the trees, watching him tear after it in a brown blur, bounding through ferns, until he was lost among the tall pines creaking overhead.

'Mum said to tell you she's on her way.'

Holly had stopped a short distance back from me, picking at the crusted bark of a pine trunk. She was dressed in a long-sleeved pink top over hot-pink tracksuit bottoms and spotted wellington boots. She hadn't bothered to dry her hair.

She looked sad and sullen, and something about her attitude made me uneasy.

'Has Brodie gone?' she asked me.

I nodded. 'How are you feeling, sweetheart?'

'Mum's given me more painkillers.'

Not exactly an answer.

'Listen, Holly, I'm here if you want to talk about what happened, OK?'

My daughter pulled a face like I'd farted. 'Dad, you do get that I'm a teenager now, right?'

'Sure.'

'Because – speaking as a teenager – it's kind of my duty to point out that telling me you're here now sort of only emphasizes how you weren't here, you know, *before*? When you walked out on me and Mum?'

Oof.

Holly's gaze was unsparing, even through the bruising to her eyes. I felt a flash of panic, like she'd tossed a stick of dynamite down next to my feet, the fuse burning rapidly away.

Holly has always been clever for her age. Even as a young kid she'd had an advanced vocabulary. Normally, that was a good thing. But it also meant her tongue could be sharp enough to wound.

'Holly, I—'

'Relax, Dad. I'm just saying, if I *wanted* to have a major teen sulk about it, I totally could. I mean, it would be totally justified.'

As Holly talked, Buster reversed backwards towards us with a completely different stick to the one I'd thrown. It was much bigger, for starters, coming in at approximately twice his body length and weight. It was also far too heavy for him to carry, so he was having to drag it across the ground, ass-backwards, snarling in the back of his throat. And yet, out of the two of us right now, I still felt like he was the smarter one.

'OK,' I said, carefully. 'And are you having a major teen sulk?'

'Right now, I'm pretty much still deciding.'

'Then can I just tell you that I think I have some idea of

how tough things have been for you and I'm sorry about it. But the situation between your mum and me is complicated, Holly. I wish it wasn't, but it is. I never wanted to move out. I only did it because—'

Holly sucked air through her teeth and tore a strip of bark off the tree. 'Now see, Dad? Teenage Holly would have to let you know that you totally walked into that one. She'd probably say something like, Yeah, I got it. Mum explained it to me *after* you'd gone.'

I felt stranded. I wanted to go to Holly and close the distance between us. But I also instinctively knew that would be the wrong move to make. And still that stick of dynamite burned down fast.

I fumbled for the right thing to say. I was pretty sure I didn't have it, but I gave it a shot all the same.

'Then I suppose I would have to tell Teenage Holly that I deserve that. But I'd also want to tell her that I didn't only come here this week because she got hurt.' I leaned to one side to catch Holly's eye but it was a difficult thing to do while she focused on her hands, tearing and crumbling the flake of bark. 'That would be something really important for Teenage Holly to know. And I'd want to emphasize that it's been a trial separation between her mum and me. Because we are trying to fix things. We want to fix things. And, Holly, sweetheart, I never stopped loving you or missing you when I moved out. Not ever. Not once. I couldn't. OK?'

Holly hitched her shoulders. She was silent a long time. When she eventually spoke, the wobble in her throat made me want to hit myself about the head with the branch Buster was playing with.

'I'm mad at you, Dad.'

'I know,' I told her. 'I'm mad at me too.'

'And at Mum and Michael?'

'I try not to be.'

Holly nodded, taking that in. 'I'm going to go for a walk now.'

'Can I come?'

'I think I just want Buster with me for a while.'

She slunk by me without pausing, then grabbed one end of the branch Buster was gnawing on and dragged it away across the forest floor with Buster prancing alongside her, his tail wagging and the branch bumping off tree stumps and roots.

'Is she giving you a hard time?'

I spun round, my heart in my throat. Rachel ducked low under the pine limbs hanging over the edge of the deck. She had on a patterned sweater and mud-smeared hiking boots. Thick woollen socks were rolled up over her ankles. And yes, she was tired, she was anxious – and we were only tentatively feeling our way forwards here – but still, when I saw her, I felt a fast ticking in my blood and everything else seemed to fall completely away.

'Nothing I shouldn't expect,' I said.

'I wasn't prying, Tom. I was trying to give you two some space. She'll come round. She loves you.'

'I've missed her.'

'And she's missed you. We both have. You know, I never asked you to leave.'

But she hadn't asked me to stay. When Rachel had found me packing my things in our bedroom, she'd taken one look at my bags and turned without a word, crossing the hall into Michael's room and shutting the door behind her. I'd tried knocking. Rachel hadn't answered. When I'd gone in, she'd been sitting on Michael's bed with her back to me and his old dressing gown pressed to her face. She wouldn't look at me when I asked her to. It was as if she'd travelled somewhere else entirely. Locked away.

'Michael would have loved it here,' she said now, and I followed her gaze to where Holly and Buster were walking. The melancholy tone in her voice told me she was picturing him with them, and for a moment I could almost see him too.

He would have been larking around. They would have started a game of tag. Michael would have run up tree trunks, flipped backwards athletically, swung from high branches like an orangutan and whooped with crazed laughter.

Grief is a strange companion. I know it will accompany me until the day I die, a shadow on my heart. Most times when I think of Michael now it feels like I've run into an invisible wall that knocks the air clean out of me. But it doesn't always grind me down. In some ways – strange ways – it can also buoy me up. It felt that way today, imagining the ghost of my dead son hurtling through the woods with his sister and our family dog for company – forever sixteen in my mind.

'Are you OK?' Rachel asked me.

I turned to her and nodded. I couldn't talk right then, but Rachel saw the truth in my eyes.

'I miss him so much,' she said. 'And it never stops hurting, does it? All the things he's missing out on. So many things we'll never see. And the horrible truth is that we couldn't and didn't help him. We were his parents, Tom. We were supposed to keep him safe.'

My wife loves helping people. She has a kind soul. If she has one flaw as a GP, it's that she cares about her patients too much. So hearing her say those words didn't surprise me, exactly, but I'm really not sure there was anything she could have done to prevent what happened to our son.

When Michael was killed, Rachel's grief was all-consuming, like her whole world had collapsed into a black hole. I'd tried everything I could think of to pull her out again – for Holly, and for me – but it was hard to escape the feeling that too much of the old Rachel was gone now. Until coming here, I wasn't sure we'd ever get her back.

Then she stepped forwards into my arms, and suddenly the simplest, most ordinary things felt so sharp and so real. The shape and warmth of Rachel's body. The drumbeat of her heart. The smell of chlorine on her skin. I looked up at the treetops, green and blurred overhead. They seemed to tangle and spin.

From a distance, I could hear Holly's voice calling to Buster, but when I turned my head I couldn't see them. They were lost to me now – like Michael – somewhere far off in the woods.

Rachel sniffed and moved clear of me, wiping at her eyes with the heel of her hand.

'Was Brodie bothering you?' she asked me.

'No. Was he bothering you?'

She shook her head and smiled, like it was nothing she wasn't used to handling. 'Something to tell you,' she said, and the nervous look on her face made something inside me tighten and knot. 'Lionel wants to expand my role at JFA. He wants me to join the board as an executive director. He'd like me to become the main spokesperson for the charity.'

The forest floor seemed to fall away from beneath my feet.

'You hate the idea, don't you?'

Yes.

And I did. I *really* did. Because Michael had killed someone. He'd stolen my car. He'd crashed it into a tree. And he'd killed someone. And now Rachel wanted to take on a more high-profile role at a charity aimed at rehabilitating criminals.

Like my son.

It's an odd thing for your wife to become a stranger to you. Odder still to be so in love with the person you remember that you'll do almost anything to find your way back to them again.

Somehow, I dredged up the words I knew she wanted to hear from that pit of fear and horror in my gut. 'If it's what you really want, I'll support you.'

'You will?'

I nodded, feeling a tumbling sensation deep inside of me. Rachel squeezed my hand and looked up into my face. I saw tears of surprise in her eyes. And maybe even – though perhaps I was overreaching here – a new kind of fragile belief too.

'Will you do me one more favour?' she whispered. 'Just while we're here? Will you think about forgiving Michael?

Just . . . can you allow yourself to think about how that would feel, OK?'

And there it was again. That invisible wall. I felt like I'd run into it flat out. I felt like there was no air in my lungs at all.

I didn't say I would do it. I didn't know if I could stand to try. Right then, it was a struggle even to speak.

'Let's catch up to Holly,' I mumbled. 'She shouldn't be on her own out here.'

7

By the time we stepped out of the trees onto the shoreline the rain had swept in. It was blowing in drenching gusts off the sea. Holly was crouched next to Buster on a mound of stacked boulders in the rain. She was holding him back by his collar, like he was primed to attack. Buster was growling, low and guttural. Holly was wet and shivering, her clothes pressed against her skin.

Ahead of them was a green void in the woods.

No, something else.

A trick of the eye.

I peered harder. There was a small building at the edge of the sea, with a pitted concrete slipway leading up to it and a fieldstone base, much like the lodge. An opening was carved out at the front of the ground floor where a small boat could be berthed. But it was the upper part of the structure that was the truly remarkable part. It was triangular and faced entirely in large mirrored panels.

The mirrors reflected the landscape all around. The green trees, grey skies, slate sea. The effect was almost enough to render the building invisible. It was a strangely unnerving sight.

'He keeps barking,' Holly called down to us through the rain. 'I think the mirrors are freaking him out.'

Rachel offered me her hand and we clambered up over the boulders together, past where Buster had abandoned his branch. When we reached the top I put my palm on his head and stroked him. His growls vibrated through his skull like the buzzing of a dentist's drill.

I wasn't overly concerned by his behaviour. Buster senses danger with all the accuracy of a dog flying a plane. I've lost count of the number of times he's leaped back and barked at the wheelie bin at the end of our drive. So I was ready to dismiss his reaction and the way the hackles were raised across his back, but as I looked at the angular, futuristic shack – and the trick of light at its heart – I experienced a sensation like spiders crawling across my skin.

'What do you think it is?' Holly asked.

'No idea,' Rachel said. 'Some kind of fancy bird hide?'

'Dad?'

I turned and scanned our surroundings, trying to get a sense of how far we'd walked. Several hundred metres to the north I could see the blurred triangular point of the deck at the front of the lodge, extending out into the ruptured ocean. To the south were windswept trees and deserted strips of hardscrabble beach, hammered by the rain and the onrushing waves.

Beyond that, a gnarled ridge poked out into the sea. Running along its back was a stretch of perimeter fencing that I guessed marked the southern border of Lionel's estate. The barbed fence angled up and down over the finger of rock like the scales of some sleeping prehistoric beast, plunging under the sea.

'I don't know, Holly.' As I stared again at the hut, the

mirrored shell seemed to suck all the bleak afternoon light into its centre and I had the absurd and sudden urge to grab hold of Holly and Rachel to prevent them from being dragged in. 'Brodie didn't mention it.'

'Can we go down there?'

I contemplated the rain-greased boulders in front of us and the wash of waves at the bottom of the slipway. We were close to soaked already but I didn't want anyone to fall in.

'I just want Buster to know it's OK, Dad. If he sniffs it all out, I think he'll relax. He's got himself all worked up.'

I looked down at Buster, tugging against his collar, his teeth bared, legs trembling. Maybe it wasn't the worst idea ever. Plus, with everything Holly had been through, I didn't want any doubts about this place plucking at the strings of her mind in the small hours of the night.

'OK. But be careful.'

As soon as Holly released Buster, he shot forwards and zigzagged down the cascade of boulders with nimble ease. It took us a good while longer to catch up to him in the mooring space. It was cold down there and it echoed with a vacuum silence that seemed to absorb sound in the same way the mirrored tiles absorbed light.

Buster flitted to and fro with his nose down and his tail up, sniffing the dank, cave-like scent on the air. A flooded trench had been carved out of the cement foundations of the building. It was lined with a frothy scum of curdled black water, decaying woodland matter and litter. Beyond it was a sleek timber door faced with brushed aluminium panels. Holly tried opening the door but it was locked. When we searched around, there were no keys to be found.

I don't know why exactly, but I felt a small kick of relief to know we couldn't get in, like a sudden buoyancy in my gut. Behind us, even Buster seemed to relax. He laid down on his belly with his tail beating dust off the ground and his jaws parted in a toothy smile.

'All good now?' I asked him.

He panted and beat his tail some more.

'I wish we could get up there,' Holly said. 'It looks cool.'

'There's probably a key at the lodge. I can phone Brodie and ask him.'

'Then let's head back.' Rachel wrapped her arms around herself. 'I'm getting cold and I want to get out of this rain and into some dry clothes. I'll make us all hot chocolate?'

The hot chocolate swung it for Holly. We retraced our steps, climbing away from the shack and over the rain-dampened boulders again, then up onto the craggy shore, where Buster bit hold of his stick once more and dragged it into the trees at an angle, moving in an awkward, crabbing trot with the branch bumping across the ground.

We followed him in our damp, clingy clothes, the rain spattering against us, and were maybe a third of the way back, tracking the coastline, when Buster snarled and grunted and hunkered down on his front paws, playing tug-o-war with his stick.

'Buster,' Holly told him. 'Just leave it. Stop messing around.'

But Buster wouldn't let go. And he was getting more and more agitated. I walked up to him, ready to free the stick from whatever root or tree stump he'd got it caught up in, but when I reached down and pulled, I felt a hot wrenching pain in my shoulder.

The stick wouldn't come.

I bent and peered closer and felt something cold and greasy slip down under the collar of my shirt.

A nylon snare was attached to the end of the branch.

'Tom?'

The slight quaver in Rachel's voice matched the flutter in my heart. She'd walked ahead of me with Holly and the two of them were standing on a patch of scuffed grass close to the shoreline. The trunks of the nearby pines were bowed and twisted around them, forming a small clearing. In the middle of the clearing were the charred remains of a campfire, ringed by a cluster of sooty stones.

I pushed Buster away from the branch and shooed him on until he finally moved off with a snort and trotted over to sniff at the burned and blackened wood, the grey-white ashes. When I got nearer, I could see the remains of an empty and scorched tin can. A buckled fork.

We stood in silence, the salt wind flinging rain in our faces, the sea falling away into wide, shallow trenches and rising on vast, crested swells.

'It could have been Lionel,' Holly said. 'With some of his guests, maybe?'

But I didn't think so. The Lionel I knew was all about the fine linen sheets, statement furniture and expensive artwork we'd found inside the lodge. He wasn't the type to lay snares and sit around a campfire in the woods eating food from a tin. Besides, he had the fire pit in the deck if he wanted to do something like that. Maybe even the strange, mirrored shack.

'Seems more like Brodie's style,' I said.

He could have come out here fishing, I thought. He could have stood at the edge of the clearing and cast out a line. Put down a snare. Maybe he'd lit a fire for warmth and had hunkered down, rubbing his hands, the flames spitting and flickering across his bearded face.

'I guess that makes sense.'

Rachel nodded, like she agreed with me, but then she clenched her jaw, swiped the rain from her eyes with the sleeve of her sweater and stared off in the direction of the main lodge. Glimpses of it were just visible through the breaks in the trees.

8

Sometimes I wonder how old your kids have to be before they see clean through you. Holly might be clever, verging on precocious, but she still missed the strain in Rachel's voice and her studied nonchalance when she told Holly to go upstairs and get on with the schoolwork her teachers had set for her while we were away.

Maybe it helped that Rachel gave Holly a plate of cookies to go along with her hot chocolate, and that Buster followed her up to her room. We'd been back at the lodge for twenty minutes by then and all of us had changed into warm track-suit bottoms and hoodies. There was a laundry room just down the corridor past the kitchen where Rachel had hung our outdoor coats when we'd first arrived. She'd sent me in there to stash our muddy boots and toss our wet clothes in the tumble dryer, and before I was done, she'd snuck in for a quick, whispered conversation about how we shouldn't call Brodie until we were on our own.

The moment Holly's bedroom door closed, Rachel took down the landline phone from a cradle on the kitchen wall, put it on speaker and dialled Brodie. While we waited for him to pick up, I studied an intercom on the wall that matched the one on the front gate. It had a screen for transmitting images from the gate camera and a button marked GATE OPEN.

'Brodie?' Rachel said, when our call was answered. 'It's Rachel Sullivan. At the lodge?'

There was a confused silence for a brief moment. 'Oh. Did I forget something? Is everything OK?'

How to answer that question? If you want me to explain why we felt so unnerved by what we'd found out in the woods, it would be a hard thing to put into words. It was more of a feeling, I guess. An instinct. Like picking up on some kind of jarring cosmic hum.

And all right, maybe we were feeding off of each other's anxiety and spooking ourselves silly. It was only an old campfire and a single snare, after all. But honestly? I think perhaps losing Michael in the way we had and the attack in London had changed our perception of things. You could say it had made us more paranoid, or you might believe me when I tell you we're more attuned to potential dangers now. And to me – and I guessed to Rachel too – for reasons I can't wholly explain, finding the campfire and the snare had felt like the twitching of an invisible tripwire in my mind.

Rachel glanced at me before answering. I saw tiny crinkles of unease tug at her eyes and mouth. 'Tom is with me. We've just been for a walk in the woods. We found . . . Well, it looks like the remains of a campfire?'

Again, Brodie didn't reply right away. I got the impression he'd been expecting something else. Perhaps he'd been worried Rachel was phoning up to complain about the way he'd behaved around her earlier.

'Tom thought it could have been yours?' Rachel pressed.

'Our dog also found what looks like a snare,' I added, holding Rachel's gaze. I had the sense I was cradling her heart in my hands.

'Oh aye?' Brodie said. 'A snare, is it?' He sounded more relaxed now. 'That'll just be some of the locals setting traps. They know the lodge is empty most of the year. You've nothing to worry about there.'

I paused. 'Traps for rabbits?'

'Hares, Tom.'

I raised my eyebrows to Rachel. It made sense, I supposed. But then again, the idea of hunters out in the woods here didn't make me feel a whole lot better.

'Have you had trouble with them before?'

'Not trouble, no. It's just that they were here before the lodge and they think that entitles them to come back. Especially with the fence. Some folks view that as a kind of challenge.'

Speaking of which, the fence was pretty damn big, wasn't it? And the entrance gate was seriously imposing. Factor in the gate camera and wasn't it all supposed to add up to something capable of, I don't know, keeping people out?

'But how would they get in?' I asked. 'I thought you said the fence covers all of Lionel's land?'

'It does. But not the sea. It's easy enough to kayak in around the coast.'

I guess that was stupid of me. I should have thought of it before. More to the point, though, maybe Lionel should have thought of it before he spent all that money on a massive fence.

'What about the hut with the mirrors all over it?'

'That's the stargazing pod. Probably should have told you about it. On a clear night you can see pretty much everything from in there.'

I sensed I had to be careful here. Rachel's nerves were already frayed and I didn't want to freak her out any more than necessary. Neither Rachel nor Holly had mentioned any real concerns about the pod to me, but on this, at least, I was with Buster. There was something about it that bothered me.

'We tried to get inside. The door was locked.'

'Right. With the storm weather that's forecast over the next few days, I didn't think you'd be using it. I have the keys with me here.'

I turned my head and glanced over my shoulder. Outside, rain whipped in off the sea and spit against the big pyramid of glass at the front of the lodge. The sky was dense with cloud. Brodie was right. It was terrible conditions for astronomy.

'Trust me, these people won't cause you any trouble,' he added. 'Word gets around pretty fast up here. They'll know the lodge is occupied just now and they won't be back until you're gone. One thing, though. You might not want to let Buster wander off too far by himself. Sounds like he had a lucky escape with that snare.'

I winced as an image flashed in my mind of Buster snagged by the neck, his tongue lolling terribly, eyes bulging, paws scrabbling desperately at the ground. I was still trying to wipe the vision from my mind as Brodie ended the call with a reminder that we should feel free to call him for anything else we might need.

'What do you think?' Rachel asked me. There was a slight grimace on her face and I could tell she was still concerned.

'Are you asking me if I think it's safe here?'

'I guess I am, yes.'

'Then I'd have to say, speaking rationally, that everything Brodie said makes sense to me. Plus we didn't see anyone out there, Rachel. That fire could have been out for a long time. Weeks, maybe.'

'And speaking irrationally?'

I shrugged. 'What are you suggesting? We drive Holly out of here? To a hotel or a B&B?'

'Probably not a good idea.'

'She's going to want to know why.'

'And I don't want to scare her. We brought her here to feel safe.'

'Then let's not say anything. Lionel's never had any concerns here, I don't think.'

Rachel didn't say anything to that. Because how could we know?

'Then how about this?' I said. 'I'll go out for another quick walk. I'll head behind the carport this time. We still have a little while before it gets dark. I'll check around. Make sure we're definitely alone. Would that help?'

Rachel bit down on her lip. 'Am I being silly?'

'No. And I fancy a walk. Where's the harm?'

'Then maybe you should? Just for peace of mind?'

The dampness in my boots seeped through my socks as I put them on. I took down my big outdoor jacket from a hook on the wall of the laundry room and pulled the hood over my head. The blowing rain swirled in at me as I opened the sliding glass door. Buster watched me from one of the sofas without moving a muscle. Not even he was dumb enough to come out with me in this weather.

I lowered my hood once I was under the trees. More paranoia, probably, but if anyone *was* out here, I didn't want to compromise my hearing or my peripheral vision. The light had faded. It was murky and hushed beneath the pines.

I hiked around in loops and figure eights for thirty solid minutes. In all that time I didn't see anything or anyone to be concerned by. My boots sank deep under mounds of fallen pine needles where it seemed as if nobody had walked for many months or years until, eventually, I tramped uphill with my back to the sea as far as the fence line.

The open grassland on the opposite side looked grainy and indistinct in the damp twilight. I reached out and took hold of two of the bevelled uprights. There was no give in them at all. The gaps between the uprights were too small for even a child to wriggle through.

At the top of the fence, raindrops quivered on the splayed barbs. It would be impossible for anyone to climb over them to one of the trees, even with a ladder, and there were no overhanging branches to grab. Above me I could see a pale nub on a pine trunk where I guessed Brodie had got busy with a chainsaw. On one level it reassured me, but I still felt a chill pass over my heart. Because who builds a fence like this for protection unless they believe they have a reason to need it? Right now, ironically, the fence's very presence was beginning to make me feel *less* safe.

I looked down at my toes, where a narrow drainage gully winked with dark moisture. The gully followed the fence line and I tracked it as far as the driveway, then stepped out into a smoky purple dusk and faint evening rain.

I pulled my mobile from my pocket. Still no signal. I did the holding-it-over-my-head-and-turning-on-the-spot thing. I even stuck my arm through a gap in the fence up to my shoulder. No bars. No reception.

The gate metal gleamed in the wet dimness when I reached out to touch it. The green paint – looking jet black in the dimming light – was waxy and thickly applied. Over to my right was another short pole with another cigar-shaped camera fitted to it, this time pointed inwards. I crouched in the damp and pressed the recessed button on the intercom. Then I waited.

No response.

I pressed the button again, longer this time.

More waiting.

Then a brash static crackle.

'What is it, Dad?'

'Holly? Can you see me?'

'*Yes.* On the monitor thingy in the kitchen. You made me come downstairs.'

And she didn't sound very happy about it.

'Can you open the gate?'

'Why?'

'I'd just like you to open the gate for a second.'

'What are you freaking out about?'

'I'm not freak—' I paused, shook my head. 'Holly, can you please just open the gate?'

'Fine. Jeez. Take a chill pill, Dad.'

There was silence, then the same low electric buzzing as

before. The same metallic *clunk* and the same static hum. The gates trembled and separated and swung outwards on the same tight arcs.

The driveway summit appeared in the opening, looking just as empty as it had in my rear-view mirror only hours before. Beyond it, I knew, was the lonely coastal road. I saw no passing headlights skimming the tree cover. I heard no engine sounds.

I stood there, my heart beating in the dark hollow of my chest like the wings of a moth in the night. Then the gates clunked and slowed and came to a halt at their widest point and less than a minute later they hummed and buzzed and trundled back slowly together again. I watched the two metal gates form up in the middle and I heard some kind of heavy interior latch *thunk* into position.

'Dad?' Holly said, over the speaker. 'Mum says to come back for dinner now. Before it burns.'

9

I caught a puff of cooked pizza dough on the air when I came in through the sliding door fronting onto the deck. Holly was sitting at the glass dining table, biting into a slice of Hawaiian. Buster had his head propped on her thigh, his big eyes pleading.

Rachel watched me from the kitchen with a glass of white wine in her hand and an anxious look on her face. I shook my head at her quickly and smiled in what I hoped was a reassuring way, then removed my boots and walked towards the laundry room in my socks.

'Dad?' Holly called. 'We're going to watch a film in Lionel's home theatre.'

I stuck my head out. 'What kind of film?'

'Your favourite kind.'

I groaned as I hung up my coat, then sneaked out and crept up on Holly from behind. 'You're talking about one of your random romcoms on Netflix, aren't you?' I tapped her left shoulder and, when she looked round, veered right to swipe a slice of her pizza.

'Hey!'

I took a bite and spun towards Rachel with the dough dripping grease over my fingers. 'All fine,' I mouthed. 'Nothing out there.' Then, louder: 'Holly? Is it OK if I give it a miss tonight? Brodie was telling me about a fire pit out on the deck and I have this whole cowboy routine planned out.'

I was trying to keep it casual but I hoped Rachel understood that I wanted to make her feel as secure as possible here. I thought if I acted like, I don't know, some kind of lookout for a couple of hours, it might help her to relax.

'Dad!'

'I'll bring you and Mum movie snacks.'

'What *kind* of movie snacks?'

It turned out Rachel had packed toffee popcorn, Maltesers, marshmallows. Once we'd gorged ourselves on pizza, I cleaned away the dishes and tipped the snacks into bowls, then carried them on a tray towards the far end of the corridor and the door with the glass porthole in it that connected with the pool room.

The home cinema was on my right. The walls were lined with pleated fabric. There was a large screen at the front and twelve leather recliners arranged over three rows of stepped seating. A projector was spraying hot, dusty light towards the screen above where Holly and Rachel were sitting with Buster slumped on the floor in front of them. He got up and started begging as I passed Rachel the tray. She handed me her wine glass in exchange.

'Any chance of a refill?'

'For you? Anything.'

'And a can of Diet Coke for me, Dad.'

A flicker of contentment sparked in my heart. This was almost normal for us, and more than anything I wished I could savour the moment, but when I got back to the kitchen

I noticed Rachel's iPhone charging on the side. I stared at it, a hot prickle of unease at the base of my neck.

No. Not now.

I tried to ignore it as I opened the fridge, taking out a can of Coke and a chilled bottle of white. The spa hotel, though. It bothered me.

I shook my head and unscrewed the bottle, getting ready to pour.

And looked again at the phone. For the record, I don't make a habit of snooping on my wife. Even my phone call to the spa hotel had been an accidental thing. But, right now, it was hard to resist the opportunity to find out what had been going on.

I checked the corridor behind me. Empty. The neck of the wine bottle rattled against Rachel's glass. And then in one fast rush I'd set the bottle down, snatched up her phone and jabbed the home button with my thumb.

My hand shook. The lock screen on Rachel's phone featured an image of Michael with his arms draped around Holly. I recognized it from our last family holiday together to Cornwall. The kids were pulling silly faces. Michael had his tongue out. Holly's cheeks and eyes bulged.

Go ahead or back down?

Quickly now, I tapped the home button again and this time the passcode screen appeared. I typed in Rachel's code. Six numbers. The month and year of Michael's birth.

The screen shook. The speaker buzzed. The phone vibrated in my hand.

Huh?

I tried again.

And got the same result.

My heart beat painfully in my chest.

Rachel had changed her passcode.

Another time, in other circumstances, it would have been a small thing. But now . . .

Rachel has been using the same code for years, for her bank cards as well as her phone. So why had she changed it? Was there information she wanted to keep from me? Calendar entries or texts she was worried I would see?

Or was the switch entirely innocent? A simple security update? Maybe even a healthy step towards moving on from Michael's death?

My thumb twitched. I almost tried again, this time with a different code. But I didn't because I was worried of locking Rachel out of her phone and I didn't want her to know I'd been prying. I sloshed wine in her glass instead. Ignorance is bliss. Isn't that what they say? But just then, it didn't feel so blissful to me.

10

That crack about being a cowboy. Even as I'd said it I knew it was a dumb thing to say. But sitting out by the fire in the night, with the flames guttering in the breeze coming in off the ocean and the mist of rain and sea spray on the air, I couldn't escape the feeling I was on some kind of frontier, keeping watch over my family.

Such as it was.

I opened another of Brodie's beers and hunkered down in my coat, and since I was trying very hard *not* to think about why Rachel had changed the passcode on her phone, I started thinking about what she'd asked me to think about instead. I dared to imagine how it would feel to forgive Michael, to believe in him again. To know he'd been a good kid on the threshold of becoming a good man. To see that he'd simply been unlucky and that I shouldn't blame him for that.

How would it feel? It would feel like finally swimming to the surface of the deepest, darkest ocean after being submerged for too long. It would feel like breathing clean air again.

But it was only a fantasy. A fairy tale Rachel had spun for herself. Because the truth was Michael wasn't blameless.

And neither was I. And that left me down in the depths, choking on the black water that had filled my lungs.

Oh. And did I mention that my wife had changed the passcode to her phone?

'Hey, Dad.'

Holly appeared next to me with Buster sniffing the air alongside her. I hadn't heard them approach. Some lookout.

I patted a space next to me and waited for Holly to sit down while Buster went off to the treeline to pee.

'How was your film?'

'It was OK. Mum's gone to bed. She said to ask you to make sure all the doors and windows are locked before you come up. You know, because of the high crime rate around here?'

Holly bumped my hip and I half smiled, staring into the fire. But still, it burned me that Rachel felt so vulnerable here and that I couldn't do much to change that. If it was this bad at the lodge, how much worse would it get when we returned to London? I wondered if I should suggest some kind of therapy or grief counselling again. I'd tried to talk Rachel into it following Michael's death but she'd always refused point blank, as if by resisting help she was somehow showing more loyalty to Michael. I thought that was pretty dumb, but then again, I hadn't taken my own advice and gone for counselling either, so who was I to talk?

'Can I have one too, Dad?'

'One of what, Holly?'

'One of those cigarettes you're trying to hide from me.'

'Huh?' I raised the cigarette in my hand and did a double-take as if it had materialized out of thin air. I used to smoke all the time when I was younger but Rachel had made me quit when Michael was born. Lately, I'd flirted with the habit again. A classic distraction, I suppose. 'Are you going to tell Mum about this?'

'I guess that depends on you, Dad.'

'Blackmail? Really?'

'I just want to have a go.'

I peered at her, as though I was actually considering it. And you know what? It was tempting to say yes, because it had been too long now since Holly had asked me to share something secret with her. But then again . . .

'Sorry, but you know Mum would kill me.' I took a hit on the cigarette and hacked up a cough for effect, then tossed it into the flames.

We watched it burn for a long moment before Holly spoke again.

'You don't have to worry about me so much, you know?'

'Parent's prerogative, sweetheart.'

'I get that. But sometimes it feels like you and Mum are watching me for signs that I might do something like Michael did. And I'm not going to do that. I would never do that.'

'You think Mum and me worry about that?'

She nodded. I could see tiny flames from the firelight reflected in the damp glimmer of her eyes, even through the bruising to her face.

'Holly, the depth and width of what your mum and I worry about when it comes to you.' I shook my head, lost for a moment. 'It's bigger than that ocean. But that's our problem. Not yours.'

'But it is my problem, Dad. It is, because I don't want to let you down.'

I felt a pinching in my heart. 'You won't, Holly.'

'I might. He took that from me. Michael did. Because I'm not allowed to screw up now, am I? He died, so I have to stay safe. Everything I do has to be safe. That's why you and Mum freaked out so much about what happened in that alley. That's why we're here, isn't it?'

I looked into the fire some more, feeling sad and desperately sorry for Holly, but at the same time enjoying the sensation of being close to her again. And yes, I did know what she meant. And no, it wasn't fair. It wasn't rational. But in so many ways she was living for the two of them now. Her future would always – in some ways – be Michael's future too. The paths she followed. The decisions she made. I would weigh them against choices her brother might have taken if he'd lived. I knew Rachel would do the same. It was inevitable. Unavoidable.

'We want to protect you, Holly. I'm sorry but that's just how it is. And it would have been the same if your brother was still alive.'

'But not as intense.'

'No, not as intense.'

I reached inside my jacket for my cigarette packet and made a show out of crushing it and adding it to the flames.

'Neat gesture, Dad. It would be a lot neater if I hadn't seen where you've stashed another packet in the car.'

'Oh, Holly.' I pulled her into me, feeling a sudden, inexplicable compulsion never to let her go. Across the deck, I could see Buster ambling back to us from the trees.

'Are you and Mum getting back together again?'

I stilled. How best to phrase this? 'It's complicated, Hols. You know that.'

'She wants to, you know.'

'She didn't tell you that.'

'Duh. She doesn't have to, Dad. It's pretty obvious. You just have to try not to, you know, screw it up?'

11

Maybe it was obvious to Holly. It didn't seem so obvious to me.

Holly kept me company for another ten minutes before hugging me goodnight and heading up to bed, with Buster following close behind. I stayed outside for a while longer, thinking about Rachel, remembering, among other things, how we'd first met. It was in the bar of our student union. Rachel was weaving drunkenly on a table, dressed in blue scrubs with a stethoscope around her neck. She was holding a plastic syringe in one hand that she was using to squirt shots of vodka into the mouths of the medically needy below. I was the guy she accidentally squirted in the eye. It stung – though maybe not *quite* as much as I made out – and Rachel leaped down to check I was OK. She had a pretty unique diagnostic method. It involved tilting my face to the light, grabbing my backside and sticking her tongue down my throat.

The kiss was wonderfully spontaneous and overwhelming. I can still taste the cherry vodka on her tongue. When we eventually – breathlessly – pulled apart, sparks of electricity fizzed in her eyes. And then had come that giddy, cascading laugh – something I knew right away I wanted to hear again and again.

Where had that dazzling, funny girl gone? What had we done to each other?

I went inside, locked the sliding door behind me, hung my coat and stashed my boots in the laundry room, then walked the ground floor of the lodge in my socks, checking the windows in the kitchen, heading down the corridor towards the pool. A series of wall sconces glowed dimly in the cinema room and I flipped them off, then ducked down a short, dog-legged corridor opposite that had a tall, thin window at the end. A tight left turn took me down a couple of steps into a small library – a book-lined nook with wall-to-wall fitted shelving. Nothing much else to see.

In the pool room, the stink of chlorine brought tears to my eyes. The pool was lit acid green by a series of submerged bulbs and wave patterns shimmered across the walls and the night-time glass, making it feel like I was trapped inside an aquarium. I rattled the handle of the patio door on the far side of the room. It was locked, same as everywhere else.

Good to go.

I left my reflection behind me in the glass and walked back along the corridor, through the living room, up the floating staircase. The door to Holly's room was ajar and light was shining around the rim.

I stuck my head inside. Holly was tucked up under the duvet, her eyes closed, her mouth hanging open, the light from the en suite washing across her bruised face. I wobbled when I saw her sleeping that way. Holly hasn't slept with a light on in her room since she was seven years old.

Buster was curled up in a tight ball at the bottom of her duvet, trying to make himself as small and as still as possible.

I made a *tsk-tsk* noise in my throat and shook my head. Buster knew the rules. He knew he should have been in his own bed. But he also probably knew I wasn't about to tell him that tonight.

Feeling a lingering sense of dismay about Holly, I left the door slightly ajar, tiptoed back along the mezzanine and turned into the corridor that separated Rachel's room from my own. Her bedroom door was partway open. A light was on in there too.

I hesitated.

'You can come in, Tom.' Something in her voice. 'I'm awake.'

The light was from a bedside lamp. Next to it was Rachel's wine glass and the nearly empty bottle of white wine from the fridge, as well as her phone. I stared at her phone. Then I became *aware* that I was staring at it. Not a good move.

Rachel sniffed and wiped a hand across her eyes and suddenly I saw that she'd been crying, sitting there with her bare legs clutched to her chest, wearing an old, laundry-faded T-shirt from a family holiday to San Diego taken years ago. 'Are you OK?'

She peered up at me, shaking her head, her cheeks swollen and blotchy. 'Aren't you tired of all this, Tom? I'm so tired of it. I just want it to stop. I want everything to go back to how it used to be. And I want Michael back. I want him back so much.'

Her shoulders heaved and I went to her, bringing her into my arms. She felt too light. Too fragile. I had the feeling that if I squeezed her I might break something.

'I know,' I whispered. 'I know. I wish that too.'

'I've tried to be strong for Holly and I just haven't been. I don't know how to connect with her any more. With you. I've messed up so badly.'

'Hey,' I told her. 'Hey, enough. I shouldn't have moved out, Rachel. That was wrong. I was wrong. I just wanted—'

'I know.' She pressed her head against my chest. 'I disappeared,' she said, in a choked voice. 'But it's been so hard not to, Tom. And now I'm exhausted. From all of it. All of the time.'

I lifted her chin, wiped the tears from her face with my thumbs. Outside, rain fell against the skylight in the sloping ceiling above us. The wind hummed and whooped.

'Buster's on Holly's bed with her,' I said softly. 'He's watching her for us.'

Rachel nodded and backed away from me a little. 'There's something I have to talk to you about. Something important.'

Uh oh. Have you ever heard something good that started that way? I thought of the spa hotel. The passcode to Rachel's phone. *I've messed up so badly.* Everything seemed to rush in at me at once, like the walls of the room were collapsing around me. I didn't want to hear it. Not now.

You just have to try not to, you know, screw it up?

'Rachel, why don't we wait until morning, OK?'

'But, Tom, I—'

'Please, Rachel. Let's just wait, can we? I really think that would be best.'

She smiled slowly, reluctantly, then lifted her shoulders. 'Maybe you're right. Maybe right now I'm just too . . .' She shook her head, as if she couldn't find the words.

'Tipsy?'

'*Nooo.*' She smiled a little as she pressed her forehead against mine and cupped her hands to the back of my neck. 'But I do want to be thinking clearly,' she whispered. 'I have so much I need to say to you, Tom.'

I swallowed hard. 'So tomorrow, then?'

'Tomorrow.' She nodded, like she was underlining the decision, and rubbed the back of my neck. 'You could get in,' she whispered. 'You could stay. I don't mind.'

I didn't say anything to that and after a few moments Rachel sighed and let go of me, leaning back.

'You don't think that's a good idea?'

'I'd like to, if that helps,' I said, carefully. 'But maybe we shouldn't rush things?'

And maybe I should hear what you have to say to me tomorrow first.

'Eighteen years of marriage and you don't want to rush things.'

'Rachel, come on, I—'

'No. No, it's OK, Tom. You're probably right. I'm not sure I can trust my own judgement right now. Maybe it's better if I trust yours.'

I paused and found myself looking down at her phone for too long again before I snapped out of it. 'Are you going to be OK in here?'

'I'll be fine.'

'Then I should probably say goodnight now.'

'Probably.'

She gazed at me with a kind of sadness I couldn't quite interpret and I sat there awkwardly for a few seconds, almost changing my mind and staying.

'Well. Goodnight, Rachel.'

'Goodnight.'

I stood and crossed the hallway to my bedroom, where I used the en suite and shed my clothes until I was wearing just my boxers, then flipped off the light, peeled back the covers and climbed into my usual side of the bed.

I lay there, listening to the rain and the wind building outside, replaying my conversation with Rachel over and over, wondering where I'd gone wrong, where I'd gone right, wondering if I should get out of my bed and go to her room. And then, some time later – I don't know how long, exactly, though I'm guessing something like forty-five minutes had passed because I'd rolled onto my side and was nearly asleep – the springs of my mattress compressed and deflected as Rachel eased into my bed. She scooted towards me under the duvet until she was spooning me and I could feel the heat coming off her body.

'Don't think,' she whispered. 'Just go with this, OK?'

Would you be surprised if I told you that, when her hand snaked round my waist and slipped down under the waistband of my boxers, I did?

I turned to her and knotted my hand in her hair. I pulled her lips to my mouth.

Rachel. Her tongue didn't taste of cherry vodka but kissing her still gave me chills. I ran my hands over the familiar-yet-new-again contours of her body. I tugged at her T-shirt.

Like I told you before, I love my wife. Despite everything that had happened – the ways I'd hurt Rachel and Rachel had hurt me – that had never gone away.

I wanted her. That would never go away, either.

I eased her onto her back and looked down at her in the dark.

'I love you, Tom Sullivan,' she told me, her eyelashes flickering against my cheeks.

'I love you too,' I said.

Her breath mingled with my breath. Her heart beat against my heart. Lost in the moment – caught up in Rachel – it was almost possible to believe that everything really would be OK.

'Michael, watch out.'

Fiona's last words.

But it's much too late already. The road has swung left on a tight curve at the end of a long straight and the car has not swung with it.

Eyes wide, Michael saws at the wheel. The Audi lists and yaws, its tyres scrabbling on the slickened blacktop.

The suspension compresses then unloads. Momentum tips the chassis. Michael can feel the passenger side lift up until Fiona is above him, her long hair floating around her. He's suddenly sure now that the car is about to topple. Any slight touch of the brake would flip it. He turns the wheel the other way, into the skid.

A squeal. A brief rubber yip.

The car slams down and shimmies, then straightens.

Michael, watch out.

For what?

For the woods that are hurtling towards them through the black?

For the basic laws of physics?

He brakes, but there's not enough time. Not enough distance.

The reflective surface of a turn sign pulses in his vision. They smash through it and the bonnet lurches up.

'I'm sorry,' Michael says.

Sorry that this is happening. Sorry that you're here with me. Sorry that I messed up. Sorry for everything.

12

'**Tom?**'

Rachel shook my shoulder.

'Tom, wake up.' She whispered, close to my ear: 'I think I heard something.'

I groaned and mashed my face into my pillow.

'Tom, it sounded like a window breaking. I think there's someone downstairs.'

I groaned some more. Rachel is a light sleeper. She hears bumps in the night. And I'm the one she's turned to – again and again – to get out of bed and creep downstairs to investigate.

'Tom?'

It was warm and fuggy under the covers – my legs were tangled in Rachel's legs – and I could so easily drift off again. I could hear the hitch of fear in Rachel's voice but it wasn't quite enough to tug me back to full consciousness.

Then a vague distant noise made me stir. It *could* have been the sound of glass crunching underfoot.

My heart clenched as Rachel yanked on my upper arm.

'Tom? Wake up. *Please.*'

Eyes open, listening hard.

The room was black. The only light was the faint glow of my wristwatch. It was just after 2 a.m.

Another slight crunching sound.

Oh God.

I blinked and stared into the pulsing darkness as a great sucking fear invaded my chest. In my mind I was watching a kind of home movie rendered in fuzzy greyscale. I was picturing a long, uninterrupted tracking shot – the visual equivalent of the auditory hunt I was carrying out with my ears. The camera in my mind's eye went snuffling across the carpet and out of the bedroom door. It sped low along the unlit hallway, sweeping left and right in small, tight arcs, like a bloodhound following a scent. When the camera reached the mezzanine it pitched up and then down over the polished steel banister rail overlooking the vaulted space below. It dropped on a wire, spinning and sweeping, sniffing out the source of the gritty crunching I had heard.

'I'm scared, Tom.'

'Shh.'

Was that the whisper of the sliding glass door on to the deck being pulled back? And now the dull thud of the door hitting the rubber buffer?

Rachel clutched my arm again. I didn't have any clothes on under the covers. And all right, it shouldn't have been a big deal right then, but it's amazing how being naked can make you feel more vulnerable.

Silence.

I waited.

My heart jackhammered in my chest, pushing me up off the mattress. Rachel's fingers dug into my flesh.

The silence persisted, but this was no natural hush. It felt loaded. Felt forced. Like somebody was holding their breath downstairs.

I was listening so intensely it was as if I could hear the throbbing of the very air itself – the sound of millions of tiny molecules rubbing and vibrating against one another. It was a sound like no other. The sound of pure fear in the middle of the night.

And before Rachel had woken me, had I heard something else? I could dimly remember a noise from the deep recesses of my dreams. A keening, buzzing whine like a tumble dryer thrashing around on a fast spin. Like a chainsaw felling a tree.

Real or imagined?

Intruder or not?

'Footsteps,' Rachel whispered.

'You think?'

'*Yes.* Downstairs. And voices, I think.'

Cold sweat sluiced across my forehead, down my neck.

But there was nothing now. Nothing other than images of an empty room transmitting back from the imaginary camera feed in my head. All I could hear were the muffled night noises of a house at rest. The bluster and whoop of the wind outside. The drumming and lashing of rain on the roof.

And the hammering of the blood in my ears.

OK, think.

Think.

Maybe I hadn't locked the sliding door quite right. That was possible, wasn't it? It was my first time locking the door and I could have made a mistake. I'd been preoccupied. I'd been drinking. So maybe I hadn't locked the door right and the wind had buffeted and sucked at it. Or maybe a fallen branch had cracked a glass pane.

I waited.

Hard to know what was worse. Part of me craved confirmation, however bad that might be. Parted of me absolutely dreaded it.

My mouth was dry. My chest very tight. My mind still caught in the gummy bind of sleep.

But my instincts were alive to the threat. I could feel the hairs on the backs of my arms standing to attention.

Rachel flinched and spun towards the doorway, the mattress springs creaking too loud. Had she heard something? She was clenching my hand very tight now. It reminded me of the way she'd held it when she was in labour with Michael and Holly.

Holly.

'Could it be Holly?' I whispered.

'Why would she go outside?'

So Rachel had heard the sliding door too. Or thought that she had. A deep, penetrating chill engulfed my heart.

'Maybe she can't sleep.'

Or maybe she was sneaking out onto the deck, down by the fire. Maybe she had a cigarette she wanted to smoke. She'd told me she'd seen my stash in the car. I guessed it was possible she could have taken one earlier. Unlikely, but possible.

But no, that didn't add up. Holly had a door from her bedroom that opened on to the balcony connecting her room to Rachel's. If she wanted to smoke one of my cigarettes, it would be easier for her to go out there. But why go outside in this weather?

And besides, no matter how much I wanted to believe it, the entire scenario was unlikely. A product of my groggy mind. I couldn't think of the last time Holly had stirred in the night. Not since the weeks after Michael had died, I didn't think. She was a deep sleeper. Always had been. Even as a young child, she'd only woken if she was scared or sick.

Then a new thought struck me. Could it be Brodie? But why would he come here in the middle of the night?

'Put on a light.' The scratch of fear in Rachel's voice was like fingernails on a chalkboard. 'Please, Tom.'

I stayed dead still. The more we talked, the more we could be heard. And I had the feeling Rachel's voice had masked another slight noise from downstairs. A kind of ripping, tearing sound, but muffled and slow.

Something cold and slick coiled up in my stomach as I remembered the break-in at Lionel's home in London and the brutal attack on Jennifer. Her murder had been the result of a botched robbery. I thought of the artwork on the walls here. Was that what this was?

Then, something else: the campfire in the woods.

Had there been someone out there after all?

I clenched my teeth, feeling the muscles in my neck pull taut. I told myself that maybe if I didn't move – if I stayed hunched up in my bed – it wouldn't be real.

I didn't want for it to be real.

'Fine. *I'll* put on a light.'

Rachel lunged for the side of the bed. The sudden *click* of the switch on the bedside lamp sounded like a gun being cocked.

Not that I know anything about guns. But times like this, the mind goes where it must.

Light exploded around the room. Too bright. Too soon.

I listened for a response from downstairs.

Nothing.

Rachel turned to me slowly, her eyes lit black in the sudden glare. Her jaw was slack, her skin shiny and bloodless. She looked terrified.

'Maybe it's Buster,' I said.

Normally, if Buster got up during the night he'd stretch and flap his ears, scratch his hind quarters, grunt and rub his head on the carpet, lick one of our hands, do *something* to wake one of us up because he knew he wouldn't wake Holly and pretty much the *only* reason Buster moved during the night was if he needed to be let out to relieve himself. But we were in a strange house. Maybe he couldn't find us.

'Do you think he went downstairs?' I whispered.

Rachel didn't answer. Something crossed her face. She turned and stared at the open door again. The glow of the bedside lamp was slanting out into the hallway. I saw her rise up a little, like she'd heard something out there. My heart beat hard in my chest.

'What is it?'

'I don't know. I'm thinking.'

Of the sliding door, I bet. I was too. Because there was no way Buster could open it on his own.

So OK. Maybe for the first time in Buster's life he'd managed to wake Holly instead of one of us. He'd been in her room, after all. So maybe Holly had got up with him instead of calling to us.

There was a first time for everything, right? Or maybe Holly had woken in pain from her facial injuries and had needed a glass of water to swallow a couple of pills. Maybe Buster had gone downstairs with her. Maybe Holly had dropped her glass on the floor.

Made sense.

'I'll go and take a look.'

'Be careful.'

I threw back the covers and sat on the edge of the bed. The night air was crisp. Goosebumps sprouted across my arms, shoulders and legs.

My boxers were twisted up on the floor. I slipped them on. Then I crouched next to my suitcase, put on some jogging trousers and a vest and padded across the room in my bare feet. I paused at the doorway, listening, then slipped out into the corridor beyond. Exactly like the journey I had followed with the camera in my head.

Only the corridor wasn't unlit. Not completely. There was the soft glow of the bedside lamp in Rachel's room bleeding into the black across the way. And at the end, beyond the mezzanine, the wavering halo effect from the downstairs lights. Holly must have flipped them on.

I felt a sudden surge of relief. A slackening of my limbs.

She was a good kid. Considerate not to wake us. Brave, when I thought of all she'd been through recently.

But she'd nearly given her parents a coronary.

I strolled on towards the light burning up from the living area. I was rubbing at my eyes. Stifling a yawn. I was getting ready to talk with my daughter.

But when I reached the front of the mezzanine and took

hold of the banister rail a sudden electric charge ripped through me.

It wasn't Holly down there.

It was far, far worse than that.

13

Fear chased me back to my bedroom – that disabling, mind-jamming, heart-pumping kind of fear that only comes during a true crisis.

'What is it?' Rachel asked.

She was kneeling on the bed in her T-shirt, tugging and twisting the hem in her hands. The moment she saw me her eyes went huge. I was wearing my fear like a heavy coat.

'What's wrong?'

How to tell your wife this? How to begin to say these words?

My head was pounding so hard my vision shook.

'There are two men downstairs.'

'*What?*'

'Shh. They've hurt Buster.'

'What do you mean they've hurt him?'

I meant that one of the men had been stooped at the waist, dragging Buster across the floor by his hind legs. I meant that Buster had been limp and inert, his tongue hanging from his mouth.

The other man had been standing by the open door to the deck, facing out to the storm. The wind was driving against him, carrying with it a hard rain that scattered across the wooden floorboards like spilled salt.

My pulse beat in my throat.

'Tom, please. Is Buster OK? What's happening?'

'I think they've killed him.'

'*What?*'

Rachel rocked forwards onto her hands and knees and bowed her head. It was hitting her hard now, reality beginning to buck and swell beneath her like a boat on the sea.

I thought of the hunters Brodie had told us about. Was that who the two men were? The callous way one of them had been dragging Buster – like he was a hare caught in one of their snares – seemed to fit with it.

Brodie had said they wouldn't be back while we were here. Word would get around. But what if word *had* got around and they'd come here because of that?

Or – and this was worse, I think – what if they'd been here from the start? What if they'd been here all day? Waiting.

'Oh God, Tom. Where's Holly?'

'I'm going to check. I'll go outside, along the balcony from your room to hers. They can't see me that way. You need to get dressed, Rachel. Do it now.'

But Rachel wasn't listening to me. She sprang off the bed, barged me out of the way and darted across the hallway into her room.

I chased after her. She was already on her way out through the glass door on to the high balcony. As she released the door the wind snatched at it and I had to catch it to stop it from slamming with a bang.

I pressed it closed behind me, the wind blustering against my back. The storm was wild outside. Sheets of rain pelted down hard. The balcony was drenched. A watery film gleamed blue-white in the moonlight, kicking up in fans from Rachel's heels as she ran. I splashed after her, my heart knocking against my ribs, watching as she grabbed the handle to Holly's door and rattled it.

Locked.

Rachel whined in panic and used her forearm to swipe rain from the glass as she peered inside.

'She's in there.' Her hands squeaked down the soaked pane. 'I think she's asleep.'

I looked around me in a hurry, then reached back and grabbed for one of the metal patio chairs. The rain hammered down like falling silver coins, bouncing off the chair as I lifted it and twisted and got ready to punch a metal leg through the glass.

'*No!*' Rachel blocked me with her arms crossed in front of her face. 'Too loud.'

She swiped the rain from her face, staring at me. She was right. The men would hear a sudden, brash *crack* in the quiet of the lodge. Same thing if we knocked on the door and tried to wake Holly. What if she startled and said something? Chances were the men would respond before we could get her out.

I looked back along the balcony. Rain had beaded on the lengths of high-tensile steel cable that had been threaded horizontally beneath the banister rail. The cables quivered in the wind.

I leaned out and looked over the yard, rain whipping in my face. The only vehicle I could see was our Volvo, down in the carport. It looked small and very far away.

'This way, Rachel. Hurry.'

I ran back along the balcony, my hand up in front of my eyes. The tops of the nearby pines thrashed and shook. The rain splattered down hard.

'We can't just leave her, Tom.'

I spun back and stared at Rachel, my chest hitching and falling at an irregular tempo. How could she think that? How could she even begin to believe—?

'I'm not going to leave her,' I said. 'I'm going to get her. I promise. But we have to hurry. *Now*.'

I grabbed her and dragged her after me into her bedroom. Her mobile was on the side. I pressed it into her hands.

'Get the police. Message someone. Anyone. Get help.'

Rachel clutched the phone and jabbed at the screen.

I turned, searching around me for an improvised weapon. The room seemed to blur. I was having difficulty thinking straight and my whole body seemed to pulse with the beating of my heart. I saw the table lamps on either side of the bed. But if I grabbed one I'd be trailing flex. And they were chubby and unwieldy. The wine bottle, then?

'Wi-Fi's not working.'

I spun back. Rachel was pressing a hand to her forehead. I felt an emptiness open up inside of me.

'It's not working, Tom. There's no signal.'

'Wait here.'

I blundered across the hallway into my own bedroom and picked up my phone from next to the bed.

Please work. Please work. Please—

But when I powered it on, I got the same result.

No Wi-Fi. No signal.

My lungs shut down. I looked up, feeling the room begin to spin. Rachel was blocking the doorway, her T-shirt soaked, clutching at her hair.

Two strange men. Two intruders in the dead of night. Rachel's worst fear made real. Her own personal nightmare.

But it was worse than she knew.

A cold numbness spread through my body as I pocketed my phone and pushed her back into her room.

'Listen to me, Rachel. I have to tell you this. They're wearing suits.'

'Suits?'

'Coveralls. The disposable kind that zip up the front. They have hoods on. Masks on. Plastic gloves.'

And they were wearing ankle-high rubber boots. Like government scientists sent in to clean up a chemical spill. Like workers in an abattoir.

Rachel sagged. I held her up by her arms. She looked bloodless and stricken but she understood what I was saying. I almost wished she didn't.

'This isn't a burglary, Tom. Burglars don't come dressed that way.'

I stared at her. Maybe. But then again, maybe not. I thought once more of the botched robbery at Lionel's London home that had led to Jennifer's death. I thought of the police's main suspect, Tony Bryant, and how he'd never been caught. Then I thought of the Damien Hirst print over the floating staircase. Had Bryant come back for more? Maybe with an accomplice? If the men were here to steal the print, they'd be coming upstairs soon.

The temperature in the room – cool to begin with – seemed to drop about ten degrees.

We had no mobile signal. The Wi-Fi wasn't functioning. The only landline handset I was aware of was downstairs in the kitchen. Our coats and boots were in the laundry room. We were isolated by geography, cut off by the storm.

Oh God.

I needed some kind of weapon and I needed it now.

'Keep trying your phone.'

I stepped into the en suite. The air seemed to crackle. There were nail scissors in Rachel's washbag. I gripped them in my clammy fist but it didn't feel like enough. I stashed the scissors in a pocket of my jogging trousers, the opposite side to my phone, then stepped out and threw open the doors to the wardrobe, pushing aside a terry-cloth robe.

There.

A long metal pole. It had a hook on one end, rubber grips on the other. There was a crank handle at the base. It was the pole for opening and closing the skylight in the sloping ceiling overhead.

I pulled it out and held it crossways in front of me, testing its heft. It felt too heavy and too light all at the same time. Too heavy because my arms were weak with fear. Too light because I wasn't sure what damage it could do.

'I'm going to get Holly.'

My voice sounded like it was coming from somebody else – someone who didn't fully believe what he was saying. I moved past Rachel towards the bedroom door. I was breathing so hard I was close to hyperventilating.

'Are you crazy? They'll see you.'

But if I didn't go now, I was afraid I wouldn't go at all.

'They didn't see me before. I'll be careful. Get dressed. Keep trying the Wi-Fi. And lock this door behind me. Push that dresser across behind it if you can.'

The dresser was a mighty thing. It was made of solid mahogany with five curved drawers on the front. I wasn't sure Rachel could shift it by itself but if she could then it would make for a reasonable barricade.

'Hunt around you for a weapon. Anything you can find. Hairspray. A razor. Anything.'

'Tom.'

'It's going to be OK, Rachel.' I blinked and black spots danced before my eyes. 'We're going to be OK.'

'Tom, please. Just wait.'

But I didn't wait. I was gone.

14

Out of the bedroom. Along the hallway. Following the same path as the imaginary camera in my head. Keeping low. Staying tight in to the wall and crawling along on my hands and knees with the metal pole gripped lengthways in my right hand and my pulse jumping in my throat.

I had no plan. I had no idea what to do. Should I try to attack the men, shout at them, scare them? Or should I stay hidden and try to get Holly and Rachel away?

My elbows shook and buckled. Tremors passed through me.

Noise. Ahead and below. Nothing identifiable. Just the muted, indistinct sounds made by two strangers stalking around and trying to keep sound to a minimum. There was the occasional rasp and crackle of their disposable coveralls. The dull tread of rubber boots on the wooden flooring. The whoop and bluster of the wind outside.

The rush of my breathing was making it difficult to hear. I was panting very fast but it didn't seem to be helping. There wasn't enough air in my lungs.

Sweat prickled through my hair as I craned my neck and looked down. Far below me, the sliding glass door was still open, rain spraying in like it was coming from a hose. No sign of Buster. Or Holly.

Was this a mistake? I hoped so. Maybe the men believed the lodge was empty? Or had they come because they knew we were here?

Questions. Too many of them. Too scary to handle. And I had no time for them now.

I swept my gaze to the left, towards Holly's bedroom. Her door was hanging ajar, the same way I'd left it earlier.

Don't come out. Please don't come out. Keep sleeping until I get to you.

So get to her now!

I crawled on. First sliding my right hand and knee forwards. Then my left. My shakes were becoming more exaggerated and I had a sensation like vertigo – as if I was crawling along a narrow beam above a deadly drop.

Another angle on the living space. I cautiously raised my head. My breathing stopped. The two men were squatted next to one another, unzipping three large sports holdalls. The holdalls were laid out on a square of blue plastic sheeting. Two of them were empty. One was not.

My heart pounded even faster.

The empty holdalls looked – and believe me, I really didn't want to be thinking this way – like improvised body bags.

I closed my eyes and felt the cold numbing sensation seep in from my extremities, pooling around my heart and lungs.

Calm down. Think. Holly needs you to calm down.

A slight clinking and my eyes sprang open again. The men were emptying equipment out of the third holdall onto the plastic sheeting. My vision throbbed. There were ropes and restraints. There was a double-barrelled shotgun and a handgun. There was a pry bar, a short-handled axe, a roll of gaffer tape, a claw hammer and a rubber mallet.

Oh Jesus. Not good. Really not good.

Three body bags. Three members of my family.

The plastic sheeting. The disposable coveralls. The firearms and the sinister DIY equipment.

This isn't a burglary, Tom.

I had to get my family out of here. I had to do it now.

The men stood suddenly and I sprawled forwards, lying flat on the ground, my chin grazing carpet.

A scuffing noise behind me. It sounded like Rachel was shunting the dresser behind her bedroom door.

Good.

Did the men hear it? I looked up. No, it didn't seem so. Their heads were close together, like they were whispering through their masks. Their masks were cupped shells of paper with elasticated straps that stretched around their plastic hoods. The height I was looking down at them from warped their dimensions, but I could tell that one of the men was taller and broader. The other was slighter and shorter.

I focused in on the bigger man and a dizzying thought struck me. Could it be Brodie? Was that why he was in coveralls, hiding his face? He looked roughly the right build, right height. And he'd know about the Wi-Fi. He'd know how to disable it.

Was Brodie bothering you?

I'd told Rachel no, but the truth is his interest in her *had* bothered me. There'd been an odd kind of furtive quality to it – an energy it was hard to put my finger on. What if he'd taken offence at Rachel's brush-off? What if I'd angered him when I'd made it clear it was time for him to leave? What if he'd come back tonight for my wife?

I held my nerve and kept watching. It seemed like the smaller man was in charge. He had his hand up, shielding his masked mouth, like he was the one issuing instructions and the bigger man was receiving them and nodding along.

So not Brodie, then?

A short pause and then the bigger man crouched and picked up the handgun and the short-handled axe. The smaller man selected the shotgun. I felt a hot buzzing in my veins. Then the men swivelled and gazed up at the mezzanine.

I flattened myself, pressing my body into the thick carpet fibres. My pulse pounded in my ears. Beyond it, I could just about hear the faint swish and crackle of the men's coveralls. Then footfall, the note changing from a dull, brittle percussion to the hollow thud of a careful rubber tread.

On the stairs.

I swallowed something about the size and consistency of a golf ball.

I couldn't stay here. I had to move. But I couldn't stand up and run because the men would see me.

So crawl on your belly.

I squirmed forwards, rocking my hips, digging into the carpet with my elbows and fingers.

The men's slow footfall made me believe I hadn't been seen. Then, with a cold jolt of adrenaline, I realized: *They think we're asleep. They don't want to wake us. They're planning to sneak up on us.*

How many stairs were there? Fifteen at a minimum? Maybe as many as twenty, twenty-two? If the big man was coming first, his line of sight could be level with the floor of the mezzanine once he was seven or eight steps from the top.

I guessed he'd climbed four or five steps already. More if he was coming up two treads at a time.

I scrambled past the top of the stairs, tucked my feet up behind me and pressed my body against the wall. My heart skittered and thumped. I was breathing hard and sweating harder, blinking cold perspiration from my eyes.

Think.

Holly's bedroom door was just a few metres away. I could see the light from her en suite on the inside. If I was quick I could dart through and slam the door behind me. Turn the key in the lock.

And then?

The men would hear me. They had guns and axes. A lock wouldn't do any good against that. And what about Rachel? She'd be on her own. A chest of drawers wouldn't protect her for long. I'd told her to arm herself with hairspray and razors. *Hairspray,* when these men had *guns.*

And that's when I knew. That's when it hit me for real. I couldn't just hide from this. I couldn't just run. I had to defend my family. And right now – no matter how scared I was – defending my family meant I had to attack.

But how?

I pictured myself standing up with my back flat against the wall and the metal pole held back behind my shoulder. When the lead man came into view, could I swing with everything I had?

But what if he ducked? Or I missed? What if I didn't hit

him hard enough? I'd never attacked a man before. And there was still the second man to think of.

Time was almost up. My blood rushed in my ears but I could just hear the men's slow footsteps, getting closer.

So I gambled and went with a compromise. A classic lawyer's solution. A fudge.

I stood quickly, my legs like rubber, and flattened myself against the wall.

Wait.

My lungs were two heavy bags of damp sand.

Wait.

There was more sweat in my eyes but this time I didn't blink it away. I stared wildly through the stinging burn.

Wait.

The gloved hands of the lead man appeared holding the handgun and the axe.

Oh God.

Now.

I stepped out and faced him.

And almost fell back.

Almost dropped the pole.

It was the bigger man. Up close, he was enormous. A great big bear of a guy.

He had one foot planted. One foot in the air. Which meant – for that split-second – he was naturally off-balance.

Time slowed down. That tiny split-second stretched and stretched, becoming endlessly elastic, until I experienced each separate moment of it with stark and terrifying clarity.

I saw the man's masked chin tilt upwards. I saw his eyes widen in surprise from inside the elasticated hem of his hood. *Definitely not Brodie.* That's what my instincts told me. This was somebody else.

Then time sped up again and I saw him crumple forwards from the waist, as if a giant bungee cord attached to the base of his spine had suddenly reached its outer limit and retracted very fast, snapping him backwards, pulling him back. He bent that way because I'd jabbed him with the end of the skylight pole – almost without thinking about it, in a kind of nervy, jerking flinch – in the centre mass of his chest.

The blow wasn't huge but it did more than I could have hoped because it reversed the bigger man's momentum just as he had one foot in the air. And now he was rocking back.

His gun arm went high to compensate but all it did was generate more momentum. His hand holding the axe followed suit. I watched, stunned, until he let go of the axe and made a wild grab for me, his fingers tightening on the front of my vest.

He yanked me towards him. It felt like he was pulling out my heart. He couldn't prevent himself from falling but he could take me with him, maybe push me off the staircase, a mighty drop to the ground below.

And he would have done, except I swept up fast with the skylight pole in another desperate, jerking strike that smacked against his forearm and knocked his hand away.

His gun flashed and sparked. It was blindingly bright. Something zipped past my head. There was an enormous, percussive explosion and – as I ducked and clasped one hand to my scalp, terrified I'd been shot – the recoil was enough to send him crashing backwards into the smaller man following from behind.

A bullet *thunked* into the pitched ceiling somewhere overhead. Chunks of ceiling board clattered down. I heard the crash and crunch and grunts of the two men colliding and tumbling down the stairs.

But by then I was already swerving into Holly's room, my legs going from under me, slamming the door closed.

I turned the key in the lock.

15

'Dad? What was that bang?'

I flipped on the ceiling light. Dropped the skylight pole. My chest was heaving. I was twitching. Flinching. Scared out of my mind.

I could still feel the grip of the man's fist on my vest, pulling me forwards, like I was teetering even now. The racket of the gunshot seemed to be trapped inside my skull, thrashing around. I patted my hands across my torso and head. Hard to believe I hadn't fallen with him or been shot. It didn't feel real. None of this felt real. I kept waiting for it to stop. Like I could somehow wake up from a bad dream or reset the night and start it over.

'Dad!'

Holly peered at me from behind the bruising on her face. She was half out of bed, her covers thrown back, her legs hanging over the side. I saw her, and felt a sharp pinching in my chest. Her pink pyjamas were twisted and ruffled, one pyjama leg pulled up over her knee.

'Holly, you have to get up. Find some shoes.'

'What?'

No time. I rushed over and grabbed her, lifting her out of bed and carrying her to her suitcase. I could feel my heart bouncing back off her ribs. But when I tried to lower her she clung on to my neck, just like she had when she was a little girl.

'Holly, please. Listen to me. Just do what I say.'

'I don't under—'

'There are two men in the house,' I shouted, louder than I'd meant to. 'Bad men. We have to get away from them.'

The shock was immediate, like I'd slapped her in the dark. Her arms slipped from my neck and she stumbled backwards as I reached into her suitcase and flung clothes aside.

'Where are your shoes?'

'Where's Mum? Is she OK?'

'Your shoes, Holly.'

'I want to know where Mum is.'

Banging on the glass door behind us. It was Rachel, out on the balcony, in the rain. She'd put on a red turtleneck sweater and dark jeans. There were old running shoes on her feet.

I think seeing Rachel – seeing the frenzied panic she was in – finally convinced Holly how serious this was. She doubled over and clutched her stomach as Rachel banged on the door again – furious now – shouting for us to open up. She must have heard the gunshot too, I realized. No way she could have missed it. The massive *bang* was still bashing around inside my skull.

Rachel's mobile was in her hand. Please God, I hoped she'd got hold of the police.

'Dad!'

Heavy footsteps in the hallway. I turned and watched the internal wall shake. My heart seized. The handle of the bedroom door rattled hard. Stopped. Rattled again. Then there was a single massive thump on the timber, like one of the men had driven his fist into it.

'Open up!' he yelled. 'Open this door.'

For some reason, hearing his voice took my fear up another notch. It made it even more real.

'Shoes, Holly. Now.'

She didn't react right away. She was just staring at the door.

'Holly! Where are your shoes?'

'Here.' She ducked towards the foot of her bed, clutching a pair of pink trainers like she didn't know what they were.

'Put them on. Go to Mum.'

And then what?

I didn't know.

Rachel slapped her palms on the glass again. The men beat on the bedroom door. I swivelled my head between them, my legs buckling horribly as I pushed up to my feet.

Even if Rachel had managed to contact the police, we had to be miles from the nearest station. Out in the wilds, they probably only had a handful of men available. And they wouldn't get here any time soon.

The bedroom door handle rattled again, so hard now I thought it might fall off. Then the door bulged sickeningly against the frame. A shoulder barge. Maybe a kick.

'Holly. Go to Mum. Get out of here.'

From the corner of my eye, I saw her hopping across the room, struggling to put on her second shoe.

I spread my feet and hands out at my sides, trying to make myself as wide as possible. If they were coming through

I was going to have to tackle them. Futile, maybe, but right then it was the only plan I had.

Another huge thump in front of me. It felt like I'd been punched in the gut. The bedroom door was made from oak. Like everything in the lodge, it looked as if it had been expensively crafted and expertly fitted. But it wouldn't withstand a sustained attack.

How long could I stop them for? A second? Maybe two? Even with my life on the line – with Holly and Rachel's lives on the line – I knew I needed a better plan that that.

I looked to my right. There was a big wardrobe next to the door. Dark timber. A burnished, reddish gleam. I rushed to it, braced my feet wide apart, pulled.

The wardrobe tipped slightly, barely a tremble, then rocked back again. I pushed against it a second time, gurning and straining every sinew. My back burned. My hands quaked.

The wardrobe wouldn't budge.

Another crash against the door. It sounded like both men this time. I flinched. The door flexed and the frame bowed and swelled. Part of the frame had come away from the wall with a puff of dust, prising screws and Rawlplugs with it.

I stared, filled with an absolute, vibrating dread that the men were only seconds from getting through.

Then I felt a cold draught behind me and the next thing I knew Holly and Rachel were grabbing hold of the wardrobe on either side of me, bracing their feet, slanting their bodies, grunting and screaming and pulling. I pushed and strained even harder. I heaved with my arms. Thrust up with my legs.

The wardrobe tipped . . . and tipped . . . and . . .

Rachel yelped as the wardrobe tumbled down hard, tearing a gouge out of the wall and hitting the ground with a solid *whump.*

We fell into each other, crashing to our knees, holding each other, crying. I could see Holly's heart beating against the fabric of her pyjama top. Rachel was clutching me tight.

The wardrobe was butted up against the door. This time, when the men attacked, the sound of the impact was firmer. More secure. The wardrobe barely moved.

And there was an angry roar from out in the hallway. Like one of the men had hurt themselves. I pictured them on the other side. Rearing back. Rubbing their arms. Regrouping. Then I thought of the handgun and the shotgun. I thought of the men firing at the door.

A terrible clamour of fear.

'*Move!*'

I dragged Holly and Rachel up, scooping my arms around them and urging them on across the room towards the glass door swinging in the wind.

Holly's legs gave way. She crashed to her knees. I shoved Rachel on ahead of us, then ducked low and picked Holly up by her waist in a fireman's lift with her body jack-knifing over my shoulder and the backs of her legs clutched in my arms. Blood throbbed behind my eyes. I could hear the men kicking and banging on the door as I chased Rachel out onto the soggy balcony, splashing through the rain.

16

We ran into Rachel's bedroom. There was nowhere else to go. I put Holly down. Rachel immediately took her into her arms and let go of a sob as I ducked back and looked along the balcony, my heart in my throat.

No sign of the men. Not yet.

When I stepped back into Rachel's bedroom I could see that she'd dragged the dresser unit across behind her door like I'd told her to. It wasn't pushed quite flush against the door and I ran over and shoved it hard. My hands slipped because I was sweating so badly.

'Are you OK, baby?' Rachel smoothed her hands over Holly's hair, looking deep in her face.

Holly was sniffling and shaking her head but not saying anything back. Rachel looked at me from over her shoulder, her face scraped white by fear.

'Did they shoot at you?'

'Yes.'

'They have guns?'

'*Yes.*'

'Did they say what they want?'

I shook my head.

But whatever it was, it wasn't good. I thought again of

the empty holdalls and a fresh chill swept across my heart. How could I tell Rachel about that? How could I begin to tell Holly?

'Where's Buster?'

Holly leaned back from Rachel and stared at us both. There was a tremor in her cheek.

'Dad, where is he? He wasn't in my room.'

A fast ticking in my blood. My daughter spun and looked between us again until horrified understanding burst behind her eyes. Her throat bulged and she clapped a hand to her mouth, her shoulders rounded and her body all bunched up, as if she was bracing for another hard punch like the one in the alley.

'Where is he?' she wailed.

'We don't know,' Rachel said, and shot me a warning look. *Don't tell her. We can't tell her.*

And how could we? Things were bad enough already. There was no way we could send Holly into a spiral now.

I hate lying to my daughter. I've never been good at it. Even when she was little, she'd quiz me if she doubted something I had to say.

'Holly, we'll find him.' I went over and squeezed her arms. 'We'll find Buster and make sure he's safe.'

'Find him where? How?'

'Wherever he is. Holly, listen to me. The first thing we have to do is protect ourselves. Do you understand?'

She didn't say anything. She just stared blindly into the room. She was shaking and trembling and then she jumped, wildly, when we heard another crashing thud from down the hall. The men were attacking Holly's door again.

I stepped out onto the balcony. Like that would help. And seconds later I startled and spun back.

An even louder bang had started up against the door to Rachel's room.

My heart iced over.

The men had split up.

Holly wailed and clamped her hands over her ears. Rachel hugged her tight, turning her back to the door like she was trying to shield Holly from a bomb blast.

The dresser unit bounced and trembled. It wasn't as solid as the wardrobe. It wasn't as big.

And it wouldn't hold out for long.

'What do we do?' Rachel screamed.

I turned around, seeking inspiration, and ran out onto the balcony again, taking another look down past the thrashing treetops towards the ground. My stomach fell like I was cresting the top of a roller coaster and beginning the big drop. I already knew what I'd see. A nasty fall onto soaked gravel and puddles of mud. Enough, easily, to break legs and ankles. Or maybe something worse.

I leaned out, craning my neck, looking through the pounding rain towards the timber carport and our Volvo. An idea skittered across my brain. If only we could get to it, we could drive it.

The roof, then? I turned and looked up. Rainwater sluiced off of the glimmering black tiles, washing down in sheets and splashing in the gutters.

I jumped and gripped hold of the overhang, but even as I clung on desperately with my fingertips, I lost grip and fell back.

It wouldn't work. The roof would be treacherous to climb. And even if we managed it, where would we go? The winds were ripping and tearing around us. The rain was slamming down hard.

More banging from either side of us. It sounded even angrier and more frenzied than before.

Again, I looked at the balcony railing. Rainfall bounced off it. I reached out and plucked one of the tensile wires. Water sprang away from it, but there was almost no give in the wire at all.

Then I heard Rachel scream my name and I rushed back into the bedroom. There was more banging against the door.

'We have to hide Holly, Tom. We have to do it now.'

But hiding her wouldn't help. Hiding was futile. Our only options were the wardrobe and the bed and the en suite. And I'd seen the three holdalls. Three body bags. For us. If Rachel knew about those, she wouldn't be trying to hide.

'No.' I shook my head. 'We can get to the car.'

'What?'

I ran forwards and dived over the bed. Rachel's handbag was on the far bedside cabinet. I snatched for it as I crashed into the wall, yanking open her bag and grabbing her car keys from inside.

I was just pushing myself to my knees – just twisting to make my way back around the bottom of the bed – when a splinter of wood exploded from a panel in the middle of the door. Fear ignited my nerves. The blade of the axe was sticking through.

I watched as the blade twisted and was yanked back out

and a sliver of the bigger man's face appeared, one red eye bulging above his mask.

'What do you want?' I yelled. 'Leave us alone.'

He didn't answer. He just struck with the axe again, spitting more wood into the room, forcing his gloved hand through the split timber. His forearm and upper arm followed, sheathed in his white plastic suit. I could hear him grunt. And I realized, with cold plunging fear, that he was feeling around for the key with his hand.

He almost had it and I was too far away to stop him.

But Rachel was closer.

She darted forwards and seized the man's hand before it clamped on the key. Then she bent back his fingers. Hard. I heard two distinct cracks. Like the noise of Holly's nose being realigned. Only sharper. Cleaner. The ruthless expertise of a medical professional.

The man yowled and snatched his buckled hand back out.

'I'm gonna kill you, you bitch.'

Rachel snagged the key from the lock. She turned to me, shaking.

'Tom?'

I jumped onto the bed and bounded across the mattress, leaping down and grabbing hold of Holly, pushing her ahead of me out onto the balcony, with Rachel following as another axe blow chewed into the door.

We slipped and fell on the greased timber. My bare feet had no traction at all.

'Wait here,' I told Rachel, hurtling on into the rain.

I leaped over the patio chair I'd dropped earlier, stuck

out my hand and swung myself around and into Holly's room.

Where was it? Where was it?

There.

The skylight pole.

I lunged for it and was just turning to go again when I heard an ominous, metallic *crunch-crack* from the other side of the door. It sounded like a nut being crushed. Or like a piece of mail being run through an old-fashioned franking machine.

I shuddered.

A short pause followed.

Then an explosion went off.

17

If the gunshot before had been loud, this was like a bomb detonating. The noise was deafening. A raging, calamitous boom that blasted out from the hallway and pulsed through the door.

Smoke and the stink of gunpowder hung in the air.

I was face down on the ground, coughing and spluttering. Hard to say if I dived there or if I was thrown. A chunk of door slammed into the wall in front of me. Fragments of wood rained down on my head and back and shoulders. Dust filled my hair.

The shotgun. Had to be.

A small voice in my head told me to stay where I was. These men weren't stopping. They were heavily armed. We were hopelessly outmatched and totally overwhelmed with terror and confusion.

But then I thought of Holly and Rachel. My family was under attack. And I had only one job now. I had to get up and out of that room. I had to get us down from the balcony. I had to get us away.

I pushed up, choking on wood dust, my ears whooshing and ringing, my balance completely thrown. I bounced off the doorway on my way out to the balcony and glanced back over my shoulder at a crunching, splitting sound from behind. The smaller man was using the butt of the shotgun to strike at the splintered remains of the upper part of the bedroom door and rake them aside.

My stomach turned to water. We didn't have long now until they'd be inside.

I felt hands grabbing me and turned to see Holly and Rachel pulling me towards them, crying and screaming words I couldn't hear over the fierce, high-pitched wailing in my head. Rachel's hair was sodden and streaking across her eyes. Holly's face gleamed in the rain.

'With me,' I shouted, into the din, and then I bashed against the balcony rail and clambered over it, clinging to the other side, fighting a sudden spell of dizziness and swallowing against the gritty dust that was coating my tongue and catching in my throat.

The distant ground bounced and tilted beneath me as I crouched in the rain and hung the metal hook on the end of the skylight pole from the lowest strand of tensile wire. The rest of the pole dangled freely below.

Again, hands reached for me and yanked at me and I looked up to see Rachel tugging at my arm. She was shouting something – trying to dissuade me, I guessed – but her words were lost to me as I lunged down with one hand on the pole, the other on the fluted metal upright supporting the banister and a swirl of vertigo stopping my breath. I took all my weight on my arms, kicked a spray of rain off the edge of the balcony and swung my legs out over the abyss.

I hung there, my bare feet kicking in the soaked darkness,

spitting rain from my mouth. Then I let go of the railing and clasped the pole with both hands. It bore my weight. I felt a small flutter of relief. I slid down it – faster than I meant to – until my fists butted up against the rubber handles.

I blinked up through the rain, twisting and flailing. I could feel the blood pulsing in my arms.

'Holly first,' I shouted.

Rachel and Holly looked at each other like I was mad. But then they flinched and turned and glanced back towards the bedrooms, and seconds later Rachel grabbed Holly, lifting up her pyjama top, urging her over the rail. My daughter half climbed, half stumbled, almost falling in an awkward somersault before she ducked and grasped for the pole.

She missed. Tried again. This time she got it in her left hand, followed by her right. I could see her knees give out and her feet drag behind her as she launched herself off, clinging on desperately, the pole swinging out and back, then bumping against the balcony edge.

She shrieked. The hook scraped and slipped. My grip began to give.

'*Move!*'

Holly slid down to me, fast now, wrapping her legs around my torso, her arms around my neck.

'They're coming through the doors, Dad. They're nearly in.'

I could feel the shakes passing through her body as she clambered on down me, hugging my waist, my thighs, my knees. My arms strained at their sockets. My fingers stretched and ached. Holly hung from my ankles, still a considerable distance up. She spotted her landing. Dropped.

She hit the ground with a soggy eruption of water and mud, rolling to one side.

'Hurry, Mum,' she screamed.

I peered up at Rachel, rainwater swamping my mouth. She was looking down at me, her hair hanging about her face.

'I can't hold on much longer,' I told her.

For the briefest second, I was gripped with absolute terror that she wouldn't come.

Then, in one fluid movement, she put one foot on the first trembling wire and swung her other leg over the banister.

'Faster, Rachel.'

That was my mistake. She was only halfway over when I said it and she didn't pause to compose herself before she jumped for the pole. She was sideways-on when she grabbed for it and her momentum made the pole slide, then twist.

The hook slipped on the wire. The wire twanged and slackened. We slumped and dropped – only by a fraction – but in that instant Rachel's foot slammed into my shoulder and her other foot scrambled against my face. She pushed all her weight down on top of me, forcing my head right back, and by the time she reached down to grab for my neck, my hands had already parted company with the pole and were clutching on air.

We fell together into the fragmented black, the rain hammering down like silver needles, the ground rushing up fast.

'Michael, please.'

Fiona stares at Michael, her eyes huge in the darkness, like he's become some kind of stranger to her. She's clenching the grab handle above her door so hard Michael can see the bones of her knuckles pressing through her skin.

'That was crazy. You're going too fast.'

He knows she's right. Touching eighty now and he's never driven beyond twenty before tonight. There's an odd levity to the suspension, like the Audi's tyres are peeling away from the road. The engine roars and the steering feels light and aimless. Trees whip by at his side.

The road surface undulates. The Audi bucks.

A flutter in Michael's stomach. Like when his dad used to accelerate over a humped bridge, just so he could ask Michael if he needed to go back to pick up his tummy. Michael always loved that. He can remember giggling and clutching his stomach, looking out the rear window as if his tummy was somewhere behind him. He wonders if his dad ever felt this out of control.

'You're scaring me.'

Michael is scaring himself. He's taken risks in the past. He's leaped between stairwells and dropped between buildings when he's free running, tumble-rolling to a stop. He's balanced on high ledges, then dangled from them with Fiona standing over him, focusing in with her camera for the perfect shot.

But nothing compared to this.

'You have to slow down.'

18

The impact was like being hit by a truck.

I landed on my back on the boggy gravel. It drove the air out of my lungs. Rachel crashed down on top of me. All elbows and bones.

She cried out and rolled off me. Raised herself to her knees. Through the heavy downpour I could see she was baring her teeth and clutching her left arm. Her arm hung uselessly at her side.

'My shoulder is dislocated.'

I tried to reply but I couldn't speak. I was doing that gasping, dry-croaking thing in the back of my throat. Any second now, oxygen would flood my lungs again. But still, that second. It was hard not to succumb to the panic.

I rocked sideways. Pain lit up across my pelvis and spine. I managed a short, halting breath, like sipping oxygen through a straw. Then another. A little more air this time. I pushed up, teetered back, pushed up again. I must have banged my head when I fell. I was groggy. We had to move – I knew that – but everything seemed to take too long.

Something twanged with a hot burst of acid in the middle of my back. It didn't stop me. I got to my knees as Holly splashed through puddles and helped me to lift Rachel. We leaned on one another, our clothes and hair drenched and pasted to our skin.

'This way.'

We stumbled and limped through the deluge and took cover beneath the balcony. Rachel braced her body against the fieldstone base of the lodge. She cowered in the murk, her face scrubbed and straining.

Footfall from above. Fast and heavy. I was sick with dread, my breathing laboured, my hearing blurry, but there was no mistaking the sound. We all looked up, shivering and scared. The timber boards shook and vibrated. Drops of rain fell down on us in clumps and loose sprinkles. More rain rinsed down in a curtain of water from the balcony's edge.

We couldn't be seen, I didn't think. Not directly.

More footsteps, this time from the far end of the balcony. We huddled in silence as the two men formed up in the middle. They talked fast but their words were snatched away by the howling wind, smothered by the downpour. I guessed they were looking out at the broad circle of soaked gravel ahead of them in the moonlight and the skylight pole twisting and swinging in the wind. I trembled. Had we left footprints leading back under the balcony? Even if we hadn't, they'd know we were close.

Holly stared at me, breathless, then something seemed to break inside of her. Her face fell and her lips peeled back in a frightened, silent scream. I pulled her into me, holding her like I could somehow smother her fear. But I couldn't and it killed me.

I didn't know why these men had come for my family. That was not my priority right now. They could have any number of reasons. They could be aiming to kidnap us to try to get a ransom from Lionel. They might be planning to kill me in order to take Rachel or Holly away for purposes I did not ever want to think about. Or maybe it was something simpler than that. Some kind of pent-up resentment that had to do with the lodge, perhaps. Brodie had mentioned that some of the locals didn't like the fence Lionel had erected. Maybe this was some sort of extreme, psychotic expression of that.

I didn't care. My only focus was on protecting my family. And that meant getting to our car.

Reaching down to my side, I peeled open a soaked pocket on my jogging trousers and removed Rachel's car keys with shaking fingers. I held them up in front of Rachel and Holly, pointed towards the carport and turned the ignition key like a mime.

They stilled, then nodded fitfully. It was clear they had their doubts. We were all very scared and afraid of being spotted. Making any decision right now was frightening.

I pushed Holly back and urged her on towards the Volvo.

'I have to help Mum,' I whispered, and then I watched, terrified, as she stumbled and weaved ahead of us, using her hands to feel along the blackened stonework like a blind person learning new terrain for the first time. I got my arm around Rachel's waist and we hobbled after Holly with Rachel cupping the elbow of her dislocated arm with her hand.

A sudden shout from above froze my blood. The balcony shook again with the thud of fast-moving footsteps. My guess was the men were rushing back inside. They were going to hurry through the lodge and down the stairs and come outside to find us. Fear pounded in my chest.

'*Run!*'

I lunged forwards and shoved Holly out from beneath the balcony into the rain-swamped yard, then ducked and lifted Rachel in my arms. She shrieked in pain. Holly cried in panic. The gravel stung my bare feet and cold rain blustered in at us, like someone was hurling crushed ice in our faces.

We were about two-thirds of the way towards the carport when I shifted Rachel in my arms and aimed the remote keys I was gripping in my fist towards the Volvo. The headlamps flashed in the gloom. The indicators pulsed orange. The cabin light shone dimly through the blackened windscreen.

My stomach dropped.

I could immediately see – with a numbing, disabling paralysis – that we wouldn't be going anywhere in our car. It was slumped lower than it should have been. All four tyres had been slashed.

My brain couldn't process it. I faltered, staring in horror at the way the rubber was pooled and spread at the base of the alloy wheels. Rachel bucked with a sudden jolt in my arms.

'Oh my God, no,' she said. 'No. This isn't happening.'

I dropped her to the ground, still staring at the car, as if somehow it would magically fix itself. Holly had stopped just in front of us, her arms out at her sides, the rain lashing down around her. For a moment I thought she was going to collapse.

My first instinct was to get in the car anyway. Gun the

engine. Try to drive. But I knew it wouldn't work. It would be hopeless in the best of conditions, and with the driveway saturated it was impossible. If we didn't get bogged down immediately, we'd gain no traction at all when the gradient started to rise. We'd be stuck.

I looked back at the lodge. What to do?

'We have to go back,' Rachel said. 'Tom, we have to find somewhere to hide.'

Slowly, my brain kicked in again. We only had seconds, but it might be enough.

'Wait.'

I sprinted to the Volvo and pressed the catch to open the boot. Pinching water from my eyes, I reached quickly inside. The first thing I grabbed was Rachel's medical bag. It was a blue nylon rucksack that I looped over my shoulder. Next was an old padded overcoat of mine that Holly could wear. After that came a small toolbox, and last, from the sculpted hollow beneath the false floor in the base of the boot, I snatched up a wheel wrench from next to the car jack. It was the closest thing to a weapon I could find.

19

We watched through a break in the trees as the outdoor lights stuttered on around the exterior of the lodge. The bulbs blazed blue-white against the saturated black, bleaching the timber walls and the gravel yard and forming a hazed border of light that throbbed and flickered in the rain and wind.

A pane of glass in the downstairs kitchen window was smashed. The jagged shards still attached to the frame shone in the light with a blue iridescence. Rachel had been woken by the sound of a window breaking. Was this was how the two men had got in?

I felt a sudden clutch in my chest as the men appeared tramping across the deck. They jumped down onto the sodden gravel. The smaller man came first with the shotgun held crossways in front of him. The bigger man followed from behind with the handgun in his left hand and his right hand tucked under his armpit. He was stooped at the waist and leaning to his left, as if trying to muffle the pain of his two broken fingers.

Holly gasped. I reached over and pulled her down next to me. She'd put on my old coat but she was trembling hard. We were hidden behind a screen of trees and bushes opposite the carport.

I tightened my grip on the wheel wrench. My knuckles pressed down into sodden mulch. My breath came in fast pants. I was wearing Rachel's backpack by both shoulder straps. There were pain meds inside and Rachel was going to need them. Right now she was lying prone on the ground, writhing in discomfort. Her head was pressed up against a fallen log. She put her fist in her mouth and bit down on her knuckles to keep from making any sound. I looked at her, saw her pain, and felt something inside me tear and give way.

The men plodded forwards, jutting their chins into the dark. The rain lashed against them. The plastic coating of their disposable coveralls glistened in the outdoor lighting with a wet liquid sheen.

Something inside my stomach tightened and quivered, like a string plucked on a guitar. I'd thought of something. What was it? My groggy mind couldn't complete the thought. I strained and thought harder. The near-thought repeated itself, like a faint, scratching sensation at the back of my head. It was something about the men. But what?

I studied their dimensions. Their body language. Their outfits. White plastic coveralls with their hoods up. Blue nitrile gloves on their hands. Blue rubber boots on their feet. Surgical masks over their faces.

Still I pursued the thought, chasing it around and around my mind. The thought scratched, and scratched, and then . . .

Blue gloves.

Both men were wearing them.

Just like the mugger in the alley had worn.

A shudder ripped through me.

And they were covering their faces. In the alley our attacker had worn a pair of tights over his head. Here, the men had on cupped paper masks and a hood.

Was it possible there was a connection? I'd thought of the attack in London as a random act of violence. One of those unfortunate, albeit terrifying, I-hope-I-never-experience-it-for-myself side effects of living in a big city. But what if it *hadn't* been random? What if there was a line running from that incident to this? Because, really, what were the chances of these two things happening to us in such quick succession?

Hold it. Don't jump to conclusions. People sometimes talk about confirmation bias – the phenomenon of believing something you want (or perversely, maybe really *don't* want) to believe. I don't know a huge deal about it, but my guess is the effect is more pronounced when you're trying to make sense of something that's essentially nonsensical. The kind of experience, say, that involves a sustained overload of shock and fear on levels you've previously never come close to being exposed to before. Plus, I was basing this on gloves. Cheap disposable gloves. I could go into any DIY shop in the country and buy a box of gloves just like them. Same thing with the masks.

But still.

Again, I studied the build of the two men. Could one of them have been the mugger? The smaller one, possibly. The mugger hadn't struck me as particularly big at the time. But why would he follow us here?

My head crackled with electric fear. I wanted to ask Rachel and Holly about it but I was afraid to talk or move. The men were close enough to hear any sound we might make. To spot any disturbance in the trees.

I looked again at Rachel. Her face was scrunched up tight and she was having to fight not to cry out in agony. It was a reminder of just how tough and resilient my wife really was.

The men stopped in the middle of the yard, peering blindly into the night. They spun a complete 360, the smaller one turning clockwise, the bigger one anticlockwise. The rain beat hard against their coveralls with a sound like ball bearings dropped onto a metal tray.

I didn't breathe. Didn't blink. I just stared through the saturated foliage and reached over to squeeze Holly's hand as the bigger man squinted right at us, trying to wish myself invisible as I struggled to get a handle on what was going on here. Thinking clearly was difficult because, well, I'd banged my head, I was petrified and that same electric crackle raged on in my skull. My body was flooded with adrenaline and the same mix of fear-or-flight endorphins that had overwhelmed me during the mugging in the alley. So maybe *that's* all the connection I was feeling really was. A chemical echo. Maybe the two incidents *weren't* linked. Maybe we'd just been incredibly unlucky.

No. I didn't buy it, either.

Something about the set-up, the men, had to be connected.

But why?

The bigger man's gaze swept on past us. He hadn't seen us. Then the smaller man nudged him with his elbow and gestured at the Volvo. I'd left the boot open, hoping to lure the men away in the opposite direction to where we were.

Holly stifled a whimper as they advanced on the car. The smaller man adjusted his grip on the shotgun and raised it under his chin, sighting along the barrel. The bigger man followed from behind with the handgun braced over his right forearm.

'You can come out,' the smaller man shouted, suddenly. 'We won't hurt you, I promise.'

I reached up and placed my muddied fingers against Holly's lips. Her skin was cold to the touch.

Again, thoughts hurtled inside my head. These men had come here to kill. They were violent. They were armed.

I thought of the way the mugger had punched Holly in the alley. It had been an extreme and brutal act. At the time, I'd thought he'd wanted to silence her to stop her from screaming or shouting for help, but what if his intentions had been more sinister?

Take it a step further. The man had put his knife to Rachel's throat. What if he hadn't been planning to simply mug us? What if he'd been intending to kill us there and then? What if they'd come here tonight to finish the task?

Also: *why?*

Why would anyone want to terrorize my family like this? Why would they want us dead?

PC Baker's words came back to me again. *Do you have any enemies at all, Mr Sullivan? Does your wife?* But we didn't. Oh, there were people we didn't get along with. The odd distant relative who'd slighted us or we'd vaguely insulted over the years. Colleagues at work who bore petty grudges, maybe. But this? No, nothing like it.

'We just want to talk,' the smaller man yelled.

I peered at Holly and shook my head. *Don't fall for it. Don't speak.* She swallowed and blinked, trembling hard, like it was taking all her willpower not to scream out in the night.

A cold shiver ran down my spine.

The men looked at one another. They waited. The wind tore at their coveralls. The rain splattered back off the waxy plastic coating of their hoods.

The smaller man's body was all hunched up against the damp and the cold. The bigger man appeared better equipped for the conditions. Maybe he had a jacket on underneath. That could account for some of his bulk, I supposed.

When the men got no response they continued on to the threshold of the carport. Then they split up. One crept to the left of the Volvo. One crept to the right. They circled wide and took their time, sighting along their weapons, checking the front seats through the passenger windows, then the rear cabin.

They neared the back of the Volvo and paused, then moved very fast, jumping sideways and aiming their weapons into the space behind the boot.

Holly clapped a hand to her mouth.

Neither man fired.

They remained still for a long, tense moment, and then they relaxed and shook their heads and scuffed the ground with their boots, just two guys acknowledging with an 'aw shucks' kind of embarrassment that maybe we'd fooled them this time.

I watched in a strange kind of wonder as they relaxed a little and lowered their firearms and moved back towards the threshold of the garage to huddle up just out of the rain. The smaller man cupped his hand around his masked mouth and raised himself on his toes to talk into the bigger man's ear. The bigger man nodded along, then turned and strode away, tramping back across the gravel yard in the direction of the lodge.

'What's he doing?' Rachel whispered, through gritted teeth.

I held up a hand, wanting her to be quiet. She stared at me, dark eyes flicking side to side in the black.

The bigger man was using short, choppy strides. I guessed his boots were built for indoor terrain. Maybe there was no tread pattern on the soles. Better to be sure and keep his balance than to slip. Falling down onto two broken fingers would be bad.

'Tom? Please. What's happening?'

'Shh.'

The bigger man crossed to the broken kitchen window, rose up on his toes and peered inside. Then, when he failed to spot us, he turned and jogged away to his right, stepping onto the deck and heading around towards the front of the lodge.

'Is he going back inside?' Rachel hissed. 'Why's he doing that?'

Again, I didn't answer. I was thinking. Hard.

If they split up, it would be bad in some ways. Bad because splitting up might increase their chances of finding us. Bad because we'd have to contend with two separate threats instead of one consolidated threat.

But it could be good in some ways too. Good because the chances of our survival in a three-on-one confrontation were a little better than our prospects in a three-on-two confrontation. Good because a lucky swing with the wheel wrench, if it came to it, might just be enough to take out one of the men. Assuming that man happened to be isolated. Assuming I could sneak up on him unseen. Especially if he had two broken fingers and a handgun instead of a shotgun.

But all of that – crazy as it was to even contemplate – turned out to be irrelevant. Because shortly after we'd watched the bigger man hurry into the lodge he emerged again to reteam with the smaller man.

This time, he was carrying a torch.

20

The torch was long and black and the shiny metal casing gleamed in the hard outdoor light.

I watched, barely breathing, as the bigger man stepped into the gravel yard with the torch held up by his head and his arm bent at the elbow. He pressed a switch with his thumb and a powerful beam punched a cone of light through the black rain into the smaller man's masked face. His white hood flared and winked in the gloom as he reared back and put his gloved hand in front of his eyes.

My body tensed. What was their plan here?

The bigger man lowered the beam and tramped on through the saturated gravel, the torchlight jinking side to side with his stunted strides. There was a weighted bulge on the right-hand side of his jumpsuit trousers. The butt of his handgun was poking out of a pocket there.

When he reached the middle of the yard he swung at the hips and started another careful 360, this time with the torch. We ducked even lower. The teeming rain swirled and glittered in the dazzle. The torch carved a funnel of bright light through the blackness, probing among bushes and trees. It lit up the steep gradient of the driveway, then swept over our heads, staining the foliage around us a livid, pale green.

My lungs screamed for air. I held my breath. Holly pressed her face into the dirt. She was shaking all over. The beam passed on, paused, jinked back, then whirled on again like a lighthouse lantern.

I inhaled and started to breathe more easily, but not for long. They weren't giving up. They were determined to find us.

Again, I wondered why. And again, I had no clue. I can't tell you how much I wished they would just leave us and go. But then, maybe they knew – as I'd begun to understand with a numbing dread – that we were essentially trapped here. Our car was undriveable. We couldn't call for help. And sure, the grounds of the lodge were large and we could try to hide, but ultimately the estate was bordered by the sea on one side, the gate on the other and a fence everywhere else. That fence. Something that was designed to keep threats out was now keeping us *in*. Not exactly a comforting thought, and not one I had much success pushing out of my mind.

Very gently now, I placed my hand on Holly's back and began to rub it in small circles. I don't know if it helped. Probably not. But I didn't want her to think she was on her own.

Once the bigger man had completed his sweep, he tramped on towards the smaller man. The smaller man pointed at the Volvo and the bigger man splashed torchlight over it. He stepped in under the shelter and took his time opening the passenger doors. He checked the front footwells and the cavity in front of the rear seats. He crouched and shone the light under the chassis. The men were being very deliberate and very thorough. I didn't like that at all. In my mind, it added credence to my theory that this was somehow linked to the mugging in London. Maybe the mugging hadn't played out how they'd wanted, but they were intending to see it through to whatever grisly conclusion they had in mind here. I don't know if thinking that made things worse or better. I did know I wanted us to survive and, right now, trying to think of an angle – any angle – that would give some insight to what was going on here seemed like a good move.

Eventually the two men congregated at the open boot and spent some time there, probably asking themselves why we'd opened it and what we'd taken. There was a good chance they'd spot that the wheel wrench was missing. After that, it was guesswork.

Holly shifted beside me, raising her head. I was squatted low and my thighs tingled with an acid burn. Rachel tilted her head back and strained to look out through the undergrowth, her breath steaming in the dank forest air. She was grinding her heel into the ground against the pain from her shoulder. I didn't know how much more she could take.

I took my hand off Holly and rested it on Rachel's stomach. Her abdominals were all clenched up. I leaned down close to her ear.

'Is there anything I can do to help?'

'You can . . . pop my shoulder . . . back in.' She gritted her teeth and whined faintly. 'But it's . . . going to make some noise.'

I glanced out through the trees to where the two men were conferring in the carport. 'I think we have to wait. I'm sorry.'

She nodded, pressing her lips tightly closed and shutting her eyes against a fresh surge of pain.

'What about painkillers?' I whispered. 'Have you got something in your bag?'

'Afterwards.'

I gave her hand a quick squeeze. Rachel squeezed me back, blinking against the tears that had sprung from her eyes as she gazed up at the canopy of trees overhead. She swallowed again, like she was about to say something more.

'What is it?' I asked.

Her eyes flickered. She shook her head quickly.

'Rachel?'

I moved even closer, until I was looking down at her face. But Rachel wouldn't meet my eye.

'Tell me.'

She shook her head again and, as I stared at her, I felt a pair of invisible hands close around my throat and slowly begin to squeeze.

Did Rachel have some idea of what was going on here? Could she know why these men had come?

I felt a queasiness in my gut as my mind flashed on her response to finding the remains of the campfire and the snare out in the woods. And true, I'd been thrown by it, but really wasn't it Rachel's unease that had been the catalyst for my own? It was Rachel who'd pushed ahead with calling Brodie to try to find out more. And wasn't the main reason that I'd gone out into the woods to reassure her?

Then there was last night. I'd found her in tears in her bedroom. She'd even – and here, I didn't want to dwell on my own behaviour too closely – probably slipped into my bed as much for comfort as anything else.

What was it she'd said to me in her bedroom before that?

There's something I have to talk to you about. Something important.

I do want to be thinking clearly. I have so much I need to say to you, Tom.

I've messed up so badly.

I felt a terrible tremor in the base of my skull. Had she known, on some level, that this threat existed?

No. Surely not. Rachel would never have let us come here if that was the case. I may not know *everything* about my wife but I do know this: she loves Holly without limit. She'd wanted us to come to Scotland for Holly's sake. If I was honest with myself, I was pretty sure she'd been willing to take another pass at mending our relationship for the same reason. Losing Michael had come close to destroying Rachel. There was no way she'd risk losing Holly too.

But still, I sensed there was something there. Something just out of reach.

Torchlight flared again in my peripheral vision. It swung around from the rear of the car and whirled and blazed directly at us. I stopped breathing again. I stayed dead still. I had this terrible, game-over sensation – like I was an inmate caught attempting a prison break, pinned by a searchlight glare.

But no, the dense foliage must have shielded us because the bigger man didn't react in any way. He simply arced the torch beam down at the ground and then the two men stood together in its glow on the concrete plinth under the carport roof, talking and looking around them as the rain fell thunderously down and bounced and splashed in the puddled gravel.

I peered closer. The smaller man was now holding a torch of his own and I realized with a sinking feeling that it was the old spare I keep in the boot of the Volvo. I hadn't thought to grab it myself.

He clicked it on. The filament stuttered and cut out. He slapped the torch against his thigh. It flickered to life but the beam was yellow and weak. Small mercies. I'm not the most organized, most practical guy. Rachel often gives me hell for it. I couldn't remember the last time I'd replaced the batteries.

The smaller man shook his head, as if dismayed by my tardiness, and issued more instructions to the bigger man. This time, his movements were more abrupt and severe. Like he was starting to lose patience because things weren't going according to plan. Then he nudged the bigger man with the back of the hand he was holding the shotgun in and he jabbed the muzzle into the trees behind the carport.

You go that way.

The bigger man nodded and the smaller man raised the hand holding the torch and inverted his wrist and bounced the lens off his chest. He straightened his arm and pointed the watery beam up the driveway.

I'll go this way.

Another brief conference and they parted company.

I shifted position, my muscles cramping with fear, and watched as the bigger man skirted around the side of the carport with the blazing industrial torch. He stood still for a long moment, searching the woods across from us. The torch beam winked off tree trunks and undergrowth. It illuminated the dense canopy above. Then he set a course with the beam and took a series of long, exaggerated strides into the woods, pausing briefly between each one. Maybe he was afraid I was hiding close by with the wheel wrench cocked behind my shoulder. Or perhaps he just didn't want to rip his coveralls on the brambles and thorns.

The smaller man watched him go, then turned and marched up the driveway, the weak beam of his torch blurring the darkness around him into a faint orange dim. I waited until I was sure they were both out of earshot before whispering again.

'I think the smaller one's going up to check the gate.'

'How do you know?' Rachel asked me.

'Because it's the only way out of here.'

Holly whimpered and cradled her head in her hands. I looked at her, wanting so badly to change what was happening, knowing I couldn't.

But maybe there was something I *could* do.

I peered forwards again, pushing aside branches and leaves to see clearly out into the driving rain. The bigger man appeared to be striding on into the trees. The light of his torch was visible as a lurid greenish haze moving away from us deep into the woods. The smaller man was approaching the top of the driveway gradient and the faint light of his torch was dipping over the humped rise at the summit.

If there was any window of opportunity, this might be it.

'Are they going to keep looking until they find us?' Holly asked.

'That's not going to happen,' I told her.

'You don't know that, Dad.'

'I won't allow it.'

I don't know if Holly believed me. I barely believed it myself. But I did know one thing. The smaller man wouldn't stay at the gate for long. He'd probably check it and make sure we weren't there and then he'd come back again. And when he did, we needed to be able to get to the gate and get out.

I looked at Rachel. 'Tell me how to fix your shoulder,' I said.

21

Rachel told me. The procedure sounded equal parts daunting and sickening. I'm not like Rachel. As a doctor, she's pretty much immune to gore. I remember when, aged six, Michael fell off his skateboard one Sunday in front of our house and ripped open his knee. The cut was so deep you could see the bone. When I heard his screams and went out to check on him, I didn't know if I was going to throw up or faint. Rachel, though, had been eerily calm. She'd scooped Michael into her arms, his blood leaking over her clothes, and had carried him inside to the kitchen, where she'd hummed along to an ABBA song on the radio as she cleaned and stitched the wound like it was a minor everyday chore.

I tried to channel some of her strength now as I sat next to her on the matted ground, lifted her bad arm carefully by the wrist (she wailed, I apologized) and slipped my foot underneath. I told Holly to go around the other side of Rachel to support her head in her lap. I had to tell her twice before she lowered her hands with jerky terror and finally started to move. I knew she was scared but I thought that maybe giving her something to do might help.

'Don't let go,' Rachel reminded me, through gritted teeth. 'We don't want to do this twice.'

I grimaced and tried not to look away as I nestled my toes deeper in her armpit, squeezing her wrist between my hands as her breathing hitched and modulated and she began to whine. I was about to get to the next stage and start pulling when she stopped me.

'Wait.' She felt around in the undergrowth and grabbed a gnarled stick that she held crossways in front of her mouth. 'OK?'

Not really.

'OK,' I told her.

'Go.'

She placed the stick between her teeth and bit down hard. I started pulling, raising her arm towards me, aware of my face twisting and contorting in a similar way to Rachel's. She'd told me to apply constant pressure with no sudden yanks. Which sounded fine, in theory, but somehow witnessing her slow agony was so much worse in practice.

She grimaced and made a high, choked gargle in the back of her throat, biting down on the stick so hard it started to splinter and snap. I leaned back, used my foot for leverage and pulled even harder. Holly caught her breath and turned away.

For a horrible moment, I didn't think it was going to work. I didn't think Rachel's arm would move any further. But then her shoulder suddenly extended, the joint slipped, popped, clunked, and Rachel groaned.

I let go and sprawled backwards in the soggy earth, an uneasy sensation flickering across my back. Rachel twisted sideways, pressing her face into Holly's lap. Holly cradled her head, biting her lip.

For several seconds, Rachel didn't move. Then, gradually,

she seemed to relax, her body sagged, and she pivoted up into a sitting position, spitting out fragments of stick.

'Is that . . . better?' I asked her.

'So much. Thank you. Pass me my bag?'

She let go of a long breath, unzipped her bag when I handed it to her and removed some pills in a foil pack. She dry swallowed them, and meanwhile I patted the ground around me until I located the toolbox in the saturated undergrowth.

I undid the plastic catches on the front and flipped back the lid. It was only a small toolbox with a limited selection of tools. I keep it in the Volvo in case a minor mechanical problem crops up. Maybe a windscreen wiper comes loose. Maybe a bulb needs replacing.

Or, I don't know, maybe I need to get out through a high security gate.

I felt around in the uppermost tray until my hands settled on a crosshead screwdriver. I held it in my right fist with the wheel wrench in my left. Then, very slowly, I crawled forwards on my hands and knees towards the driveway.

I pushed aside a fern and looked out. Rain rattled against the roof of the carport and blew in violent shimmies through the outdoor lights shining around the lodge. Nobody around.

'Tom?'

I heard a gurgling in front of me. When I patted the ground, my fingers came away wet. A drainage gully. It was flooded now.

'Tom, what are you doing? Come back here.'

'We have to be able to open the gate, Rachel.' I glanced to my left, towards the broken window in the side of the lodge. 'There's a button on the intercom in the kitchen. Holly used it for me yesterday evening. But I don't think it will help us. The gate only stayed open for a minute and then it closed again. We wouldn't get to the gate in time.'

'So?' Holly whispered.

'There's a camera on the inside of the gate. It's pointed inwards. I saw it. I think it'll recognize our number plate like the camera on the outside did.'

Silence.

'We can't drive the car, Dad.'

But I wasn't planning to. The gully was filled with leaves and brackish water. I slid forwards into it. The water oozed beneath me, foul and icy cold.

'Tom,' Rachel whispered. 'Please. It's not safe.'

I looked back over my shoulder. I'd only gone a short distance but it was already nearly impossible to see Rachel or Holly in the dark.

I knew there was a good chance Rachel was right. This probably *was* a bad idea. But two things made me want to go ahead anyway. One, the two men were still searching for us. And two, it was the only idea I had. I'd failed Rachel and Holly in that alleyway. I had no intention of failing them now.

I pushed up out of my prone position – my legs heavy with nerves – and broke across the yard, running at a stoop. I zigzagged and jumped between puddles. The rain drilled into my bare shoulders and arms.

I'm pretty sure Rachel did a kind of shout-whisper thing to me, telling me to come back, but it was too late.

The distance wasn't far. Maybe forty metres, at most.

It felt like running forty miles.

My legs gave out as I neared the carport. Too much fear. An overload of adrenaline. My ankle buckled and I skinned my knees and fell just short of the front number plate on the Volvo.

It was smeared with mud and dead flies. Filmed with rain. Two screws held it in place, concealed behind white plastic plugs. I put the wheel wrench down and tore my thumbnail unsnapping the first of the plugs, then freed the second with shaking fingers.

I got busy with the screwdriver. It wasn't easy getting it lined up with the first screw because my hands and arms were convulsing with the heavy beating of my heart. I had to force myself to clamp down on my fear and really concentrate to get the screwdriver to fit. At every moment I expected the men to shout and rush in at me.

It took over a minute to get both screws undone. The aluminium bolts on the back fell and jangled softly on the concrete plinth, bouncing and rolling into the darkness under the car. The number plate came loose in my hands.

I was just turning to get up out of my crouch and sprint back across the driveway when a pale wash of torchlight arced and tilted against the trees in front of me. It was coming from behind the carport.

The bigger man was on his way back.

My body shut down then. My brain just stalled. I knew I was stranded. I knew I couldn't risk running back to Rachel and Holly because I didn't know how long it would be until the bigger man emerged from the woods and I had no way of telling what his view of the driveway was like right now. But I couldn't stay where I was.

Hide. Do it now.

The passenger doors were still open on the left of the Volvo. I darted around them, then doubled back for the wheel wrench I'd left on the ground, looked in at the seats, changed my mind about hiding *inside* the car and dived *under* it instead.

I squirmed forwards on my elbows and belly, into the stink of cold rubber and engine oil, the chassis pressing down on my head. It was a tight squeeze because the car was slumped so low on its alloy wheels.

Something jabbed into the back of my neck. Something else jelly-like and greasy smeared the side of my cheek. I lay there, my heart jolting me up off the ground, every nerve end twitching and alive, waiting for the bigger man to come.

His torchlight got brighter. Nearer. Then I heard the clomp and splash of his rubber boots on the gravel close by. He paused in front of the Volvo. I could see the toes of his boots and the elasticated hems at the ankles of his white plastic coveralls.

I waited for him to cast his light my way and notice that the number plate was missing.

His feet didn't move.

Very carefully, I slid back a fraction and, too late, noticed that one of the tiny bolts from the screws was nestled by the front left tyre, just ready to sparkle in the glimmer of his torchlight.

But the torch didn't swing my way.

The bigger man was moving forwards across the driveway.

Towards where Rachel and Holly were hidden.

22

The bigger man must have decided there were only four broad directions we could have gone in. Into the trees behind the carport, where he'd already checked. Up the driveway towards the gate, where the smaller man had headed. Back to the lodge, which he'd returned to not long before. Or into the trees on the other side of the gravel yard.

Fear crawled up my spine. I lay there, not moving, not making a sound, when all I wanted to do was yell at him to stop.

Do something.

But what?

I slid backwards on my belly, squeezed out from under the Volvo's exhaust and pushed up into a squat. Again, I moved painfully slowly. Trying not to make any sound. Trying to disturb the air around me as little as possible. I leaned to one side – knees wobbling – and peeked out from behind the rear of the car.

My breath caught in my throat.

The bigger man was facing away from me with his hood up. The rain and wind were blasting against him, riffling his coveralls. And suddenly, I was seized by a horrible dread that he would somehow sense my presence, spin, dazzle me with his torch and go for his gun.

But he didn't turn. He advanced on across the driveway instead.

I wiped the grease from my cheek – like that was a concern right now – and stalked out from behind the car.

My bare feet were so numbed from the mud and rain it felt like I was walking on two frozen turkeys. I edged sideways across the rippled concrete, slipping the screwdriver into my left pocket, holding the number plate by my thigh and raising the wheel wrench in my right hand.

The bigger man was perhaps ten careful steps ahead of me. Or four quick strides. If I could sneak up on him I could club him over the head. I could strike him again and again and again.

Two problems with that.

One, he looked like an absolute giant standing out in the open. He was tall and broad with wide shoulders, a thick neck and big wrists and hands. In the movies, if the hero hits a bad guy with something heavy from behind, the bad guy drops instantly. He doesn't fight back. But what if I hit the bigger man with everything I had and it wasn't enough? What if he simply absorbed the blow and then shot me?

And two, those ten slow steps or four quick strides would be across saturated gravel. I was barefoot but it would still be noisy.

And he had a gun.

I hesitated. I could feel those invisible hands again. Only this time they weren't slipping around my neck. They were pawing at my clothes, yanking me back, trying to save me from myself. Was not attacking the man an act of cowardice or the sensible move?

He strode on.

I stood there, gripped by indecision, the fierce wind tugging at the wheel wrench in my hand like a nagging doubt.

Think.

I looked over at the lodge, shining brightly in the wind-swept gloom, the shattered kitchen window glittering with a blued dazzle. Then I crabbed away to my right, very fast now. Foot over foot. Towards the far side of the carport.

I took two steps out onto the gravel, then two steps back and around the side until I was standing up to my ankles in soaked nettles, in the darkness under the trees, using the wall of the carport as a blind.

My breath rattled in my lungs. I looked at the lodge again. From the angle I was on I could only see a slim wedge of the decking at the front. It was lit starkly by the powerful outdoor lights, like an empty stage.

The bigger man paced relentlessly on. He was only two or three steps from the trees on the far side of the driveway. All he'd have to do was cross the gully, push through the foliage and then . . .

I blocked the thought from my mind, weighing the wheel wrench in my hand. My arm trembled. If this was a mistake . . .

Drawing my arm way back, I stuck my other arm out for balance and threw the wrench with all my might.

It arced through the air, turning over and over, slicing through the rain, buzzing in the black. The wrench struck the top corner of the lodge with a loud thud, pinwheeled on across the roof, then clattered and clanged and dropped, unseen, onto the decking with a heavy *clump*.

I didn't wait to see how the bigger man reacted because I was already streaking into the trees behind the carport, tramping through nettles and ferns. I hurried to the far side of the structure and peered out. The bigger man was at the edge of the gravel yard, close to the decking. He looked long to his right, as if sensing someone was watching him. Then he leaped onto the deck and ran towards the front of the lodge.

The second he was gone, I sprinted across the driveway with the number plate. I didn't slow up for the gully. I didn't slow up at all. I just leaped into the woods.

23

'Don't you *ever* do anything that stupid again.'

Rachel thumped me. We were creeping uphill through the darkness under the trees, trying to keep parallel to the driveway. I was carrying Holly in my arms, stumbling under her weight. My feet were cut. I could feel blood between my toes.

Rachel walked alongside me with her left elbow cradled in her right hand, cursing whenever she got tagged by an unseen branch or slipped on the uneven terrain. It was so black under the trees I could only see a few metres in front of us and what I could see was blurred and shadowed. The men could have been standing under the trees a short distance away, watching us, and we wouldn't have known.

'Do you have *any* idea how close he was to finding you?' Rachel hissed.

I didn't say anything.

'Seriously, Tom. We had to watch it.'

And I had to live it. And if I hadn't, he would have found you, I thought.

But I didn't say that. I told Rachel I was sorry instead. And the truth is I was sorry I'd taken such a gamble. But, even so, I couldn't deny the slight buzz of exhilaration that was humming in my veins now it was over. The number plate dangled from Holly's hands and tapped against the backpack I was wearing – a constant reminder that gave me hope.

'This is going to work,' I said. 'We're going to get out of here.'

It was Rachel's turn not to say anything. Maybe she wasn't prepared to allow herself to believe it. Or maybe – after what had happened in the alley – she didn't fully believe in me.

I boosted Holly in my arms, trying not to let that thought twist in my mind. Holly was clinging to my neck, her legs dangling at my side. Fathers and daughters. I know it's a cliché, but Holly would always be my little princess. Carrying her like this reminded me of all the years I'd carried her when she was younger. The way her hair grazed my face. The way she hung her chin over my neck.

'OK, sweetheart?'

'I'm worried about Buster.'

That got me. I'd been trying not to think about Buster, or what had been done to him, and I didn't want my upset to show. Rachel shot me a quick, conflicted look.

'We're all worried about him,' she said.

'I want to find him.'

'We know.'

'Do you think he just ran off somewhere? Maybe he'll find us.'

How to answer that? I didn't know what was worse. The fact Buster hadn't been moving the last time I'd seen him, or that the bigger man had been dragging him across the floor by his back legs like he was a piece of rubbish to be flung outside.

Then a new thought hit me. The sea was so close to the lodge.

Oh God.

'We'll keep an eye out,' I said, and tried to block the harrowing images that were filling my mind. 'If we don't find him before we get to the gate, we'll call the police the second we're out of here. They'll send people back to find him. OK?'

Yes, I felt terrible for lying to my daughter, but in my defence I knew what the truth would do to her because it was already gnawing at me. I loved Buster. He was a big, affectionate, dopey lump. He'd snoozed on my feet when I watched Sunday football on the TV. He'd always been the first to greet me when I came downstairs in the morning or when I got home from work. I'd loved walking him to the pub, sneaking him treats.

But most of all I loved him for the complete and unconditional love he'd shown my children. I couldn't begin to imagine what life was going to be like without him, or how I would explain to Holly that he was gone. I guess that's my way of saying why, for the time being at least, I didn't try.

'If anything happens to him . . .' Holly said. And then she started to cry.

I held her, feeling her tears against my face, wishing so badly I could somehow deny what I'd seen with my own eyes – or that I could go back in time, maybe. Save Buster. Stop any of this from happening.

Whatever *this* was.

We tramped on, climbing steadily, pausing every now and again to catch our breath, check our bearings. I didn't think it could be far now. And it was much quieter, because the hard rain had slowed, sputtering out into faint sprays and intermittent drops. The wind was still blasting through the trees overhead but the background deluge had faded, like turning off a television that was screening only static. I stilled, feeling like someone had hit pause on the world.

A few seconds passed and then Rachel grabbed hold of my backpack and yanked me and Holly down to the ground. I knelt in the mud, staring wildly at Rachel in the dark. Her eyes were black and lidless. She put a finger to her lips. Holly clung to me tighter, shaking, burying her face in my neck.

Fear shrank my scalp.

Nothing happened.

Long seconds went by.

I was starting to think that Rachel had just got freaked out by the silence and the dark.

Then my heart jolted.

The smaller man was just visible through the breaks in the trees, hiking downhill along the driveway in his white coveralls. Cold terror washed over me, like someone had burst a water balloon over my head.

The smaller man's torch was shining faintly. The batteries were almost gone. He was clutching the shotgun by the barrel in his other hand. I supposed he must have checked the gate and satisfied himself it was secure. His boots crunched on in the quiet.

Then stopped.

He was almost level with us. Had he heard a noise? Maybe just the creaking of my kneecaps was enough to give us away.

I watched him, silently urging him to move on, holding Holly so tight I could feel her heart banging away.

She flinched. A sudden loud shout had ripped through the dark from the direction of the lodge. If we'd been in the woods in the daytime, it was the kind of noise that would have made birds scatter. Now, it just seemed to echo into the night.

We watched in breathless silence as the bigger man's hooded head bounced up over the humped summit of the driveway. He jogged closer to the smaller man, pulled up, clutched his knees and tugged down his mask to catch his breath. I strained my eyes to try to get a clear look at him but it was no good. He was angled away from us, his massive shoulders turned. The one thing I could see was the wheel wrench he was carrying. He showed it to the smaller man, gesturing back down at the way he'd come.

The smaller man snatched the wrench with the hand holding the torch. He shook his head and began to jab and gesture with the wrench. The two men had a heated discussion. At the end of it, the smaller man shook his hooded head once more, like a disgruntled employer, and marched on down the driveway alone.

I guessed he'd told the bigger man he'd fallen for a diversion. He probably wanted to be shown the area of woodland the bigger man had been heading towards when he'd become distracted. A thought struck me then. We'd left my toolbox behind. If the men found it, they'd know we'd been there. But what difference could that make now?

We were so close to the gate. So close to getting out.

After several long seconds of standing and watching the smaller man walk off, the bigger man's shoulders finally dropped and he shook his head. Then he refitted his face mask, pulled his big industrial torch out of his pocket, switched it on and jogged after the smaller man with the beam lancing into the night.

Time slipped by. We crouched there. Waiting.

24

'How much longer do we stay here?' Holly whispered.

'Not long.'

Do you want to know something bizarre? Just then, I wasn't in a total hurry to move on. We'd been waiting for eight minutes by my watch, sitting largely in silence in the dark under the trees. We didn't want to make a move towards the gate too soon in case one or both of the men were still around. But at the same time, we didn't want to leave it too long, either, in case they came back. And the wait was, yes, terrifying and, yes, nervy as all hell, but it was also – and here's the bizarre part – kind of special.

Fatherhood is a puzzle to me. It's one I feel like I'll never get close to solving. I can remember when I first found out Rachel was pregnant with Michael. We were thrilled, of course. Like most couples who'd been trying to conceive for a while, we'd hugged and cried and talked for long hours about how excited we were for the future. And I was excited. I had all these images of me being this Great Dad, like those snapshots you see in catalogues and magazines. You know the ones I mean. Arty, black-and-white shots of Bare-Chested Dad cradling his baby infant for the first time, the little one curling his tiny fist round Dad's finger. Or sunny, beachside shots of the whole family together with Holiday Dad carrying one of his gorgeous kids on his shoulders and Holiday Mum swinging a wicker basket filled with perfectly packed picnic things. Memorable moments. Quality time with the family. That's what we all want, isn't it? But too often, it hadn't been that way for me.

The simple truth was I hadn't spent enough time with my kids or my wife. And yeah, that was particularly true lately, but the seeds had been planted long before Rachel and I had split. I'd worked endless hours as a corporate lawyer in a City firm when I'd first started out on my career and then even longer hours for Lionel. I'd wanted to get ahead, make good money, provide for Rachel and the kids. But I know now that what I'd lost sight of – what we all probably lose sight of too often – was that I could never get that time back.

If I reflect on my own childhood, some of my most cherished moments were spent camping in some local woods with my dad. I close my eyes and it's not hard for me to remember the smell of woodsmoke and sweat in his shirt when he hugged me, or the sound of his gentle snoring in the forest night.

I'd wanted to share moments with Michael like that too. I'd wanted for us to create our own memories. But I wasn't as good a father as my dad was. I hadn't made the time. And now that Michael was dead, I knew I never could.

Was that one of the reasons why he'd gone off the rails? Was it why he'd gone joyriding in my car and had wound up dead? These were the questions that haunted me in the sleepless hours of the night.

So forgive me for the interlude, but sitting here with

Rachel and Holly, holding hands in the stillness . . . I don't know how to explain it in a way that makes sense. I did know, of course, that this was ridiculous. Context is everything and we were in the woods hiding for our lives. But, even so, I felt this incredible closeness between us like I hadn't in too long. It was as if all my nerve endings were stripped raw and tingling. As if I was feeling the bonds between us with a pure intensity that reached back far beyond whatever problems had pushed us apart.

'Tom? Can I talk to you a second?'

'What is it?' Holly asked, stirring.

'It's nothing,' Rachel told her. 'Wait here. Your dad and I will be back in just a sec, OK?'

'I don't want to be left on my own,' Holly pleaded.

'You won't be. We'll stay close. Tom?'

There was a no-nonsense quality to Rachel's voice that I recognized. She put her hand out to me and I let go of Holly and took it, wondering what exactly she was leading me away to.

We walked a short distance into the trees, then stopped and looked back to where Holly was sitting on the ground with her chin propped on her knees and her arms around her shins. She watched after us, looking almost as worried about what Rachel was about to say to me as I was.

'What's the problem?' I asked her.

Rachel released my hand and rubbed her bad arm. I got the impression she wasn't sure how to begin. 'What's your plan when we get out through the gate?'

'How do you mean?'

'Just . . . tell me what we do next.'

Even in the darkness, I could tell how guarded she was acting. It unnerved me.

'I don't know, Rachel. We get to the road. We flag down a car. Or we find a house. Somewhere with a telephone.'

'And then?'

'We call the police, of course.'

'And what do we tell them?'

A strange quiver in my heart. I was missing something here, but I had no idea what.

It was odd to think that just hours ago I'd held Rachel in my arms. We'd made love and been more intimate than we had been in months. Being together like that, wanting her so badly and feeling like she wanted me in return . . . I don't know. It had felt like we'd found our way back to each other. But now, all I could sense was the chasm opening up between us again.

'You're really going to make me say it, aren't you?' She raised her eyes to the treetops as though exasperated and, when she spoke, I could hear the constriction in her throat. 'Do you know who these men are, Tom? Do you know the reason they've come here?' She eyed Holly and lowered her voice still further. 'Does it have to do with what happened to us in London?'

A tumbling sensation, like I was falling into a pit in the ground. I thought of how Rachel wouldn't meet my gaze just a short while ago. I'd wondered then if it was because she'd had some idea what this was about and she wasn't telling me. But no, apparently she'd been wondering if *I* was the one who'd caused this.

'Does it have to do with your work for Lionel? Is that what this is?'

'*Sorry?*'

'I want to know what's safe for us to tell the police, Tom. I don't want to put Holly in any more danger.'

I stared at her, feeling like my lungs didn't work any more. How could she think this? But then, hadn't I thought the same thing about her?

'Rachel, I don't know why these men are here. I have no idea what they want with us. It could all be a horrible mistake.'

She considered me cagily, not saying anything right away, just studying me for any kind of slip or tell.

'Come on, Rachel. Who do you think Lionel is? He makes money off of people who have good ideas. I help him to do that. We don't do anything illegal. That's not who Lionel is. It's not who I am. I thought you knew that?'

She squinted at me some more. I'm not sure she was convinced. And, on balance, I suppose I could understand why. After all, it's not as if I hadn't had my suspicions about her.

'I promise you, Rachel.' I took her hands. 'I don't know anything to tell the police other than how scared I am right now.'

She was silent a moment, then she nodded. 'OK.' She worked a small, rueful smile. 'Then let's get out through this gate and away from this place, can we?'

I stumbled after her back to Holly, but it was only when we'd helped her to her feet and moved off towards the driveway that I realized I hadn't turned Rachel's question back on her. I hadn't asked if there was something she wasn't telling me.

25

I ventured out of the trees at a stoop, scoping out the driveway. Once I was sure it was clear, I beckoned for Rachel and Holly to join me. I shied away from looking at Rachel directly. I was still troubled by our conversation in the woods.

The wind blustered against us, pushing us up the last stretch of driveway to the gate and the fence. The gate looked about a hundred feet tall in the darkness. The spiked barbs running along the top cut into the sky like thousands of knives.

We stopped and stood together in roughly the spot we might have slowed up in the Volvo. The number-plate camera was on the post to our right.

I got down on one knee, the wind streaking around me, and gestured for Holly to pass me the number plate. I took it in both hands and angled it towards the camera.

My heart rose up into my mouth.

Rachel and Holly watched me.

We waited. And waited.

But nothing happened.

The camera stared blindly ahead. No lights blinked on. No hidden mechanism whirred. There was no humming surge of electricity.

Don't panic.

I wiped the number plate on my soaked jogging trousers and tried again. I tilted and tipped it. I moved it side to side and up and down.

'It's not working,' Holly said. She cringed and looked back down the driveway, like she expected the men to appear any second.

'Maybe it's a weight thing,' Rachel suggested. 'Maybe there are sensors under the ground.'

'To get out?' I shook my head. It felt like someone had fitted a giant vice around my chest and was slowly tightening it. My ribs strained. My lungs shrivelled. 'Here, you hold it.'

I passed Rachel the number plate and crossed to the camera, taking a quick look at it from behind. An unsettling thought had formed in my mind. Maybe *this* was what the smaller man had been doing up here. If he knew that the gate was the only way out of here, then maybe he'd sabotaged it. But no, there were two thick black cables plugged into the back of the camera. Neither of them were cut or disconnected in any way.

My eyes slid to the intercom. I knew that if I pressed the button then the unit in the kitchen of the lodge would ring. I knew there was a button there to open the gate. I'd said before that the controls in the kitchen wouldn't open the gate for more than a minute, but obviously I hadn't paid that much attention to the unit before. Now I was asking myself if there was an override or some other way of keeping the gate locked in the open position. Maybe if you pressed and held the GATE OPEN button in the kitchen for longer it would do the trick.

I glanced back at Rachel and Holly. Rachel was angling the number plate in all kinds of directions, getting frustrated and desperate. Holly was keeping watch, bending forwards from the waist, clasping her arms around her for warmth.

Could I make it back to the lodge and into the kitchen without the men spotting me? Would Rachel and Holly wait here without me while I tried? If I managed to trigger the gate for them they could get away and summon help. I could hide until the police came.

If I was lucky.

What else?

I got up out of my crouch, walked over to one of the gate panels and shoved it with the flats of my hands. It didn't budge. There was no give in it at all. I looked up, but even if I cupped my hands and tried to boost Rachel or Holly, there was no safe way for them to make it over the barbs at the top.

'Headlights,' Holly hissed.

I spun, eyes wide.

'Dad, it's night. If we were in our car, we'd have our headlights on.'

I felt a surge of blood push through my veins. Maybe she was right. Maybe at night the gate camera was light sensitive. Fumbling in the pocket of my jogging trousers, I pulled out my mobile phone. It was coated in moisture, slippery to the touch. I walked close to Rachel and got down on one knee, shielding the phone with my body as I turned it on.

The screen glowed with a watery blue light. I cupped my hand around it and checked there was still no signal, then flicked at the bottom of the screen with my thumb and called up the torch app.

The flashbulb on the back of the phone blazed down at the ground. Rachel swallowed hard and looked behind us, then nodded at me slowly. Again, I wondered what she was thinking. Did she still suspect me? Should I suspect her?

Carefully now, I moved my hand until the beam shone brightly against the reflective surface of the number plate. Rachel angled the plate towards the camera.

And . . . Nothing.

No clunk. No whirring electric mechanism.

In a fit of frustration, I almost threw my phone down at the ground.

'Try shining the light at the camera,' Holly said.

I immediately turned and swung my phone towards the lens – forgetting to shield it with my body – and that's when the first shot rang out.

Not that I knew what it was. Not at first. For those initial blurred moments it was just a brash *crack* in the blackened silence. Until something *whanged* off the gate in a shower of sparks.

I remained frozen for far too long. It seemed to take an age for my brain to catch up to what was happening. Then a judder of absolute terror tore through my body. I twisted round and – from the corner of my vision – glimpsed a bright flash from the tree cover down the driveway to our left.

A puff of muddy dirt kicked up from the ground two metres in front of Holly.

She screamed and leaped back.

'*Gun!*' Rachel yelled.

I grabbed for Holly, snatching fistfuls of her pyjama top, hauling her roughly away towards the trees on the opposite side of the driveway.

There was another huge bang. Another puff of dirt. Gravel spattered my calf. I launched myself forwards with Holly. Saw Rachel drop the number plate and dive forwards in a blur at my side.

A tree trunk exploded close to us in a raging burst of splinters.

We tumbled and fell forwards through bushes and ferns, then pushed up to our feet and scrambled on into the trees. Into the dark.

26

We ran hard and blind and breathless, reaching out and calling to one another, tearing through the blackness, fleeing like wild things. I didn't know where the men were. I didn't know if we were about to run into them. Each time a twig snapped I thought it was a gunshot.

Trees and bushes zipped by and jolted in my vision. Rachel was in front, using her good arm to push aside branches that flicked back and struck my face. I held Holly's wrist and wrenched her forwards, ducking and swerving, stumbling, fighting to stay up.

My bare feet pounded the forest floor. It was a world of sticks and thorns and brambles. Pretty much every step hurt me. I didn't care. We only got faster. Desperation can do that for you. Adrenaline. Fear. I could feel my heart hammering in my chest. Behind me, Holly was making frenzied yelping noises. Rachel was swearing over and over.

She was leading us downhill and I guessed that was the right move. We were faster with the ground falling away beneath us, so long as we didn't trip or fall.

I glanced to my left and felt a hollowness open up in my gut as I saw the bright dazzle of the industrial torch bouncing and flaring in the dark. It looked like one of the men was racing down the driveway. He was yelling for us to stop and cursing and swinging the beam in through the trees, but I didn't think he could see us. The beam arced and jagged and probed the woods around us. It flashed only once on Rachel, then was gone. But the look of terror on her face pierced me.

The two men shouted to one another, asking each other if they'd seen us, where we had gone. They sounded panicked and furious. Based on the way their voices carried, I was pretty sure one of them was somewhere in the trees behind us. Hard to know for sure. The woods and the wind seemed to distort all sound. I looked behind me but all I saw were the rows of pines, the endless darkness, and then Holly flinching and shrieking as a branch scratched her face and tore at her hair.

Maybe I should stop. Maybe I should hide. If I found a place where I could duck behind a tree trunk, it was possible I could wait and jump out on the man who was following us. I had the screwdriver in my pocket. If I was quick enough maybe I could jab it in his neck, his side, anywhere soft and vulnerable. Maybe I could get hold of his gun.

Those guns. Whatever this situation was – whatever had caused it – one thing was clear to me now. When the men had shot at us, they hadn't been aiming at any of us in particular. Their bullets had sprayed us indiscriminately. They could have hit Rachel or me or Holly. I had to believe – no matter how much I didn't want to – that their intention was to kill us all. And that meant that if we couldn't get out through the gate or the fence, then either we had to hide somewhere there was no chance of the men finding us or, somehow, I had to try and stop them.

But crouching behind a tree? Taking that chance? It seemed like too big a risk right now. And I didn't want to leave Rachel and Holly on their own. I wanted to make certain I'd got them away from these men.

We ran on. Something crunched into my chest. It stopped me in my tracks. It felt like I'd been hit with a cricket bat. I teetered backwards and went down on one knee. Breathing was difficult. There was a stabbing pain in my ribs.

I'd run into a tree.

Holly clattered into me, almost falling. I put my hand on her back, urged her on, staggered after her from behind.

My breathing grew funny. I was starting to pant, and not just from my man-on-tree incident. I'm not all that fit. I don't go to the gym on a regular basis or jog around my neighbourhood. My stamina was starting to let me down and my legs were doing that rubbery exhaustion thing. I got a stitch in my side.

I wouldn't stop.

Then, out of the dark, fractals of light shimmered through the trees to our left. The lodge. It was coming up fast, the outdoor lights shining around it in a wavering blue orb, getting nearer, brighter, until the dark husk of the carport flashed by in the night.

We ran on. The trees started to thin. I could hear and smell the sea. Another glance behind me, back to the driveway. And a strange, empty sensation, like looking into a black void in the night.

There was no sign of the man with the torch. I couldn't spot the beam at all. Had he come into the trees after us? Had he stopped further up the driveway because he was being cautious, afraid we'd doubled back? Or had he switched off his torch to sneak up on us?

'Watch out.'

In front of me, Rachel grabbed for a tree trunk and yanked herself to a stop with a pained cry. Holly skidded and slid down onto her side on a ledge of hardscrabble grass next to the shore. I pulled up into a stagger, clasping my aching ribs, sucking down air. It didn't help. There wasn't enough oxygen in my lungs. It felt like I'd been inhaling helium from a balloon.

Sea spray showered us. It was icy cold. The tide was high. A major storm surge. Frenzied waves clashed and collided, throwing up twisted ropes of foam. Immediately below us was a cluster of boulders, black and waxy in the moonlight. More waves burst against them, spray hammering down.

I spun and looked at Rachel. Her face was clammy and grey. Behind her I could see the decking in front of the lodge, lit starkly by the outdoor lights, and the yawing hole where I'd left the fire pit uncovered. More lights glowed from inside the towering wall of tinted glass at the front of the living room. Boiling surf gushed in under the deck, coiling around the sunken pilings and girders that supported the structure.

I stood there, my breathing shallow, my heartbeat flickering against my ribs. Holly pushed up to her knees, spitting up phlegm and fear. Rachel clutched her bad arm and turned to search for the men.

My family. Under threat.

I searched the trees too, but all I could see were shades of black and near-black and the regimented grey streaks of the endless rows of pines. I needed a better angle. If I clambered out onto the boulders it might give me a clearer view of the deck and the driveway. I ducked low and crawled out on all fours. The sea roiled and rushed in at me. Foaming suds swamped my ankles and wrists, pooling under my chest. I leaned out, my elbows trembling, the tide sucking and draining away.

A stutter of torchlight. The slick gleam of white coveralls. I shuddered. The smaller man was standing towards the base of the gravel yard, between the lodge and the carport, flinging his torch around. I felt a stabbing pain in my ribs again as I saw the shotgun held down by his leg. I guessed he'd ditched the wheel wrench. Maybe he'd tossed it into the trees.

As I watched, he leaned his head back on his shoulders and shouted, 'Do you see them?'

If the bigger man responded, I couldn't hear him. I turned and looked back at Rachel and Holly. Fear shook me. I wanted them safe. We couldn't stay here. We were too exposed. But I thought there was something we could do. Maybe.

'We have to go in the water,' I said. 'We have to get to the other side.'

'You're not serious.' Rachel pushed off from the tree she was leaning against and moved towards me, staring at me like I'd lost my mind. Holly wouldn't look at me. It was like she was trying to hide from what I had to say.

'We have to get back inside the lodge. We can release the gate from in there. There must be a way to make it stay open.' I pushed up into a crouch, my upper body trembling and frozen, the salt water pushing and pulling at my lower legs. Another wave detonated behind me as I pointed to the lodge. 'If we get inside we can get to the phone in the kitchen. We can call the police. The gate and the phone. That's what we have going for us right now. If you want, I can try by myself but—'

'*No.*' Holly looked between us, shaking her head. From the angle she was on, I could see that my old coat had been ripped on her left side. Stuffing was poking out of it. 'No, Dad. No way.'

I peered towards the driveway and the trees again. It bothered me that we still hadn't spotted the bigger man.

'One of them is by the carport,' I said. 'I'm not sure where the other one is but we can't go over the deck. It's too brightly lit. Right now they know we're somewhere over this side of the driveway. The best thing we can do is get to the other side in a way they won't be expecting.'

Rachel stepped closer. 'They won't be expecting it because we won't make it.'

I didn't reply.

'It's too rough, Tom. And I can't swim with my arm like this. The joint's still unstable.'

'You won't be swimming. You'll be wading. If we stay close to the deck, it shouldn't be too deep.' I didn't dare look at the water too closely. It was impossible to tell if that was true or not. 'We can get to the rocks on the far side. They'll be out of sight from the driveway. We'll get into the pool room from there. We'll use some of the towels that were outside the sauna to dry ourselves. We can warm up. Grab our clothes from the tumble dryer in the laundry room. Our coats. Our boots. Get to the phone.'

Rachel let go of a withering breath. She looked away from

me at the waves pawing at the decking, shaking her head. I knew what I was demanding of my family. I knew I was asking for their trust and that, maybe, after everything that had happened, I didn't deserve it.

'Dad's right, Mum,' Holly said, and I felt something shatter inside of me – something that had been clenched up for too long. 'I think we can do this. I think we have to try.'

27

I slipped Rachel's backpack off in a hurry and jammed the items from my pockets inside – my mobile phone, Rachel's car keys, the screwdriver, the nail scissors. Then I zipped the backpack closed and fed Holly's arms through the straps. Her breathing was shallow and fast, like she was having some kind of asthma attack.

'You'll go on my back,' I told her. 'I'll carry you. OK?'

She nodded but she looked scared. I went down on one knee and waited until I felt her weight on my back, her hands around my neck. I took hold of her legs. They were shaking. From the cold or from fear? Probably both.

'Rachel?'

I turned to her. Her jaw was locked. She was rocking forwards and backwards on her toes as she focused on the sea, like she was trying to psych herself up.

A shout ripped through the dark.

'If you come out, we can talk. We can help you.'

It was from the smaller man. I inched forwards with Holly on my back and peered towards the carport. He was staring blindly into the trees. He had no idea where we were.

'If you keep hiding you'll just make it worse on yourselves. We can let the girl go.'

'He's lying,' Rachel whispered.

I thought so too. I knew that if I had to lay down my life to save Holly right now, I'd do it, no question. But not if I didn't believe she'd be safe. And there was no way I could trust the word of these two thugs.

I waited for the smaller man to say something more, but instead he stiffened and pushed his face forwards into the darkness. He stared for several seconds, then bolted into the trees with his torch. Maybe he thought he'd heard something or seen something. Maybe the bigger man had signalled to him.

Time to go.

'He's gone into the trees,' I told Rachel. 'We can't stay here.'

I rose up and stalked out onto the rocks, picking my way between them, slipping and teetering with Holly on my back, venturing as close as I dared to the edge of the lighted deck. Black water swelled up towards me, circling my ankles. Rachel was close behind us, shaking her head.

'Two minutes, Hols. Then it's done.'

Holly squeezed my hips with her quaking thighs by way of answer and I plunged in, hearing Rachel splash down and cry out to my side.

At first, the cold was so brutal and immediate I felt almost nothing. Then it bludgeoned me. A terrible numbing chill that stole my breath and coursed up through my gut and spine as an incoming swell washed in, swamping Holly's legs. She whimpered and clung to me tighter.

'It's OK. It's not too deep.'

A lie. The icy wash was already as high as my chest. A

black wave rushed in, the swell much deeper than I'd anticipated. My feet scrambled for grip on the vanishing seabed. We were pushed towards a metal girder braided with rivets. I thrashed and kicked my legs, twisting at the waist. Then the wave washed out and I bounded forwards in its wake. Holly pressed one hand onto my forehead, half covering my eyes. Her teeth chattered close to my ear.

Another wave raised us up and tipped us. We were only a few metres across with a long way to go. Rachel appeared at my side, splashing forwards with an awkward kind of scissor kick, using her good arm to scoop handfuls of water ahead of her. She looked clumsy and desperate.

I was the one who'd made us do this. What if it was a mistake? I was afraid we'd be washed under the decking and pummelled against the metal girders. That the men would appear on the shoreline and spot us.

The water nudged my chin. It had to be close to Holly's shoulders. Any deeper and we'd be forced to swim for it. Holly still had my coat on. That wouldn't help. But with my next leap forwards the seabed sloped up a little to greet me. My toes scrabbled for grip.

The tide washed out, dragging at my waist and legs. Rachel kicked and flailed at my side. I heard her gargle something. She spat and pointed. I turned.

And froze.

A huge black wave was rolling in.

It hurtled towards us. Rising up. Cresting over.

I turned sideways on to it, clamping down on Holly's thighs with my arms, bracing my feet.

No time left.

The wave barrelled into us, thundering and raging, almost peeling Holly away from me while her fingers clutched at my mouth and eyes. I took two involuntary steps backwards, holding fast to Holly's legs. I staggered. Dipped. The water rushed and gurgled in my ears and mouth. I struggled to stay upright. Lights flashed in my vision.

I saw Rachel go under, vanish, fight her way back to the surface, spluttering and spitting. I snatched one hand away from Holly and reached out to Rachel, clutching her fingers. I gritted my teeth and strained to hold on to them both.

The wave rushed on, swamping the underside of the deck with a terrific gushing roar. And with it, I saw something rise up in the dark behind Rachel. A slick, grey shape, like a whale breeching the surface.

My pulse spiked. I let go of an involuntary gasp of surprise.

That sound from the deep well of my dreams.

The keening, buzzing whine like a tumble dryer thrashing around on a fast spin. Like a chainsaw felling a tree.

I knew now what it had been.

An outboard motor.

Holly flailed towards me and tightened her grip around my neck as I turned Rachel to see.

A rubber dinghy was moored to the timber steps leading from the deck into the water.

28

I boosted Holly and Rachel into the dinghy, then heaved myself up and rolled in after them, with both of them pulling on my arms. I was drenched. My ribs hurt. I was stunned and breathless from the cold. But I felt another small hum of elation. A boat. We could get out of here now.

The dinghy rocked beneath us, bumping against the mooring post. Rachel was cradling Holly to her. Their clothes and hair were saturated. Their faces and lips were blue. They shivered. Holly had lost one of her shoes in the water. They looked so scared, so broken and lost.

Night steam wafted up from our bodies and clothes. When I raised my hands in front of my face, my fingers were numbed and bloated. It was difficult to form them into fists.

Brodie's words came back to me again. *It's easy enough to kayak in around the coast.* Stupid. We should have thought of looking for a boat before. And what else? Something about the boat. A loose thought I couldn't quite grasp jangled in my mind.

'Dad? Can we go?'

I held my clawed hands in front of me – a bit like a surgeon who'd scrubbed in and was waiting for a nurse to slip on some gloves – as I stumbled past Rachel and Holly to the outboard motor at the stern. I'd never operated a dinghy before, but in my head it was going to be straightforward. We'd start the motor like we were cranking a lawn-mower engine, then we'd race away. Even if the men heard us, we'd be gone before they could stop us.

I should have known better.

The moment I looked at the engine I felt a terrible knocking in my chest. There was a keyhole for an ignition key. But there was no key to be seen.

Panic swelled in my lungs. Did one of the men have the key in a pocket of their coveralls? I ducked to search beneath the engine. Nothing.

'What is it?' Rachel asked.

The fear in her voice cut me on the inside. I thumped a deadened hand off the engine casing and told her. She said nothing. She was stunned. I told them both to help me search for oars.

We got on our hands and knees and felt all around us. Nothing. Holly found a metal equipment locker tucked into the prow of the dinghy. It was probably where life jackets and flares were stored. But it was secured by a padlock. No way of opening it.

'Wait here,' I said.

'Tom.'

'Just trust me, Rachel.'

I eased up to my feet, the boat swaying beneath me, and gingerly raised my head. I had to squint because the light shining on the decking was so bright. My eyes stung and watered. I shielded them with my hand. I couldn't see any sign of the men beyond the deck. I couldn't see the light of their torch. I hoped they were still searching the woods. Maybe they'd headed back up to the gate.

I crabbed sideways, placing one foot on the wooden steps. A blue rope had been looped around the mooring post. Next to it, Brodie's plastic leaf rake had toppled in the wind. I freed the rope, grabbed the rake and jumped back aboard the dinghy, pushing off from the steps with my foot.

'Will that work?' Rachel asked.

Hard to say, but it was worth a shot. I got down on my knees and started using the rake as an oar. If we could somehow get the boat out to sea without being spotted we could work our way along the coast. And even if the men *did* spot us, as long as we got enough distance between us and the shore, I hoped we'd be safe from being shot at. I didn't think they'd swim after us. The waves were too violent, the tide too strong, the water too cold. We'd only waded a short distance across the inlet and I was almost completely spent, my body bucking and cramping from the intense frigid chill.

'Help me.'

Holly reached over the side and paddled with her hand. Rachel stood with her head bent low and clutched the timber deck with her good hand, grimacing and shivering as she pushed us along.

We nudged into the swell. A wave slammed in, buoying the front of the dinghy, knocking Rachel off her feet. She crashed onto her back, jarred her shoulder, cried out in pain.

Holly and I watched her. She winced and nodded that she was OK. We splashed on. We couldn't afford to stop. We were in danger of being pushed under the decking and getting beached down there.

It didn't help that the rake made for an unwieldy oar. The plastic blade was about three times as wide as a typical spade. It was designed to be flexible, which made it flimsy in the water. It kept being bent and snatched sideways by the shifting tides. Plus, of course, my hands were numb.

The next wave twisted us to our left. The one after that turned us to our right. I tried fighting against it with my floppy rake-oar, digging hard on either side of the dinghy as the wave washed back out.

'You have to paddle again,' I shouted to Rachel.

She grunted and got back up, then leaned over the side of the boat up to her elbow and scooped handfuls of water with her good arm.

My head pounded. It was tough going but we seemed to be making progress. Another few strokes with the rake and we neared the front of the deck. I raised myself up and checked for the men again. Still no sign of them.

'Keep it up,' I said.

'We're trying, Tom.'

I plunged my rake-oar in again, pulling with one long sweep after another. My arms and back ached. My muscles quivered. The next wave was bigger than any we'd faced before. It thundered towards us.

'Hold on.'

The wave slammed against the boat, shunting us back. The rear of the dinghy bounced hard off a metal girder with a groan and a twist. Again, I worried about being sucked under the decking. But there was one advantage to the wave being so big. When it washed back out, it carried us with it. And the next few waves were smaller. Just. I paddled harder. Rachel and Holly did the same.

Five minutes of frenzied exertion. Maybe longer. I didn't look up through any of it. I just paddled and pulled. Paddled and pulled. In my mind's eye, I pictured us together when this was over. I could see Holly and Rachel sitting with blankets over their shoulders in the back of a police station somewhere, mugs of hot tea in their hands. I could see them looking up at me with tears of relief in their eyes. Safe now. All of it over. A chance to move on.

I wanted it over.

The boat jostled and rocked, dragging me back to reality. My ribs stung and ached. My arms were on fire. I made myself take five more strokes before I finally turned and looked back.

My heart sank.

We were barely fifteen metres from shore, rocking out in the open, close to the deck. Stuck. Rachel and Holly must have noticed the slump in my shoulders because they turned to look too.

'Oh God.' Rachel hung her head. 'We're not going to make it.'

Holly just stared. Then she leaned forwards, clinging to the rear of the boat.

'Buster,' she muttered.

'What?'

'Buster!' She pointed. 'Dad, I see Buster!'

Horror clawed at my heart. Another wave tilted the boat as I pushed my face into the darkness, peering towards shore.

Please don't let her see what they did to him. Please not that.

But the more I looked, the thicker the darkness became. Was Holly imagining it? We were all suffering from shock and exhaustion. No way we couldn't be. Perhaps Holly was just seeing what she wanted to.

'I don't see anything,' Rachel told her.

'*There.*' She pointed again, more insistent now. 'Near the boulders. Under that tree.'

I squinted, following her finger. And then something buckled inside me. I felt my body sag.

Buster.

They'd dragged him out onto the rocks at the edge of the deck. He was lying with his face hanging down, bedraggled and limp. I felt a hot spike of anger, like someone had stabbed me between the shoulder blades. Our family dog. He deserved so much better than this.

'Dad, we have to go back for him.'

I slumped more, feeling the physical drag in my arms, the tug in my heart.

'We can't,' I told her.

'Yes we can. He looks hurt.'

I didn't say anything. I just shook my head.

'Dad! Go back! We have time. He can see us!'

I shook my head no. Holly's eyes went wide. Confusion twisted her face. Then she stood and made a grab for the rake. I didn't release it. We looked at each other, our faces only inches apart. How much more could Holly take?

'Mum, tell him.'

She glanced down at Rachel, a pleading expression twisting her face. But Rachel wouldn't look up at her. I think it was then that Holly started to understand. I saw a tremor in her cheek. Her lips shook.

'W-why won't you go back?'

Tears pricked her eyes.

'Dad?'

'Please, Holly. Please don't ask me that.'

'Dad!'

I looked away, off to the deck. My throat felt raw. It hurt when I swallowed. I snatched a ragged breath, shaking my head.

I was going to have to tell her now. I didn't see that I had a choice.

'Buster's dead,' I whispered. 'I'm sorry, but they killed him. I saw them.'

'*What?*'

She stepped backwards, but she didn't let go of the rake.

'You said he was OK. You promised me we'd come back for him.'

The pain in my throat was even worse now. 'Because I lied. I had to. I didn't want to but I had to. I'm so sorry, Holly. There's nothing we can do.'

I saw her shock. I saw her despair and betrayal. All of those years of telling her to trust me. All of it wiped out in an instant.

'Mum?'

This time, Rachel lifted her face slowly, as if her head was weighed down. Her eyes glimmered darkly. Her mouth was slack.

'I don't believe you.' Holly's voice shook. 'I don't believe either of you.'

'Why would we lie?' Rachel asked her.

'I want to go *back*.'

She made another grab for the rake, harder this time. The dinghy had twisted sideways and I had my back to the sea, so I didn't see the wave coming in. It rocked the boat hard, tipping us up.

A lifting sensation. My bare feet slipped. I toppled forwards, letting go of the rake as Holly fell back.

I heard her yelp. Heard Rachel shout.

There was a splash.

I crashed to my knees, grabbing hold of the side of the dinghy.

But when I looked up, Holly was gone.

29

Three seconds. That's how long – give or take – I stared into the sea. That's how long the worst, most crippling kind of fear can grip hold of you for.

I couldn't spot Holly anywhere. It was like she'd vanished. The waves were wild, the tide was strong. She had my outdoor coat weighing her down, my backpack on her shoulders.

I thought of her sinking, fighting to get back to the surface. I felt like unseen hands were reaching up through the bottom of the dinghy and gripping hold of my ankles, pulling me down with her.

Where was she?

Rachel leaned over the side of the boat, searching the water. The long seconds ticked on. The dinghy twisted and rocked.

'I don't see her,' she screamed. 'I don't see her, Tom.'

Panic took me then. It flooded my system, like a raging electrical storm.

Think.

What about the rake? If I used it as a pole, maybe we could find her and pull her out. But as I looked around, I saw that the rake was gone too. Holly must have fallen with it.

She had to come up. She had to. She . . .

There.

A hand broke the surface maybe five metres in front of us, between the boat and the shore. Holly's face briefly appeared with a flash of white. She gulped air and went under again. I dived in.

Icy blackness tore through my head. It rippled over my skin. I pulled with my arms and kicked with my legs. My jogging trousers dragged against me. I swam to where I thought Holly had been and came up, looking madly around. Black waves jostled me. The deck loomed high overhead. The dinghy bobbed up. Rachel was watching me, shaking her head in rigid fear.

Oh Jesus, no.

I sucked air and went under again. I pulled down hard, feeling the waves and the tides tussling with my body. I opened my eyes into the salty sting but the absolute black was impenetrable, like not opening my eyes at all. I stretched out my hands as far as I could. I did the same with my feet. I floated there, star-like, waving my fingers and toes around at the far extremes of my reach, straining to feel for Holly, for anything.

The ache built in my lungs, but I wouldn't come up yet. I couldn't. I craved air but still I hung on.

Then I felt it. *Something.* A leg? A waist? It was above me.

I kicked up. But when I broke the surface and grabbed with my arms, another jolt of panic ripped through me. It wasn't Holly. It was Rachel.

'She's over there, Tom.'

Rachel wiped water from her face and pointed to shore. I whirled around, my heart in my mouth, and saw Holly staggering and stumbling up the stacked boulders fronting the shoreline, waves crashing against her, water draining out of her coat and the backpack she had on. She'd made it in. My brilliant, stupid, headstrong girl.

'I was afraid you wouldn't come up without her,' Rachel said. 'I was worried you'd think she was still down there.'

'Can you swim?'

'I think so. With the waves, I can.'

Rachel did her one-handed crawl next to me, turned onto her side. I swam beside her in a clumsy breaststroke, the massive waves bundling us up and tumbling us on. Far off to our right, the dinghy skimmed by, then faltered and rocked back with an outgoing wave before being gathered up and skimming forwards again.

'I couldn't stay in the boat on my own, Tom. I didn't want to leave you and Holly alone.'

I nodded, spitting water, pulling and kicking towards shore. I could see Holly ahead of us. She almost fell back in exhaustion, then pressed her cheek to a rock and clung on for a few seconds before climbing again. I didn't know how she'd react when she saw Buster, and I was afraid of the men getting to her before we could.

'Should we have told her sooner?' Rachel asked me.

I shook my head no. And even if we'd told her, I was pretty sure she would have dived in anyway. She wouldn't have left Buster on these rocks.

'We couldn't,' I said.

'Because we were protecting her.'

'Yes.'

'You wouldn't change it if you could do it again?'

I stared at Rachel. Why was she asking me this? Again, I felt a quiver of uncertainty as I thought of the question I hadn't put to her earlier. *Do you know what this is? Do you know why these men are here?*

Ask it? Or don't ask it?

But what could it change now?

Waves crashed around us. We were close to the shore. I pushed up to my feet. My legs shook. My arms trembled. I grasped for the boulders and helped Rachel to climb.

'Tom?'

I looked back. Rachel was reaching up to me with her good arm.

'You know I love you both? You know I love you both so much?'

I swallowed.

Don't ask it.

Not now.

'We love you too, Rachel.'

I grasped her wrist and heaved her towards me. There was a blur of grey behind her as the dinghy rushed in on a wave and blasted against the rocks. It rose up wildly, hovered, plunged back down.

Another wave rocked it, even more than before. This time, water breached the sides and gushed in. The boat juddered and groaned, beginning to flex. It sank backwards, until just the prow was sticking up at an awkward angle, pinned against the rocks, waves hammering against it.

I watched the dinghy and knew – with a sinking sensation

of my own – that it would be almost impossible to relaunch it until the sea calmed and the tide went back out, and perhaps not even then.

'Dad?'

Holly was crouching over Buster at the top of the boulders, her hair hanging wetly over her face. Her jaw wobbled.

'I'm sorry, Holly.' I scrambled up the last boulder to join her and kneel at her side. 'I am so, so sorry, my love.'

'No. I *told* you, Dad.' Her eyes were red and lost, searching my face. 'Look.'

She placed my hand on Buster's flank. I felt everything I didn't want to feel. He was icy cold. His fur was saturated and dense with salt and mud.

She can't accept it, I thought. *She just can't. It's all too much.*

But then I felt something. The vaguest stirring. A slight, wheezing expansion of Buster's chest.

What?

I lowered my face towards his muzzle. A wisp of air escaped his nostrils and grazed my cheek.

My body went weak with relief and sadness. Buster. He'd held on all this time. He'd waited for us to come.

I think that's what was about to finally break me. The fact Buster had been so strong, that he'd been suffering alone. That I'd been going to leave him behind.

'This was in his leg,' Holly said.

My eyesight was hazy from the salt water and fatigue, so it took a few seconds for focus to come.

I peered closer. Holly was holding some kind of feather. Red, with a sharp steel point on the end.

'What is that?'

'A dart.' Rachel had levered herself up the rocks in front of us. She panted, then reached out to peel back Buster's eyelid. 'I think he's sedated. I think they shot him with a tranquilizer gun.'

30

A *tranquilizer* dart.

I felt conflicted by that. On the one hand, yes, I experienced a huge swell of relief, because they'd subdued Buster instead of killing him. But, on the other hand, I felt a deep trill of fear. Because didn't their use of a tranquilizer gun suggest some really detailed planning? And didn't that mean either the men had been spying on us or they'd been tipped to expect a dog?

By Brodie? It had to be possible. And now the loose thought that had jangled in my mind about the dinghy came to me fully formed. It was Brodie who'd suggested the only way in here without coming through the gate was by boat. He could have told these men the same thing. And it was Brodie who'd told me where to park our car. So maybe he'd told these men exactly where our Volvo would be. Maybe that was how they'd known to slash our tyres.

Which made him, what? Some kind of spotter for these men? He knew how isolated it was here. Maybe he'd waited until the right family came along and then . . .

No. Stop it. Don't go there. Not now.

I had to focus on getting us to safety.

Lifting Buster in my arms, I ran with him towards the

south side of the lodge with Rachel and Holly stumbling alongside. Buster's head drooped over my forearm. His legs bounced and jolted. His fur was soaked and cold. Rachel had said we needed to get him warm and dry, fast. Same thing with us. We were all pale and shivering and I knew we couldn't stay outside much longer. I wanted to get to the phone in the kitchen. We had to try calling for help.

The side door to the pool room was out of sight of the far side of the lodge. It was made up of two panels of reinforced glass separated by a horizontal strip of oak in the middle. I laid Buster on the ground and grabbed the screwdriver from the sodden backpack Holly had on. There was a rock nearby. I used it like a hammer on the end of the screwdriver and punched out the glass in the bottom panel of the door, timing my blows with the crashing of the waves.

After six or seven strikes I cleared the last remaining shards away with the rock and then Rachel stuck her head inside and crawled through, sweeping the shattered glass into a pile with the side of her shoe. She reached back out for Holly's hand and I followed after them, stooping low with Buster sagging in my arms.

The pool room was lit green from the lights submerged in the pool. My skin flushed and tingled in the sudden dense heat. We stood there, listening, but the only noise was the hum of the boiler unit for the pool.

'Where first?' Rachel asked.

'Laundry room. We get dry. We get dressed.'

She nodded and loaded Holly up with towels from the rack outside the sauna. They hurried around the pool. Holly was limping because of her missing shoe. She looked dazed and wiped, like she'd been awake for days.

I scanned the deck outside. There was no sign of the men. Hoisting Buster in my arms, I jogged to where Rachel was waiting at the door into the main part of the lodge, peeking through the glass porthole.

'I don't see anything,' she whispered. 'Are you ready?'

Probably not.

She opened the door and I stepped through with Buster, pausing in the corridor. My nerves prickled. The lodge almost sounded *too* silent.

There was no movement. No noise. Nothing to indicate the men were close.

Water dripped out of Buster's coat, running along my arm and splattering on the floor.

Now or never.

'I think it's clear,' I said, and padded along the corridor in my bare feet. Past the cinema room and the corridor leading to the library. The kitchen up ahead.

I stopped outside the laundry room. Rachel and Holly caught up to me and moved inside. I backed in after them, hitting the light switch with my elbow and pushing the door closed with my foot. Aromas of detergent hung in the air. Rachel looked around her in a hurry, grabbed a mop, wedged it beneath the handle.

I felt paralysed with fear. I seemed to have forgotten how to breathe.

Rachel spread a towel on the floor in front of me and handed me another. 'You need to get him dry. Rub him down. Hurry, Tom.'

The laundry room was only a small space to begin with and it felt much smaller now. Holly staggered backwards into the far corner as I set Buster down. I'd never seen her look so sickly or so pale. A squiggle of purple veins pulsed slowly in her temple, behind the dark bruising to her eyes. Her lips were cracked and blue. She reached out a hand to Buster as she continued to shuffle backwards, a pained look on her face, like she couldn't bear to touch him just now.

'He's going to be OK, Holly. Mum's checked him over.'

She nodded, but I could tell she didn't believe me, and I could understand why. I rubbed him down while Rachel opened the tumble dryer and yanked out the socks, trousers and tops we'd spun the previous afternoon. Buster was floppy and inert. He didn't show any indication of coming round from his sedative.

I stuck at it as Rachel took the rest of the towels from Holly and began to help her out of the backpack and the old coat she had on. Already I felt like we were taking too much time, making too much noise. I kept expecting the door to crash open any moment. I kept hearing phantom footsteps out in the corridor and that awful *crunch-crack* of the shotgun being pumped.

'Tom?'

I looked up and almost fell back.

Oh God.

Holly was coated in blood. So much of it. Her pink pyjama top was drenched red and ruffled up on one side, adhered to her skin. Holly touched a hand to her tummy. It came away coated in blood.

'Holly?' My voice sounded funny.

She raised her head, bewildered, and Rachel peeled up her pyjama top until we could see blood oozing from the left side of her abdomen. I teetered. Rachel smeared the area with a towel. There was a hole about the size of a penny just below Holly's ribs. Blood squirmed out of the puckered hole, dark and thick, dribbling down.

'It's some kind of puncture wound,' Rachel said.

She let go of Holly's top and snatched up her backpack. I rushed forwards and picked up the coat Holly had been wearing. I fed the material through my hands. Looking. Looking. *There.* The ragged hole I'd seen earlier. The puff of white stuffing. I poked my finger through the hole and showed it to Rachel.

'Do you remember being hit?' I asked.

'No.'

I felt a ringing cold in my head. 'What about when the men shot at us?'

'Is that what this is? Have I been shot, Mum?'

Rachel gave me a hard look. I could tell she wanted me to back off. She didn't want me to upset Holly more. But I was scared out of my mind.

I stared at my finger poking through the hole in the coat and felt my darkest fears sweep inside the room as Rachel used the pair of nail scissors to snip away Holly's top.

'How's your breathing?' she asked.

Holly stared forwards without answer.

'Holly. Your breathing.'

'Um. OK. I think.'

'Any pain? Any flaring in your lungs?'

'It hurts a bit now. I didn't notice before. I was kind of numb.'

Rachel snapped on plastic gloves, tore open a sterile pad and pressed it to the wound. Holly sucked air through her teeth. Blood bubbled out over the pad and trickled over Rachel's fingers. She increased the pressure. This time Holly whined.

'Lean back against the sink behind you,' Rachel said. 'Tom, open me more pads. Those ones. The big one. And wipes.'

I dropped the coat and did as Rachel told me. My hands were shaking. My ears whistled. I felt faint.

'Holly, listen to me.' Rachel took hold of her wrist with her spare hand and felt for her pulse. 'If you start to feel queasy, or different in any way, you tell us, OK?'

'OK.'

Rachel looked at me. 'I don't think she's been shot,' she said, in a low voice. 'A tiny bit of shrapnel, maybe, but I doubt it. Her pulse is fast but I'd expect that right now.'

I wiped my hand across my mouth and nodded back. I was thinking of the tree trunk that had burst with splinters when we'd dived away from the gate. Had a fragment of wood pierced her side?

'It could be a branch jabbed you when we were in the woods,' Rachel said to Holly. 'Or maybe a stone or rock when we were in the water?'

'No,' I said. 'I saw the hole in this coat before we went into the sea.'

'So probably a stick then. That's all. OK?'

Rachel pulled the bloodied pad away and immediately pressed another to Holly's side. The bleeding didn't seem to have let up at all. I didn't know how much blood she'd lost, but I was starting to wonder if that was why she looked so pale.

I tried to catch Rachel's eye for some indication of how serious this really was, but she kept avoiding me and focused on Holly instead.

'You're going to be fine,' Rachel told her. 'I'm going to patch you up for now and we'll keep an eye on it. OK?'

Holly nodded vaguely.

'Tom, I'm going to need your help.'

I did what I could. Mostly I passed Rachel things. The sterile pad she stuck to Holly's side made her look like she'd been patched up after a shark bite. Fresh blood began to bloom through the gauze dressing, but the plastic coating on the outside held it in.

Rachel and I worked together to dry Holly and dress her in her clothes from the tumble dryer while she kept pressure on the dressing herself. When we were done, we put on our own clothes. Holly watched us, swaying, gripping hold of the sink with one hand and her side with the other. I got her into her wellington boots and put on her outdoor coat. Then I pulled on my own boots, not bothering to lace them, and shrugged on my coat. Rachel was the last to get her coat on over her sweater and pull on her boots, abandoning her soaked running shoes. She passed me her backpack and I slipped it over my shoulders before wrapping Buster in our last two towels and lifting him again.

'Ready?' I whispered.

Holly closed her eyes and nodded, like she might be about to pass out. Rachel locked her gaze on me, her eyes focused and intense. Behind her, the floor was a mess of bloodied medical supplies and saturated clothing.

'We'll get to the phone,' I said. 'We'll call for help. Then we'll find somewhere to hide. OK, Holly?'

'OK, Dad.'

I flashed her a fleeting smile, trying to mask the terror that was weighing me down. All I wanted to do right then was rush her to a hospital, get her to A&E. I thought of the blood trickling out of her side. How much could she lose before she got really ill? How much had she lost already? I wanted to ask Rachel those questions, but not in front of Holly.

Rachel took the mop from under the handle and cracked open the door.

Silence on the other side.

I stuck my head out. The corridor was empty. Cradling Buster to me – like an oversized baby swaddled in towels – I swept out to my right, towards the kitchen and the land-line phone and the controls for the main gate.

I took four, maybe five, steps with Rachel and Holly close behind me, then glanced to my left.

And froze.

My heart thumped once, very hard, then tried to thrash its way out of my chest.

Through the bars of light towards the bottom of the floating staircase I could see a pair of legs in white coveralls. Blue rubber boots.

Oh no.

One of the men was inside with us.

I spun back, shaking my head wildly, my eyes wide with

fear. I jutted with my chin back along the corridor and watched as Rachel flinched, then yanked Holly to one side. I darted by them, leading the way, the corridor tilting and lurching in my vision.

The door with the glass porthole in it was directly ahead. I hoisted Buster onto my shoulder and snatched it open.

And froze a second time.

Terror ripped through me.

The bigger man was at the far side of the pool room. He was stepping through the shattered glass door in his white plastic suit with the handgun in his gloved fist, looking down at the ground and inspecting the drifts of broken glass.

Something – some strange, cosmic tether – made him look up in that exact moment. He saw me and did a double-take, his eyes widening in surprise above his mask. Then he jerked his head back, straightened his shoulders and bellowed, 'THEY'RE HERE!'

I swung around, horror clawing at my heart. Rachel's face was stiff and strained. Holly's eyes were two dark pools of nothingness.

In the light at the end of the corridor, the smaller man skidded to a halt at the threshold of the kitchen. His rubber soles squeaked on the timber flooring. He dropped the torch and raised the shotgun in both hands.

Rachel whirled around to look at him. Then she swung back and tugged on Holly's arm, pulling her to her left, knocking into me as she ran.

'This way,' she screamed.

I saw the smaller man raise the shotgun as if in slow

motion. The muzzle came up past his knees, his thighs, his waist, like it was moving through water, taking a long, long time to be pointed at me.

I swivelled through air thick with friction and watched as the bigger man swung his gun arm forwards, his other arm back, bearing down on his front leg like a sprinter leaving the blocks, his back foot slipping on glass.

I was already leaning to my left. Already shifting my weight. Already pumping my knees and rocking my shoulders with Buster in my arms.

But the smaller man didn't shoot and, as I tore along the dog-legged corridor after my wife and daughter, I thought I knew why. He was afraid of hitting his partner. And all that was ahead of us was the library. A dead end. A trap.

I crashed into the narrow glass panel at the end of the corridor, bounced sideways and stumbled down the stairs into the reading nook.

And saw something I couldn't process right away.

Rachel was bent at the waist, her hands clutching at a central bookshelf, her feet spread shoulder-width apart and digging into the ground like she was trying to pull the shelf down on top of her. Maybe, in desperation, she was thinking of hiding under it.

But no, the shelf didn't fall. She heaved and grimaced until it swung out and opened on a tight, controlled arc.

Because it was a concealed door. And behind it was another door. Glossy white. A soft, metallic gleam. Centred in the middle of the door was an electronic keypad.

I felt myself teeter again.

'Wine cellar,' Rachel panted.

She punched in a fast code. Six digits.

I heard a muted beep. Then the door buzzed and dropped on its hinges and Rachel threw her weight against it. The door smashed open. Deep gloom on the other side.

Rachel reached back out for Holly and yanked her in.

I hesitated a second longer, then stumbled in after them and tripped down a short flight of concrete steps with Buster in my arms. Rachel streaked up past me and slammed the metal door closed behind us.

The door was many inches thick. At least three bolts slammed home with rapid, percussive *clunks.*

I shuddered. There was a sudden hard clang against the door. It sounded like the smaller man was hammering on the metal with the butt of his shotgun.

All around us, automatic lights twitched on, flicking glare and shadow around the cellar. I flinched and turned with Buster in my arms, taking in the subterranean, oak-lined space and the bottles of wine gleaming in the dazzle. There had to be 500 bottles in here. They were shelved in an elaborate, hexagonal racking system. Like the walls of a beehive.

Blood pounded in my ears. Hot sweat broke out across my back and scalp.

Behind me, Rachel groaned and hung her head at the top of the steps, the flat of her hand pressed against the back of the door.

The smaller man was still battering on it. But now it sounded like the bigger man had joined him and was kicking it too. The door was sturdy and the metal was almost thick enough to muffle the sounds of their attack.

'Mum?' Holly touched spread fingers to her mouth and

took a step backwards, her other hand still clutched to her dressing under her coat. 'How did you know this was here? Brodie didn't show us this. How did you know the code?'

I stared at Rachel. She was holding her head in her hands, tugging at the roots of her hair, groaning more.

Amid the shock and fear and confusion of the past several seconds, I'd been asking myself the same thing.

And the answer, when it came, hit me like a punch to the throat.

Rachel had lied to us.

This wasn't her first trip to Lionel's lodge.

The haulage truck thunders towards them. The mighty cab is an abrupt wall of steel and glass. The tarpaulin at the side shimmers in the dark.

The truck's headlights blare. Its horn moans.

And still Michael doesn't move.

The driver is a big man. Wide shoulders, bull neck, thick arms. The steering wheel sways and chatters in his hands. Like there's somewhere to go. Anywhere to go. The terror on his face is shocking to see.

'Michael!'

Fiona's scream is an ice pick in his ear. She grabs for the wheel and the Audi rocks and sways.

Michael shoves her away. Harder than he means to.

Headlamps slam into the truck driver's eyes. Full beam. Something the driver will remember. Something he definitely won't forget.

'Michael!'

He's played chicken before. On bikes when he was a kid. Once on a train track.

He knows that to win you have to wait longer . . . longer . . .

The truck driver brakes and locks his arms for impact.

And Michael tugs at the wheel, feathering the brake.

The Audi lurches, the truck horn blares again and then there is the rush and thunder of the truck slamming by. The shimmy of moving air.

The empty road ahead.

31

'It's not what you think, Tom.'

The men stopped attacking the door. The thick cellar walls seemed to amplify the quiet all around us. The cellar had an airless, muted quality. Like being sealed inside a vault.

I stared at Rachel. Buster hung heavy in my arms. All my strength seemed to just . . . leave me. Like I was wilting. Fading. Blinking out.

I shook my head, edging backwards, as Rachel moved down the steps in her big outdoor coat and her hiking boots, pushing her hair out of her face and tucking it behind her ears. Holly was standing to my side but, for the moment at least, Rachel's attention was fixed only on me. She tipped her head to one side. Her eyes were swollen with tears.

'None of this is going to be easy for you to hear, Tom. I'm really sorry about that.'

My heart crumbled. My breathing had grown funny. The room didn't spin or tilt, nothing like that, but I had a sensation like everything had become hyperreal. The colours in the room seemed too bright. The details too sharp. My hearing too acute.

The situation too real.

'I'm going to tell you everything I can, I promise. But first I want you to know – I want you both to know – that this room is safe. There's no way those men can get in here.'

'I don't get it, Mum. How do you know?'

'Because Lionel's wine collection is worth hundreds of thousands. The security system is state of the art.'

'Great.' Holly moved over to the wall of wine bottles behind me and slumped to the ground. She pulled the hood of her coat up over her head. 'Then I guess that means we're stuck in here.'

I swallowed and stared at Rachel. I felt like I was looking at a completely different person.

'You've been here before?' I asked her.

'Yes.'

'With Lionel?'

A slight pause. 'Yes.'

'What about Brodie?'

'He was here too.'

'Mum! I thought you didn't know him!'

I felt as if Rachel had cracked open my chest, reached in through my ribs, taken my heart in her hand and squeezed.

She raised her eyes and watched me, her pupils flicking left to right very fast, like she was trying to gauge my response. I had no idea what my response should be. I felt overwhelmed by what she was telling me. By everything, really.

'When?'

'Just over three weeks ago.'

I nodded, numbed. Just over three weeks ago was the weekend when Rachel was supposed to have been at the spa hotel that had had no record of her stay. If she'd been here instead, it explained why I hadn't been able to get hold of her because her phone would have been out of signal.

But why had she come?

I shook my head and turned around slowly. The wine bottles shimmered and gleamed in the hard, bright light. The oak shelving was ornate and expertly fitted. Down on the ground, a handful of wooden wine boxes had been stacked on top of one another. The temperature was noticeably chill and much cooler than the rest of the lodge. There were no windows and only the one door. I remembered seeing how some of the earth had been banked up against the fieldstone walls on this side of the property. It made me wonder how deep underground we were.

Details, you see, can help. Details can be a distraction. But no distraction could last as long as I wanted this one to.

'Tom.' Rachel tugged on the sleeve of my coat until I faced her again. Her soft brown eyes were edged with pink. 'I love you. I've always loved you. You might not want to hear that right now but it's true. And you might not want to hear this, either, but everything that has happened here tonight is because of how much I love you.'

I shook my head, feeling my throat close up.

'It's true, Tom.'

She took a step nearer, peeled back the towels from around Buster and checked his breathing and his pupil response. She was so close I could feel the warmth of her breath on my hand, but I'm not sure we'd ever been so far apart.

'You know me,' she whispered. 'Remember that.'

Did I?

I honestly didn't know any more.

I was just about to tell her so when a faint, shrill, beeping noise made me jump. It had come from behind the metal door. Fear vibrated inside me. I heard Holly catch her breath. It sounded like one of the buttons had been pressed on the electronic keypad on the outside.

'They can't get in here,' Rachel said again.

There was another faint beep. And a third.

'Daddy?'

Holly looked up at me from inside her hood. Her face was drawn, her skin waxy. I moved towards her and laid Buster down on the ground next to her, resting his head on her lap. Then I pulled a bottle of wine from one of the racks, took up a position in front of Holly and raised the bottle over my shoulder like a club.

My body quaked.

The men entered a fourth and a fifth digit.

Rachel faced the door, her arms out at her sides, fingers flexing.

A sixth shrill beep.

Please, no.

My stomach clenched. I waited for the locking mechanism to release. For the handle to turn and the door to drop on its hinges and crash open. For the men to bundle inside with their guns raised.

'I'm scared,' Holly whispered.

I reached back for her hand.

Then there was a sudden odd, discordant buzzing, followed by muffled swearing and the thud of the door being kicked or punched. A red diode started blinking on a control panel just inside the door.

I let go of a small breath. I waited. My heart banged against my ribs. Slowly, I crept across the room towards the blinking red light, still afraid the door might crash open any second.

'I told you,' Rachel said, exhaling hard. 'They can't get in here. They don't have the code.'

But just then, I was more interested in the control panel to the right of the door.

'Do you know how to use this?' I asked.

The control panel featured a keypad like the one outside the door, except there were several additional buttons and an inbuilt speaker. One of the buttons was marked GATE OPEN. It looked similar to the intercom in the kitchen.

Rachel didn't answer. I asked her again.

'Rachel, can we open the main gate from in here?'

A beat. 'In theory, yes.'

'Why only in theory?'

She moved up alongside me. My skin prickled.

'The unit also doubles as a telephone.'

'Then let's call the police.'

'But that's just it, Tom. I don't think we can.'

I looked at her and thought again of how she'd pulled me to one side in the woods. When Rachel had asked me what I'd tell the police if we got hold of them, she'd made it seem as if she'd suspected me of doing something illegal that had led these men to attack us. But now I wondered: had she been afraid of contacting the police for another reason? And if so, what could that reason be?

A clammy coldness seeped across the back of my neck, like someone had pressed a wet flannel to my skin.

'Rachel? The sooner we call the police, the sooner we get out of here. The sooner we get Holly to a hospital.'

'I know that. Don't you think I don't know that?'

'Then help me.'

'It's not working.' She tapped a couple of buttons on the control panel, shaking her head. 'No dial tone. They must have cut the line. I'm sorry.'

'Probably why there was no Wi-Fi, either,' I muttered.

'Maybe. But this is a separate system. A backup.'

And the men had known about it. They'd known how to cut the wires. The cold sensation at the base of my neck spread down my shoulders and across my back as I thought again of how much they appeared to know. My doubts about Brodie were resurfacing in a big way.

Then a new, more horrid thought crashed over me. Lionel knew all those things too. And he was the one who'd pushed for us to come here . . .

'What about the screens?' I pointed to the wall. 'This is more than just a wine cellar, isn't it?'

Alongside the panel was a bank of nine flat-screen monitors laid out in a three-by-three grid. They were greyed and unlit.

Again, Rachel didn't answer right away and I had to press her. 'Rachel?'

'They're linked to security cameras,' she said quietly.

'At the gate?'

'Some of them.'

'And the rest?'

Nothing.

'Rachel? What about the rest?'

'They're hidden throughout the lodge, Tom, OK? Everything here is recorded.'

I stared at her, reeling now.

'Mum! That is so messed up.'

Everything was recorded? Why? And why hadn't we been told?

'Switch them on.' I pointed again. '*Now*.'

She didn't move.

'Rachel, switch them on! We might be able to see what's going on out there.'

'They should be on already, Tom. That's why I thought something was wrong with the phone line and the gate controls. It looks like everything's been disabled. Look, let me try my mobile. It's in my bag.'

She moved behind me and unzipped a pocket on the backpack I was wearing. I felt her fumble around inside it as I stared at the banks of unlit monitors. My skin itched. Had we been filmed here? Had our conversations been recorded? What about when we'd had sex?

I heard a crinkling noise and turned to see Rachel removing her mobile phone from inside a clear plastic bag. She must have slipped it inside the bag as a precaution against the heavy rain when I'd left her with the backpack on my quest to recover the Volvo's number plate. I watched her power on her phone and enter her passcode. Her *new* passcode, I reminded myself, with a jab of resentment.

'No signal,' she said.

She paced the cellar, lifting her phone high, checking all

four corners of the room. I watched her like I'd never seen her before. Once she was done, she returned to me and shook her head, her lips pressed together.

I slipped the backpack off my shoulders and pulled out my own phone. But when I raised it in my hand, my head fell. The screen was cracked and a film of water was trapped beneath it. I tried turning it on. It was dead.

'Anything?' Holly asked.

'Not right now, sweetheart.' I slipped my phone away before she could see. 'We can try again later.'

'Brilliant. So now what?'

She had to ask.

From out of the silence, we heard another beep on the other side of the door.

The men were trying to get in again.

32

They tried twice more. Each time, we listened to the same six shrill beeps. Each time, there was the same terrible pause before the control panel emitted its grating, discordant buzzing. When they failed to get in on their third attempt, I slowly put down my wine bottle and stepped closer to Rachel.

'Six digits,' I said.

'What?'

'They punched in six digits. Whoever is out there knows this door is locked by a six-digit code.'

She shook her head, like she was stunned by the idea. 'I don't think so. I think they punched in random numbers and the system cut them off at six digits. Lionel changes the code all the time.'

'Does he?'

'He texted me the new code before we came up here. He said we should help ourselves if we wanted wine. Just not the really rare stuff.'

Generous of him. Maybe Lionel thought it was a fair exchange for helping to get us into this mess.

I closed my eyes. Tried not to let the bitterness cloud my thinking. Lionel couldn't be behind this, I thought, because he would have given the men the correct code. But, still, it was difficult not to let the anger consume me. On top of everything else, I hated the idea that Lionel had invited Rachel here in secret. Bad enough to be betrayed by my wife. But I'd also been lied to by the man I'd confided in most during the past year.

Take a breath. Think.

Holly had told me at the charity gala that Lionel had been dropping by the house to check in on her and Rachel. But was there more to it than that?

I looked at the phone in Rachel's hand, wondering what secrets it contained. Wondering if I could stand to know them.

'Rachel?'

'Shh.'

She raised her finger, like she'd heard something on the other side of the door. She climbed the steps and pressed an ear to it.

I looked back at Holly. Her face was angled down inside her hood and she was listing to one side. Buster was breathing deeply in what could have been a gentle snore. Holly's breathing, on the other hand, was fast and shallow. There was a shimmer of sweat on her skin.

'How are you feeling?' I whispered to her.

'I'm OK, Dad. It just hurts a bit.'

'You'll let us know if that changes?'

She nodded. 'What is it, Mum?'

'I'm not sure. I'm trying to—'

Rachel stopped talking and frowned. Then her eyes widened and she beckoned me closer. I climbed the steps and pressed my ear against the metal beside her. To begin with, the only sound I could pick up was the echo of my own pulse, like listening to distant sonar.

'Do you hear that?'

A cold trickling in my stomach. I nodded. There was a faint scraping, scratching kind of sound, like somebody was scoring the paintwork on the outside of the door with the blade of a knife.

'What is it?' Rachel asked.

Nothing good, I thought.

'They can't get in,' she said again.

Then a brittle snapping sound made us both rear back. I stared at Rachel, her eyes blinking rapidly, her face stained red by the blinking diode. I felt my heart drop.

'I'm pretty sure that was the keypad,' I told her carefully. 'I think they prised it away. Maybe they think they can short the wiring.'

'Can they?' Holly asked.

'No.' Rachel shook her head. 'No way.'

Holly hugged her arms around herself, rocking forwards with her chin propped on her knees. In her big outdoor coat and hiking boots, she looked like she'd found her way into a storm shelter in the middle of a tornado.

'This room is a safe space,' Rachel said. 'Lionel had it designed after what happened to Jennifer. He told me the system that protects it is state of the art.'

So state of the art that the men had been able to disable the emergency phone line and the security monitors. So state of the art that the only thing that stood between us and them was a thick metal door.

A slow minute tripped by. Then another.

My pulse slowed way down. My body was flushed with sweat, tensed all over. The back of my tongue still tasted of sea salt and I felt like I was burning up under my coat. It was probably only my imagination, but I was starting to think the cellar air had a slight taint to it. I wondered how much oxygen the room contained and how quickly the three of us could burn through it.

There were no more sounds from the other side of the door. The door didn't budge. But the silence and the stillness were a strange kind of torment. I found myself wishing we were out in the woods again. Under the trees, it had felt like the danger was everywhere, but at least we'd had the darkness to run into. At least we had fresh air to breathe.

Another minute tripped by.

I leaned towards Rachel. 'Nobody is coming here for four days.'

She looked down without meeting my eye but she understood my meaning. We were in the middle of nowhere. We had no way of signalling for help. The only person we'd seen since getting here was Brodie and, supposing he *wasn't* conspiring with the two men who were terrorizing us, he wasn't planning on returning until Saturday when we were scheduled to leave the lodge.

That meant the men had four days to get into the wine cellar. If they wanted to, they could dismantle the walls brick by brick by then.

'How is she really?' I whispered, tilting my head towards Holly.

Rachel's eyes went big, her skin pulled taut. 'At the moment, I think she's OK. But let me check her again.'

She moved down the steps and knelt beside Holly, touching her hand to her forehead. She pulled aside her coat, lifted Holly's top and checked the dressing. Blood squirmed under the plastic coating, thick and purple.

'Holly, sweetheart, when you keep pressure on, it has to be like this.' Rachel took Holly's hand and pressed it to her flank. Holly whined and scrunched up her face in pain. Rachel took Holly's other wrist and felt for her pulse, timing it against the clock on her phone.

My heart beat slower and slower.

I watched them both, feeling weak and unsteady. I hated that we were stuck here. I really didn't like that Holly was bleeding so much. I thought again about what the smaller man had shouted just before we'd gone into the water. *We can let the girl go.* I hadn't believed it then, but maybe – *maybe* – there was a chance they meant it. Perhaps, if it came to it, we could bargain with them.

'Rachel.' I waited until she looked up at me. 'You have to tell us what's going on. We need to know what you know.'

She raised her hand in a give-me-a-second gesture.

'Rachel,' I said again, harder this time.

'I heard you, Tom.' She cupped a hand to Holly's cheek. Then she rocked back on her heels, pressed her palms against her thighs and took a deep breath. 'But first, I need you both to understand something. These past eight months. Since Michael died. I've been a mess. I know that. Sometimes I feel like I lost my mind. I've done things I wouldn't normally do. Things I regret.' She paused and wafted a hand in front of her eyes to stop her tears. When she spoke again, her voice was tight and high. 'And not just because we lost

Michael but mostly because of *how* we lost him. I couldn't accept it. I couldn't believe what he'd done. What we were *told* he'd done. It just went against everything I knew and understood about my son.'

I swallowed. I knew all this. Or thought I did, anyway. Now I watched as she turned to me with a look that was sadder than anything I'd seen in a long while.

'And that's what I found so hard. That's what I couldn't begin to adjust to. Because I *knew* Michael, and if he did what we were being told he did, then that wasn't the case. It couldn't be the case. And if I didn't truly know my own son . . .' It was her turn to swallow. 'If I didn't know him, then what kind of mother was I?'

'We've been through this, Rachel. The coroner's hearing—'

'The coroner's hearing was a sham.' Her anger flared and she lost control of the pitch of her voice for a second. She raised her hand. Started again. 'The coroner's court didn't have access to all the information they should have had. They didn't know the full truth.'

I felt myself teeter. For a moment I thought Rachel was talking about Michael's personality again. I thought she was saying that if only the coroner had known Michael in the way she had, then he would never have passed a verdict of unlawful killing. He would never have determined that our son was responsible for his own death and for killing Fiona.

And, as I thought about that, I found myself wondering for the first time if Rachel had begun to lose grip of her sanity. I was thinking I might have to stop her from saying too much more in front of Holly.

'I knew you didn't feel that way, Tom. And I understand

why. I do. But yesterday I asked you to think about how it would feel to forgive Michael. To believe in him again. Do you remember?'

I glanced at Holly. She stared back from behind the bruising to her face. Her eyes were red, her gaze a little vague but, somehow, I had the feeling she was staring deep inside my heart.

'I remember.'

'Did you do it?'

I nodded slowly.

'And how did it feel?'

This time I shook my head. Not because I had nothing to say but because I knew my voice wouldn't work right if I tried. I could feel my throat closing up. The shakes starting to come.

'I did this for you,' Rachel said again. 'Lionel and Brodie helped me.'

'Helped you with what, Rachel?'

'Getting to the truth. Tom, you can believe in Michael again. He didn't kill himself joyriding. Those men out there – the monsters who've been chasing us – I think they killed our son.'

The unlit road is a fast unspooling ribbon of tarmac. White lines and cat's eyes zip by under the front tyre as the Audi drifts left, into the oncoming carriageway.

Michael squints and covers the rear-view mirror with his hand. His heart leaps into his throat. The headlights from behind are blinding. Switched to full beam, they illuminate the cabin of the Audi and the bare autumn trees stretching over the road ahead.

Michael squeezes down on the accelerator. If he can put enough distance between himself and the car behind then maybe he can see more clearly. Maybe he will spot a place to turn.

But the bright lights stay with him, blaring closer. He glances down at the lit dials on the dash, his vision blurring.

Sixty-eight miles an hour and the speed limit here is sixty.

Fiona turns in her seat to peer out through the rear window, her face stripped white by the glare.

Michael makes a decision then. He pushes down harder on the accelerator.

The needle creeps higher.

Seventy.

Seventy-one.

And flash. *He's blinded by the stutter of another fierce light.*

33

People sometimes talk about the power of words. But honestly, I don't think I'd ever come close to understanding the true meaning of that phrase until Rachel said those words to me. I felt like she'd placed both her hands on my chest and shoved me across the room.

'This is what I was going to talk to you about, Tom. This is what I needed to discuss with you. I never imagined it would happen like this. I thought we'd have time. That I could build up to it gently.'

'Gently? Do you even hear yourself? Do you have any idea what you're saying right now?'

'I do. Believe me, I do.'

'Mum, if this is some kind of sick joke . . .'

'No,' Rachel said. 'No. Holly I would never—'

'Then who are they? What makes you think they killed Michael?'

'It's better if I show you.' She lifted her phone, looking sheepish now. 'Tom, come over here by Holly. You both need to see this.'

Maybe. But I didn't feel ready for it. Perhaps I never could be. Even if I didn't believe it right then, the enormity of what Rachel was suggesting was too huge.

Somehow, though, I found myself moving forwards, almost against my will, until I was crouched by Holly's side with my back against the racks of wine bottles and my hands hanging between my thighs. Seen from above, a stranger might have thought we were about to share a sweet family moment. Maybe we were going to look at old videos on Rachel's phone, or FaceTime an elderly relative.

I felt breathless, scared, my emotions unravelling. I was terrified about the men getting into the cellar with us. I kept thinking about the wound to Holly's side and how bad it might get. And I was angry with Rachel. She'd lied to me. Betrayed me. Put us all at risk. And now here she was, getting ready to show me something that scared me almost as much as the men who'd come here tonight.

Tom, you can believe in Michael again. He didn't kill himself joyriding. Those men out there – the monsters who've been chasing us – I think they killed our son.

Could that really be true? Did I want it to be? Because if there was any truth to it whatsoever, then what kind of father was I? How badly had I failed my son?

I clasped a hand to the back of my head and stared over at the door to the wine cellar as Rachel switched on her phone. There were no sounds at all coming from the other side now. Was that a good thing or bad?

'This is not going to be easy for either of you to look at,' Rachel said.

'Just show us, Mum.'

She took a deep breath and angled her phone so Holly and I could see.

I didn't focus in to begin with but I was aware of something bright flashing up on screen. I heard Holly catch her breath.

Then I finally looked and my heart crumbled to dust.

'What is this, Mum?'

'It's a still taken from a speed camera.' Rachel's careful tone was maddening to me. 'This camera is just over a mile from where Michael . . .'

She didn't finish the sentence. She didn't have to.

I shook my head, a deep chill permeating my lungs. I felt like the wall of wine bottles had turned to rubber behind me; like I was sinking backwards into them.

I knew the camera Rachel meant. I'd passed it numerous times on the lonely drives I'd taken out to the spot where our son had died. A time and date stamp on the bottom right-hand corner of the image told me the picture had been taken less than thirty minutes before Michael's official time of death. His recorded speed was seventy-one miles an hour.

The image itself was not very clear. It was hazed and milky, like it had been harshly lit or badly overexposed. In the foreground, I could see Michael clutching hold of the steering wheel of my Audi, sitting bolt upright with his chin raised high and his neck muscles pulled taut, like he was bracing for impact. Fiona was frozen in a pose looking half over at Michael, half out the rear window, twisted sideways in her seat with her hand flattened against the dash. They could have been arguing. Fiona could have been in the process of telling Michael to slow down or turn back. The rest of the image was a bright white haze, like backlit fog.

I had a harrowing thought then. *This is the final image*

of my son alive. It was almost enough to make me roll away and curl up into a ball.

'How did . . . ? When . . . ?' I shook my head. This was too much. Too raw. I didn't understand why this image had only surfaced now. To my knowledge, it hadn't formed part of the investigation into the crash or the coroner's hearing. Where had Rachel got hold of it from?

The coroner's court didn't have access to all the information they should have had. They didn't know the full truth.

'Is this real?' I asked.

There were tears on Rachel's cheeks. 'It's real.'

'This is horrible, Mum. I don't get why you'd want us to see this.'

I didn't, either. Because even through the emotional haze I knew this wasn't evidence of Michael's innocence. The only logical conclusion to draw from this image was that Michael had definitely been speeding shortly before his death.

'Just wait, OK? There's more.'

Rachel swiped forwards on her phone. She showed us a second image that also appeared to be taken from a speed camera.

It was a shot of a different car. A silver Vauxhall. The number plate was clearly visible. Again, it was travelling at over seventy miles an hour.

'This was taken from the same speed camera,' Rachel said. 'See the time stamp?'

And the date stamp. The image had been taken on the same date as the shot of Michael and Fiona. According to the time stamp, it had been recorded just seconds afterwards. I shook my head. I could tell Rachel believed this was significant, but I still didn't get it. What were we supposed to be seeing here?

She swiped again. This time she showed us a different shot of the same car. It was a close-up of the front cabin, taken on a similar angle to the image of Michael and Fiona.

I had a pretty good idea why there were two images. A few years back, I got hit with three penalty points for triggering a speed camera close to Holly's school. When the penalty notification had come in the post it had included a website link where I could view pictures of the offence. There'd been two images. One of my Audi shot from the front. Another of the cab to prove that I was the one doing the driving.

This image was clearer than the one of Michael and Fiona. I could see two men in the front of the Vauxhall, neither of them familiar to me, and a third man sitting in the rear left. All that could be seen of the figure in the back was an arm in some kind of black top and a sliver of jawline. The driver was thin and stern-looking with a rat-like face. He was wearing a black coat zipped to his chin. His front passenger was dressed in a black windcheater. He was bulkier than the driver and he had a square jaw and a boxer's nose, sunken eyes. He was so tall that the upper portion of his forehead couldn't be seen from the angle the image had been captured on.

A smaller man and a bigger man.

I felt my knees begin to flex. My backside hit the floor.

I didn't know how to respond or what to feel. I felt like a stranger in my own body, all of my movements jerky and uncoordinated, all my thoughts jumbled and confused.

'Michael and Fiona were being followed,' Rachel told us.

That seemed like a stretch to me. These men looked to have been speeding, yes. But that didn't necessarily prove they'd been pursuing Michael. I guess Rachel must have seen the doubt in my face.

'These men were chasing them,' she said, and I could hear her belief in the theory cutting through the pain that was tightening her voice. 'You saw how the picture of Michael and Fiona wasn't as clear as this, right?'

I nodded vaguely, still gripped by the strange sensation that none of this was real. And all right, so far I didn't have the full picture. And maybe I could tell myself that Rachel had always wanted to believe that something else had happened that night so badly that she'd chosen to interpret these images to support that viewpoint.

But there was also something that cut against that. Rachel is the cleverest person I know. Emotional? Yes. Broken? No doubt. But I couldn't believe she'd be laying out this theory for me – and especially not for Holly – unless she had some evidence to back it up. Rachel is a doctor, after all. She's built a career from accurately interpreting symptoms and facts.

Rachel, I think sensing how badly this was hurting me, reached out to place a hand on my knee. I surprised myself by not pushing it away.

'We think the car that was following Michael had their lights on full beam. We think they were trying to blind Michael and that's why the camera image is overexposed.'

'And by "we" you mean you and Lionel?'

'And Brodie.'

Brodie.

'He's an investigator,' Rachel explained. 'Lionel hired him. He's worked for Lionel before.'

As soon as she said it, I believed her. For one thing, there was that story Brodie had told me about his sister. Wasn't that the kind of incident that would drive someone into that kind of work? But more to the point, I knew for a fact that in the years after Jennifer's murder Lionel had hired a stream of high-end private investigators who'd been tasked with attempting to track down Tony Bryant, Jennifer's suspected killer. Some of them were ex-cops. Others were ex-security services. Lionel had kept the hunt for Bryant going long after the police had abandoned their enquiry. It hadn't worked, but Lionel had pushed things as far as he could.

Now, I felt a tightening in my chest as I thought about how he'd done the same thing for my family too.

'*That's* why I was here three weeks ago. Lionel invited me here so Brodie could update us both on what he'd found. Lionel thought it would be good for us to be somewhere I could think clearly. He knew I'd need time and space to get my head around everything, to try to come to terms with it. You shouldn't be mad at him, Tom. He knew we'd disagreed about . . . all of this. About Michael. He actually started out on your side of things. He thought Michael did what they said too. Brodie's been working on this for months now. He's been keeping me informed. I think Lionel thought if he could prove to me, once and for all, that nothing happened that night . . .'

Then maybe he could fix our marriage. She didn't have to say it. She didn't have to say *I told you so,* either.

The silence in the cellar seemed to swirl around us. If

these images were authentic – if Rachel's theory was true – then I'd been wrong about Michael. I'd stopped believing in my son. Since his death, every time I'd thought of him I'd experienced a painful stab of guilt. Guilt for what he'd done. Guilt for how he'd snuffed out Fiona's life along with his own. Guilt for how I'd let him down.

I'd shied away from thinking of my son to avoid that hurtful stab. Eight months when I hadn't allowed myself to mourn Michael properly. Eight months when the truth behind his death had remained hidden and untold.

I thought of everything Rachel had wanted to believe. Everything she couldn't let go of. Her stubborn refusal to accept that Michael had taken my car without permission and had driven it illegally simply to impress his girlfriend.

She'd kept believing in Michael, even when all the evidence went against it. Even when I'd begged her to give it up and accept the truth for what it was.

I looked at her now, my eyes stinging, my throat raw. I felt scraped clean, hollowed out. Rachel had been there for Michael. She'd tried to bear witness to who he really was. I should have done more to help her with that. I should have given her my support.

And yet still I felt angry with her. Still I'd been hurt and tricked. It was a difficult mix of emotions to get my head around.

'But these pictures?' Holly said. 'Why didn't the police just look at them?'

'Because they were deleted. That same night. Someone went into the police system and erased any images the camera took between 9.18 and 9.36 that evening.'

I felt a banging against my ribs, like someone had injected adrenaline right into my heart. 'Then how did Brodie get them?'

'There's a backdoor into the system. He found a backup of all the stored images.'

I opened my mouth to say something more but Rachel shushed me and cut me off. She turned and stared at the cellar door, keeping very still.

The door was motionless. Soundless.

Rachel passed Holly her phone, got to her feet and crept closer to the door.

'I don't hear anything,' she whispered. 'Do you hear anything?'

I didn't respond. Neither did Holly. I was too focused on Rachel's intensity. Still reeling from her deceit. I saw how completely she'd lived this. How thoroughly she believed the men outside the cellar door were two of the men from the speed camera image she'd shown us.

'Do you think they're still out there?' she asked.

Again, I didn't say anything. There was no way to tell. And I wasn't sure what difference it could make.

'We could open the door,' she said, looking back at us.

'No.'

'No way, Mum.'

'Just a crack. We could do it quickly. Tom, you could be ready to slam it shut if they're still there.'

'They have guns, Rachel.'

'Don't open it,' Holly said. 'Please don't open it. Just . . . come back and tell us the rest. What else is there you haven't told us?'

Rachel studied us a moment, biting her cheek. She looked back at the door. I could tell she wanted to open it. She wanted to take the chance that we could slip out and get away. That told me something about how concerned she was about Holly's injury right now and about what she believed these men would do to us if they got in here. I found myself reaching over to squeeze Holly's arm.

But still, I didn't think we should open the door. My guess was this was just a tactic the men were using. If they knew they couldn't get in here, then making us open the door was their next best move.

'Mum, please. Seriously. I can't stand it.'

'OK, sweetheart. We'll wait. OK?'

Her shoulders dropped and she returned to us, kneeling next to Holly and taking another quick look at the dressing on her side. She stroked Buster's head and readjusted the towels that were wrapped around him. Then she took her phone back from Holly, tucked a strand of hair behind her ear and flicked at the screen once more.

'There's one last thing you need to see. Brodie was able to adjust the speed camera image of Michael and Fiona. He used a computer program to reduce the headlamp dazzle, change the contrast settings. He was able to bring out a lot more detail.'

'And?'

Rachel took a deep breath and showed us, and my whole world tipped on its axis yet again.

'Keep going.'

Michael tries to see behind him in the rear-view mirror. But the dazzle of the headlamps from behind is too bright. All he can see is a dark outline of head and body.

'I told you. Stop looking back here.'

Michael glances at Fiona instead. She's sniffing, her face smeared with tears. He wants to tell her it's going to be OK. Wants to say he knows what to do.

But he doesn't.

Sixteen years old and he feels like such a boy.

'Is she your girlfriend?'

Michael waits, then nods.

'You should start thinking about what you need to say to each other.'

'What do you mean?' Fiona asks.

But Michael knows. He wishes he didn't, but he does.

'I mean your goodbyes. You understand? I'm sorry, but that's just how it is now. There's no other choice.'

Darkness hurtles by outside. Everything is out of control. This situation is so far beyond their control.

Michael's skin prickles. He feels very cold. His heart thumps like a machine in his chest.

'Hey. Hey, slow down. Don't do anything crazy.'

But in all the things Michael can't *control about tonight, this is now the one thing he can control.*

'Slow down!'

Michael hunches his shoulder, grips the steering wheel and stamps on the accelerator.

34

With the contrast adjusted and the dazzle minimized, it was possible to pick out vague, blurred details in the whited-out space between Michael and Fiona. Like the smudged outline of a head and shoulders. Like the blocky rendering of something dark gripped in a hand sheathed in what appeared to be a blue glove.

I rocked back and jammed my fist in my mouth. My whole body shook.

This is how it happens. This is how your life changes in an instant. You believe the things about your child you really don't want to. *Michael is dead. It was his fault. He killed his girlfriend.* You force yourself to confront that reality and you accept it even though it wounds you deeply. You know immediately a part of you died that night too. You know you will never recover from it. Your world can never be the same. Because what kind of son did you raise who could do something like that? What kind of father are you?

And then, suddenly, you're exposed to a new truth. A different reality. Like stepping into a parallel – equally horrifying – world.

Someone had been in my car with my son and Fiona.

'Brodie thinks the black shape in that image is a gun.'

I bit down on my knuckles. I felt like my jaw might crack. A gun. It looked plausible. I thought of the men who'd come here tonight and the firearms they'd been carrying. A swell of hot rage and regret sloshed around in my chest.

Had Michael known the same fears we'd faced tonight in the moments before he died?

'Who is this?' I asked, pointing at the blurred figure in the photograph.

Rachel just looked at me with tears in her eyes.

I jabbed my finger towards the cellar door. 'Who are they, Rachel?'

'Just . . . let me explain in my own way, OK? Lionel wanted my go-ahead, Tom. When I came here three weeks ago Brodie showed me these images and they asked me to think seriously about whether I wanted him to probe further. He warned me it could be dangerous.'

Dangerous.

I went to interrupt but Rachel raised her hand, asking for more time.

'It's like I said earlier. I was always going to tell you about this, Tom. That's why I said we needed to talk. I knew this decision was too big for me to tackle by myself.' Rachel glanced at Holly, not quite meeting her eyes. 'And once we'd talked, your dad and I could agree whether to tell you too, Holly. At least, that was my idea . . .' She shook her head and searched my face again, fighting back tears. From the way her expression stilled and she leaned back, I guess my reaction was worse than she'd feared. 'You have to understand, Tom. I wasn't shutting you out. But I was . . . hurt. And confused by what's been happening between us. You moved out. We didn't talk about it. I don't know. I wasn't sure if you'd be prepared to listen to me.'

And honestly? Maybe I wouldn't have been. But she still should have tried.

'He was our son, Rachel. *Our* son.'

'And my brother,' Holly told her.

'And that's why we're here now. That's why all of us are here. So I could tell you. So we could decide what to do next.'

'What's to decide?' Holly asked. 'You should have just gone to the police with these pictures.'

But I knew that wouldn't be straightforward for Rachel. Not when her opinion of the police was so low. Not when they'd failed to dig for a deeper truth the first time around. I could see why Rachel might have believed she'd have more chance of finding out what really happened by sticking with Lionel and Brodie. Particularly when the police's own speed camera system had been compromised.

'You still haven't told us who was in my car with Michael and Fiona. Who are the men here tonight?'

Rachel glanced towards the door again. Then she closed her eyes and, in a low, modulated voice, she said, 'I don't know.'

'You don't know?'

'Because I was going to find out this week. Once I'd spoken to you about it. Once we'd both decided if we wanted to know more. Brodie was going to report back to us. If we wanted to hear it.'

If we wanted to hear it.

I didn't believe Rachel would have accepted it if I'd said

we should walk away. She'd craved an explanation for Michael's behaviour too badly. She'd needed it too much.

Whatever the risks to her family.

I cradled my head in my hands and thought some more about Brodie's role in all this. I was beginning to wonder if it cast a new light on that moment when we'd first arrived at the lodge. I'd thought Brodie had looked down and away when I'd introduced him to Rachel because he was attracted to her. But maybe he'd acted that way because he'd been conscious of the real reason why all of us were here. He knew Holly and I didn't have a clue about it. Maybe he'd been feeling uncomfortable about that.

'And the mugging? How does that fit into it?'

Rachel glanced at Holly, then looked away to her side. 'It's possible that was a warning. I'm so sorry, Holly. If you only knew how sorry I am. I'm—'

'It's *possible*?'

Rachel startled at the fury in my voice. 'OK, maybe more than possible. I don't know, Tom. Don't you think I feel bad enough about it already?'

I glared at her.

'Look, you noticed that Brodie was trying to talk to me, didn't you? When you were bringing things in from the car?'

This time I didn't say anything. I waited for her to go on.

'He was warning me, Tom. He was telling me things had escalated. He was saying that I – that *we* – had to make a decision soon. I don't know. Maybe he pushed too hard. Maybe he alerted these men that he was on to them, somehow.'

'Oh, well, that's just terrific, Rachel. And yet you and Lionel still thought it was a great idea for us all to come out here to the middle of bloody nowhere?'

Rachel raised both hands like I'd slapped her. 'I didn't think they'd come here, Tom. That never occurred to me. This place was meant to be safe. There's the fence. The gate.'

'*Safe.*'

I closed my eyes and squeezed the bridge of my nose between my finger and thumb. It was all so confusing. I was hurt and angry, but I also knew that part of my anger was really directed at myself. Because if I'd been a better dad – a better husband – maybe none of this would have happened in the first place. It was a lot to try and digest. Too much, just then.

And even as the anger swarmed inside my skull, I was straining to think and join other dots together. How had the men tracked us here? If they could delete footage from speed cameras it suggested they had a level of technical expertise. Same thing with disabling the telephone and the security system linked to the wine cellar. So had they tapped Rachel's phone? My phone? Had they put some kind of GPS tracker on our car?

Or was it a lot simpler than that?

'How do you know you can trust Brodie? How do you know he didn't sell us out to these men?'

'He didn't.'

'Maybe he's the one that told them to bring a tranquilizer gun for Buster. Maybe he's the one who told them about this room and how to cut if off. He could have told them the six-digit code for the door, Rachel. How was he to know Lionel was changing it?'

'Lionel trusts him.'

'Do you?'

Silence. Rachel didn't respond. But I could see that some of the doubts I'd raised had hit home. She got to her feet, wobbling a little, and moved a few steps away. She raised her hand to her mouth, lowered it again. I was beginning to think that maybe she was adding some doubts of her own and it bothered me that she wasn't sharing them.

Next to me, Holly groaned and buried her face in the sleeve of her coat. I put my arm around her, hugging her tight. I hated that this was happening, but the part I hated most of all was that it was happening with Holly here. It seemed as if these men really had been involved in my son's death. I didn't know why but I thought I knew that much. And I also knew there was a good chance one of them had punched Holly in London. I swore to myself I wasn't going to give them a chance to hurt her again.

That was when a sudden, loud *clang* made us all jump. Holly whimpered and clung to me. We all stared in horror at the door.

The clanging noise came again.

The door thumped and trembled.

It sounded to me like one of the men was ramming the door with something heavy. Maybe even the sledgehammer I'd seen among their equipment. But surely they didn't think they could get in here with something as crude as that?

Another blow. We heard the smashing of plastics. The crunching of circuitry and wires. The utter obliteration, I guessed, of the keypad on the front of the door and the electronics connected to it.

My eyes went to the red light that was still flashing on the control panel. To the phone system that didn't work. I felt my stomach twist and knot, and a sudden flush of fear, like I'd fallen in an ice-cold bath.

'What are they doing?' Rachel asked.

'Keep back from the door,' I said. I stood up and pulled Rachel away by her arm. 'Both of you, stay back.'

'I told you, Tom. They can't get in here.'

I turned and scanned the cellar again. I looked at the uniform racks of bottles. The boxes of wine. The four solid walls.

My legs buckled. I lunged towards the wine boxes and pushed them aside. There was only the cement floor beneath.

'Rachel,' I said, standing quickly, 'you need to start helping me to take down these wine bottles. We have to search this room for an air inlet. A vent. Anything.'

'I don't understand. Tom? What is it?'

'Why, Dad?'

I stared at them both, trying to block the sensation of the walls closing in, the ceiling pressing down, my throat closing up.

'Because your mum is right. They can't get in here. Only, I don't think they want to. They just want to make sure we can't get out.'

35

Four days. No food. No water. Just bottles and bottles of wine.

I looked at Holly. I wanted so badly to lift her in my arms and hug her. We couldn't just stay here doing nothing. We couldn't risk her condition deteriorating or her bleeding getting worse without any way to get out.

'Check everywhere. Do it now.'

'It's pointless, Tom. I told you how secure this room is.'

'Rachel, please.' I seized her by the upper arms and moved her over to the shelves of bottles next to the control panel and the security monitors. 'Just try.'

She shook her head, staring forwards. 'We should have opened the door when I said.'

'Trust me, Rachel. You don't want to start playing should-have-done with me.'

I backed away from her before I lost it completely and crossed to Holly. Slipping a hand under her armpit, I helped her to her feet. She blinked and swayed and leaned into me.

'OK?'

'Yes. Just dizzy.'

'Do you need to sit down again? Mum and I can do this.'

'No, it's OK. I want to help, Dad.'

I gave her another quick hug, then swept her hair clear of her damp forehead and positioned her facing the opposite wall to Rachel. I waited until I was sure she was steady, then I took the wall at the back of the cellar for myself.

Rachel began slowly, begrudgingly, like the task was futile. Holly worked with only one hand, slipping out a bottle and setting it carefully on the floor, keeping her other hand pressed to the dressing on her side. My pace was much faster. I got into a frenzy. Snatching two bottles from their hexagonal racks. Ducking and setting them on the floor close to where Buster was laid out. Then snatching another two. And repeat.

The floor filled up around me. I kept nudging bottles with the toes of my boots. Pretty soon I had to take my coat off because I was getting too warm. But all I uncovered were empty wine racks and the bare cement wall behind them. Panic crowded in on me.

A wet thud made me turn.

'*Sorry*.'

Holly grimaced. She'd dropped a bottle. The glass had splintered and spread, red wine pooling around her boots.

We all glanced at the door. There was no reaction from the men.

'Doesn't matter,' I said. 'Keep looking.'

'I don't see any vents, Tom. It's just brick.'

'Don't stop.'

I was starting to think I'd underestimated the number of wine bottles. The way it was going, pretty soon we were going to have to start reshelving the bottles we'd cleared to make space for the ones we hadn't taken down yet.

I had another two bottles in my fists when Buster began to snarl and flinch. I looked down at him. He flexed his front legs, kicking off the towels I'd laid over his body. He rasped air through his nostrils. He bared his teeth and snarled some more. I felt a little more of my strength go out of me as I watched him, scared he was having a bad reaction to whatever sedative the men had given him.

'What's wrong?' Holly asked. 'Is he OK?'

Rachel put down the wine bottles she was holding and went to him. She cupped one hand under his head to stop him from hurting himself on the floor. She placed her other hand on his side, under the towel. She shushed him, stroked him. His paws thrashed against her and some of the bottles I'd stacked close by. His head jerked and flinched. I took a step towards Holly, ready to block her view if it got any worse, but after a few seconds Buster began to calm and relax.

Rachel exhaled. 'Just a bad dream, I think. Probably worse because of the sedative.'

We watched Buster jerk a few more times, less frequently now, then he fell mostly still, his legs barely moving. Rachel covered him back over with the towel. Holly bit her lip.

'OK.' I let go of a breath and wiped my face with the back of my hand. 'Let's get back to it.'

Rachel went over and faced her wall with a shake of her head and a sigh. Holly resumed plucking out one bottle after another, sneaking lingering glances at Buster. I went back to working as fast as I could.

Two minutes later, Holly said, 'Over here, Dad. I think I've found something?'

She was on tiptoes, reaching up with her right hand and carefully sliding out a portion of shelving from a sculpted hollow among the hexagonal racks. The section was large enough to hold perhaps a dozen bottles.

I moved closer. Behind where the portion of shelving had been was the fluted metal grill on the front of a white cooling unit. I felt a small surge of hope. The unit was a little bigger than a standard household microwave. I don't know a lot about storing wine, but I do know that controlling temperature and humidity is important. This unit looked a bit like one of the through-the-wall air conditioners I'd seen on apartment buildings and motels in the United States.

'Let me see.'

I took the section of shelving from her and set it on the ground, then climbed the empty racks to Holly's right and placed my left hand in front of the grill. A current of cool air wobbled against my palm.

The unit was fitted flush to the wall, set back behind the shelving surrounding it. I jammed my fingers through the vent on the front and tugged. The fascia deformed but didn't budge. I could see several flathead screws holding it in place. There were eight screws in total. Two on each side. Two on the top. Two on the bottom.

'I think we may be able to get out this way.'

'But do we want to?' Rachel asked. 'They might leave soon.'

'You don't believe that, Rachel. And how would we know?'

'But if you remove it,' Holly said, 'won't they be able to get in at us?'

'Maybe. But that might be a risk we have to take.'

I tried turning one of the screws with my finger and

thumb, but it was useless. Human fingers are not designed to function as screwdrivers and I'd left the screwdriver we'd used to break into the pool room outside in the dirt.

'Your backpack,' I told Rachel. 'You must have something we can use.'

'Tom, I really don't—'

'Just humour me, Rachel. If it doesn't work, where's the harm?'

She threw up her hands, shaking her head, but then she ducked down next to her backpack and unzipped a compartment on the front. I could see a collection of syringes, vials, antiseptic wipes.

'You could try this, I suppose.'

She handed me a disposable scalpel without much enthusiasm. It had a sculpted plastic handle and a metal blade with a safety cap on the end. I pulled the cap off with my teeth and aligned the flat of the blade with the head of the first screw.

The blade was thin. The screw wouldn't budge. I moved my finger and thumb down low on the blade and tried again. Nothing. I spit on the screw. Twisted some more, harder this time. The screw shifted a tiny fraction with a scraping, grinding noise.

It was something. But it was slow, laborious work. I didn't know how long ago the lodge had been built. Five years? Six? My guess was this cooling unit had been installed at the same time and these screws hadn't moved since.

I thought of the two men outside the door again. What were they doing? What would come next? Had they really killed my son? Michael was just sixteen. And yes, he'd had a wild streak. He'd got into trouble from time to time. Sometimes at school. Sometimes outside of it. But how could he have become involved with violent thugs like this? I just couldn't see it.

And I still didn't know why they were here. Why did they want us dead? Were they afraid that we were going to expose them? Were they trying to kill us before the truth of Michael's death could get out? Surely they had to know Lionel was involved too. Killing us would only solve part of their problem. So was something else going on? Was there more Rachel wasn't telling me?

I gritted my teeth. Pinched my finger and thumb hard. Rachel and Holly watched as the screw turned in slow increments and the scalpel turned with it, scratching the fascia of the cooling unit. I adjusted my grip and kept twisting. Now things were getting a little easier. The screw was starting to emerge.

It was awkward working with my left hand instead of my right, which was still gripping tight to the shelving. My fingers were cramping. I could feel tremors passing down through my hands and wrists. But after several more painstaking turns I was able to pop the handle of the scalpel in my mouth and use my fingers to loosen the screw all the way.

I dropped it on the floor and began working on the next screw.

'Got any more of these?' I asked Rachel.

'Two.'

'Then climb up here with me. You can get started on the screws on the other side.'

At first I thought Rachel was going to ignore me or refuse. But she climbed up and got to work. A few seconds later, Holly wandered over to stroke Buster. We both took a moment to watch her. Holly still looked pale and her movements were stilted, but I thought she must be doing OK because she was able to move around and talk with us. Buster simply dozed on.

After something like ten minutes, a lot of swearing and even more sweating, we had seven of the screws loosened and released. The eighth screw, located in the top left of the fascia, was proving more troublesome. Rachel had snapped her scalpel blade on it. She'd been lucky not to slice open her thumb. I told her to hop down while I tried yanking on the fascia but it wouldn't come free. Maybe if I used my right hand? I scrambled over to the empty wine racks on the left of the unit. But before I could get started, there was a hollow *clang* from the metal door.

The noise reverberated inside my chest.

I turned and looked. There was nothing for several long seconds. I remained clinging to the shelving as electric fear pulsed down my arms.

Then another *clang*. And a third.

Something jabbed beneath the base of the door.

I felt like a blade had been pushed between my ribs.

What was it?

I jumped down from the shelving and climbed the concrete steps. The object was a tongue of black metal. Slightly chipped and oxidized. Something vaguely familiar about it. I reached towards it. It was cold and hard to the touch and it twisted slightly under my fingers.

I snatched my hand away and looked back at Rachel. She rolled out her bottom lip, nonplussed. Then a deep, screeching, cranking sound made us both cringe. The noise seemed to *creeeak* inside my teeth. The metal door strained and groaned. The cranking sound came again, that desperate *creeeak* drilling through my gums into my jaw. My hand trembled as I placed my palm on the door. I could feel all kinds of stresses and strains passing through the metal. A sprinkle of dust rained down from the lintel above.

Nerves scattered across my back.

I recoiled at the sound of a splintered crunch. When I looked down, a tiny crack and a small crater had appeared in the painted concrete floor just beneath the tongue of metal.

'Tom, what is it?'

I backed away on my heels, crossing the room in a hurry. I scrambled up the shelving and focused on the screw again. The screw still wouldn't turn. I swore and tried spitting on it. I shifted the angle of the scalpel blade. I tugged crazily on the fascia.

More cranking from behind. More straining and groaning and dry crunching sounds. More *creaking* inside my molars.

'Tom, talk to us.'

'I think they got the car jack out of the Volvo,' I panted. 'I think they're trying to lift up the door.'

Holly stood slowly. 'Will that work?'

I didn't answer. I gritted my teeth and exerted more pressure on the scalpel blade instead.

The blade snapped and shattered.

Damn.

'Another one.' I clicked my fingers. 'Now, Rachel.'

But Rachel didn't react. She seemed transfixed by the door. Her hands tightened into fists. The muscles of her jaw bunched and clenched.

'Rachel,' I hissed. 'Another scalpel. Quick.'

Holly shot past her and fumbled in her bag, passing one to me.

'That's my last one,' Rachel said. Her voice sounded hollow.

Again, I pulled off the cap with my teeth. Again, I got to work.

The cranking and creaking sounds continued. The metal door wailed and protested. The sound seemed to penetrate down through my teeth into the nerves in my neck.

Then there was a sharp, searing, buckling noise that made me almost let go and fall back, followed by a sudden brash snap and a metallic clatter and some loud, aggressive swearing from outside the door.

I guessed the jack handle had come loose or sheared clean away. I didn't want to turn and look, but when I did I could see the metal fascia of the door had crinkled very slightly in the middle. It was as if there was a tiny vertical crease low down on the panel. But worse – much worse – was the crack of light now visible beneath the door. It was maybe five centimetres long. A few millimetres high.

Staring at it, I felt like a little kid hiding under my bed, just waiting for the bogey man to lift up the covers and shout 'boo'.

Muffled sounds carried through the crack. I could hear the men stomping and talking on the other side.

Then I heard something different. A hollow, guttural

sloshing that made my intestines quiver and contract. It was followed by a splash and a glug and a spatter.

A finger of dark, oily liquid seeped under the door. I felt like someone was pouring iced water down my neck.

Rachel climbed the steps very slowly. She touched a fingertip to the liquid and raised it to her nose. Then she sniffed and I watched her face fall.

'Oh God, I'm so sorry. It's petrol.'

'Drive.'

Michael's sweaty palm slips on the gear lever. His leg feels heavy and dull as he presses down on the clutch. He tries to control his panic as he looks around him at the street where he's parked. Badly, as it happens, with one wheel mounted on the kerb. But the only witnesses are three teens in tatty hoodies, one of them on a BMX, likely stolen, who have their hands in their pockets so as to conceal the drugs they're dealing, and the peaks of their baseball caps tilted down to hide their faces. He could blast his horn, only . . .

'I said, drive*.'*

. . . there's that hot itch on the back of his neck from where the gun is jabbing into him. And what are the chances of anyone responding here, in this place; a shabby backstreet next to a dismal multistorey car park and an empty council office building?

'Michael,' Fiona says. 'Just do it. Hurry.'

So he does. Too abruptly. The Audi bunny hops forwards and thumps off the kerb.

'Take it easy.'

And maybe Michael would. But tonight is the first time he's driven on real roads and without his dad alongside him. He doesn't know what he's doing. Doesn't want to risk getting into any more trouble than he's already in. Maybe it's a good thing he can pass off his inexperience as panic.

'Where to?' he asks now, his voice wavering as he snatches second gear.

'Take a right at the end here. Head back to the train station.'

His eyes flick to the rear-view mirror. 'And then?'

Behind them, Michael sees a silver Vauxhall swoop down the exit ramp at the front of the parking structure. Three men are sitting inside, dressed in dark clothes.

36

The fuel spread and probed and branched off in oily rivulets. It drained down over the top step and crept towards the next. Rachel moved backwards into the cellar, her arms out at her sides to keep Holly behind her.

'Use the towels,' I said. 'From Buster. Don't let that petrol get any further.'

I could smell the fumes now. They perfumed the chilled cellar air, as if we were standing on the forecourt of a filling station in the dead of night.

'They're just trying to scare us,' I said.

But it was working. If they set fire to the cellar, we'd be trapped.

Rachel and Holly hurried to unwrap Buster. I watched as Rachel rolled the towels up and packed them against the base of the door before backing away again. A temporary solution but not a perfect one. The towels would soak up the fuel like a sponge. If the men set light to them, they'd ignite like a torch.

'The police are on their way,' Holly yelled, suddenly.

She clamped her hand to her mouth, like she couldn't believe she'd said it, and we looked at one another in the brittle silence that followed.

The men had to be able to hear us now they'd raised the door. For just a second, I couldn't tell what would be worse: a response, or no response at all.

'Bullshit,' one of them yelled back. 'Open this door or we'll torch you.'

Holly cried behind her hand and leaned into Rachel. I felt my knees begin to flex.

Death by burning, or death by gunshot if we opened the door. Not a choice we could make. And not a choice I wanted Holly to be confronted with.

'It's OK,' I whispered to her. 'It's not going to come to that.'

I waited until she raised her head from behind Rachel and then I pointed to the ceiling, where two small sprinklers were located. I didn't know if they'd offer us any real protection from a petrol fire, but I wanted her to see them. I wanted her to have something to believe in. She swallowed and nodded at me.

'I'm going to get us out of here,' I whispered. 'I am.'

Rachel turned to me with her good arm around Holly. Her skin was white and bloodless, her lips pulled back over her teeth. 'Hurry.'

I returned my attention to the final screw, concentrating everything I had on transmitting all my strength down into the scalpel blade.

Still nothing.

Still nothing.

And then . . .

The screw budged.

I felt a humming in my temples. It only moved by a minuscule amount but that was all it took to get it started.

I redoubled my efforts and kept working with the scalpel, kept grunting and hanging my tongue out of the side of my mouth, until I had the screw loosened enough to use my fingers. My pulse throbbed in my fingertips. I could hear my breathing, loud and fast.

Over by the door, the towels were yellowing. Petrol was slowly oozing beneath them and spreading across the concrete, trickling down to the lower steps.

I tugged the screw free, plunged my fingers into the vents on the front of the cooling unit and pulled hard. The front panel clunked, then wrenched free with a faint metal-on-metal screech, trailing dust and cobwebs from behind.

I froze and looked over to the door, my heart hammering in my throat.

No response. At least not as far as I could tell.

A musty smell wafted out from the cooling unit. The interior was filled with component parts that were furred with dust and grime. I passed the front panel down to Rachel, fitted my hand inside the unit and heaved.

The metal edges were sharp and unfinished. They cut into my fingers. I didn't care. The unit screeched outwards a fraction and again I stopped and checked the door for any response from the men. Nothing obvious. I thought there was a good chance they couldn't hear inside clearly, especially with the towels packed against the door.

No sense doing this slowly now.

Fitting both hands inside the unit, I walked my feet up the shelving racks until I was bent at the waist with my knees up by my chest, like I was about to surge backwards from the end of a swimming pool.

I pushed with my toes. Heaved with my arms. Felt the burning strain in my lower back.

The unit scraped towards me, scraped again, then came free and plunged a short, sharp distance until I was hanging from it with the back end of the unit butted up against the top of the wall cavity that had been carved out for it.

'A little help.'

Rachel and Holly rushed over and took hold of my legs and waist. Rachel used one foot to scoop a wooden wine box closer. I placed my toes on it and Rachel climbed onto the box next to me so that we could work together to wrestle the unit free.

She wailed and ducked down on one side. Her shoulder wasn't up to the task.

'It's OK,' I told her. 'I've got this.'

The unit was heavy and cumbersome, but now that I was standing on the wine box I was able to ease it out the rest of the way and bear its weight as I lowered it to the ground. It wouldn't come all the way because of an electrical cable trailing out the back, but the cable gave just enough slack for me to be able to balance the unit on the ground on its front edge.

I wiped the dust and muck from my lips and eyes, then stood on the back of the unit and peered into the cavity.

It was a rectangular ventilation tunnel faced in metal sheeting. I could see for three or four metres but then the cramped tunnel disintegrated into gloom. I felt a tingling in my scalp. How far did it go on for? Its dimensions were much tighter than I'd anticipated. A small child could crawl through unhindered, but me?

I swallowed.

'Pass me your phone.'

Rachel pulled her phone out of her back pocket and handed it to me. I pressed the home button. The lock screen lit up with that same picture of Michael and Holly fooling around. My heart clenched when I saw it. Michael. I missed him.

I shook the thought from my mind and thrust my arm down the tunnel, the glare of the phone screen bouncing and reflecting off the metal sheeting with a bluish gleam. In a strange way, it felt like Michael was guiding me out. I could see a little further but not all the way. Surely the shaft couldn't go on that far?

'I have to get a closer look,' I said. 'Keep an eye on the door. Watch Buster. Shout me if anything changes.'

And then, bracing my forearms just inside the opening, I sprang off from my toes and squirmed up and in.

I banged my knee. The sides of the tunnel compressed my shoulders, chest and hips. I knocked the back of my head off the top. The polished sheeting deformed and deflected under my weight. The dimensions were so tight I couldn't crawl forwards. All I could do was squirm and wriggle. Holly and Rachel grabbed at my legs and pushed on my feet. I squirmed some more, until my toes tapped against the metal sheeting. Then I made the mistake of thinking of all the earth that was probably piled on top of the shaft. The shaft wasn't designed for people to slither along. What would happen if the tunnel collapsed?

My lungs emptied of air. Pressure built inside my chest. Rachel's phone screen dimmed, then powered off, plunging me into darkness.

Don't panic.

I hit the home button. Blue light shimmered around me. Michael and Holly, showing me the way.

Breathe.

I felt the vaguest flutter of cool air against my face. It smelled of the night forest and the taint of rain.

I pulled my chin down and scrambled on, digging in with my elbows, scraping my hips and knees, thrusting from my toes, until, eventually, I saw a reflective glimmer from what had to be the end of the tunnel, no more than a metre ahead.

I should have been relieved to see it but right then I experienced a sudden shortening of my breath, like someone had clamped a hand over my mouth and jabbed an elbow into the back of my neck. It looked like a dead end.

Until I got there. Until I craned my neck and looked up.

A half-metre above me was a slatted metal grill. Dark shapes swayed and shifted above it. I felt a small flutter of relief as I realized I was looking up at the canopy of pines.

I thrashed and fought to turn myself around with the metal banging and deflecting underneath me until I was lying flat on my back and I could stretch my hand up towards the grill.

I couldn't reach.

Gritting my teeth, I closed my eyes, then raised my head slightly and looked back down the tunnel past my toes. The lights of the cellar shone brightly. I could see Holly's face in the opening. She was peering in at me, her hair tangled, chewing her lip.

'It's OK,' I whispered to her. 'Are you and Mum all right?'

She nodded.

'Buster too?'

'Yes.'

My lungs felt like they were shrivelling. Cool air pressed down on me, but still I sweated badly.

Carefully now, I balanced Rachel's phone on my chest, the blued dazzle reflecting back off the metal, then flattened my hands on the sides of the tunnel and shunted myself back even further. My neck was contorted. The back of my head and shoulders were mashed up against the end of the shaft.

I had to scrape my elbows and squeeze in my shoulders until I was able to thrust both my arms up past my ears. I stretched and jammed the heels of my hands against the grill.

Grainy detritus showered my face. Seed pods and pine needles. I blinked and spat them away.

I was anticipating stubborn resistance from the grill, because nothing so far had been easy. Maybe it was screwed down from the outside. Maybe it was packed down beneath a dense seam of wet earth. But to my surprise the panel flipped outwards, trailing threads of rubber sealant and sprinkling more dirt on my face.

For a terrible second, I had a vision of a gun muzzle appearing in the opening, pointed down at me, with one of the masked men on the other end of it. The scenario seemed so plausible I was almost reluctant to move.

I swallowed my fear, fitted my hands around the wet earth at the opening, sucked in my stomach and heaved myself into a sitting position. My arms and shoulders shook and trembled. The top of my head emerged from among the forest floor.

There was nobody around.

The trees shook and swayed. Wind ruffled my hair. I was roughly ten metres away from the lodge.

I tipped my head right back, letting go of a long breath, and took a big gulp of the sweet woodland air. Then I tensed the muscles in my stomach and shuffled down inside the narrow shaft again, bending my neck, pressing my chin against my chest, flattening my palms against the metal sheeting and wriggling and clunking my way back towards the cellar and the heady stink of petrol.

37

We got Holly out first. It wasn't easy. The pain from her side was manageable until she stretched or caught herself, but when that happened she had to stop and lay still inside the ventilation tunnel until the aching passed. Rachel was worried about her aggravating her wound and making the bleeding worse. But what were our options? We couldn't stay where we were. Not with the men pouring petrol in under the door. They were taunting us. Shouting at us to open up. We didn't reply. Not once. I thought it was better that way. Because what if we started up a dialogue and then the men got suspicious about why we'd gone quiet?

I stared down the ventilation shaft, wincing each time Holly hurt herself, whispering encouraging words to get her to move on. When her head was finally free and only her feet were left in the tunnel, I lifted Rachel up and into the hole and she scrambled after Holly with the backpack, pushing herself along with her good arm and her feet.

The hardest part was moving Buster. He was heavy and floppy and his weight sagged against me as I heaved him towards the shaft. I propped his head inside, then braced my shoulder under him and checked behind me. The petrol had soaked through the towels completely. My breath quickened.

The fuel was pooling over by the door, draining down the steps. The scent of it was heavy on the air and I knew it would take just the smallest spark to ignite it.

I shoved Buster forwards. His wet fur left damp streaks on the metal sheeting. His front legs got snarled and tangled up. I reached in past him and freed them, then put on my coat in a hurry, clambered in behind him and shoved him on.

I was out of breath and sweating hard by the time I got him to the end of the shaft. I paused to gather my strength while Rachel reached down for the scruff of Buster's coat. It took an enormous effort to lift him from the angle I was on and Rachel was compromised because of her shoulder. Holly had to help.

Once he was finally out, I lay back, spent and breathless, peering down the shaft past my toes. I couldn't see any flames but I wasn't about to hang around.

Thrusting my hands up, I pulled with my arms, kicked with my feet and wriggled my hips until my head was free of the opening. Finally, I used my elbows to prise myself out onto the forest floor like a man climbing from the cockpit of a crashed aeroplane.

I rolled onto my side and ground my face into the earth. I'd been woken up in the middle of the night and shot at. Chased through the woods. Driven into the sea. I'd fallen from a balcony. Crawled through a tunnel. All I wanted to say right then was, *Enough*.

'Now what do we do?' Rachel asked.

I groaned and reached out to Buster. The ground between us was wet with damp, even under the trees. I kept expecting to hear a whoosh of flames from the wine cellar. I could imagine a waft of sudden heat escaping the ventilation shaft and smoke billowing out into the night.

Buster was still out cold. When I rested my hand on him, the matted fur of his chest rose and fell in time with his laboured breathing. I looked past him towards the lodge. The tall, thin window at the end of the corridor that linked the cinema room with the reading nook was lit yellow in the gloom. Neither of the men were visible through it. I knew what I had to say next, and even I didn't like it.

'I have to take a look in through that window.'

'What? Why?'

'Because we need to know they're both still in the library, Rachel. I don't want us to go running into one of them.'

'We should get away from here while we still can.'

'Yeah? Where to?'

She didn't answer. She just knelt in the darkness, her bunched fists pressing down into the wetness, her lank hair hiding her face. I didn't know how to feel about Rachel right now. My thoughts and emotions were totally scrambled. I knew she'd lied to me and Holly. I knew she'd placed us at enormous risk. And yes, I was furious about that. Especially when I thought of how we'd made love just hours ago now. How I'd laid there afterwards, thinking this was the start of a new beginning for us both. But at the same time, I also understood that Rachel had acted out of love for Michael. Right now, I wanted nothing more than to protect my family. Rachel – however misguided – had been trying to fix us.

She raised her head and looked at me. 'Maybe if we follow the fence, we'll find a spot where my phone will work?'

'Brodie told me there was no signal anywhere around here.'

Unless Brodie was working with these men. Unless he wanted us to think that.

I closed my eyes, pushing the thought from my mind. For so much of our marriage I'd trusted Rachel's judgement. We'd made so many decisions together over the years that had seemed vital at the time. Decisions about what house to buy and which mortgage to take out. Choices about which school to send the kids to, what holidays we should go on, how to handle delicate situations with colleagues or friends. But, in reality, none of those decisions had mattered in anything like the same way the choices we made tonight would count. And at the same time, I had the gnawing suspicion that Rachel hadn't told me everything yet. Was she keeping more from me and, if so, what?

'What about the stargazing pod?' Holly asked.

Silence.

Wind shuttled through the trees overhead. I found myself looking past the lodge in the direction of the pod, thinking it through. Would the men know about it? Would they find it? Maybe if Brodie had briefed them . . .

'Dad, come on, we could totally go there.'

'The door was locked, Holly.'

'We can try and break in. There might be stuff inside we could use. Maybe even a phone.'

I looked at Rachel. She could see the question in my eyes.

'I've never been there,' she told me. 'I didn't know it *was* there. Honestly. But if you're asking me what I think, I think it's a good idea.'

'*If* we can get in.'

But even as I cast doubt on it, my thoughts turned to the practicalities of accessing the pod. The door had looked too substantial to barge or kick our way through. But perhaps there was another way.

'Your toolbox.' Rachel sprang to her feet. 'We left it next to the driveway, didn't we?'

Holly got up alongside her, wiping the dirt from her palms and slipping one hand under her coat to hold against her side. It was difficult to tell if she was deteriorating at all. Even without her injury she'd be pale and exhausted right now. But it was another reminder that we needed to keep a watch on her.

'Wait,' I told them.

'Tom, there must be something in your toolbox we can use. There has to be.'

Maybe. Maybe not. Most of the tools I carried were pretty small. There was nothing that could be relied on to force a door open.

'Dad, come on. Let's at least check it out.'

'Just . . . let me see where they are first, OK?'

'Tom.'

'One minute, Rachel. That's all I'm asking. I'll run over and be back as soon as I've seen where they are. *Then* we go.'

Rachel winced and looked off through the trees towards the driveway, then back at me.

'OK, but hurry.'

I got up from my crouch and moved forwards at a stoop, stepping out from under the trees onto the raised grassy bank that butted up against the fieldstone base of the lodge. On the opposite side of the wall, I now knew, was the wine cellar. And next to it the reading nook where I hoped both men still were.

I crabbed sideways towards the window, the nylon of my outdoor jacket rasping against the brickwork. When I got there, I stopped and looked back. Rachel and Holly were holding hands and watching me. I counted to five in my head, then rocked to my right and took a quick peek inside.

The corridor leading to the cinema room was empty.

I rocked back and waited a few seconds more. Then, before I could lose my nerve, I took one long stride past the window.

My skin crawled. Beneath the trees, Holly was covering her eyes with her hand, afraid to watch. Rachel stared at me, her mouth hanging open, the wind tugging at her hair. I nodded to her like everything was OK – who was I kidding? – and turned to look in through the glass.

My heart raced. I could see a segment of the shelves of books, a vertical portion of the closed metal door and the buckled car jack that had been wedged beneath it. And I could see the smaller man in his white plastic coveralls.

A surge of white-hot anger lit up my spine.

He was down on one knee with his back to me and his hood up. His gloved hands were flat against the floor, shoulder-width apart, and he was pressing his face to the crack under the door. Next to him was a red household bucket. It looked like the bucket the mop had been standing in inside the laundry room. I guessed it contained the fuel the men had been pouring under the door.

A small part of my brain said: *If it was really fuel.* But

why would Rachel lie? And no, I'd smelt the petrol myself. I was letting paranoia get the better of me.

There was no sign of the bigger man.

If only I was in there now, I could whack the smaller man over the back of the head. I could strike him again and again and . . .

I snatched my head back and flattened myself against the wall. My chest heaved. I shut my eyes.

Where was the bigger man?

Please tell me he isn't outside already.

I lifted my right hand in the air and motioned for Rachel and Holly to duck low in case he was close by. They crouched instantly. In the dark under the trees, they were hard to spot.

Better.

I motioned to them again, this time spreading my fingers in a gesture that was designed to say: *Stay put. Bear with me.*

Rachel fixed her jaw and shook her head resolutely. Holly mouthed the word 'No' and beckoned me back by waving her hand.

I showed them my palm again. Spread my fingers again. *Stay put. Bear with me.*

'It's OK,' I mouthed, and wondered who exactly I was trying to convince. If I ran into the bigger man right now, I'd likely collapse to my knees.

No. Don't think like that.

I pressed my cheek to the wall and crept towards the southerly corner of the lodge. There were two more panels of rectangular glazing ahead of me. No yellow light was shining through them. There was just a kind of gaseous, turquoise glow shimmering against the glass.

The windows looked in on the pool room. I paused by the first panel and sneaked a glance. The only movement was from the swimming pool waters, lit vivid green against the black.

I let go of a breath and crept on towards the second panel. I saw the exact same thing when I snuck a look inside.

Three more cautious paces took me to the corner of the lodge. I placed my hands and face against the brickwork and inched my head around.

An icy judder coursed through me.

It was the bigger man. He was standing outside the shattered side door to the pool room, looking off through the trees in the direction of the stargazing pod.

38

His back was to me, his hood was up, his blue rubber boots were planted in the saturated dirt. The wind rippled against his plastic coveralls with a fast, abrasive droning.

He had the big industrial torch in his hand. As I watched, he turned – my muscles tensed – and swept the beam over the waves towards the side of the timber deck. He played the beam casually over the dark waters.

At the area where their dinghy had been.

I saw him stiffen and lean closer, then sweep the torch beam around in a widening arc. I could almost imagine the thought process running through his head: *Our dinghy has gone? Where has it gone?*

My heart was pumping so wildly I clamped a hand over my chest for fear he might hear it. I watched the bigger man edge forwards, away from the lodge. He crouched and played the torch beam down under the deck.

I snatched my head back, rested a moment against the brickwork, then scurried up the grassy bank through the trees to Rachel and Holly.

'What is it?' Rachel asked me.

I stood there, hunched over, panting. 'The smaller one is

still in the library. But the bigger one is outside. He's just over that way.'

Holly reared back. 'Is he looking for us?'

'No, I don't think so.' I explained about the missing boat. 'But, Holly, sweetheart, I don't think we should try and get to the pod just now. I'm not saying it's a bad idea, just that we shouldn't head in that direction while he's out here.'

I lifted Rachel's backpack from the floor and fed my arms through the straps. I didn't look at Holly. I didn't want to see the disappointment on her face.

I tugged back the sleeve of my coat. The time on my wristwatch said it was approaching 4 a.m. Almost two hours had passed since the men had broken in. It felt like so much longer. I was drained. My head was fuzzy. I was breathless and strung out from all the adrenaline that had been coursing through my system.

How long now until it got light? I didn't know. An hour? Maybe an hour and a half? And then? Hard to tell. But I knew we'd be easier to spot if the men worked out we were no longer in the wine cellar and they came looking for us in daylight.

'Let's go and find the toolbox, OK?'

'OK, Dad.'

I bent down and scooped up Buster, then tramped through the trees towards the gravel yard, keeping close to the lodge. My skin tightened across my back. I was terrified that the bigger man would come round the corner and see us. I followed along beneath the balcony. The skylight pole was still dangling high up in the wind.

I paused and adjusted Buster's weight. I was trying to orientate myself. Holly must have picked up on that.

'It's this way,' she whispered. 'We were near that tree with the split branch on the side.'

She led us across the yard, between some trees and through waist-high bracken and ferns. It looked like the right spot. When I crouched and peered towards the carport, I recognized the angle of the view.

But no matter where we looked or how desperately we felt around us with our hands and feet, we couldn't find the toolbox. It was gone.

'They must have taken it.'

My heart sank. We hadn't just lost a set of tools. We'd also lost a stash of potential weapons.

Rachel and Holly were silent. They were probably thinking, like me, that our chances of getting into the stargazing pod were even slimmer now. First, the bigger man was in our way. Second, the door was locked and we didn't have any tools to attack it with.

'Let's keep moving,' I said.

Because if the men had found this spot before, they could find it again. And also – thinking about it now – because the toolbox wasn't the *only* stash of weapons I'd seen tonight.

'We can't go back, Tom. Not if you saw one of them over there.'

'We're not going to. Come on. This way.'

My biceps were aching from holding Buster for so long. I hoisted him again, until his face and forepaws were up by my right shoulder, my hands on his soggy rump. I'd have to lay him down soon. I had a pretty good idea where.

I stalked forwards through the drainage gully, branches tearing at my hands and legs. Rachel and Holly joined me and then, on the count of three, we bolted across the yard, streaking through the halo of blue light shining around the perimeter of the lodge and passing in front of the carport.

I glanced at our Volvo as we ran. The paintwork shone darkly in the wash of the security lighting and I noticed, with a stab of anger, that the fuel cap was open and a length of plastic piping was curled out of it, dripping fuel on the ground. The two men hadn't only threatened to burn us. They'd planned to do it with the fuel from our family car.

I lumbered into the trees behind Holly and crashed to the ground with Buster weighing down on top of me. Branches and foliage cracked and snapped. Rachel got down on her haunches by my side.

We had a pretty clear view across the gravel yard towards a corner of the deck. The timber looked bleached and scrubbed in the hard glare of the outdoor lighting. The black seawater dipped and surged.

We couldn't see the bigger man from the angle we were on and I wondered if by now he'd found the dinghy. Or could he have gone back inside to tell the smaller man their boat was missing?

Buster's head drooped over the crook of my arm. I hugged him to me, staring intently at the portion of the deck I could see. I thought about the open sliding door at the front of the lodge. Then I glanced sideways at the shattered kitchen window and the luminous, jagged shards sticking out of the frame.

Could I get in there? *Should* I go in there?

My scalp tingled.

There were some plusses to the move. There was the phone in the kitchen, for one. If it was working, I could call for help. There was also the control unit for the gate. Again, if it was functioning and I could find a way to keep the gate open, we'd have a way of getting away from here. And lastly, there were the weapons and tools the men had brought with them, laid out on the plastic sheet in the middle of the living room. If I could get to them, I could arm myself.

And the cons?

Well, those would be the two men I might run into who wanted me and my family dead.

But, honestly? In some ways, a tiny part of me wondered if that was even a con.

Does that sound crazy? I guess it does. But based on what Rachel had told me and the images she'd shown me, I believed these men were somehow responsible for killing Michael and Fiona. They'd lied about it. They'd concealed the truth. They'd allowed the world – and me – to believe that Michael was to blame. And then, when they were in danger of being exposed, they'd come here and hunted down my family. They'd terrorized my daughter and my wife. They'd hurt my dog.

And no, it wasn't rational. It wasn't wise. And truthfully, I knew I was mostly kidding myself when I thought about confronting them. Because what were the chances I'd come out on top?

But here's the thing: I was angry. No, scratch that, I was furious. I wanted to save my family. That was priority one. But I also realized something else: I might think of myself as a coward, but for eight months these men had hidden in the shadows. Tonight, they'd hidden behind hoods and masks. So, yes, there was a part of me – a more primitive, hot-headed version of myself – that wanted to go after these men. To attack them. To make them pay for what they'd done.

'Tom?'

Rachel reached up to the nape of my hair and rubbed the skin at the base of my neck with her thumb. It was something she'd done a lot during our marriage when I'd been stressed or tired. She'd done the same thing last night after we'd made love. Right now, I didn't know whether to lean into it or pull away. I settled for not showing any reaction at all.

'What are you thinking?'

Where to begin? Because in truth, I was thinking of a lot of things. For example, I was trying to decide if it would be possible for me to climb in through the kitchen window without injuring myself or making any noise. I was wondering how long it would take me to try the phone and the gate controls. How long to grab a weapon from the men's stash? How long to get back?

And suppose I didn't come back? What if I snatched up a weapon, crept into the library and bludgeoned the smaller man while the bigger man was outside?

But what if the smaller man saw me coming? What if he shot me? Or what if the bigger man spotted me running into the lodge, and so knew we'd escaped from the wine cellar and came looking for Rachel and Holly while I was gone?

But mostly, truthfully, I was thinking about Rachel rubbing

my neck. About how angry I was with her for the danger she'd placed us in tonight and for the secrets she'd kept. And, mixed in with that, I was thinking about Michael and my own particular burden of guilt. Because it wasn't only Rachel who'd kept secrets. It wasn't only Rachel who'd made mistakes.

My mind kept looping on how terrified Michael had looked in the image captured by the speed camera. And I wondered: had he been thinking then about his phone call to me?

Because the truth is Michael had called me just over an hour before the time the coroner had ruled as his official time of death. Just under thirty minutes before the time stamped on that speed camera image. It was a phone call I'd never told anyone about. Not Rachel. Not anyone.

Why?

Because I hadn't answered my son's call. I'd seen it flash up on my mobile and I'd diverted him to voicemail. I was in my office, in the middle of writing an email to the lead lawyer on the other side of the deal Lionel was pushing to close. I didn't want to be interrupted.

I know, I know. But if you think that makes me a terrible person, it's nothing to what I think of myself.

Later, when I was flaked out in the back of a cab home – little more than half an hour before the two police officers turned up to tell us Michael was dead – I'd remembered his call and checked my messages. Three short seconds of my son's breathing on the end of the line. That was all there was. That was all he'd left me.

In the time that had passed since Michael's death – and, just possibly, to ease my guilt – I'd assumed he'd been calling me to try to get a read on when I'd be coming home from the office that night. I'd thought he'd been trying to figure out whether he had a clear window of time to drive his girlfriend somewhere in my car with the idea of fooling around with her before I got home and before Rachel brought Holly back from gym practice.

But now I had to ask myself if he'd been calling for another reason. If he'd needed my help. If he'd known he was in trouble. If he'd waited those three precious seconds, debating whether to say something to me, and had ultimately decided it wasn't something he could say in a voicemail.

I was wondering if I could have saved my son's life.

'Don't move and don't speak.'

'Please,' Fiona begs. 'Don't hurt him.'

'That includes you. Keep quiet.'

The gun muzzle drills into the back of Michael's skull. His head is forced forwards against the steering wheel. Michael keeps very still as hands reach around him from behind and pat him down.

'Where's your phone?'

'It fell out back there.'

The gun is jabbed harder against his head.

'Don't lie to me.'

'I'm not.'

Silence for several seconds. Then, 'Unlock this.'

Fiona's phone is tossed into her lap. She raises it to her face with shaking hands. The facial recognition software unlocks the phone.

'Show me the call log.'

She hesitates, then does.

'Messages.'

She does that too. Text messages, then WhatsApp. Even Snapchat. Why not? Fiona's chat with Michael has already been erased. There's nothing to suggest that she's contacted anyone.

Her phone is snatched back.

'Start the car.'

The gun eases off a fraction. Michael lifts his head, though he can still feel the gritty kiss of the muzzle pressing against his scalp.

Slowly, he reaches for the ignition key with his right hand. He turns it, then lowers his hand to his lap and carefully slips his fingers under his thigh to where his phone is hidden.

His phone is a generation older than Fiona's. He's been bugging his parents to update it, though he's glad now he can use his thumbprint to unlock the device. He delays for a moment longer, peering down at the concealed screen as he navigates to the phone menu. His chest feels very tight.

He could try 999, but that requires more taps on the keypad. And he can't speak to tell the control centre what he wants.

His mum has taken Holly to gym practice. She'll be chatting with the other parents, her phone buried in her handbag.

Michael calls his dad, pressing the green icon on the phone screen at the exact same time he revs the engine, like a nervous twitch, to mask the muffled sound of the phone ringing.

And it works, for a second or two.

Until the engine note drops and the phone's low droning vibrates against the seat cushion. An angry grunt from behind and the gun pushes much harder against Michael's skull, smashing his forehead against the steering wheel as hands reach around him to claim the phone.

He just glimpses the screen before it's gone. Call answered.

Michael can hear heavy breathing behind him. Two, maybe three, seconds of it.

Then a beep as the call is cancelled.

'You're really going to regret doing that.'

39

Movement on the deck in front of the lodge pulled me out of my thoughts. My heart stuttered. Through the scatter of branches and foliage in front of me I could see the bigger man striding towards us.

My hands made fists in Buster's fur.

'No,' Holly breathed.

Rachel reached over to clench her arm.

The bigger man kept coming. The wind flattened his plastic coveralls against his body and riffled his hood. The shotgun was in his left hand down by his leg. The big industrial torch was in his right hand. The light from his torch jinked and bobbed and swayed with his movements, rocking side to side in stunted arcs as he leaped down onto the soaked gravel yard. He looked enormous. Like a yeti in a storm.

We crouched, holding our breaths.

The bigger man stopped walking and stood absolutely still. He titled his hooded head to one side, like he was listening intently for a minor disturbance in the air.

All three of us remained motionless.

Until Buster jerked in my arms.

His body spasmed once. Twice.

Terror coursed through me. I squeezed Buster tight and

stared in horror as the bigger man leaned forwards, little more than twenty paces away.

Had he heard us?

Buster juddered and whined. His nostrils flared. Panic swelled in my chest.

Not now. Not now. Not . . .

The bigger man took a slow step forwards, peering into the black. Holly tentatively reached out and rested her hand on Buster's side. I could feel the tension coming off of Rachel like heat from a fire. Buster kicked at the towels that surrounded him with his forepaws. He started to thrash. I clung to him even tighter.

The bigger man kept staring. I could see his paper mask move inwards and outwards in time with his breathing. Then – just as I felt sure he was about to rush us – he turned away and swiped his torch off towards the wooded area on the far side of the carport.

There was a furious rustling of foliage. A ragged slapping noise. A bird broke out from the tree cover in the wet glitter of the torch beam. It flew up through the torchlight into the trees.

I felt a sudden, heady lightness as the bigger man's shoulders dropped and he swung his torch beam down at his feet, then tramped off up the driveway, moving at pace.

I sagged. My body went limp. Holly let go of a sigh and collapsed into me. Rachel covered her mouth with her hand, shaking her head wordlessly.

I would have said something, but Buster chose that moment to start jerking more. He inhaled and exhaled rapidly through his nostrils. His chest rose and fell.

I peered after the bigger man. He didn't turn back.

Buster's eyelids snapped open. He raised his head and stared at me with crazed eyes. He blinked. Blinked again. Then he grunted and kicked and thrashed until I released him and he staggered off my lap towards Holly.

'It's OK, boy,' I whispered, tapping his quivering side, craning my neck to watch the bigger man continue on his way.

Buster took two unsteady steps, paused for a long moment, tried shaking the wetness from his coat. His back legs gave out. He crashed onto his rump.

'Can we do anything for him?' I whispered to Rachel.

'Not a lot. It could take him a while to come round properly. Whatever they gave him . . .' She blew air through her lips. 'It looks like it was a heavy dose.'

Holly hooked a finger through Buster's collar and stroked his head. She hushed him. She didn't seem to be in any pain or discomfort from our run across the yard. She hadn't mentioned feeling queasy or faint.

'Do you think he was looking for us?' Rachel asked me. She kept her voice low. I could tell she was uncomfortable discussing it in front of Holly.

'No.'

'It didn't feel that way to me, either.'

I craned my neck. The bigger man was maybe a hundred metres away now, leaning forwards as he climbed the steep driveway gradient. His torch beam swung side to side with his movements, but not like a searchlight. He wasn't probing the treeline with intent.

'They must think we're still in the cellar,' I said, half to myself. 'If they knew we were out here, they'd both be searching for us. They'd be rushing around. Like before.'

'Then what's he doing?'

'It looks like he's on his way to the gate.'

'The gate is locked. They already checked it.'

'Yes. But Holly told them we'd called for help.' I looked back at her. 'You shouted it to them, remember? "The police are on their way."'

'They didn't believe me, Dad.'

'They *said* they didn't believe you. But maybe that's not a risk they can take?'

Or maybe he's going to the gate for another reason.

Buster let go of a whimper. He stretched out his front legs until he was lying on his stomach. Seconds later, he curled up and tried to lick the spot on his hind leg where the tranquilizer dart had hit him.

'Hey. Hey, stop it.' Rachel moved forwards to drag his head away. 'Don't do that, Buster.'

He started licking Rachel's hand instead. He was so groggy I wasn't sure he knew the difference. His eyes rolled like he might fall back to sleep.

I looked over at the lodge again. Time to make a decision.

'Listen,' I said. 'Our best move right now is for me to try to sneak into the lodge and use the phone.'

'No. Dad, that's crazy.'

'They cut the phone lines, Tom. You know that.'

'Did they? All of them? Then why's he going to the gate?' I pointed after the bigger man. 'Think about it. We know they cut the line into the wine cellar. But before we got into the cellar, they found us sneaking around the lodge. We were close to the kitchen. Maybe they *think* we used the landline there. Maybe they hadn't disconnected it. And if they think we're still in the cellar . . .'

'Then maybe it still works,' Holly finished.

A tiny spark of hope flickered in her eyes. Rachel's expression was more stoic. She didn't shake her head. She didn't tell me I was wrong. But she didn't encourage me, either.

I pressed my case. I reminded her about the controls for the main gate and the stash of weapons in the living room. I told her we had to take a chance.

Then I peered out from behind the woodland foliage at the saturated yard and the deck. There was still no sign of the smaller man. When I looked to my left, the wash of the bigger man's torch was just wavering over the summit at the top of the driveway. If this was our opportunity, it wouldn't last long.

'You two keep hold of Buster,' I said. 'I'll run in there and take a quick look. If it's safe, I'll go for the phone and I'll try the gate controls. If it's not, I won't.'

'I don't know, Dad. It's really dangerous.'

'Is it? We know the smaller one is in the reading nook. If the bigger one's going to the gate, he won't be back for a while.'

'You promised we'd go to the stargazing pod.'

'And we will.'

'We could go now, though.'

'Holly, we'd need to get in through the door. Here.' I pulled back my coat sleeve and unfastened my watch strap. I fitted it over Holly's wrist and tapped the illuminated dial. 'Give me two minutes, OK? If I come out and run back to you, it means I've called the police or I've found a way to keep the gate open and we'll try to get out together. If I wave you over to me, we'll head to the pod. Understand?'

Holly didn't say anything. She just bit down on her lip and gave me a shaky look. Rachel reached out and put her hand on my arm. When she met my eyes, I could see the trepidation on her face.

'And if you don't come out?'

'That's not going to happen.'

'But if it does?'

'Then you get as far away from here as you can and you hide. You do it right away. Get to the pod if you can make it. I'll meet you there.'

Rachel looked down and stroked Buster. He was panting hard, acting dazed and glassy-eyed. He didn't look capable of walking anywhere soon, let alone running, and I knew Rachel couldn't lift him with her bad arm. I guessed she was thinking the same thing.

'Maybe I should go instead,' she said quietly. 'I got us into this mess.'

'Forget it.' I got up into a crouch. 'Two minutes. Then I'll be back here with you.'

And before they could argue any more – before I could change my mind – I stepped out from our hiding place and sprinted across the yard.

Michael runs towards the car like he's running from an explosion. His trainers thump on the cracked asphalt. His vision jolts and jars.

Fiona streaks ahead of him beneath a faulty street light. She runs cross-country at county level. She has a stride like a gazelle.

'Hurry!' she yells.

By the time Michael has the car unlocked, she's already at the far side and is yanking on the passenger door handle.

Michael rushes towards the driver's door and hauls it open. He drops inside, slams the door.

The car key slips in his sweaty fingers. He keeps fumbling as he tries to jam it in the ignition.

'Faster.'

Finally, the key fits.

'Go!' Fiona screams.

And Michael would, except for the tapping on his window.

He turns his head to see a gloved hand holding a gun.

40

Gravel flew up from my heels. I splashed through puddles. I ran into the wind. My instincts told me to avoid the kitchen window. With the bigger man on his way to the gate, the front of the lodge should be clear. It would be quicker.

I veered onto the deck and into the blinding white light. My legs were so heavy with nerves I felt like I was running through sand. The open fire pit smelled faintly of dampened woodsmoke. The big pyramid of glass glowed yellow at the front of the lodge.

Twenty seconds gone.

I guessed.

My arm shook as I braced a hand on the sliding glass door and kicked off my hiking boots. My palm left a sweaty print on the glass.

The timber floor inside the lodge was wet from rain scatter and the treads of the men's rubber boots. I snatched a breath and crept inside in my socks, looking jerkily around.

The living space appeared empty, upstairs and down, but a tremor passed through me when I saw the ragged, scorched hole in the plasterboard above the mezzanine, just back from the staircase. The hole was from the bullet the bigger man had fired when I'd prodded him with the skylight pole. Looking at it now, I could almost feel the whisper of the bullet tearing past my head.

Thirty seconds gone. Give or take. I felt like I'd been holding my breath the entire time.

I almost lost my nerve then but I forced myself on, locking my eyes on the entrance to the corridor leading towards the pool room. I listened for any sound from the smaller man. I was ready to turn and flee. A big part of me wanted to go right now.

I startled as my toes crinkled the edge of the blue plastic sheeting the men had laid on the floor. My mouth went dry. The three holdalls were still there. But most of the equipment was gone. I tried to focus and remember what I'd seen before. Like a split-second memory game. There was the double-barrelled shotgun and the handgun. The pry bar and the short-handled axe and the claw hammer. But all that was left now were the ropes, the restraints, the roll of gaffer tape and the rubber mallet. There was no sign of the toolbox I'd taken from the Volvo.

Not good.

I bent on quaking knees and snatched up the mallet, weighing it in my hand. My grip felt weak. The dense rubber head vibrated with the shakes running down my arm.

Forty seconds gone.

I knuckled the sweat from my eyes and peered towards the corridor again. There was a sharp pain in my chest when I inhaled. Still no sign of the smaller man.

I checked behind me. Nothing.

Go for the phone?

My legs buckled. I forced myself on, shaking all over and moving with a sort of involuntary stutter.

Fifty seconds.

Just over a minute to go.

Assuming Rachel and Holly stuck with my plan – which they maybe wouldn't – I guessed they'd want to give me a little leeway. And I knew Holly wouldn't want to leave Buster behind.

I saw the phone ahead of me in the kitchen. It was still fitted to the bracket on the wall.

I tightened my fingers around the mallet and moved towards it, feeling badly exposed as I tiptoed in front of the corridor to my right. I knew, from when Rachel had called Brodie, that the phone made a cheery, two-tone beeping noise when you lifted it from its cradle. It was the kind of noise I didn't want to be making right now.

I gazed down at the mallet in my hand, thinking. Would it be enough to smash our way through the door to the stargazing pod? Should I just go?

My pulse thumped in my ears. I put a hand to my chest.

The Wi-Fi router on the kitchen counter beneath the handset was dark and unlit. No diodes flashed on the front of it.

Don't panic. You knew that already.

Perspiration prickled across my neck. I looked again to my right. The door to the laundry room was ajar. The door to the pool room was closed. The corridor remained empty.

To my left, fragments and nuggets of glass littered the kitchen countertop and the timber floor from where the window over the sink had been smashed. The shards still attached to the frame shone softly.

One minute and ten seconds.

My spine trembled and my sight blurred. I snatched a breath. Closed my eyes. I thought of Holly and Rachel. I pictured myself making the phone call. I imagined the police racing here through the night. Then I opened my eyes, strode forwards very fast and snatched the receiver off its plastic bracket.

There was no cheery, two-tone beeping noise.

There was no sound at all.

My heartbeat slowed. My pulse became sticky. The room seemed to contract around me.

The LCD screen on the front of the phone was blank and unlit. And the handset was too light. I turned it over, frowning, and looked at the back. The plastic cover on the battery compartment had been removed. The battery was gone. The handset was dead.

Oh man.

One minute and thirty seconds.

I looked up at the intercom unit for the front gate. The button marked GATE OPEN was immediately below the speaker console, next to the button marked TALK. If the bigger man was there now, how would he react if the gate swung open? Would he hide and wait for us to come?

I raised a quaking finger. The air felt dense as water. It seemed to shimmy around my hand. But before I could press the button, the gate camera fuzzed and flickered to life.

I jerked back.

Hazed lines of static appeared on screen followed by the bloom of a brilliant white light. Something bulged inside my throat. The light dimmed. Then the feedback to the small

LCD screen redrew itself and settled into a blurred night-time image rendered in shades of grey.

My body shut down then. My breathing. Heartbeat. Everything.

I swayed.

The light had dimmed because I was looking at two car headlamps that had been switched from full dazzle to dipped beams.

Someone was at the gate waiting to come in.

41

The vehicle was a Toyota Land Cruiser. The driver was Brodie.

I rocked back. All my suspicions crashed in at me again. Because what else could he be doing here at four in the morning, dressed in a dark fleece jacket zipped up to his beard with a woollen beanie tugged down on his head?

My body went numb. A bolt of anger tore through me. I put my fingers to the monitor as Brodie powered down his side window and hooked his elbow out over the sill. His eyes flashed bright in the infrared glare, like the eyes of a woodland predator filmed on a nature documentary.

Had the two men summoned him? Was that why the bigger man had hiked up to the gate?

The monitor fuzzed again. The greyscale image was grainy and indistinct. It was hard to get a read on Brodie's demeanour and attitude. Was he relaxed or tensed? Did he know what was going on here?

I stared at the intercom and thought about pressing the button marked TALK. In my mind, I was running through everything Rachel had told me. She'd said that Brodie was an investigator. Lionel trusted him. Rachel trusted him. Brodie had warned Rachel that things were escalating. Could he be here to help us?

I stood there, clenching and unclenching my hands. The gates slowly separated and swung apart. The Land Cruiser eased forwards. Brodie drove out of shot.

My chin dipped to my chest. My brain felt sluggish. I had no idea what to do, how to respond. The monitor continued to transmit sketchy darkness and a wash of faint grey tree cover for several more seconds. Then the feed blacked out.

I stepped back. Thoughts and theories hurtled through my mind but none of them would stick. Across from me was the shattered kitchen window. I stared at it, trying to get a handle on what it meant. The men wouldn't have needed to smash it if Brodie was part of this. He could have given them a key to get into the lodge. So did that mean Brodie was in the clear? Or was it a bluff – a way to hide his involvement from a police investigation?

I didn't know. I was terrified of getting it wrong.

I stepped towards the window with the rubber mallet in my hand, being careful not to tread on any glass. I listened for the Land Cruiser. For the clunk of a car door opening. For the murmur of hushed conversation between Brodie and the bigger man. Or for the explosion of a shotgun cartridge in the dark.

All I could hear was the bluster of the wind outside.

My two minutes were up. I thought about running outside. If I sprinted for the woods right this second, maybe I could let Rachel and Holly know what was happening. I could warn them not to approach Brodie until we knew if it was safe.

But it was already too late.

The jagged window glass glittered in the dazzle of the Toyota's headlamps.

I ducked and cowered against the cupboard beneath the sink. I could hear the low bass idle of the Land Cruiser's engine. The pop and crackle of gravel under big rubber tyres.

The engine stopped. There was the slow creaking of a handbrake cable. The sound seemed to crawl up my spine.

Silence.

I inched up and peeked out. Brodie had parked in the middle of the gravel yard between the lodge and the carport. He opened his door and stepped into the bright outdoor lighting with his bearded face to the wind and one hand on the roof of his car.

I wondered if Rachel would call to him. I hoped not. It wasn't a risk we could take.

My chest tightened as I thought about Buster. What if he barked?

But no, normally he would have done that by now. He would have darted from the tree cover, yapping and bounding. So perhaps Rachel and Holly were pinning him down, gripping hold of his muzzle. Or perhaps he was too punch-drunk from the tranquilizer to respond.

The bigger man wasn't with Brodie.

Was this a trick? A lure?

Brodie swivelled in my direction. I crouched and huddled, trembling so hard the cupboard door rattled.

Footsteps approached. I heard the crunch of gravel. Then a lull.

There was a long, long moment where nothing happened. I was pretty sure he was right above me but I was too afraid to look.

Then the footsteps started up again, receding this time.

I heard the clunk of a door latch and a wheezing, pneumatic hiss.

I closed my eyes and told myself to stay where I was. Didn't work. I had to know. I eased up from my thighs, wrapped a hand around the porcelain sink and peeped out again.

Brodie had opened the Land Cruiser's boot. He removed something from under a blanket or a coat. The object had a blackened finish that shone wetly in the hard outdoor lighting.

My stomach quivered.

A pistol.

My legs almost gave out. I jumped as Brodie closed the boot and shut the driver's door. He locked his car. Then he set off towards the deck with the gun held out in front of him in a two-handed grip, damp gravel rasping under his boots.

Think.

A private investigator with a gun? It was possible, I supposed. But a bad guy with a gun? I'd already seen two of those tonight.

I slumped to the floor. I had nowhere to go. Brodie would be inside before I could make it to the stairs. If I rushed down the corridor to the pool room the smaller man would hear me. I could try climbing out through the kitchen window, but what if the bigger man was waiting for me out there?

Think.

The laundry room? I could just about make it. Maybe. In another lifetime, with legs that weren't locked with fear.

I glanced around me, my breath hot and heavy. I looked at the fitted cupboards and drawers. At the cooker and the big American fridge freezer.

At the pantry cupboard.

Go.

I dived, scrambling inside the cupboard on my hands and knees, pulling the door closed in front of my face.

It was dark and cramped on the inside. The walls that surrounded me were lined with shelving. The shelves were stocked with groceries and kitchen supplies.

I waited.

My heart beat in my ears.

The darkness seemed to close in around me. It crept inside my eyes and mouth. The space seemed to shrink. The room felt airless, weightless. Like a portal to another dimension. One where there was only me and the darkness and my own breathless fear.

I had that feeling – the one where you know you're at a fork in the road. I had a choice to make now. A big one. An impossible one. Did I trust Brodie or not? If I got it wrong, it would cost me my life. And worse, it would leave Rachel and Holly to fend for themselves.

Shout out a warning? Or stay hidden?

Think.

I went with another compromise. Another lawyerly fudge.

I cracked open the pantry door until a blade of light sliced through the gap. I put my eye to it and looked out.

Brodie crossed in front of the wall of glass at the front of the lodge. He crabbed sideways with the barrel of the pistol up by his face. He paused at the open door, saw my hiking boots, the spill of rain on the timber floor.

'Rachel?' he whispered. 'Tom?'

Don't fall for it. It could be a trick.

He scoped out the room. His gaze lingered on the plastic sheeting and the holdalls. He frowned.

Was he genuinely surprised, or was it an act?

If he was working with the two men, why hadn't he been here from the start? Maybe to deny any involvement. But maybe that had changed when we'd locked ourselves inside the wine cellar. Maybe the men had summoned Brodie because he knew a work-around for the system. But if that was the case, why was he whispering our names now?

'Rachel? It's Brodie. Are you here?'

That fork in the road.

Trust him or don't trust him?

I eased back from the gap in the door. Wiped the sweat from my face. This decision felt too weighty. I couldn't afford to get it wrong.

There wasn't any sound now except my own breathing. I put my eye to the gap again. Brodie was climbing the floating staircase. He passed out of sight. I listened to his footfall on the treads. There was brief spell of silence when he reached the top. Was he looking at the damage to Holly's bedroom door? The bullet hole in the ceiling?

I almost opened the door and stepped out but then I flinched and ducked as the ceiling boards above my head shook and flexed. It sounded like Brodie was pounding along in the direction of our bedrooms.

Was he really here to help?

Again, I was poised to step out. But then I saw something else and a jab of fear stopped me.

The bigger man had walked in through the sliding glass door in his mask and coveralls.

42

He was holding his shotgun crossways in front of his body.

Oh no. Please tell me he didn't find Rachel and Holly. Please not that . . .

He scanned the room, checking every angle. Then his hooded head snapped up towards the top of the staircase. He started to climb. He was fast, but careless. His rubber boots hammered on the polished timber treads. The noise rebounded in my heart.

I thought of darting out of the pantry. Out through the window. Tearing into the trees.

'Rachel?'

It was Brodie, calling from above.

I cringed in the darkness, unsure what to do. If I warned him, the bigger man would hear me. He had the shotgun. All I had was a mallet. And this could still all be a trick.

I opened the door. Took two shaky steps towards the window. And stopped.

There was a grunt of surprise above me. A blunt, plosive gasp. Like one of the men had been hit hard in the stomach.

I looked up towards the mezzanine, then back at the window.

Go for it or don't go for it?

I flinched. Something – or someone – had crashed into a wall. There were scuffed footsteps, grunting, a struggle.

A gun went off.

I crouched. The noise was shocking and enormous. A roaring, sharp clap in the stillness of the lodge. I stared in horror down the corridor towards the pool room, feeling like my feet were nailed to the floor.

There was scuffed footfall, grunting, then a ringing clang against the banister rail that fronted the mezzanine.

After that came a choked shout.

Something heavy slammed to the ground in front of me.

I jumped back inside the pantry. But not before I'd seen who'd hit the ground.

Brodie.

He was lying on his front, his arms splayed, groaning. His pistol had sprung out of his hand and skidded away across the floor towards the plastic sheeting near the log burner.

I stared after it from the crack in the pantry door.

That fork in the road.

I'd messed up badly. He'd come to help.

I could see blood. Lots of it. Brodie looked to be bleeding from somewhere low down on his left calf. The blood was seeping out through the jeans he had on, dark and glossy against the pale flooring.

I didn't breathe. Didn't move.

I stared at the gun.

Brodie wheezed out a breath and tried pulling himself forwards. He didn't have the strength. I knew he was going for his gun. I knew he wouldn't get there. If I was braver, stronger, maybe I would have run out to help. But I didn't.

I didn't know how to shoot.

The bigger man was charging down the staircase with the shotgun.

And I could hear shouting and footfall from along the corridor. It was the sound of the smaller man rushing this way.

I cringed, then reached up to pull the door closed.

I didn't manage it unseen.

Brodie glanced back just in time to spot me. His eyes widened. I went dead still.

A voice yelled, 'What's going on? What are you shooting for?'

It was the smaller man, sounding vexed and low on patience. His boots clomped down the corridor. The bigger man leaped to the ground from the stairs.

I framed a look of desperate apology and watched through the tiniest slit in the door as Brodie swung his head forwards and strained to crawl to his pistol again. The bigger man came thundering towards him. He bounded over the plastic sheeting. He swung his right foot back at the knee, whipped his leg forwards from the hip and kicked Brodie full in the ribs.

Another plosive gasp. An agonized, wheezing groan.

I hunched back, like I'd been kicked myself.

Brodie tried to cover up but the bigger man grabbed his arm and rolled him over onto his back, then placed the toe of his boot on Brodie's throat and pointed the shotgun at his face.

I went cold.

'What the fuck is he doing here?' the smaller man asked.

The two men lined up next to one another, looking down at Brodie with their backs to me. The smaller man had a pistol in his gloved fist. I felt a scratching in my scalp, like he was pointing it at my head.

'He brought a gun.' The bigger man nodded towards where Brodie's pistol had fallen. He waited until the smaller man had paced over and picked the gun up and studied it closely. 'He just pulled up right outside.'

'Yeah?' The smaller man slipped Brodie's gun into a pocket on his coveralls. Then he cast a long, questioning look along the corridor towards the reading nook and the wine cellar. He stroked his chin. 'They must have contacted him from in there. I don't know how, but they did. Right?'

The bigger man shrugged and leaned his weight down on the shotgun until Brodie's skin dimpled around the muzzle and his face tightened in pain.

So the bigger man hasn't found Rachel and Holly. They still think we're in the cellar.

The smaller man got down on his haunches. 'Did they call you? Message you? What?'

'Go to hell,' Brodie snarled.

The bigger man snatched the shotgun away, spun it in his hand and stabbed the butt down hard on Brodie's left knee. I flinched. The noise was terrible. Like a snooker ball thrown against a chalkboard. Brodie's leg bounced off the floor, spilling blood from the wound in his calf. He roared with pain and tried rolling away but the bigger man had his foot clamped on his throat.

If I was a better person, maybe I would have taken a chance on sneaking up on the men with the mallet that was shaking in my hand. Maybe I would have attacked them. Maybe, against all odds, I would have come out on top.

But the truth is, I'm not an action hero. I'm a husband. A dad.

Brodie had come here to help us. I didn't know how or why but he had. I knew I was failing him and maybe failing myself too. And yet, at the same time, I had to prioritize Rachel and Holly. If I got shot, what would happen to them?

And all right, perhaps this is a lot of self-justification to explain my actions, but that doesn't mean I didn't loathe myself for just watching as the smaller man strode off across the room, snatched up the wire recliner over by the wall of glass, set it down in the middle of the plastic sheeting and then worked with the bigger man to haul Brodie into the chair and bind his chest and biceps to it with the roll of silver gaffer tape.

43

Let me save you the gory details of what followed. Trust me, you don't want to hear about what it's like to watch someone beaten in front of you. And I don't particularly want to tell it.

One thing I can say is that it was fast. This was no prolonged torture scene.

Mostly they focused on Brodie's face. They also pummelled his chest and ribs and they threatened to gag him when he struggled to breathe. At one point, the bigger man twisted the muzzle of his shotgun into the bloody wound on Brodie's leg and he screamed so wildly I knew there was no way that Rachel and Holly couldn't have heard it. They would have heard the gunshot before that. My throat closed up as I thought about how scared and distressed they must be right now. Did they think I was dead? Probably. How would Holly cope with that? Would she be able to hold it together enough to run with Rachel to the stargazing pod? Would they leave Buster behind? I doubted it, but I hoped they'd find a way into the pod. I hoped there was a phone there. I hoped very badly they'd survive this terror, because now that I'd seen what these men were capable of, I was terrified I wouldn't.

Brodie had given us a chance to get through this and I hadn't taken it. I knew I could never forgive myself for that.

The men shouted a series of rapid questions as they beat him. First and most important, they wanted to know how to get through the steel door into the cellar. Brodie told them they couldn't if it was locked from the inside. Not even a reset code would work.

They asked him why he'd come. He told them a silent alarm had been triggered inside the cellar. The alarm had flashed up on his phone. It was his job to respond.

Then more questions, some of them overlapping. The entire interrogation couldn't have lasted more than a minute but it felt like much longer.

They asked him if the police had been notified. He said no.

They asked him if he'd called the police himself. He said no again.

Then they stepped back, panting heavily. Brodie's head lolled. He dribbled blood onto his chest through his sweat-drenched beard. His face was mashed and torn and swollen.

My stomach dropped.

He hadn't given me away and, while I was enormously grateful to him for that, I felt an overwhelming burden of guilt. I told myself that maybe he was hoping the men would leave him alone and I could untie him. Or maybe he'd lied to the men. Maybe the police really were on their way and he was trying to stall until they got here.

I hoped so. But I had no way of knowing. Neither did the bigger man or the smaller man, and that was a huge problem for them.

I hugged myself tight as the smaller man waved the bigger man towards the kitchen. They grouped up just metres away from me, breathing hard, swearing harder.

I didn't shrink back from the door. I was too afraid of making a sound. I breathed through my mouth in shallow gulps and focused on staying still, not knocking any groceries off the pantry shelves. I could feel hot sweat in my hair, under my arms, in the small of my back, on my eyelids. The mallet grew heavy at the end of my arm. I was so afraid of dropping it that my fingers cramped.

The men conferred in low whispers, like they didn't want Brodie to hear what they had to say. I tried to listen but the thunder of the blood in my ears was too loud. Soon, they moved off and returned to Brodie, standing on either side of him with the smaller man on the left and the bigger man on the right.

'You know who we want,' the smaller man said.

He took hold of Brodie's hair and tugged his face upright. His bloodied nose was putty. His right eye was a ghastly pouch of swollen and puckered skin. I flashed on what had happened to Holly in that alley. I'd thought it had been bad, but now I saw how much worse it could have been.

I waited for Brodie to look my way and tell them where I was hidden. To signal the men. To choose the obvious way out.

But he said nothing.

My heart ached.

The smaller man clipped him with his gun. A stinging backhand blow that opened a welt across Brodie's forehead and whipped his head to one side.

Brodie dribbled blood onto his shoulder. 'I don't . . . know . . . who . . . you're talking about. I don't know . . . why . . . you're here.'

'Oh, you don't? You think you can investigate us and we won't know about it?'

'I . . . told you.' Brodie raised his head and looked groggily at the two men. 'I don't know . . . anything.'

People talk about everyday heroes. You read about them in the news from time to time. They're the people who show their true mettle when it matters, in the moment, based on a split-second response to an unanticipated danger. The ones who tackle a gunman to prevent a shooting spree. The ones who run into burning buildings to rescue complete strangers. The people who *act* when someone pulls a knife on them in a darkened alley instead of being paralysed by fear.

Brodie was one of those people. I understood now that he was prepared to do what he could to shield my family from this horror. The ache in my heart got deeper as I thought about his courage. I knew I'd never be able to repay him for it.

'You should just leave,' he said.

But they didn't leave. The smaller man hit Brodie one last time and then shoved him back so hard that his chair tipped and crashed to the ground, toppling to one side. His wrists were swollen beneath their gaffer-tape bindings. His fingers were turning purple. The leg of his jeans was soaked with blood.

The men looked at him a moment more, then shook their heads dismissively and backed up into the kitchen again. This time they talked more freely. More loudly. I supposed they were no longer concerned about Brodie hearing what they had to say. There was no doubt in my mind that they intended to kill him.

'So?' the bigger man asked.

The smaller man shrugged and rubbed his chin beneath his paper mask again. 'We burn them. All of them. Problem solved.'

We burn them.

I froze. A numbing sensation started in my fingers and toes, creeping towards my heart. It hadn't been an idle threat. They really had been prepared to burn my family alive.

The bigger man fell quiet. He looked away towards the deck and the sea.

'What?' the smaller man asked. 'You think they're just going to come out? Look at us. They know what we'll do to them. They know what's at stake.'

'But come on. That's—'

'Hey, we have to protect ourselves.'

The bigger man said nothing.

'You have a problem with that?'

Still he didn't reply.

'Look, we'll give them one more chance to open the door, OK? But this was always going to end badly, one way or another. You had to know that going in.'

'Not like this. You didn't say it would be like this.'

The smaller man didn't respond to begin with. He just watched the bigger man. Then he shook his head and snatched the shotgun from him.

'You think I like this any more than you do? We don't have a choice. We can't get in there, OK? And you know we can't let them talk. This guy already turned up. Who knows who else might be coming? We don't have time to screw around here. Think about it. They all die, and there's nothing to connect us to any of this. So I say we burn them, then we search the rest of this place and make sure we didn't miss anything. You have any better ideas, go ahead and tell me. I'm listening.' He waited, but the bigger man shook his head, looking down at his boots. 'That's what I thought. So how about you do us both a favour and find me some matches?'

Fiona is huddled in the darkness under a stairwell when Michael finds her. Her phone screen is glowing. She's clutching it like a child cradling a night light.

'There you are.' He gets down on one knee and crawls under to join her. 'Are you OK?'

'I'm so frightened.' She pulls him close. He can feel the wetness of her tears on his face. 'I really thought they were going to find me.'

'They won't.'

'They're looking.'

Michael nods, feeling young and small against the enormity of the situation he's been drawn into. Until he'd got here, he'd been clinging to the hope that Fiona had somehow got spooked or mixed up. That things couldn't be as bad as she'd said.

But when he'd pulled up outside he'd seen shadowy figures running around the car park structure, leaning out to survey the drop to the parking levels below and the street beyond that. They were obviously in a hurry. Obviously looking for something.

For someone.

And now, with the state Fiona is in . . .

Michael's never seen her like this. Never seen anyone *like this.*

'We should go,' he tells her.

She shrinks back into the darkness under the stairs. It's as if she can't hear him properly. As if she's on the other side of a thick pane of glass.

'Fi. We have to move. OK?'

She moans, shaking her head. Her shoulder bag is on the ground next to her, her camera poking out. Fiona has been working on the same material for close to a year now. It's a photographic journal of Michael doing his free running.

She's good. Really good. And she's so dedicated to her art, and Michael is so in love with her that he wants more than anything for her to finish the project and maybe, just maybe, get a place at uni to study photography and a chance at a career beyond that.

That's why Fiona's here tonight, grabbing some background shots to add context to the last sequence he'd figured out – a kind of before and after effect. Fiona is obsessive like that. Sometimes she makes Michael repeat the same stunt so many times his calves burn and the skin is scraped off his palms when he gets into bed at night.

He makes a grab for her bag but she recoils instinctively. It scares him to see how scared she is.

'Fiona,' he says again.

And then they hear it. Hurried footfall. One flight up, rushing down.

Michael grabs Fiona's hand and her bag and hauls her out. He drags her to the stairs, where she's shot countless sequences of him descending before. He's performed wallflips and sideflips, aerial twists, frontflips and gainers, vaulting handrails, leaping down entire flights in one bound. On a perfect descent, he can get down faster than any elevator. But right now he feels slow, held back.

And the footsteps chasing them just seem to be getting quicker.

44

***Find me some matches.* Words I *really* didn't want to hear**
right now.

The smaller man paced off down the corridor. The bigger man stood and watched him go. He raised his gloved hand and studied his mangled fingers, like he couldn't believe the damage he'd sustained. As if maybe his broken fingers were symptomatic of everything that had gone wrong for him tonight.

Then he rested his hand crossways over his chest and returned to the living room, shaking his head.

'You don't have to . . . listen to him,' Brodie panted. 'Get out of here while you still can.'

The bigger man stood there, like he was considering it, then he grunted and stepped hard on Brodie's wrist. I winced. Brodie hissed air through his teeth. The bigger man pressed down on his foot even more as he picked up the roll of gaffer tape and tore off a strip with his teeth. He used the swatch of tape to wrap around his two broken fingers and secure them to his little finger like a splint. When he was done, he lifted his foot from Brodie, dropped the tape in his face and moved out of my line of sight. I heard the crinkle of the thick plastic sheeting deflecting under his weight.

My head pounded. I had a pretty good idea where he was going. *The log burner,* I thought. Because people with log burners and fireplaces tend to keep a box of matches nearby. But I knew he wouldn't find any matches there. I'd drawn a similar blank when I'd been preparing to light the fire in the fire pit last night.

And that was a huge problem for me. Because the only matches I'd found were in the pantry. I could see them now – a big box of 200 kitchen matches on a shelf to my right.

Fear got its claws in me then. It tore at my skin. I reached out and closed the pantry door.

Had the man heard it? I hoped not. It might have sounded like a cannon shot to me right now, but I didn't think the noise had carried.

I trembled in the dark, listening to the bigger man striding back across the plastic sheeting. He passed the pantry door. I heard the crush and crumple of glass fragments under his boots from the broken window. Then other sounds. Sudden clicks. Muffled clunks. The soft whisper of metal runners on greased bearings. He was opening and closing kitchen cupboards and drawers. Every noise made me flinch.

I stepped back. My shoulders bumped against the shelves behind me. Nowhere else to go.

A rim of light was shining around the pantry door. Footsteps approached. I saw a bar of darkness at the bottom.

He's coming in.

My heart seized. I could sense the bigger man's presence on the other side of the door. Could he sense mine?

'Hey,' Brodie hissed.

I wobbled like a wire.

'Shut the fuck up,' the bigger man growled.

'You're making a mistake.' Brodie was talking fast and urgent. 'You should listen to me.'

'You need to stop talking or I'm going to come over there and make it so you can't talk any more.'

I raised the mallet above my head. It felt like I was lifting a heavy dumb-bell. My arm shook crazily.

'You don't want to go in there,' Brodie said. 'I'll tell you whatever you want to know.'

The bigger man didn't respond. The door handle rotated. I snatched a quick breath. Then the door swung open and the rim of bright light became a rapidly widening wedge that swept in across the pantry floor and streaked up my legs and body.

I drew back.

The bigger man loomed there, staring at me from beneath the rim of his hood and above his mask. His eyes were red-rimmed, threaded with capillaries, strained and fatigued from a long, wakeful night trying to corner and kill my family.

I watched his pupils go wide. I saw the shock. He'd believed I was locked in the wine cellar. Along with my family. But now here I was.

His confusion didn't last long. Mostly because I took a swing at him with the mallet.

But I messed it up. I was too nervous. Too jumpy. And it was an awkward, truncated swing because of the cramped conditions inside the pantry. I had no shoulder room.

The mallet crunched against the side of his neck. His neck

was thick with muscle and swollen with fat. The impact was like hitting a mound of wet clay.

He barely reacted.

I stared. My knees flexed.

Then he reached in and clubbed me behind the ear. It wasn't a punch. Because of his broken fingers. But it was enough to knock me sideways. My cheek crashed off a shelf. The impact jolted me hard. I felt my right hand go light. He'd ripped the mallet from me like taking a toy from a child and now he took a swing of his own. I rocked back wildly. The mallet whispered past my nose. I started to fall and he helped me on my way by ramming the heel of his hand into my solar plexus, sending me clattering into the shelving on the back wall.

A stabbing pain in my back. I dropped down. Fear flashed like a bright light in my head. One shelf came loose at the hinges and tilted, raining tins and packets on top of me. A plastic tub cracked and spilled salt across the floor. An aerosol can of cooking fat struck my forehead and bounced into a corner of the cupboard.

I tried to get up. He wouldn't let me. He kicked at my feet. My shins. Panic filled my throat. He tried to stomp on my ankle but I pulled my leg away. Then he dropped on me, hard, landing with both knees on my stomach. I folded up like a medicine ball had been thrown at my gut.

Air gushed out of my lungs. I couldn't breathe. The panic got worse. And meanwhile he swung down with the mallet in his left hand, aiming for my skull. I just about moved my head away. The mallet clipped my ear, crunching salt. My ear exploded with pain.

Oh Jesus.

He was so much bigger than me. So much stronger. I'm not good at fighting. I don't have any experience. I don't box in my spare time. I've never tried martial arts. But I did have one thing going for me. I was desperate.

Attack something soft. Something vulnerable.

I scrabbled for his face. I tried to get my thumbs in his eyes. My ear was a raging hot nub of pain. He leaned back. I tugged on his mask. Then I changed tactics, snatching for his broken fingers, trying to wrench them back and cause him pain. He yanked his hand clear, dropped the mallet and clamped his massive left palm over my face.

More panic. My nostrils filled with the chemical stink of his glove. I couldn't breathe. He thrust all his weight down on top of me with his elbow locked, forcing my face to the side, driving my eye into the spilled salt and exerting so much force I felt sure my cheekbone would compress and fracture. My ear throbbed and swelled.

Fear ignited my nerves. It crackled across my body. I was beaten. I was suffocating. I was still trying to fight back, still scrabbling, but my efforts were getting weaker, limper, like I was trying to fight gravity itself.

I closed my eyes and thought of Holly, then. I pictured her fleeing through the woods with Rachel and Buster at her side. I imagined them getting inside the pod. Finding shelter. Getting help. I knew I couldn't hold on for much longer. I knew it was futile. But I told myself something that gave me the tiniest shred of solace. Every second I resisted was another precious second for Holly to get away from these men.

Until everything changed.

Until a rope appeared, looped around the man's neck, secured by a slip knot.

My heart stopped. I tried to kick up. How had Brodie got free?

Still the bigger man held me down. He crowded me. I couldn't see past him. My lungs burned. My eyes bulged. There was an intense pulsing heat in my throat.

The rope was tightly woven, speckled in shades of light and dark blue. It was one of the ropes I'd seen among the stash of equipment the men had brought with them.

Then the bigger man rocked to one side.

Rachel.

She was standing behind him, tugging on the end of the rope.

She'd come back for me.

My heart burst. I didn't know whether to be elated or terrified.

She had her foot in the middle of the man's back, pulling with her good arm, a mighty grimace on her face.

At last, the bigger man choked and gargled and lifted his hands off of me towards his throat. I gulped air. He tried to prise the rope away. Tried to dig his fingers beneath it and gain some slack. It wasn't easy with gloves on. Even worse with two broken fingers. Much harder again when Rachel braced the elbow of her bad arm against the back of the man's neck and the rope dug deeper.

So the man changed tactics. He tried to spin in the tight space and reach backwards for Rachel. He grasped for her coat. Her hair. He gurgled and wheezed. He tried shouting for the smaller man to come to his aid but his words were no more than a hoarse rasp. Then he tried bashing a tin off the nearest shelf.

It might have worked. Except I finally surged forwards against the lancing pain in my stomach and grabbed for his wrists. I wrenched him back around and down towards me. The hot stink of his breath was in my face. I shook and clung on with everything I had.

Rachel clenched her jaw and yanked even harder. As a doctor, she'd know all about the effects of air deprivation. I guessed she'd try and choke him out. If he went limp, maybe the two of us could attempt to restrain him, somehow.

But Rachel didn't let up. Not when the bigger man stopped fighting. Not when his face flushed and his eyes protruded. Not when he stiffened, then went slack and slumped down on top of me.

'Rachel?'

Still she pulled. I stared in horror, pinned beneath the bigger man. Rachel seemed to be in some other place entirely. Thinking of Michael, maybe. Of how much she loved him. Of how much had been taken away from us.

I felt a pang. You think you know someone. You think you know them better than anybody else possibly could. Like the way I knew Rachel. Eighteen years of marriage. Four years together before that. Two kids. Three homes over the years. A mortgage. Bills. A lifetime of shared experiences and love and pain.

Then come the secrets. The lies. The hurt. You see the parts of your lover they have tried to keep hidden from you.

But still, you don't know them. Not really. The same way I didn't know Rachel until I watched her wrench the life from a man who'd set out to kill us both.

45

Rachel let go of the rope and collapsed to one side. Her face was flushed and sheened in sweat. Her eyes fluttered closed. The straps of her medical backpack were twisted over her shoulders.

I kicked and squirmed out from under the man. My heart was beating against my ribs like a fist on a door. I had a thick ear. It was burning as if someone had rubbed sandpaper on it. I could still smell the plastic of the man's glove when I inhaled.

'Is he dead?'

Rachel opened her eyes. They were big and shiny. I watched as she leaned forwards to put two fingers to the pulse point on the man's neck. She held them there and waited. Then she lowered her eyes and nodded, slowly.

My stomach knotted. I felt the pressure build inside my head. Rachel had saved me. She'd risked her life for me. But watching her throttle the man had been like watching a different person.

She'd killed him. I'd helped her. And yes, it was self-defence, but the enormity of what we'd done seemed too big for the pantry cupboard to contain.

'Where's the other one?' she whispered, turning to look out the door.

I blinked. Shook my head. I felt cold and clammy. My pulse beat in my throat.

'Tom, where is he?'

'Outside the wine cellar.' I swallowed. 'He's expecting this one to bring him matches.'

Rachel stilled. Her face hardened. She was probably running the implications through her mind. Maybe she was picturing what it would have been like to be inside the cellar when the flames took hold.

'Where's Holly?' I asked. 'Is she safe?'

It only took a second for Rachel to respond but the wait felt like a lifetime to me.

'She's on her way to the pod.'

I let go of a breath. I should have been relieved but I wasn't. 'You let her go on her *own*?'

'Buster is with her. He's more alert now.'

'That wasn't the plan, Rachel.'

'The plan changed when we heard the gunshot.' She stared at me and her mouth began to tremble. I thought she might cry. 'You have no idea how scared we were. The only way I could stop her from running in here was if I came instead.'

I could believe that. I could imagine Holly running in here in much the same way she'd dived out of the dinghy to get to Buster. I was glad she hadn't. But the idea of her alone in the woods, running scared, not knowing if we were coming for her . . .

'I can't believe we killed him.'

Rachel was quiet a moment. 'He would have killed you if we hadn't.'

Would he? Hadn't there been a window when we could have subdued him?

'These men came here to murder us, Tom. You know that. You know what they did to Michael too.'

Did I? I gazed at the dead man, feeling an enormous weight pressing down on me. His cheeks were mottled and berry-coloured above his mask, his throat grossly swollen around the climbing rope that circled his neck. I took a halting breath, then reached out tentatively and tugged down his mask. I pinched the top of his hood and peeled it backwards over his sweaty hair.

A shudder passed through me. Rachel had been right. I recognized the man from the speed camera images.

'He was in the car that was following Michael,' I said. My voice sounded like it belonged to somebody else. 'He was the front passenger.'

Rachel looked at the man without saying anything. Something flashed across her eyes, but I wasn't sure what. Not guilt, exactly. Maybe sadness?

'I didn't know what to do when Brodie showed up,' she whispered. 'You'd put so much doubt in my mind about him, Tom.'

'I was wrong about that. He saw me in here. He didn't tell them.'

She paused. 'They shot him?'

'His leg.'

She closed her eyes, like she didn't want to imagine that right now. 'What about the phone?'

'It didn't work.'

'The gate?'

'Brodie showed up before I could try. He said we'd triggered a silent alarm. In the wine cellar.'

Something else crossed her face. Again, I wasn't sure what exactly. It bothered me. What more did she know that I didn't?

As I thought about that, I also thought about Brodie's Land Cruiser. The gate had already opened for it once. Maybe we could try and get out in it. But at least one of us would have to go into the woods to find Holly. By the time we got back, the smaller man would be looking for his partner. Once he found him dead, he'd be looking for us. There was no way we could leave Brodie behind after what he'd done for us, but I couldn't see how we could take him with us, either. We couldn't lift him. I doubted he could walk. We had to try something else and we had to do it soon.

'Go to Brodie,' I said. 'Take a look at his leg.'

'What about the other man?'

I swallowed. 'I'm working on that.'

46

By the time I stepped out of the pantry, Rachel had loosened Brodie's arms and was cutting open his jeans with the scissors from her backpack. She'd slipped on a pair of blue rubber gloves and she was applying pressure to his bloodied leg with another sterile pad. Brodie sucked air through his teeth, then made a grab for Rachel's wrist. She stilled and gradually looked up at him, and I felt a sudden painful squeezing in my chest.

The way Brodie stared at my wife – I'd looked at Rachel too many times like that myself. And sure, I'd begun to suspect Brodie had a thing for her, but this seemed like something more than just a crush. And maybe – though I really didn't want to have to acknowledge this right now – it wasn't entirely one way.

'Listen, Rachel, I—'

My foot scuffed the floor and Rachel jumped and turned, lifting the scissors above her shoulder like a dagger.

'Easy,' I told her. 'It's me.'

She thrust her face forwards, her body stiffening, and I patted the air with my hand until she lowered the scissors in degrees. Her face became slack. She shook her head slowly. Then she seemed to become conscious of the way

Brodie was holding her wrist and she pushed his hand away.

'No, Tom,' she said. 'No way.'

I looked between them, my mind still buzzing from what I'd witnessed. Was Rachel the real reason Brodie had come back to the lodge? What had he been about to say to her?

'That's a really . . . bad idea,' he panted.

Probably Brodie was right. Probably it was a bad idea. And it's possible I was being churlish, but I didn't feel all that inclined to listen to his advice right now. Besides, it was the only idea I had.

I looked down at the outfit I had on. I was wearing the dead man's white plastic coveralls, his surgical mask, his blue rubber boots. It had been tricky to undress him in a hurry inside the pantry. Space was tight. His body was heavy. The cheap coveralls were designed to be disposable and I'd torn a gash in the seam behind my right shoulder.

Also, the coveralls were too big. To try and compensate, I'd put them on over my outdoor jacket. The dead man's boots fitted me like clown's shoes. And I only had on one glove, not two. The blue nitrile glove on the man's right hand had been torn and shredded around his broken fingers, gummed up with tape.

'Hey! What's the hold-up?'

My scalp prickled. My heart squeezed painfully again. I turned. It was the smaller man, yelling at me from the end of the corridor. I stared at him from over the mask I had on. Sweat broke across my face.

Would this work? *Could* it work?

Very carefully, I eased my bare hand behind my back. I

was trembling. From the angle the smaller man was on, he couldn't see Brodie or Rachel.

My throat had gone dry. Every instinct told me to grab Rachel and run. To get away to Holly.

No. Wait. Be strong.

The smaller man folded his arms and shook his head, like he was weary and weighed down by his crushing disappointment with the bigger man. I waited for him to see me. *Really* see me. To notice how my pulse was throbbing in my neck. How my fingers were twitching. How my breathing was too shallow, too fast. But all he saw was my outfit from a distance. All he saw was the bigger man he'd expected to see.

Slowly, jerkily, I raised the box of kitchen matches in my gloved hand. I felt like I was holding a mirror up to my face.

I waited.

'Finally!' he shouted. 'Then stop stalling and get back here. Now!'

He beckoned me with a dismissive sweep of his arm and headed back to the wine cellar. I watched him go, my heart flip-flopping in my chest. Once he was gone I hunched forwards, and grabbed my stomach like I had a bad cramp. I felt limp and weightless. I wasn't getting enough air through the mask.

'Give me a glove from your bag,' I said to Rachel.

'Tom, no.'

'He'll kill you,' Brodie warned.

I looked down at him, still bound to the chair, his battered face pressed against the floor, his beard speckled with blood. The white of his left eye was stained red. His swollen right eye looked like a baseball mitt.

I swallowed and tried to keep my shakes under control. 'Are the police on their way?'

Brodie hung his head. 'No.'

I didn't move for a second. I'd been hoping for a different response. There was no question in my mind that I had to do something. For Holly. For us.

'Give me a glove, Rachel. Please.'

'You're being crazy.'

'This whole night has been crazy. Why should now be any different?'

My wife turned to Brodie again, her jaw clenched, her eyes wide, as if she was urging him to intervene. But Brodie just peered at me for a long moment without saying anything until I broke the pause by moving forwards and reaching into Rachel's backpack for a glove. I stretched it over my fingers. The glove was a shade darker than the one on my left hand. Nothing I could do about that.

'How's his leg?'

Rachel considered the wound again and shook her head, like she didn't know or couldn't tell. As a GP from a practice in a wealthy residential area of London, I was pretty sure she'd never had to deal with a gunshot wound before.

'I think the bullet went right through. Maybe. I can pack the wound. Try to stem the bleeding. If we're lucky then—'

'OK.' I nodded and snapped the glove against my wrist, releasing a puff of talcum. I kept my face down, not looking at either of them directly because I was afraid of what my eyes would reveal.

Then I turned to the corridor, squared my shoulders and

took a series of fast breaths, like I was psyching myself up to run head first into a wall.

'Tom?'

Rachel reached up for my hand. I was aware of Brodie watching us closely but I tried to block that out as I stared into my wife's beautiful brown eyes. I was so very, very afraid, but I wanted to be brave for Rachel. I wanted to be the man she needed me to be.

'It's OK, Rachel. Everything is going to be OK.' My throat burned. Tears pressed against my eyes. 'We'll go and get Holly soon. We have to protect her, right?'

I tried smiling through my fear. Rachel couldn't see my smile from behind my mask, but part of me hoped she'd know it was there anyway.

Then I stepped into the corridor. It seemed to stretch ahead of me for miles and miles.

47

I'd had this nightmare before. The corridor that never ends.

My breath washed back at me, hot and humid from the mask. My ear stung and throbbed. The hood muffled my hearing. My steps felt clumsy and exaggerated inside the bigger man's boots. All things considered, I felt a lot like a diver wearing deep-sea apparatus, wading along the ocean floor.

I tramped on down the corridor, aware that every step was taking me further and further from Rachel. Aware that I was leaving her on her own with Brodie. It seemed to take far too long and no time at all until I reached the reading nook.

Be brave.

Protect Holly.

I snatched a fast, airless breath and stepped inside.

A spasm tore through me. I almost dropped the matchbox. The smaller man was on his hands and knees, with one eye pressed to the crack at the bottom of the door to the wine cellar.

Could I attack him now?

'They made their choice,' he said. 'They're not coming out.'

I didn't respond. Terror and rage pounded in my head. This man was ruthless. He was planning to burn my family alive, and now he was trying to justify it to me.

The car jack was pinned under the metal door. The door had been wrenched forwards from its lowest hinge. A smashed green circuit board hung from the middle of it on a strand of electrical wire.

Next to the red plastic bucket with the petrol in it was the claw hammer. Next to that was the sledgehammer. The man's handgun and Brodie's pistol were close by his right hand. The shotgun was resting by its stock against a bookshelf to the side of the metal door.

I stared at the shotgun. My vision throbbed. Could I get to it? It would take three, maybe four strides into the room. A lunge. A grab. And then? Turn with one finger on the trigger, the other supporting the stock? And . . . *boom*?

Maybe. But maybe it wasn't as simple as pulling the trigger. Maybe I had to pump the action first. That awful *crunch-crack*. Was there some kind of safety to disengage? I didn't know. I'd never fired a shotgun before. Same thing with the handguns.

So the sledgehammer? I wavered. It was long and heavy. If I went for it and the smaller man noticed, he might shoot me before I could swing down at him.

The claw hammer, then? Possibly. But it was an extra stride away. And even now – even with all that was at stake – I didn't know if I could bring myself to club him with it. I was a dad and a husband, not a savage.

I stood there. Sweating. Trembling. Trying to think. Trying to be certain. But every move seemed to contain its own pitfalls.

Do something.

The smaller man stayed on his hands and knees, squinting,

straining. I was just about to move when he yelled under the door.

'Listen up. Last chance. Let us in now or you're going to burn.'

I shuffled half a step forwards. My legs shook. I blinked the sweat from my eyes and then, just as I was about to take another step, the smaller man backed up from the crack and glanced around at me.

My blood turned to ice.

It was a fast, sweeping movement of his head and neck. And his gaze was mostly on my torso and legs. Partly because of his positioning, but also partly because his attitude towards me was still dismissive. As if the bigger man's performance had been so poor he couldn't bring himself to look at him fully.

I stood there, quaking. An impostor. The box of matches shook in my left hand. My right hand was tucked behind my back.

My legs trembled. I was levering myself slightly up off my heels. Trying to make myself appear taller. And I was pulling back my shoulders. Trying to make myself appear broader.

But there was no need. It seemed like I was little more than a blurred set of white plastic coveralls to the smaller man. His glance swept one way, fast. Then back the other way, equally fast. Then he put his ear back to the crack under the door again.

'I can't hear a thing in there,' he muttered. 'Can't see them. They've pushed something up against the gap here. Clothing, maybe.'

Again, I didn't respond.

'OK. Hand me the matches. Enough of this bullshit.'

He beckoned to me. A curling of his fingers. Still not prepared to look at me directly.

Now what?

Did I cross towards him? Get closer?

I got closer.

Three steps. I was near to his side now, by his waist, a little behind him. If I wanted to, I could reach out and touch him.

I shivered.

From the angle he was on, it would be awkward for him to turn and look up at my face. But I still couldn't risk that happening. So I stretched out my arm and waggled the box of matches at his side. I waited. He reached up over his shoulder for them in an overhand, backwards grab. His fingers brushed my fingers. Could he feel my shakes?

My eyes slid to the hammer. It was so close now. Near my foot. And, with the matches in his right hand, going for a gun would take the man fractionally longer. First, he'd have to drop the matchbox. *Then* go for the gun. A two-step process, instead of a one-step process. Did that matter? It did to me.

My knees flexed. I clenched my teeth and started to dip. To go for the hammer.

Closer . . . Closer . . .

The smaller man removed a match from inside the box.

'Remember, they asked for this.'

I faltered.

He scrubbed the match head against the strike. There was

a spark. A flame. It guttered in a slight, imperceptible breeze creeping under the door of the wine cellar, squeezing by the packed and soaked towels, probably originating from all the way down the ventilation shaft we'd opened up into the woods outside.

The smaller man cupped his gloved hand around the flame. The light danced and peaked, casting ghoulish shadows across his masked and hooded face.

Remember, they asked for this.

This man.

Hot rage crackled in my mind.

He'd caused my son's death. He'd terrorized us tonight. And now he was casually planning to set fire to the rest of my family and burn us alive.

I stopped bending for the claw hammer. Because that was going to involve a slight, improvised, two-step process of my own. And instead I whipped my right hand around from behind my back. With the aerosol can of cooking fat in it.

I aimed the nozzle at the flame and sprayed.

Michael's parents' house recedes in the rear-view mirror. The night-time road feels too narrow. His dad's Audi too wide. The headlamps don't seem to give him enough light to see by and he wonders if he should switch to full beam. But he remembers you probably shouldn't do that in a residential area. And Michael can't afford to draw attention to himself. Besides, in the darkness of the car, all the controls feel alien to him. It's overwhelming. He's suddenly sure he'll crash.

He can picture himself clipping every wing mirror of the long line of cars parked ahead of him. The vision is almost enough to make him stop.

Hands jittery on the steering wheel, Michael glances down at the screen of his phone. No more messages from Fiona. Not yet. He doesn't know whether to be relieved or afraid.

In the deepest folds of his heart, he knows this can't be a trick. Fiona wouldn't do that to him. She wouldn't ask him to take his dad's car and risk getting caught like this. But part of him wishes it was *a trick – a part of him that wants it so badly he begins to weave a narrative for himself where he can tell Fiona he was so convinced it was a prank he didn't come. A narrative where he turns back and she forgives him for letting her down. Where everything works out OK. Where she understands.*

A sudden huge thump. The steering wheel jumps from Michael's hands and the Audi's headlamps strafe the trees overhead.

It takes him a second to realize he's taken a speed bump too hard.

He grips the wheel, lets off on the accelerator, stares intently at the road leading into town.

Come quickly.

That's what Fiona's most recent message said.

And before that: Please. I'm begging you.

And before that: So scared.

48

There was a motif on the reverse of the spray can of a black and yellow flame inside a yellow triangle. Beneath the motif were two words: HIGHLY FLAMMABLE.

The misted spray condensed around the match flame and ignited in a gaseous flash. The flame mushroomed, smoked and expanded. The heat bundled back towards me in a wobbling, roaring jet.

Dread surged inside me. I flinched and covered my face with my forearm. But I continued to spray, dousing the man and his plastic coveralls, painting the air with dancing flames that twitched blue and yellow and orange and white.

The man's suit went up like it was beaded with gasoline. The flame was ghastly and riotous. It started at his wrist and streaked up his sleeve.

He screamed and slapped at his arm, batting it hard, but the fire scrabbled at the side of his face and ignited his hood before whipping around to the back of his neck and upper back, ripping up and down in an angry surge.

Too hot.

Too close.

I dropped the can and moved clear, the heat raging in my face. The man bucked and twisted, howled and flailed. He threw himself against the ground and thrashed. I stared in horror. For a brief moment, it seemed as if the fire had extinguished, but then the front of the man's coveralls ignited with a sudden *whoosh* of flame.

He pushed up to his knees, eyes crazed and straining from above his mask. He stared at me, incredulous, and streaked out of the room.

I didn't pause. Didn't think. I grabbed for his handgun and ran after him in my oversized boots, my heart hammering in my chest.

He was still alight as he fled down the corridor and blasted through the door with the porthole of glass in it. The door swung back at me as I chased him through.

He leaped for the swimming pool. His feet dragged on the surface. Then his knees folded and he toppled forwards, the bright flames spreading and hissing as he plunged face down.

I skidded to a halt, planted my feet and juggled the gun in a hasty two-handed grip.

Could I do this? Could I shoot him?

Yes.

For Holly, I could.

I aimed. Squeezed the trigger.

The gun flashed and boomed inside the echoing, tiled space. My hands leaped with the recoil. The bullet went spiralling through the water off to the man's right.

I swallowed my heart back down out of my mouth. My hands trembled wildly. The man was horribly burned, flailing in the water. I tugged the mask off my face. Fired again.

Another gigantic boom. It echoed inside my chest.

The bullet clipped off a floor tile at the far end of the

pool, then skipped on and obliterated a panel of tinted glass. I ducked. The glass exploded and fell down in one collapsed sheet, like a shower curtain dropping from a railing.

My hands jumped with my racing pulse. I gritted my teeth and fired a third time.

A dry click.

The gun was out of bullets.

A void opened up inside me. I wavered, knees quaking, wondering what the hell to do. The man was swimming towards the side of the pool. He looked angry. Looked livid.

Do something *at least!*

I tossed the gun to one side, dived into the pool and immediately realized my mistake. I still had on the plastic coveralls over my outdoor jacket. Plus my jeans. Plus the too-big rubber boots.

Terror gripped me. It dragged me down. I floundered and sank, kicking off the boots, pulling up desperately towards the surface just as the smaller man reared around and put two hands on my head, forcing me down.

I was twisting. Writhing. Clawing for the surface.

It was unreachable.

My toes grazed the bottom of the swimming pool. I sprang up and felt the immense drag of my clothing pulling against me.

And the man's knees on my shoulders. His hands on my head.

Pure panic overwhelmed me then. It sparked in every fibre and synapse of my body. It flooded my brain.

I went nuts. Full-on frenzied. I flapped and grappled for a handhold, my fingers tearing free from his waxed coveralls.

It had no effect. The man pushed down on me even harder, thrusting with his legs, bouncing from his knees.

I sank way down and looked all around me. Terror swelled in my chest until it felt like my heart would explode. Chlorine stung my eyes. The submerged bulbs shone murky and green. I could feel an immense and urgent pressure building inside my lungs. The desperate, pulsing, life-defining need to breathe.

Get away from him. Do it now!

I sculled backwards along the bottom of the pool, staring up wildly at the man's legs scissoring and kicking.

Somewhere behind him there was a sudden pluming froth of bubbles. The bubbles spun and twisted, then hung suspended for a moment before fizzing and dissipating to reveal Rachel swimming underwater, her sweater bulging around her, her hair floating about her face.

I screamed underwater. My wife had come to help me again. But this was too dangerous. Too much. I couldn't let him hurt her.

I pushed off from the bottom, spearing upwards, scooping great handfuls of water with my palms.

I broke the surface close to the end of the pool. Too close to the man.

He was on me instantly. He grabbed for my throat, my face, forcing me down, cracking the back of my skull off the tiles.

My sight went hazy. My eyes roved. I gurgled water. Coughed. Swallowed water again.

Through the boiling green waters, the man's face was a vivid red, his eyes shining black and beady against the peeled skin all around.

My legs and arms felt so heavy.

Then his hold on me loosened.

I saw legs. Arms. Twisted. Combined. A churning of water. Feet, kicking.

Rachel. I had to help her. I had to . . .

But my body wouldn't obey. My movements were so limp and weighed down. I kicked for the surface. It took an age for me to get there.

When I finally broke through, I grabbed for the side and gulped air.

Rachel and the man were in the middle of the pool. She had her arms around his neck. Her legs circling his waist.

Like a role reversal from what had happened in the alley.

Because the man's mask was fully down now. The blistered and blackened remains of his hood were melted onto his skin. And no, he wasn't wearing a pair of tights under a hoodie. His face wasn't squished and contorted. And he was terribly burned. But there was no question in my mind that he was the man who'd mugged us. He was also the driver of the car that had followed Michael.

Oh God.

My heart plummeted as he reached up and backwards for Rachel. He took a fistful of her hair, dragged her face down underwater, held it there.

I dived towards him. A surge of water came with me. I swam and floundered.

They were still several strokes away.

Rachel thrashed and fought.

The man bared his teeth and snarled. He would drown her. He would kill her. There was no doubt in my mind about that.

Help her. Get to her. You have to . . .

I saw her reach up, hopelessly. I saw her hand grasp air once. Twice. Her fingers went limp.

A terrible chill spread through me.

No. Not now. Not when we were so close to surviving this.

I took two more strokes, then lashed out with my right fist and connected with a weak punch to his right temple. My knuckle cracked. His face splashed into the water but he didn't let go of Rachel's hair.

Panic swirled in my mind.

How long had she been under? Thirty seconds? A minute? But time had no meaning now. Because any time at all was too long. Had Rachel got any air before he'd forced her under? I didn't know.

The man snarled, baring his teeth. I hit him again. And again. In the eye. On the mouth. I rained down on him with a series of blows.

When Michael and Holly were young, I bought them an inflatable toy they could hit that would always bounce back up. This man reminded me of that. Or maybe my punches were pathetic.

He didn't release Rachel. He pushed her down even more, grinning horribly like he was enjoying it. I pulled my fist back again for another punch. But before I could throw it I heard two loud, concussive thuds and the man convulsed twice in a fast jerking movement, like someone had grabbed him by the shoulders and wrenched him violently to the left, then to the right.

He pitched sideways. He lolled face down.

I turned, my body locked with fear, and saw Brodie leaning

against the tiled wall to my right. He clutched his bloodied calf in one hand, lowered his gun in the other, slid to the ground.

For what could only have been a split-second – but felt much, much longer – I stared at the dead man sinking below the water; at the fine scarlet threads weaving up from the wounds in his chest and at the scorched fragments of plastic drifting around. Then I took a breath and dived, grabbing for Rachel's sweater, her arms, lifting and dragging her, pulling her up with me towards the surface as fast as I could.

49

I mentioned before about Rachel holding my hand when she was in labour with Michael and Holly. What I didn't explain was that Michael's birth was complicated. Rachel was nearly two weeks overdue. She had to be induced. She was in active labour for more than nine hours with no sign that the baby would come. Then a new consultant came on shift, checked in on Rachel and immediately ordered an emergency caesarean. Her vitals had crashed. Mother and baby were in danger. In the moments after the epidural went in, I stroked Rachel's face and – for the first time in our marriage – confronted the very real possibility that I might lose her. She was so weak. So disorientated. I had visions of the midwife handing me our baby in the moments after my wife had passed. I knew I couldn't cope without her. I had no idea how I would go on.

This felt like that, only worse. I heaved her out of the pool onto her back. Her skin was translucent. She wasn't breathing. She was so terribly limp.

Oh, please, no.

Why had she dived in after me? She shouldn't have done that. I'd wanted her to be safe.

Fear paralysed me then. I had no idea what to do. I looked

over at Brodie. He stared back, his face tight with horror, shaking his head with wild urgency. There was no team of trained medics around me. There was only Rachel, lying unresponsive on the cold tiles.

Don't let me lose her. Not now.

It was too cruel.

I tilted her chin up, pinched her nose. Rachel was the doctor. She should be the one telling me how to do this. I leaned down to give her mouth-to-mouth and . . .

Her chest bucked, her throat swelled and she coughed up half the swimming pool.

I rocked back and looked up at the ceiling. I cried. I heard Brodie exhale with a pained groan of relief. I choked out Rachel's name and rolled her onto her side, patting and rubbing her back. She coughed and spat and gasped, curling up into a ball. I cleared her hair from her mouth. I stroked her face. She reached back and clenched my hand.

If I hadn't got her out of the water when I did . . . Well, I don't really want to think about that.

I knelt on the tiles, still holding her hand. Darkness faded in from the corners of my vision. My head dipped. My eyelids drooped.

I don't know how long I stayed there exactly. Long enough for Rachel to stop coughing and for her breathing to become less hoarse. Long enough for the questions to begin to swirl in my mind. Questions I didn't want to confront. Questions I knew I had to.

I thought about Brodie and the feelings he seemed to have for my wife. He hadn't called the police before coming here but he'd turned up with a gun in the middle of the night.

Why? What had he expected to find? And he'd shot a man. Cool and collected. As if it was something he'd done before.

The smaller man was dead, drifting and bobbing in the swimming pool. The bigger man was dead in the pantry. Maybe I should have felt bad about it but the truth is I didn't. They'd tried to kill my family. They'd terrorized us. I thought about the sick smile on the smaller man's face when he'd been drowning Rachel. The way he'd dashed my head against the side of the pool. The chemical stink of the bigger man's glove as he shut off my air. I still didn't know either of their names. I didn't know why they'd pursued my son to his death or why anyone could have wanted to kill Michael or Fiona. Rachel had said they'd come for us tonight to prevent the truth getting out. But I still wondered if there was more to it than that.

Who had been sitting behind Michael in my car? What was their connection to the smaller man and the bigger man?

I suspected Rachel and Brodie knew at least some of the answers to those questions and others besides. I was going to have to insist they told me. But first, I needed to race into the woods and find Holly. I wanted to tell her she was safe, wrap her in my arms and never let her go.

'Tom?'

Rachel pushed up on her elbow and leaned towards me. She put her hand on my chest and rested her forehead against mine. Her dark eyes searched me for something – some kind of understanding or forgiveness I wasn't sure I was ready to give. That could come later. Maybe. I hoped.

From across the room I heard Brodie grunt and grimace. We both turned and looked towards him. The tender spot on the back of my skull throbbed and bulged. The room slid in and out of focus. Brodie was pushing himself up with his back against the wall, his legs splayed, blood trickling across the tiles beneath his left calf. His face was bruised and weeping.

'You saved us,' I told him.

He stared back, but not at me. His attention was focused solely on Rachel. That strange energy again. The yearning in his eyes. He panted hard, grimaced, then something in his face began to break, as if he might weep, and he shook his head, like a wordless apology.

For what?

A hand touched my cheek. Rachel was pulling me back to look at her again. I fell into her eyes.

'I thought I'd lost you,' I whispered.

'You did. But only for a little while. And I'm not just talking about tonight.'

I felt the love spread all the way through my chest. I lifted my hand to the back of her neck. She closed her eyes. A tear rolled down her cheek. I pulled her towards me. Her lips parted. I loved her. I loved her so much.

But we didn't quite kiss.

Before our lips touched, we both startled and broke apart.

From somewhere out in the woods, a sharp bang echoed.

It sounded like the roar of a shotgun blast.

50

I sprang to my feet. The room teetered and swayed. The shattering bang repeated in my head. It seemed to get louder, brasher, more terrifying. The pain at the back of my head bulged and swelled but I didn't care about that right now. I thought about Holly and the gunshot and my throat closed up as my mind shut down.

I wanted to run out into the woods but I was so very afraid of what we'd find. Two men had come for us. Two men had hunted us. Both were now dead.

What was going on?

'Did you see anybody else out there?'

'No,' Rachel told me.

Her dark eyes were blank. Horrified. When she got to her feet, it was like she was collapsing at the same time.

'Brodie?'

He didn't respond to begin with. He was too busy staring at Rachel, slack-jawed and beaten up. He tried to push himself to his feet. His elbows shook wildly. Then he groaned and his arms gave out and he slid back down.

'Brodie! Listen to me. Did you see anyone else?'

'No.' He snapped out of it. 'No one.'

Rachel turned from him to stare out at the woods. I

watched her. She looked like she was staring into the darkest folds of her heart.

'I'm going to find her,' I said.

'I'm coming with you.'

'No.'

Rachel had almost drowned. I wasn't sure she had enough strength to cross the room let alone help me to find Holly.

'I'm coming,' she said again, sterner now, beginning to push her way past me.

'Wait!' Brodie yelled.

He flopped to one side and stretched for his pistol with a mighty groan. His fingers brushed the barrel. He stretched even further, then gathered the gun in to his stomach and bared his teeth as he pressed a recessed button on the side of the grip. A magazine dropped out into his lap. He reached inside his fleece for a replacement and slapped it into the butt with his palm, then beckoned Rachel towards him.

When she was close enough, he pressed the gun into her hands, clasping her fingers over it. She tried to turn away from him. He clung on.

'Nine rounds,' he told her. 'You just point and shoot. OK?'

She looked down at the gun without speaking.

'Rachel. You can do this.'

Enough. We didn't have time. I rushed over and pulled her away from him, snatching the gun for myself.

'Hey, Tom, don't—'

'Come *on*, Rachel.'

She tripped and stooped low as I yanked her after me, grabbing up her hiking boots from where she'd kicked them off before diving into the pool. She stopped briefly to pull them on and I picked my way between the broken glass onto the deck.

The wind scoured against us. The sea clashed and raged. The saturated white plastic suit I had on clung to my body like I'd been shrink-wrapped. I tore it from me in strips, then turned and looked all around, listening for anything. For Holly. Some noise.

Rachel peered into the dark. Her face was pinched and urgent. She wouldn't look at me right now.

'Did the gunshot come from the stargazing pod, do you think?'

'I'm not sure,' I told her.

I closed my eyes and tried to tune in to the trace of the bang that still lingered in my mind. I was shaking all over. I couldn't be certain where the sound had originated from. And I didn't want for us to run off in the wrong direction.

So I took a chance. I squared my shoulders and I yelled Holly's name.

Nothing.

Just wind and waves. Just silence. It seemed such a sad and ominous thing, shouting my daughter's name into the void.

I shouted again.

The woods swallowed my words.

I was wracked with fear. It crackled through me. Rachel bent at the waist and covered her mouth with both hands like she might retch. I'd seen her do that before – when we'd gone together to view Michael's body. Even after everything we'd been told. Even knowing our son was dead. I don't think either of us had truly believed it. There'd still been that ridiculous, faint hope that maybe there'd been a mistake. Maybe it wasn't Michael. But of course that hadn't happened. We'd looked down at our son and it had been real. And Rachel had covered her mouth just like this.

Please, God, we'd lost one child already.

'I don't know where she is.' Rachel sagged at my side.

I grabbed for her and held her up, staring into the trees. I felt helpless. Lost. Unsure what to do.

Then a deep, bass *woof* exploded through the night and Buster broke out from the woods to the south. He bounded, lopsided, towards us, his tongue hanging out.

My heart burst. The moment he saw us, Buster skidded to a halt, his claws scrabbling for grip on the decking. He wheeled around and barked some more, looking back over his shoulder as he raced again for the trees.

We sprinted after him. I didn't know whether to hope or not. It seemed like too big a risk. Because, maybe, if I prepared myself for the worst. If I braced myself for it . . .

No, there could be no shielding myself from this.

All we could do was run into the inky black. The forest floor was dense and spiky under my stockinged feet. My soaked clothes clung to my skin. I held on to Rachel and dragged her along beside me. Sometimes Buster was visible in faint splashes of moonlight. Mostly we tracked him by sound.

To the pod.

It stood alone and quiet by the raging coast. The trees overhead teetered and groaned. The pod's silvered surface shone darkly. I shivered in the cold.

Buster was silhouetted on a massive boulder close to the shoreline, standing bow-legged and quivering.

'All right, boy. All right.'

We scrambled over the rocks towards him, into the streaking wind. The pod wouldn't give up its secrets to us from the outside. The mirrored surface meant there was no way to see in. The raging sea clawed and pawed at the slipway, and I thought, with a deeper judder, of how Holly had fallen in earlier.

'If anything has happened to her . . .' Rachel tugged on the sleeve of my coat, biting her lip. 'I'll never forgive myself, Tom. I'm sorry. I'm so, so sorry. For everything. I just want her to be safe.'

I stared at her, feeling my insides contract.

'It's OK,' I told her. 'We have the gun. It's going to be OK, Rachel.'

Buster bumped the back of my calf, nudging me on.

'All right, Buster. We're going.'

We clambered down onto the flooded slipway. Waves rushed in. The black water rose over our knees and slapped and echoed against the dank concrete foundations of the pod.

'Look.'

I followed Rachel's finger to where the timber door was hanging wildly askew. A crater of brickwork had been blown into the wall next to the latch. A splintered chunk of the door was missing.

From a shotgun blast?

My mind raced. We'd only heard one shot. Had this been it?

Light spilled out from beyond the door. I aimed the pistol ahead of me, my arm jolting and drifting. We ventured in.

A sleek timber staircase wound around tightly to the right. I looked up, leading with the gun. The staircase was narrow and steep. There was more light spill from a doorway at the top. No sound. No movement. No sign of Holly. Just the soft yellow light and a creeping fear that whispered in my ear: *She's dead. You've lost her.*

I climbed. The barrel of the pistol bounced and swayed. Sweat greased my palm. Rachel followed, her hand on my shoulder, her breath on my neck.

Please let her be alive. I'll do anything if she's alive. I don't think I can cope if . . .

One quick step took me in through the doorway. The world opened up overhead. The pod was walled in one-way glass. Mirrored on the outside. Clear on the inside. The effect was disabling, like walking out onto a ledge in the sky. On a starry night it would be spectacular. Like floating through space. Right now, with the storm clouds gathered low overhead, the effect was more oppressive.

'Don't move.'

The voice came from behind me.

Rachel bumped into my back.

'I said, *don't move*.'

Fear scattered across my body. The voice was male. Tight with stress.

Something metallic and solid had been rammed under my jaw, forcing my head up at a crunching angle. The muzzle of a shotgun, I thought.

'Tom?' Rachel whined.

'Shut up,' the voice barked. 'You. Hold that gun out. Slowly.'

My bones turned to lead. I swallowed awkwardly against the obstruction in my throat and did exactly as the voice told me, but it seemed to take all my strength to lift my arm.

'And *you.*' Rachel stumbled past me, almost falling to the ground. The man must have pushed her. 'Take it from him. Go over to that window. Throw it outside.'

Rachel hesitated.

'Mum, please, just do what he says.'

Holly.

Relief quivered through me. I tried to turn to her. But the man used the shotgun muzzle to lever my chin even higher. My neck strained. I went up on my toes in an attempt to ease the pain. It was horrible. I wanted so badly to see that Holly was OK.

'Listen to your daughter,' the man said. 'Open the window. Throw the gun out. Do it now. I won't tell you again.'

Rachel's jaw trembled as she reached for the gun. She took it from me with a look of pinched apology and crossed to a slanted, glazed panel with an aluminium bar at the bottom. There was a telescope on a tripod close by. Rachel pressed down on the bar and opened the window. Black sea glittered beneath.

A flick of her hand and the gun was gone. I heard a faint splash. It seemed to ripple inside my stomach.

'Turn around,' the voice said.

Rachel swivelled and stared. A shudder passed through her. Then her eyes jinked to her left, my right, and I could tell from the sudden softening of her face and the tears that brimmed over in her eyes that she was looking at Holly.

Then her pupils flickered once more. Her gaze darted on around the room. And something changed. A sudden, dire confusion twisted her brow.

I felt a jolt of panic.

What's wrong? What's she seen?

'Take a seat,' the man growled.

Rachel didn't move. She just stared.

'I said, *Take a seat.*'

'Mum, seriously. Listen to him.'

The man drove the shotgun even harder into my throat. I gargled and scrabbled against the glass. Finally, Rachel got the message and edged forwards.

'Now you,' he said. 'Turn around.'

51

The panels of one-way glass shone with a dim lustre as I swivelled, stiff-necked, with my arms up in a position of surrender. The muzzle of the shotgun slid around to nestle at the base of my skull. I wobbled. The horizon see-sawed in front of me.

A new segment of room and sky swung into view. The moonlit sea swamped the coast. The trees thrashed outside. Then I saw Holly and something collapsed inside of me. It was a struggle to stay upright and hold it together. She was sitting on an old velour sofa, hugging her knees to her chest. There were tear tracks on her face.

Rachel lowered herself in stages into the seat next to her. She reached for Holly's hand but Holly shirked away. I saw Rachel flinch and readjust. Holly's reaction had stung her.

'Move.'

The shotgun prodded into me, forcing me to bend at the waist. But not before I'd spied the bank of monitors fitted into the space behind the sofa. My heart flipped over. They looked just like the monitors inside the wine cellar. With one difference. These monitors were working.

Eight bright, flickering screens. Eight fuzzy images from inside and outside the lodge. A slanted desktop was fitted beneath them with a set of controls embedded in it. The controls featured dials and sliders that reminded me of the kind of set-up a film editor might use.

What the hell?

I stared at the monitors, light bouncing back off the glass. One screen showed an angle on the swimming pool shot from above the sauna. I could see the dead man floating in the water and Brodie sitting propped against the wall. Another monitor featured a wide shot of the main living area, empty apart from the plastic sheeting and the sports holdalls. The camera in the kitchen showed the broken window above the sink and the open door to the pantry. It wasn't possible to see the bigger man's corpse. An icy shiver gushed down my spine. Had Rachel made a mistake? Had he survived? Was he holding the shotgun on me now?

My stomach cramped. I tried to keep the fear at bay and focus on what I was seeing but it was difficult to wrap my head around. Other monitors showed the interior of the wine cellar and Rachel's bedroom. Outside, there was an infrared shot of the gravel yard with Brodie's abandoned Land Cruiser in it, one door open at the rear, and the carport with our Volvo slumped low. Lastly, there was a shot from among the trees aimed up the driveway towards the closed gates and the fence.

It was unnerving. Chilling.

'Hello, Tom.'

That voice. A different voice.

A sickening, spiralling confusion swamped my brain.

'Lionel?'

I whirled sideways, feeling as if the ground was rushing up to meet me.

It couldn't be.

But it was.

He raised his hand to a nasty bruise by his temple and winced. He was sitting on a single bed at the far side of the room. He had on a rumpled flannel shirt, worn corduroy trousers, thick woollen socks and hiking boots. His grey hair was tufted up at one side, his face glazed in sweat. There was an angry red welt and a wet gash on the cheek below his left eye.

He was supposed to be in London. He wasn't meant to be . . . How had he . . . ?

'What the hell are you doing here?'

'I came to help you, Tom. I heard the gunshot. I got here just as Holly—'

'It's true, Dad. He did. He tried to sneak in after us.'

'No talking,' the voice behind me growled.

I felt the hairs stand up on the back of my neck. When had Lionel arrived at the lodge? How long had he been here?

I couldn't breathe. Couldn't think.

Lionel held my gaze with sorrowful green eyes. He framed a look of pained apology and pressed his palms tight together, like he was begging me for a chance to explain.

My boss. My mentor.

I felt the rage start deep inside me and begin to spread. All the secrets. All the lies. They might have begun with Rachel but Lionel had been a massive part of it. This was his lodge. He was the one who'd approached Rachel offering help without involving me in any of this. He was the one who'd hired Brodie to dig into the circumstances surrounding Michael's death. Who'd spent a weekend here with Rachel.

Who'd lied to me directly or by omission. Who'd talked about saving my family just as he'd set us down this bloody path.

And now this.

I'd dedicated six years of my working life to him. I'd shared my grief about Michael with him, my worries about Rachel. Just how misguided had that been?

On a small side table next to the bed was a silver picture frame. The photograph inside was a replica of the shot of Jennifer that I'd seen on the dais at the charity function.

A fierce whistling started up in my head as I glanced again at the monitors, trying to piece it all together. Then I remembered something Brodie had said about the pod when I'd mentioned it to him on the phone.

On a clear night you can see pretty much everything from in there.

Had it been a sick joke? A taunt? Was Lionel some kind of twisted voyeur who liked watching his guests at the lodge? Was all of this some horribly depraved stunt?

No. One look at Lionel's slumped pose and the livid welt on his face told me that couldn't be it.

'Sit down.'

A sharp jab from the shotgun and I twisted and collapsed onto the sofa next to Holly.

My head pounded like I had a migraine. I felt sick.

The gates. The security fence. The cameras.

What *was* this place? What had Rachel done? Why was Lionel here now? And who was the man with the shotgun?

Holly leaned into me, sniffing back tears. I slipped my arm around her and then, finally, I looked up at the tall, broad man towering over us.

I saw his blue rubber boots, his white jumpsuit, his bulk. But it wasn't until I saw his gloved hands that I understood our error. It *couldn't* have been the bigger man we'd seen hiking up the driveway towards the gate. The man who'd passed us had been carrying an industrial torch in one hand and the shotgun in the other. How could the bigger man have done that with two broken fingers? And how had he got back to the lodge so soon after Brodie had entered?

The answer was he hadn't.

Because there were never just two intruders. There were three.

Michael looks at himself in the dim light of the hallway mirror. He's aware that he's changing in this moment, transforming into someone other than the person he was before tonight. Someone who will do things the previous Michael wouldn't contemplate.

Like when this new Michael snatches open the little drawer in the hallway dresser and takes out the keys to his dad's car. The keys seem to have an added weight to them. An extra burden. Michael's hand doesn't shake but the air feels hot and scratchy in his lungs.

He lets the keys dangle from his fingers as he looks up slowly into the glass. For a harrowing second, it's as if he's staring at a ghost.

52

The sofa opened up beneath me. I felt like I was tumbling back, sinking down. The man was dressed exactly like the other two, right down to the hood over his head and the paper mask. If anything, he looked even taller now than the bigger man – though perhaps that was just the sensation of him standing over me. I locked on to his angry eyes and held them. I wanted to show courage for Holly and Rachel. But inside I could feel myself shrinking back.

'Why are you doing this to us? Why target my family this way?'

He snorted from behind his mask.

'He doesn't know,' Lionel told him.

I stilled. 'Know what?' I asked, but even as I said it, I felt a slippery unease creep under my skin.

The man peered at me before glancing at Lionel. 'Show him.'

Lionel didn't move.

'Show him now or I'll hit you again.'

The man feigned a step forwards, raising the shotgun like a club, and I watched as Lionel recoiled, turning his back, then got up slowly, shame-faced, not meeting my stare. He wavered a moment before crossing to the controls for the monitors and punching a button.

'Take a look for yourself,' the man told me.

Something in his voice warned me I wouldn't like what I was about to see. I was aware of Holly and Rachel twisting around beside me, but I waited for Lionel to move back and look at me instead. He shook his head slowly, and when he lifted his face there was a wet glimmer of regret in his eyes.

'Who is that?' Holly asked.

My skin prickled. It wasn't her question so much as the tremor in her voice that finally made me turn and stare.

The images on the monitors had changed. They were screening different angles on different rooms and exterior views, cycling between them on regular intervals. There had to be many more than eight cameras fitted around the lodge.

The image Holly was talking about was on the uppermost monitor at the far right. I squinted at it and felt a chasm open up inside my chest. The infrared picture was rendered in flickering shades of grey. The focus was blurred and the light reflecting off the monitor made it difficult to pick out details. But I could see enough to tell it was an interior view of a room I hadn't seen before. There was no furniture. The floor appeared to be bare cement. The walls were unadorned.

Like a cell.

I stopped breathing.

The chasm inside me began filling with an icy trickle. In the foreground of the image was a paler blob. Someone was huddled face down on the floor in a dark tracksuit and pale socks.

They appeared to be asleep.

Or drugged.

Or worse.

I squeezed my eyes tight shut. The icy liquid rose up in my lungs. I could feel a terrible chill as I exhaled. And I knew in that moment – right there and then – that we'd crossed an invisible threshold. Whatever this was – whatever it had been – I understood instinctively that it had just become something far worse.

We have to get out of here. We have to get away. Somehow. We have to . . .

'They weren't supposed to be here yet!' Rachel spun towards Lionel and stood up. 'This wasn't the plan! I didn't agree to this.'

The crack in Rachel's voice lodged like a splinter in my heart. I spun to face her, dread knocking against my ribs. *I didn't agree to this.*

Oh God. What *had* she agreed to?

'I know that, Rachel,' Lionel told her. 'Don't you think I don't know that?'

'You told me you'd wait for my go-ahead. You promised me you'd let me talk with Tom first.'

There's something I have to talk to you about. Something important.

Oh Christ, no, please, no, not this. She couldn't have. Could she?

'Mum? Who is it? You have to tell us!'

But Rachel didn't answer. She just dug her fingers into her soaked sweater and tugged on the fabric, tears springing from her eyes.

And I didn't think I needed her to answer now anyway. I had an awful feeling I understood.

There'd been one man in the car with Michael and Fiona. The one with the gun.

There'd been three men following in the car behind.

Four men in total.

Two of the men were dead inside the lodge. One of them was holding a shotgun on us. My guess was the fourth man was inside the secret room.

The fence. The gate. The isolated lodge.

They weren't supposed to be here yet. This wasn't the plan.

Oh no, no, no, no . . .

The icy liquid bubbled up into my throat until it felt like I was drowning on the inside. I stared at Rachel, but all she could do was shake her head and drop onto the sofa with her face in her hands. When I turned to Lionel, the truth was plainer to see. He closed his eyes as if in pain and nodded slowly.

They say money can't buy you happiness. Speaking as a bereaved parent, I can tell you that's true. All the money in the world could never compensate for the pain of losing Michael. But the time I'd spent in Lionel's company had taught me something else: a rich man can get most things he wants, any way he wants, any time.

You know who we want.

That was what the smaller man had said to Brodie when he was tied to the chair.

At the time, I'd assumed he was talking about Rachel, about us, but I realized now – with a slow, choking dread – that I'd been wrong.

53

Rachel believed the men had come here to stop her from investigating Michael's death, and maybe that was part of it. But it wasn't their only reason. They'd also come because of the man held captive in that room.

My head spun. I thought again about the questions the smaller man and the bigger man had asked Brodie. They'd wanted to know how to get into the wine cellar. *Because they'd believed this man was locked inside with us. They'd wanted to free him.* But when Brodie had told them there was no way of getting into the cellar, the smaller man had been prepared to burn everyone on the other side of the steel door. And the bigger man had been willing to go along with that. Reluctant, but willing.

Why? Why try to rescue someone you were prepared to let die?

My eyes slid to the framed photograph of Jennifer. I felt another jolt. The man who'd murdered her had escaped unpunished. According to Rachel, Lionel hadn't wanted us to suffer the same fate.

They weren't supposed to be here yet.

So, what exactly? Rachel, Lionel and Brodie had discussed a plan to abduct the man and hold him captive here? Why?

So they could make him own up to his role in Michael's death? Record his confession on the camera in the secret room?

The idea made me feel physically sick but I supposed it was possible. Outlandish? Yes. Wildly irresponsible and dangerous? Undoubtedly. But possible, and the smaller man and the bigger man must have thought so too. Perhaps that's why they'd been willing to let him die. Maybe they'd wanted their secret contained here, whatever it took.

I didn't know how to feel about what I'd seen on the monitor. Disgusted? Appalled? Or something else? Was there a tiny part of me – a part I didn't want to recognize right now – that might have wanted ten minutes alone in a room with that man?

And what about Rachel? What had she wanted from this? She was a mess next to me, clawing at her hair. It hurt me to see it. One look at her could trigger so many memories. The way she used to curl up in front of the TV under a blanket on Sunday evenings. The way she'd comb the tangles out of Holly's hair after a bath. The smell of her skin when I kissed the freckles on her neck. And now . . . *this.*

The man in the coveralls jerked his shotgun towards Lionel, snapping me out of my thoughts.

'I'm going to need you to take me to that room now.'

'You know I can't do that.'

'I could shoot you.'

'You could.' Lionel nodded and gazed up at him. Lionel wasn't a short man, but he appeared slight in comparison. 'But then how would you find it?'

My body went cold. Rachel lowered her hands from her face and looked up.

'Lionel,' I pleaded. 'Just tell him what he wants to know.'

'I can't, Tom. Don't you see? I'm trying to protect you. All of you. You have to believe me when I tell you I have your family's best interests at heart here. I know that may be a hard thing to accept right now, but it's true.' He didn't look at me as he spoke. His attention remained on the man with the shotgun, like a referee studying a wrestler in the middle of a bout.

'Here's what I think,' he said to him. 'If you really wanted to shoot me, you would have done it already. You could have shot Holly out in those woods. But you didn't, and I bet if I played back the footage from all these cameras we'd see that you spent most of your time outside the lodge. I'm not sure you want any part of this. I wonder if you ever did.'

I thought about that. If my thinking so far was right – if the man with the shotgun was one of the men from the silver Vauxhall that had followed Michael and Fiona – then he *had* to be the one who'd been sitting in the rear. In the image taken from the speed camera, only his shoulder and upper arm had been visible because he'd been leaning back from the men in front. He hadn't been crouching forwards between the two front seats. He hadn't been talking with them. He hadn't been *participating.* And, unlike the man who'd been in my car with Michael and Fiona, he hadn't held a gun on my son.

So maybe – *maybe* – Lionel was on to something. Maybe the man was just a reluctant player in all this.

'For what it's worth,' Lionel told him, 'I didn't want to be here tonight, either. Things have spun . . . out of control. But together we can resolve this mess. These are good people.

You know the trauma they've been through as a family. Holly here is just thirteen years old.'

The man watched Lionel carefully, like he was considering his words and trying to spot the hidden trap that lurked within them.

'Tom,' Lionel said, from the corner of his mouth. 'I think it's probably time I gave you some answers. And perhaps I should begin by introducing our guest here. Though, of course, the two of you have met before.'

54

***Met before?* I felt a rush of fear and confusion as I stared** at the man in the coveralls. I strained to form some kind of picture in my mind. All I could see were his eyes, eyebrows and cheeks as he loomed over us. It wasn't enough.

'You don't think I know who you are?' Lionel asked him, shaking his head. 'Who all of you are? Or, in the case of your two friends, perhaps I should say *were*.'

The man stiffened at the shift in Lionel's tone. He took a step towards him, crowding him, like he'd finally felt that hidden trap begin to snap closed.

'Lionel,' I warned.

I didn't know why he was pressing the man's buttons like this. It was almost like he was being deliberately antagonistic all of a sudden.

Almost deliberately . . .

Tingles of unease streaked up and down my arms and legs. I glanced past Holly towards Rachel. She was inching forwards on the sofa, one leg twisted at the knee, a look of tense anticipation on her face.

Oh, hell.

'You know,' the man said to Lionel, 'you're really beginning to—'

I moved before Rachel could, launching myself off the sofa as the man took another step forwards.

'Dad, no!' Holly screamed.

The man swivelled. I panicked. I had no kind of plan. But I was committed now and I made a grab for his shotgun, clamping both hands on the barrel. I felt like I was looking up at a giant. My heart thumped in my chest. My palms were slick with sweat. I pushed up with the heels of my hands, shunting the gun crossways against the man's wide chest, trying to slam him back against the wall behind him.

He didn't budge.

Rachel got to her feet, watching us, taking little half-steps forwards and back.

'Tom, he's going to shoot!'

The panic in Rachel's voice was like a shrill alarm bell in my head. The man was so much bigger than me. It felt like I was trying to hold up a wall. I could feel his immense strength as he pushed down against me. My biceps burned. I tried another kind of ramming, shoving move, aiming to force the shotgun up towards his throat.

Didn't work. The shotgun didn't move.

Then a searing white flash of pain filled my head and the next thing I knew I was down on my backside on the ground. I must have blacked out for a half-second or so because it took me a moment to realize the man had headbutted me. The crunch reverberated through my skull. It felt like my forehead had split open.

I peered up, groggy now, my head throbbing. I could see two hazed men in white coveralls, two shotguns, two muzzles swinging my way.

Terror exploded in my chest.

I glimpsed a pink blur of movement. I heard Holly's frenzied scream.

'*Stop!*' the man yelled, and he turned with the shotgun, swinging it fast.

My vision snapped back into terrible focus. A judder of pure horror tore through me. Holly crashed to her knees, her hands in the air. The muzzle of the shotgun was pointed down at her chest. The man hadn't pulled the trigger. Yet.

'Don't shoot!' Rachel screamed. 'Oh my God, don't shoot!'

Time stopped.

Everything – my whole life – suspended in a moment.

Rachel looked down at Holly, pure black terror in her eyes. My body went numb. My heart simply ceased beating. Every detail became vivid and clear. The snag and catch of Holly's breathing. The soundless scream that was frozen on her lips. The way the shotgun was digging into her coat, pushing her backwards from her hips. The way the man's finger was tightening on the trigger.

Limitless space opened up between the seconds. It was a space where my deepest fears lived.

We think we have so much time in life. Time to make mistakes. Time to fix things that go wrong. But every so often it hits us – the worst things happen when we have no time at all.

I watched.

Paralysed.

My daughter didn't dare move.

'Baker,' Lionel said, his voice very tight. 'Wasn't that the name of the officer you impersonated?'

My vision seemed to warp and distort. My ears hummed at a disabling frequency.

Baker?

The man growled and shook his head, sighting down the barrel. His swollen knuckles bunched around the shotgun. Sweat coated his brow.

Holly was blinking her eyes over and over. Tears streaked down her face. Rachel tried to reach out to her, but when the man told her to stop and demanded again that we tell him where the secret room was, she stepped back, her face collapsing, clutching her hands to her mouth.

I looked between Holly and the man, the barrel of the shotgun connecting them in the worst possible way.

Baker.

Thoughts cascaded in my mind. I realized I'd mistaken the third intruder for the bigger man earlier because, well, he was big. Broad shoulders. Large hands. A thick neck. I thought of how imposing Baker had looked in his uniform in the hospital. Of how he'd seemed to tower over me. This man was the right size, right height, right weight.

And, thinking about it now, he'd only spoken to me at the hospital, not Rachel or Holly. He hadn't asked me to sign a statement. He hadn't suggested photographing Holly's injuries. He hadn't swabbed any of us for DNA.

Because he was never investigating the mugging. He already knew what had happened. He'd wanted to find out how much I *knew. He'd wanted to stop us from filing an official report.*

The smaller man had held a knife on Rachel in that alley. He'd punched Holly. And this man – whoever he was – had been sent in to clean the incident up.

It was grotesque. Appalling.

Then I thought of something else. The phone call from Baker I'd taken on speakerphone in the Volvo on our way here. *Is there anyone you know who might want to harm you or your family? Do you have any enemies?* Again, he'd been trying to gauge how much I knew. How much we, as a family, knew.

'Enough!' Rachel slashed her arms through the air. She shook her head frantically. 'That's enough. Stop this. I want you to stop pointing that gun at my daughter. I'll take you to the room. I'll show you where it is.'

55

We scaled the boulders at the side of the pod and stepped onto a patch of soaked grass next to the woods. Holly was in my arms, her face nestled in my shoulder. She was crying silently. My forehead ached. My thick ear burned. My back and arms were straining. But it was nothing compared to the cramping pain in my chest whenever I thought of that shotgun barrel being pressed into my daughter's body. It killed me that, no matter how tightly I held her, I couldn't stop her from shaking.

I'll take you to the room. I'll show you where it is.

It was like I'd feared. Rachel had known a lot more than she'd told us. How much more was there still to come?

Above the trees to the east, the sky was beginning to lighten from the full black of night to a watery grey dawn. The storm winds had faded but the early morning air was damp and chill. I shivered in my soaked clothes, feeling dazed and undone, like a stranger blundering around in my own skin.

Rachel stepped up next to me and reached out to Holly, but Holly pulled back again. I saw the hurt bloom in Rachel's eyes. I felt the ache in my heart. Rachel had been so focused on trying to redeem Michael. Maybe now, for the first time, she was starting to understand how much Holly had suffered because of it.

'Holly, please. I never wanted you to get hurt in any of this.'

Holly hid her face. Rachel looked at me bleakly. I didn't know what to say to her. Michael's death had broken her. I suppose I'd known that already, but I hadn't come anywhere close to appreciating quite how badly. I knew she was responsible for a lot of what had happened here tonight but the truth is I felt responsible too. Maybe if I had got her help at the beginning. If I'd been there . . .

'You're making a mistake, Rachel.'

Lionel was standing a short distance away from us, the breeze lifting his hair, the swelling to his temple beginning to yellow above the weeping cut below his eye. He hadn't looked at me directly since the man had held the shotgun on Holly and I hadn't been able to bring myself to approach him. Even thinking about it made me shake with rage.

'No,' Rachel muttered. 'My mistake was trusting you.'

'Not me,' he said, and shot her a loaded look.

I waited. Rachel held her ground for a few seconds, then stared down at her feet.

'I wanted you to do this,' Lionel told her. 'You know that. I don't deny it. But I was waiting for you to decide. Like you wanted.' He paused. 'Not everyone was so patient.'

Rachel slumped, like she was wilting, and I found myself thinking again of the way Brodie had looked at my wife. According to Rachel he'd been reporting back to her for months now, giving her hope, restoring her faith in Michael during the same period when I'd bailed on my family. I could see how that kind of commitment would be seductive to Rachel. And I could easily understand how Brodie might fall for my wife.

I've done things I wouldn't normally do. Things I regret.

Oh, Rachel.

The pounding in my head got worse. I could feel the bitter logic of it all hardening like a tumour in my brain.

Rachel had told me that Brodie had warned her the situation was escalating when we'd got here, but only he'd known how badly that was true.

'The moment I found out what had happened, I travelled up here immediately,' Lionel said. 'I got to Brodie's place late last night. You can't imagine how angry I was. I told him we had to come to the lodge right away. I wanted to see for myself. We had to let you know what he'd done. He didn't like it but I insisted. I got in his car and next thing I knew . . .' Lionel touched a hand to the bruising on his head. 'I think he panicked. He didn't want me to tell you anything before he could explain it himself. I came to on the back seat. Some loud bangs had woken me. At first, I was terrified by what Brodie might have done. I saw you and Holly sprint out of the trees. I didn't know what to do. Then I heard the blast over by the pod and, well . . .' He glanced at Holly. 'I got here as soon as I could. Not soon enough.'

'Shut it!' The man with the shotgun jumped off the boulders onto the soggy ground. 'All of you shut up and just tell me where we're going.'

Rachel considered Lionel through narrowed eyes.

'Don't do this,' Lionel warned her.

'The lodge,' she said quietly, turning to the man. 'I'll show you where when we get there.'

I felt a skittering across my spine. The lodge? Really?

'Adams,' Lionel said, lifting his chin. 'Your real name is Ross Patrick Adams.'

'Lionel.' I turned with Holly in my arms to try and shield her from what I was afraid might come next. 'What are you doing?'

The man swore and marched towards him, sighting down the barrel of his shotgun. Lionel tried to hold his ground but as the man advanced on him he began to stumble backwards, raising his hands in the air.

'You can threaten us,' Lionel said in a hurry. 'You can wear those coveralls. Hide your face in front of the cameras. Put gloves on your hands. *It doesn't matter.* Don't you understand? It's not just me who knows who you are. There are others. My investigator for one. He keeps detailed records. Lots of backups. It's called a contingency.'

'Bullshit.'

'Is it?' Lionel bumped up against a tree. He rose up on his toes, turning his face from the gun. 'Are you willing to take that chance?'

The man leaned over Lionel and shoved his jaw forwards, studying him intently. He didn't say anything for several long seconds. Then he reached up, pulled down his hood, removed his mask.

I gulped air. Lionel had been right. This *was* the man who'd introduced himself to me as Baker at the hospital. The man who'd reassured me there was nothing more I could have done in the alley. Even now – even after everything that had happened – I felt ill to have been so duped.

Ross Patrick Adams.

Lionel had said he knew everything about him but I still knew very little. Who was he? Who were the other men who had come here with him? Who was the man held captive in the bare, cell-like room?

What had drawn my son into their orbit?

My head hurt, and not just from the way Adams had butted me.

Over by Lionel, Adams scrubbed one gloved hand over his face, itching at the deep marks the mask had left in his skin. Lionel inched up the tree trunk, pressing his spine into the bark.

'You really don't know when to shut up, do you?'

'You should listen to me,' Lionel told him. 'Because you still have a choice here. You can leave right now. You should just go. Because if you kill us, I guarantee you your name will be made public. You'll have nowhere to hide. You came here to cover something up that can't be covered any longer. But with my help, your name can be left out of it.'

'Your help? Really?'

'I give you my word.'

Silence.

'You're full of crap.'

'I don't think you believe that. You still have time to listen to good advice.'

For the briefest second, I saw Adams falter, and I wondered: *is he actually considering it?* Could Lionel really talk us out of this mess?

But no, Adams shook his head, refitted his mask, pulled his hood up and pointed towards the woods with his gun.

'Move. All of you.'

Nobody budged so he lifted the shotgun and pumped the action. That awful *crunch-crack* again. It seemed to echo in the trees. Holly gasped and clung to me even tighter. Rachel shuddered and looked at me. She seemed desperate. Helpless.

'Come *on*,' I said to her roughly. 'We should just go.'

I turned and tramped forwards in my drenched socks, cradling Holly. After a few seconds, Rachel and Lionel fell into step behind us.

'Where's Buster?' Holly whispered, into my ear.

I shook my head. I'd been wondering the same thing, but I didn't know the answer to her question and I wasn't going to lie to her this time. He hadn't been outside when we'd come out of the pod. I thought maybe he'd run back to the lodge ahead of us. Or maybe he was wandering around, dazed and scared silly in the trees.

'Are we going to die?'

'No, Holly. We're not going to die.'

A lie? Maybe, because I had no way of knowing how things would turn out. But there was one thing I was aware of – something I was pretty sure everyone else had missed. Before we'd left the pod, I'd snatched one final look at the bank of monitors. The camera sequence had cycled back to the video from the swimming pool. It still featured the smaller man's body bobbing under the surface. But Brodie was no longer there.

56

I thought about a lot of things as we walked into those woods. I thought about Rachel and Brodie, and what he'd done for her and why. Then, when I felt the need to shy away from thinking about that, I thought about Holly and how much I loved her and wanted to protect her, and how sorry I was for all the ways we'd let her down. Rachel and I had been so focused on our own problems, on missing Michael. As parents we like to tell ourselves our kids always come first. But that hadn't been the case with Holly, and still she'd leaped up off that sofa to try to save me, even as, I feared, blood was seeping out of the puncture wound to her side. She'd had a shotgun pointed at her. She'd placed her life on the line for me.

It made me wonder again: what kind of father was I to deserve a child like that? What kind of husband? What kind of man?

My son was dead. I hadn't been there for Michael at the end and – perhaps even worse than that – I hadn't defended him afterwards. Rachel had been so sure Michael couldn't have done what he'd been accused of and she'd been right. Why hadn't I believed in him in that way? I knew my son as well as Rachel did. I knew that he loved playing Xbox, that he could do a backwards flip from a standing start, that he was failing geography but acing maths, that he never picked up his towel after a shower, that he was in love with Fiona, that he had dreams of taking a year out and travelling when his A levels were done. I knew all that and so much more, and deep in my heart I also knew that I should have believed in him and forgiven him, the same way Rachel had asked me to, the same way she instinctively had.

Rachel had gone so far – too far – to find out the truth about Michael's death and to give me back my love of my son. I thought about how much I missed him. How much I missed my family. And yes, I asked myself if we were going to die out here among these trees. If these were the last moments I would spend with Rachel and Holly. If these were the last sights, smells, feelings any of us would ever have. Because if the man whom Adams and his two partners had come here looking for was really imprisoned inside the lodge, then what was to stop Adams from killing us and going in search of him for himself? Or maybe he'd just shoot Rachel and Holly and me, then force Lionel to tell him the truth.

We entered the clearing with the remains of the campfire in it. I felt watched. And not just by Adams. Foolish, maybe, but in that moment I swear I could feel Michael's presence. It was almost as if he was here with us, and for those few brief seconds I almost let go of my fear. I don't know if I believe in heaven or God or any of those things. But I do know that I believed in Michael again and – as I stopped and inhaled the damp forest scent – a small part of me took solace from the thought that if this really was going to be it, then maybe, somehow, I would get to see him once more.

'What have you stopped for?' Adams shouted. 'Keep moving.'

I could hear the tension in his voice and I realized, with a sinking dread, that this was a moment of intense pressure for him. He was so close to getting what he'd come here for, even after two men had died. But if we were going to make a move, he had to know that our best chance would be in the dawn gloom under the trees.

I peered forwards, to where the lights blazing inside and outside the lodge were visible in fractured patterns through the pine needles and leaves. Was Brodie making his way to us, planning some kind of ambush? He'd saved our lives at least once tonight but he'd also knocked Lionel out, abducted the man in the secret room, drawn these men towards us like moths to a flame. How unpredictable was he? How far would he go?

'Holly, sweetheart, I'm going to need you to walk for a bit.'

I set her down gently. She swayed, then got her balance. Once she was steady, I undid her coat and quickly checked the dressing on her side. A film of blood was trapped under the plastic coating, thick and dark. It squirmed under my fingers. The gauze pad was soaked through but there was no real leakage. Maybe the bleeding had slowed or begun to clot.

'That hurts, Dad.'

'Sorry.'

I replaced her coat and took her hand, then turned and reached out for Rachel. She seemed surprised by my move. I think I was too. So much had gone wrong between us. I guess I was still trying to cling to what had always been right.

Lionel hung back by a metre or so, his tufted hair and unkempt appearance making him look bleary and hungover.

Adams crabbed round to our left. His coveralls flashed white in the dim morning light. I had a sudden urge to push Holly and Rachel away and yell at them to run as fast and as far as they could. Maybe I could dive back and tackle Adams more successfully this time. Block a shot. Do *something* – anything – to get them away from this.

'Start moving or I start shooting.'

Fear quivered at the base of my spine. Holly tugged on my hand. I resisted a second more, but there was no way out that I could see. I tramped after her, pulling on Rachel's hand in turn. I heard the crunch of Lionel's footfall. Then Adams's.

The trees began to shrink in around us, becoming densely clustered, tightly knotted. Soon, Rachel, Holly and I were forced to bunch close together to fit between them. We could have let go of each other's hands but I didn't want to, and I sensed that they didn't either.

'I love you,' I whispered.

They squeezed my hands. Holly snivelled. When I looked back at Rachel, her mouth fell open soundlessly and she shook her head, like there were no words for her to explain.

A tree with a wide trunk blocked our path. There were thick brambles to the left of it. Holly veered to the right, into a trench filled with knee-high ferns. In the middle of the trench, the trunk of a long-ago-toppled pine was lying slantways a few feet off the ground. Stunted branches poked out from it. A huge clod of earth and roots had been torn up at one end.

Holly paused, as if to turn back, but I jabbed her wrist forwards. *Keep going.*

She glanced back at me, uncertain. Her face was drawn, her pupils wildly dilated from behind the swelling around her eyes.

'It's OK,' I whispered, and even though I knew she didn't believe me and I could tell how scared she was, my heart still clenched when she nodded and hoisted her front leg over the log, as Rachel bumped into me from behind.

'What's the hold-up?' Adams called.

'There's a tree on the ground.'

I faced forwards and scanned the trees in the dewy gloom. Still no sign of Brodie. Was that a good thing or bad? I didn't know how far he could walk or how much blood he'd lost from the wound to his calf. Too much, maybe.

Holly lifted her second leg over the trunk and I tracked her move. Ahead and to our right was a thick screen of brambles and bushes. To our left was another undulating trench and more deep thickets of ferns. Diamonds of blue-white light shone through the trees from the lights around the lodge. Rachel straddled the tree after me, then Lionel.

We swished on through the ferns. I heard dark muttering from behind as Adams planted one foot on the trunk and jumped down to the other side.

An owl – I kid you not – hooted from somewhere far off in the trees. As its whooping call repeated and faded away, I heard a faint rustle of foliage from the thicket of brambles and bushes to our right. Was it a woodland animal responding to the call the owl had made? One of the hares Brodie had told me about, maybe? Or was it Brodie himself?

'What the—?'

I turned and looked past Lionel to see Adams suspended in mid-movement, his body locked in an unnatural pose. His elbows were high above him, the shotgun held sideways over his head, like he was wading waist-deep in a muggy bog and trying to keep the shotgun dry. He was leaning forwards from his hips with all his weight on his lead foot, his masked face twisted and turned, looking back at his trailing foot, which was a short distance up in the air, his toe pointed down.

I watched him yank his trailing leg forwards but it wouldn't come. Something was holding it back.

A snare.

It was looped around his ankle.

My heart seized. Was this our chance?

That sound in the foliage again. It was louder now. *Snapping* and *cracking*, off to our right. The foliage shook and swayed and—

'Nobody moves!' Adams yelled. 'Don't any of you move!'

—I heard two familiar yips as Buster tore through the brambles. His barks ricocheted around the tight woodland space. He bounded forwards in a chocolate-brown blur, jaws parted, teeth bared in a primal snarl.

Adams yanked on his trapped leg again. When it still wouldn't come he hopped round on his front foot to face Buster. He lowered his shotgun.

My body shut down. I went numb all over and stared as Holly screamed in terror and something heavy and dark buzzed by my face.

*

Like I told you before, Holly plays hockey on Saturday mornings. To watch her go sprinting across a field of AstroTurf is to see a warrior princess intent on scalping a sworn enemy.

She'd picked up a branch and swung it hard at Adams's temple with an explosion of bark. He teetered backwards. A brilliant white flash stung my eyes. The shotgun boomed. Branches shattered above our heads. Adams fell backwards over the log as the shotgun sprang out of his hands and Buster slammed into his chest and spun away. The snare ripped clean out of the ground.

I still couldn't move. I just stared, gripped by horror as Adams lay still for a split-second, winded maybe, and Buster barked and growled in his face. Then Adams batted Buster away, twisted onto his knees, felt around for the shotgun.

Too late.

Lionel was ahead of him, leaping through the ferns like a much younger man. Adams saw it and scrambled to his feet. He turned and broke into a lurching run with one hand pressed to his head, the snare trailing from his ankle and Buster barking after him.

Lionel kicked and fumbled around in the tall ferns, turning in circles. Adams flitted away between the trees.

Then Brodie hobbled out through a tangle of brambles and foliage, using a branch as a crutch. There was a pistol in his hand. He aimed it at Lionel's chest and motioned with it until Lionel backed up and Brodie was able to duck awkwardly for the shotgun.

'Well, you can bloody well stop pointing that thing at me,' Lionel told him. 'Tom, Rachel, Holly, why don't we go back to the lodge?'

Michael is playing FIFA on his Xbox when his phone buzzes. His bedroom has grown dark around him. The TV flickers in the gloom.

He hits pause on his controller. It's been half an hour now since Mum and Holly went out. He remembers Mum shouted something about a pizza that was ready for him to put in the oven. When he grabs up his phone he sees that Fi has sent him a message on Snapchat.

Fiona: Hi?

Michael: Hey.

Fiona: Something has happened.

Fiona: Something bad.

Michael: U OK?

Fiona: No. I'm in trouble.

Fiona: Seriously. You have to help me.

Michael: Where are u? What's happening?

Fiona: The car park.

Fiona: I'm hiding.

Michael: From what? I told you not to go there without me.

Michael: You promised.

There's no response for close to a minute. Michael sits there, cradling his phone, looking blindly at his football game frozen on screen. Around him all is darkness. The dark is inside his bedroom and outside on the street. As he waits, Michael has the creepy feeling that the darkness is sneaking inside his lungs.

He's seen people dealing in that car park. He knows there are homeless people who sleep there.

He should put on a light. Then he'll call her.

Fiona: Don't call me.

Michael: Why not?

Fiona: Because they're looking for me. They'll hear.

Michael: Who is looking for you?

Michael: What happened?

Michael: Seriously. R U OK?

Michael: Is this a joke?

Michael gets up from the floor. He paces the room. His heart flutters like a bird is trapped in his chest.

Fiona: I need you to come and get me.

Fiona: Please.

Michael: You know I'm not supposed to go out tonight.

Fiona: MICHAEL! I NEED YOU!

Michael scrubs his palm over his face. He's never known Fiona to lie or fool around. Not like this. Part of him wishes he had.

Michael: What about your parents?

Fiona: Are you kidding? Help me!

Fiona: Michael?

Michael: OK.

Michael: Let me get my bike out.

Fiona: No. You have to get here fast.

Fiona: Like now.

Fiona: Can you bring your dad's car?

Again, Michael looks up from his screen. He has a terrible feeling about this. What she's asking him is impossible. And yet . . .

Michael: Why are you hiding?

This time, the wait is longer. Michael is aware of a slow ticking in his blood.

Fiona: They killed someone.

Fiona: I saw them.

Michael: WHAT?

Fiona: They were crowding this man.

Fiona: They forced him off the roof. From the top level.

Michael: For real?

Fiona: Yes. I was taking photos of that car. I hid behind it when they came up.

Michael's heart thumps harder, like the bird is desperate to get out. He knows the car she's talking about. There's a waist-high brick wall on the top level of the car park, overlooking a three-storey drop to a parking level below. Two days ago, Fiona took photos of Michael running along that ledge and vaulting over an estate car that's been abandoned for weeks now.

Fiona: Please help me.

Fiona: PLEASE.

Michael: Call the police.

Fiona: No.

Michael: You have to.

Fiona: I can't.

Michael: Why not?

57

'You're telling me these men are *police detectives*?'

Everything around me stilled. *Police.* I'd thought of the men who'd come here tonight as thugs. As criminals.

My temples throbbed. I couldn't control the jitters in my hands. We were sitting around the glass dining table in the lodge. Lionel was facing me. Rachel was to my left, Holly to my right. Buster was on the floor by Holly's chair.

Brodie adjusted his position behind us. He was braced against the back of the nearest sofa, wincing as he eased the weight off his bloodied leg. The shotgun was resting next to him. The pistol was in his right hand. He'd used a tea towel to smear some of the blood from his face and chest. On the surface, at least, he was keeping watch for Adams, but there was no doubt in my mind he was also guarding us.

I watched as Lionel glared over at him again. They were monitoring each other furtively, but they seemed to have reached an unspoken truce. I didn't understand why quite yet, but I had a feeling I wouldn't like it when I did.

Holly gripped my leg under the table. She was frighteningly pale. Rachel had checked her vitals and her dressing. She'd told Holly everything looked fine, but I didn't know how worried we should be. Rachel had been reluctant to unpeel the dressing to take a closer look in case Holly's bleeding worsened.

Now Rachel was leaning forwards with her head in her hands. I thought again of that moment when she'd drawn me to one side in the woods. If she'd known these men were really police detectives, it probably explained her reluctance to call the police for help.

'DC Adams you know,' Lionel said carefully. 'DC Kenny is the one in the pantry. DS Nayler is the one in the pool.'

I felt my skin cool. 'So by coming here tonight . . . ?'

'They were acting out of pure self-interest. They didn't come in any official capacity. Not by a long way.'

Police. All three of them. I tried again to adjust to that. It still wouldn't stick. Based on what Rachel had told me, they'd hounded Michael to his death. They'd come here tonight to silence my family. The thought was sickening and disorientating, and it made me just about as angry as I'd ever been in my life. But at the same time, it did explain some things.

Such as why Rachel had gone along with Lionel's plan to let Brodie investigate what had really happened, because they'd probably convinced her it was the only sure way to prevent an ongoing cover-up. And that fit, didn't it? The images from the speed cameras had been half scrubbed from the public records, and I guessed that was something police detectives could be capable of.

Then there were the firearms the men had come here with. The tranquilizer gun they'd used on Buster. Even their disposable forensics suits. It was all equipment that could be available to police officers. It also explained how Adams had been able to get hold of a uniform to carry out his impersonation of PC Baker.

'They were part of a specialist drugs task force,' Lionel said. 'Their unit has secured a lot of high-profile arrests in recent years. Lots of success.'

Drugs. Police.

I was finding it difficult to breathe.

Was the secret room close to where we were sitting? Had the man inside it been held prisoner here the entire time we'd been in the lodge? I guessed so. Brodie must have brought him here before we'd arrived. Just the idea of it freaked me out. To think of him trapped on the other side of one of these walls . . .

I shuddered.

How powerful a figure did you have to be to have three police detectives prepared to do what these men had done tonight? Lionel had mentioned drugs. Had Adams, Kenny and Nayler been on the take? Was the man in that room some kind of crime lord or drug baron?

Then there was one more question – the one I knew I had to ask, even though it scared me the most.

'What was their connection to Michael?'

'Wait.'

Brodie levered himself up off the sofa with a grimace and hobbled over to the sliding glass door. He scanned the terrain outside. Goosebumps prickled across the back of my neck. I felt my breath shorten. Daylight was blooming over a green-grey sea.

'False alarm.' He shook his head and limped back to the

sofa, baring his teeth the entire time. 'He's unarmed. I don't think he'll be back.'

His one good eye was trained on Rachel as he talked, like he was willing her to look up at him. I think she knew that. She kept her head down.

Lionel cleared his throat. 'To answer your question, Tom, they were attempting to infiltrate a major east London drugs network.'

'Michael didn't have anything to do with drugs,' Holly said. Her voice was hoarse and scratchy, but she glared at Lionel without backing down. My fierce, brave girl. She knew as well as I did that we were no longer simply guests here, but she was still there for her brother. I felt a swell of pride. 'Neither did Fiona.'

Brodie spoke up. When he talked, I could hear a background wheeze that made me wonder how much internal damage he'd sustained. 'They didn't. The man in the car park was going to be the unit's way in to the network. They had plans for him to become a confidential informer. They'd been trying to cultivate him for some time. Completely off the books.'

The man in the car park who – according to the account Brodie and Lionel had laid out for us when we'd first settled around the dining table – had taken a three-storey dive to his death. I glanced at Rachel. She wouldn't look up at me either. That worried me. What else was she hiding?

'So what are you saying? He didn't want to talk?'

'You have to understand how this unit operated.' Brodie's dismissive tone suggested I didn't know the first thing about the world he inhabited. That I didn't know much of anything, really. 'They needed this man's help and they were prepared to do whatever it took to get it. They had a lot of evidence against him. If he refused to cooperate, they would have threatened to prosecute him. Then they would have told him word could get around that he was feeding them information for a reduced sentence. With the kind of professional drug gangs we're talking about here, it would have been as good as giving him a death sentence. He would have gone into custody with a price on his head. There would have been no safe space for him.'

'So he just jumped off the roof?'

'Or walked off it.'

I felt a sudden chill sweep inside the room.

'Fiona saw everything,' Rachel muttered.

And contacted Michael.

I closed my eyes as I thought about his phone call to me. The one I hadn't answered. Those few seconds of breathing on the line.

'Without Brodie we wouldn't have found out any of this, Tom.'

I ignored that. I wanted to know more about the man who'd fallen to his death. 'Who was he?'

'Does it matter?' Lionel asked.

My anger flared. 'Oh, I don't know, Lionel. Some low-life drug dealer jumps off a roof and our son is killed because of it. These men came here tonight because of it. So, yes, on balance, I'd say it's a pretty big deal.'

Lionel waited a beat. He hitched an eyebrow. 'Rachel?'

Finally, she lifted her face just a fraction. Her eyes were

red and trembling. She glanced from Lionel to Brodie, then back down again.

'Just . . . let's take them to the room. They should see for themselves.'

58

'Take a seat. All of you.'

Lionel gestured at the tiered seating in the cinema room as he stalked towards the big screen at the front. I wavered just inside the doorway, feeling as if a physical force was pushing me back. Holly squirmed by me and collapsed into a chair. She looked exhausted; her face speckled with sweat.

In any other circumstance, I would have insisted on her staying behind so she didn't have to bear witness to this. But I was afraid that Adams might try to sneak into the lodge, and although we'd told Buster to stay put and keep watch it was safer to keep Holly close.

Rachel shuffled into the room with her face down, looking dazed and anxious. Brodie followed her in. I'd heard him whispering harshly to her in the corridor, though I had no idea what had been said and wasn't sure I cared to know. He propped the shotgun against the doorway behind him and held the pistol in his right fist down by his thigh. My eyes wandered to the shotgun. There was no easy way of getting to it. Brodie flatted his back against the wall with a grunt, then tilted his head and considered me with a slight, dismissive smirk, as if my predicament right now was nothing more than I deserved.

'Not sitting, Tom?' Lionel asked.

'I'll stand.'

Lionel nodded, as if he understood completely. It maddened me. I didn't need or want Lionel's understanding or his compassion right now.

There was a remote control in his hand. He pressed a button on it and the wall sconces glowed dimly. Then he pressed another button and a low electric humming started up above our heads. Holly flinched and looked up, and I watched with a growing sense of dread as the cinema screen began to shuffle up into a recessed slot in the ceiling.

My knees flexed. Hidden behind the screen was a large panel of thickened glass with a greyish tint. Beyond it was deep gloom. Lionel rapped on the glass with his knuckle.

'Heavily reinforced. Fully soundproofed.'

My family had watched a film in here. They'd eaten snacks in here.

I swallowed against the rising surge of bile in my throat and tried to brace myself for what had to come next. Lionel was poised to press another button on the remote when Rachel blurted out, 'Wait!'

She turned to me, reaching for my hand. I hesitated a moment before taking it and allowing her to pull me to one side. I was aware of Brodie watching us. It was obvious he didn't like what he was seeing. I didn't care. Rachel lowered her eyes as she gathered her nerves, but when she finally looked up at me and saw my expression, her face fell. My heart fell with it.

Everything that has happened here tonight is because of how much I love you.

The strangest thing – maybe the hardest thing – was that I think Rachel really meant that.

'He was twenty-eight years old, Tom. He had a young daughter.' She tugged on my hand. 'It wasn't just his life on the line when he jumped off that roof. He didn't have a choice. These drug gangs don't mess around.' Rachel paused and looked off to her side. 'Brodie can tell you a lot more about that.'

I felt a deadening thud in my heart. It was another reminder that it was Brodie who'd found Rachel the answers nobody else could. It was Brodie who'd absolved our son. Whatever had happened here tonight, whatever he'd pushed us towards, I sensed that Rachel would always be grateful to him for that.

'He would have known they'd come for his daughter, Tom. He stepped off that roof to save her.'

I felt a heaviness in my chest. A father's overwhelming love for his child. That was something I could relate to. And look at Rachel. Look at what she'd gone along with out of love for our son.

I thought about what that man had done. Would I have been brave enough to do the same? Could I have coolly, calmly, stepped off a ledge to save Holly from harm?

'What was his name, Rachel?'

She hesitated.

'Just tell me.'

'James Finch,' she said quietly, barely a whisper.

I felt a cold tingling where our hands touched. That name. I could tell from the way she said it that it meant something to Rachel. That it should mean something to me.

I grappled in my mind, thinking back.

A spasm tore through me as I made the connection.

Rachel's speech at the gala function. James Finch had been the name of the repeat offender who'd committed suicide on the same day Michael had died. But Rachel must have known by then it wasn't a simple suicide. She'd known his death was connected to Michael's.

She looked up and watched me connect the dots. I saw the fear and the shame in her eyes.

'That wasn't just a speech you gave, was it?' I felt hollowed out, undone. 'Someone at that function knew the truth. Just like you knew the truth. It wasn't a speech. It was a taunt.'

She shook her head desperately. 'It was a test, Tom. Just a test. I was still trying to make up my mind. About all of this. About . . .'

'You told me you wanted this,' Brodie growled. 'You still do.'

She closed her eyes, as if stung. I stared at her, not quite believing what I was about to say.

'It triggered the mugging, didn't it? They came for us because you dropped that name. They came for us because you made it clear you knew.'

'*Mum*,' Holly whispered, and with that one word she communicated enough hurt and betrayal to make Rachel's legs go from under her.

'You have to believe me. I never imagined for one minute that any of this . . .'

She collapsed, sobbing, and I held her up, feeling the most enormous weight dragging down on my heart. My throat burned. Tears blurred my sight. I turned and looked over at

Lionel, feeling like I was drowning with no idea if he would throw me a rope or watch me sink.

He smiled thinly with that same infuriating look of compassion, then clicked another button on the remote.

Spotlights blazed into the space behind the glass.

The room was mostly bare. A metal toilet bowl with no seat was bolted to one wall. The cement floor angled and sloped towards a drainage grill in the middle. The walls were painted a shiny, white gloss.

My lungs stopped working. My heart banged against my ribs.

The figure on the floor woke with a start and immediately curled into a foetal position, then slowly looked up.

I'd made another mistake. Another crucial misunderstanding.

It was a woman.

59

She was hunched up and cowed, her eyes squinted against the fierce light in the room. I watched her peer towards the glass with a faraway gaze and felt the ground fall away beneath me. The short hair. The long limbs. The striking features.

'One-way glass,' Lionel said, though by now his words sounded oddly distorted to me. 'And yes, Tom. You've met before too.'

At the charity gala. Lionel had introduced us. Rachel hadn't been looking at me when she'd been standing on that dais making her speech, I now realized. Not exclusively. She'd also been looking at this woman.

In her dress uniform.

DCI Kate Ryan.

I felt winded and there was a sudden intense swarming noise inside my head, growing louder, more crazed.

The same thing must have been true of Brodie, I thought. He hadn't been looking at me or at Lionel from across that room. He'd been studying Ryan's reaction when Rachel dropped James Finch's name.

An enormous swell of suppressed rage expanded in my chest. Ryan had been the blurred figure sitting behind Michael and Fiona in the speed camera image of my car.

She'd held a gun on my son. She'd scared Michael so badly he'd driven into a tree. She hadn't pulled the trigger, but she may as well have. Without that, my son would still be here.

And yet, at the same time, I also knew that whatever this was, it wasn't right.

'This is so messed up,' Holly said.

I stared at Lionel, feeling an overwhelming sense of waste and despair. 'You can't force a confession out of someone like this and use it in court. You must know you can't.'

Tiny frown lines appeared on Lionel's forehead.

'Why do we need a confession, Tom? We have all the facts of the case. Who said anything about court?'

The swarming inside my head grew even fiercer as I stared at Ryan. A hero cop. A rising star of the Met. She placed her quaking hands flat against the glass and stared blankly out. Bewildered. Terrified.

'JFA, Tom,' Lionel said carefully. 'Did Rachel tell you I invited her to join the board in an executive capacity?'

I turned to look at Rachel again. She stumbled away from me, backing into the wall. My heart contracted.

'You know how the board is currently structured,' Lionel continued.

I did, even if I didn't want to think about it right now. There were eleven members on the board of Justice For All. Seven of them, if you included Lionel as chairman, were executive members. I knew this because I'd helped to draw up the governing documents for the charity. I'd handled the board minutes and other administrative work on a pro bono basis.

I also knew that, in practical terms, it was the seven executive members who took all the key operational decisions behind JFA. And they all had one thing in common that had led them to become involved in the first place. Each of them had been the victim of an unsolved crime. Some had suffered directly. For others, a family member had been harmed. Appalling rapes. Tragic hit and runs. Murder. Grievous assault. Stalking.

While the details of their own individual stories differed, they'd all experienced some of the anguish Lionel had known. It was a similar torment, I now knew, to the agony Rachel, Holly and I had experienced at the hands of Kate Ryan and her fellow officers. Then there was Brodie. Hadn't he been haunted by whatever unknown horror had been visited upon his sister?

'I take extreme care when I appoint any new executive director, Tom. There's a rigorous vetting process. To get a seat on the board I have to know that a candidate is suitably driven. That we share the same world view, I suppose.'

I snatched a breath. It felt like I was inhaling dry ice. What was that world view exactly? I was beginning to sense it wasn't simply that all seven existing directors had been victims of unsolved crimes. It had to be something more than that. And even more worrying, it was a world view that my wife – hurt and broken as she was – had apparently come to share.

Lionel raised the remote and clicked another button. Rachel startled and swung away from the wall. Behind where she'd been standing, a concealed panel had slid away to reveal a hidden recess.

I stared into it. I had the feeling I was staring into the darkest, most damaged corners of Lionel's mind.

You think Lionel needs therapy, much?

I'm just saying, after what happened to his wife . . .

I actually shivered. The bronzed gleam. The elegant lines. Inside the recess was a statuette of a dancing ballerina. I had an awful suspicion it was the lost Degas that had been stolen from Lionel's home on the night Jennifer was murdered.

Oh no. No. Not this. No.

It felt in that moment as if one door had slammed shut in my mind and another had flown open on to a yawning, black hole. I had the sensation I was toppling. That I was about to plummet so far and so fast that I'd never climb out again.

The remote location. The isolated room. The fences. The gate. Didn't that sound a lot like a prison?

Seven executive board members. Seven families let down by a justice system that had failed to punish those responsible for causing terrible harm.

The swarming in my head became a dizzying roar.

The room behind the glass wasn't a holding cell. And this was something far more sinister than a home theatre.

'Tony Bryant never made it to Spain, Tom. He was the first.'

I reached out to steady myself as the room around me began to dip and swirl.

Oh God, no. Please no.

This was a viewing gallery.

The secret room was an execution chamber.

60

I looked at Rachel. It felt as if someone had ripped out my heart. She was so fragile. So wretched. I wanted to go to her. I wanted to keep my distance. I didn't know what to do.

'Tell me you didn't agree to this,' I said. 'Please tell me you didn't.'

Tears spilled from her eyes. 'I wanted answers, Tom. I needed them. You did too, if you're honest.'

'Not like this I didn't.'

'You can't *say* that.' Her voice cracked. 'It's not like there was another option. I wanted to fix us.'

'By killing someone?'

'Maybe. I thought if I had all the pieces I could put us together again. As a family. Maybe this would give us closure.'

Closure.

I didn't say anything. I just shook my head and took a step back. I felt weightless. Untethered. Like I was having a strange, out-of-body experience.

'And it's not as if I'd made up my mind. I was still trying to decide. I wanted to talk to you about it. We were going to talk about it, remember?'

Halting sobs took hold of her then. Her shoulders trembled. She reached out a hand to me but I took another step back.

'She killed our son, Tom.'

I felt my throat close up. There it was. That part I got.

As I stood there, thinking of Michael, every dark vision of his death I'd ever had seemed to slam in at me at once. My car hurtling through the woods. The tree towering ahead of him. The fear he must have experienced. The pain I was afraid he'd felt.

Then other memories. Brighter flashes.

The first few seconds after Michael was born. That first night cradling him in my arms as a baby. The first time he crawled. First time he walked. Leading him by the hand to primary school. Playing cricket in the back garden. His laughter. His smile.

All of them moments Rachel and I had shared in one way or another.

I looked at her and felt my heart shatter. It just broke.

'He must have been so scared, don't you think? Michael must have been so scared.'

I shook my head again, feeling groggy. There was a pulsing ache deep inside of me, spreading out towards my fingers and toes. All my grief. All my anger. Closure was a false promise. I knew that. I knew it because I also knew that my grief over Michael would never end. Oh, it might ebb over the years. Perhaps it's true what people say and the pain would start to fade with time, though I was yet to experience that myself. But I knew it would always be there – a bottomless source – ready to engulf me at a moment's notice. And that would still be the case even if the truth of what had really happened to Michael and Fiona came out and was made public. It would be the case even if we killed Kate Ryan in cold blood and never told a soul.

I looked at her now, pressing her palms against the glass, the angst and the horror on her face so clear to see. That pulsing ache. It seemed to throb around me like a force field as I moved down the steps towards her.

Lionel moved aside. I reached out my hand towards Ryan's, searching her eyes for something. I don't know what exactly. Guilt? Regret? She looked back at me – through me, really. She didn't know I was there.

You killed my son.

The thought was too big. Too absurd.

'I know it's a shock, Tom.' Lionel actually touched my shoulder. 'And yes, Brodie was hasty. He rushed things. He reacted to the mugging on an emotional level. I think you know why. He shouldn't have done that. But we are where we are. And if you think about it – *really* think about it – I think you'll see this makes sense.'

I didn't speak. I just stared.

'You've trusted my judgement in the past, Tom. Why not now?'

Again, I didn't reply.

'You'll feel so much better afterwards, Tom. I did. You can't imagine how healing it is.'

My hand shot out before I was fully aware of it. I shoved Lionel against the glass. The panel barely moved. My hand was round his throat.

'Hey!' Brodie yelled. 'Hey. Stop that.'

I didn't stop. I squeezed.

'It's OK.' Lionel wheezed. He scrabbled at my hands. I didn't know if he was talking to me or to Brodie. 'Think of it as justice, Tom. For Michael.'

I cried out then. Couldn't help it. I didn't want to hear my son's name on Lionel's lips right now, but somehow his words sneaked inside my head. And as I found myself thinking about what he'd said about Michael, another memory crashed over me.

On one of the last days we'd spent together, a fortnight before Michael's death, I'd taken him into the office with me for the day. Michael was supposed to have organized a week's work experience for school but, like so often in the past, my slacker son hadn't got around to setting anything up. I'd stepped in at the last minute and told him he could spend the week at Webster Ventures. He could shadow me and some of my colleagues.

Michael didn't like it. I knew and understood that he'd be bored. But there was one moment during his first morning in my office when we'd seemed suddenly close and Michael had asked me why I'd become a lawyer and, for just a second, I'd thought about telling him the truth. That I'd had a good degree, that I was in love with his mother, that I'd wanted to marry her and spend the rest of my life with her and I'd thought a well-paying career would help us to build a future together. But instead I'd lied. I'd told him that old chestnut about being drawn into the law by a burning sense of justice. By wanting to help defend and define the difference between right and wrong. It was nonsense, of course. I think Michael knew that. I was a corporate commercial lawyer. My job, in its purest sense, was about making Lionel – who was already incredibly rich – even richer. But still I spun Michael that line and, even though I saw a flash of what might have been disappointment cross his face, he didn't challenge me on it.

And now here I was, my arm quivering as I crushed Lionel's throat, thinking about justice and vengeance, about what was right and what was wrong. Michael was dead. Our sixteen-year-old son had been ripped from us. His future had been stolen away from him by a woman who was just inches away from me and who Lionel was inviting me to kill.

And you know what? I can't deny the lure of it. Because based on the evidence I'd been shown and the explanations I'd been given, I believed Kate Ryan was responsible for my son's death. She'd destroyed my family, and for what? Career ambition? Her own desperation to hide a major mistake? A ruthless streak? I didn't know.

So, yes, part of me *was* tempted. A sanitized killing room in a lonely place, the opportunity to avenge my son without fear of being caught. Who wouldn't be tempted by that?

'How else were you going to get justice for Michael, Tom?' Lionel's voice was a choked whisper. 'Look at her. Think of what she's already done to cover this up and what more she could do. Michael was sixteen. She's a decorated police officer with the backing of senior officers. A media darling. And look at the men from her team who came here tonight. Look at what they were prepared to do to keep their secret.'

I did look at her then and, as she stared back at me, my own reflection in the tinted glass seemed to hover behind her, as if I too was confined in that room.

'They wouldn't have come here if Brodie hadn't kidnapped her.' My voice sounded far away, like it belonged to someone else.

'You may be right, Tom. But do you really believe you'd have been safe? You saw what happened to Holly in that alley. You must know by now that Rachel was fortunate to escape with her life.'

My mind flashed again on seeing Lionel talking with Rachel in the hospital afterwards. Had he made this argument to her then? It might have been Brodie who'd forced matters to a conclusion, but it was clear to me that Lionel believed this was the right conclusion to reach.

'*Tom?*'

It was Rachel. I could hear the shattered urgency in her voice, but I didn't turn to look at her. I didn't think I had the strength to face her just now.

'Tom, please. It's Holly.'

I released Lionel – he staggered backwards, gasping – and spun around, a huge weight of dread pressing down on my chest. I couldn't see Holly. Not at first. I bounded up the stairs towards where Rachel was leaning over her, feeling like I was running the wrong way up an escalator. Then I saw her. She was slumped and very pale, her eyes blank and roving.

'It really hurts now, Dad.'

'She's crashing,' Rachel told me. 'Her blood pressure's right down. Her pulse is thready.'

'What does that mean?'

'I think she's bleeding internally. Maybe she ripped something out there when—'

She didn't have to say it. I closed my eyes, thinking of

how Holly had grabbed the heavy branch and swung it at Adams. She'd saved us, but at what cost?

That weight in my chest again. My heart felt saturated. Every heartbeat hurt.

'We have to get her to a hospital,' Rachel said. 'We have to do it now.'

I lunged forwards to lift Holly in my arms. But before I could slip my hands under her, Brodie yelled at me to stop again.

My body went cold. I lifted my head slowly. He was pointing his gun at me.

'Nobody leaves. Not yet.' His hand didn't shake. His grip was rock solid. But his eyes flicked towards Lionel. 'You know I'm right. Don't pretend that you don't.'

The gun Brodie was holding on me seemed to get bigger with every passing second. You've heard that line about a gun muzzle opening up like a tunnel. Well, this was like staring down the deepest, darkest tunnel to the worst destination imaginable. And Lionel's voice, when he spoke, was like the shrill whistle of an oncoming train.

'I'm sorry, Tom, but Brodie has a point.'

I shook my head.

'This has to happen now. We don't have a choice. You can see that, can't you? You can understand what I'm saying. It's already gone too far.'

Lionel's words hit me like a series of body blows. Again, I felt myself teeter towards that black void. How many bodies were buried in these woods? How many people had been killed in this room?

Lionel had wanted me to recognize what the men who'd

come here had been prepared to do to protect their secret. But I didn't doubt that Lionel and Brodie would be equally ruthless in protecting theirs.

'It's simple, Tom. Kill her and you can go.'

With blood on our hands. With secrets to keep.

As I stared some more at Brodie's gun, his gaze wandered towards Rachel.

'You wanted this.' His face scrunched up, though this time I didn't believe it was from the pain in his leg. 'We talked about it. You know we did.'

I reached out slowly and squeezed Holly's hand. She cried. There wasn't enough air in the room. All I wanted was to lift her in my arms, get her to a hospital. I looked around me, searching for choices. I saw Brodie, blocking the door with the pistol in his hand. I saw Lionel, rubbing his throat and trying to act like any of this was reasonable. Then I saw Kate Ryan, pinned and very scared behind the glass.

'I'll do it,' Rachel whispered, and the tremors in her voice spread like dark ripples in my heart. 'I got us into this. It should be me who gets us out of it.'

61

The room was cold, like the wine cellar. Or maybe that was just me.

I edged in behind Rachel. Every step seemed to jar me. When I lifted my legs it felt like sandbags were tied to my ankles.

The air inside was stale with a back note of bleach and adrenalized sweat. The bright halogen lighting bounced off the cement floor and the mirrored glazing with a blazing shimmer. I squinted until my eyes adjusted. There were faint russet stains on the walls.

Oh God.

Ryan recognized us immediately. She took two fast steps forwards, then stopped and rocked back as Rachel straightened her arm. The gun Rachel was holding jumped in her hand like a fish. It was Brodie's pistol. He'd hobbled down the steps and passed it to her at the threshold of the room. The door to the room had been concealed behind another hidden panel. It was metal with an electronic keypad in the middle, like the cellar door.

Brodie was now halfway up the tiered steps again, watching over Holly, slumped on the ground with his back against the wall and his hand cradling his ribs. He was canted to one side and sweating like he had a fever. His face was torn and bruised, his beard greased and bloodied. I was sure he was in agony from his leg, not to mention his other injuries. He needed a hospital too.

Lionel watched us from the doorway. Brodie had tossed him the shotgun before he'd started down the steps. Any hope I might have had that Lionel would change his mind and let us go had evaporated when he'd trained the shotgun on us with an apologetic shrug as Brodie handed over his gun.

'This might be happening sooner than we planned, Tom, but I really believe it's for the best. We're all on the same side here.'

Except we weren't.

'Please,' Ryan begged. She crossed her arms in front of her and bowed at the waist. Her short hair was scuffed and kicked up on one side. Her tracksuit hung limply off her body. Her eyes were two sunken discs. 'I know who you are. And I understand now why I'm here. I do. And I'm sorry. Truly. But it was an accident. I promise you. We never meant for your son or his girlfriend to die. We just wanted to talk to them. They got scared. That was all. It was an accident.'

'That you covered up.'

The shakes in Rachel's voice were nothing compared to the shakes in her hand. Ryan took another step back towards the corner of the room. Her breath hitched when she bumped up against the wall and the mirrored glass.

'Please. I'll do anything. Say anything. I'll confess. I'll—'

She stopped talking as Rachel whined and jabbed at her with the gun.

I felt the air still in my lungs.

Rachel's elbow was locked now but, in the long, aching seconds that followed, the end of the pistol began to waver, like an invisible wire was tethered to it, tugging it down.

Ryan hunched up. Rachel clenched her teeth and groaned. She used her free hand to help support the pistol. It didn't seem to make much difference. The circles the muzzle were sketching in the air got bigger, wonkier, more out of control.

'Listen to me,' Ryan pleaded. 'You know who I am. You know there'll be people looking for me.'

It was the wrong thing to say. I think Ryan sensed that. Rachel's feet scuffed as she took a small step forwards. She angled the gun down. It wavered again, worse than before.

I caught our reflection in the mirrored glass. All I could see was the cold room we were in. The helpless woman cringing before us. Rachel, holding a gun. And me. I almost didn't recognize myself. Red-eyed. Crazed hair. An egg-shaped bruise on my brow. And a look of absolute dread on my face.

All the things I'd allowed to happen to my family. All the damage I'd allowed to be done. I hadn't protected them. I'd abandoned them. And now this. If Rachel pulled that trigger she'd have to live with the consequences for the rest of her life. I wasn't sure she was strong enough to handle them. So should I step up? Take the gun out of her hand? Was I brave enough to make that move, even as I knew it was the wrong thing to do?

And yes, Rachel had killed a man already tonight. But that man had been attacking me in the pantry. He would have suffocated me. Rachel had acted in the moment, in a hurry. This was different. Ryan was scared and helpless.

And Holly was watching.

'Mum!' Her croaky voice was like a siren in my head. 'Don't do this. Michael wouldn't want you to do this. You know he wouldn't.'

Rachel sobbed once and covered her mouth with her free hand. We had to protect Holly. We had to get her to a hospital. But, if Rachel pulled that trigger, I think we both knew that our daughter would never look at either of us the same way again.

Ryan glanced up, like she'd sensed the smallest chance. 'Listen to what she's telling you,' she pleaded. 'I'm a police detective, for God's sake. Don't you know what will happen to you?'

'Mum, please. I can't stand this. I can't.'

'Go ahead, Rachel,' Lionel said. His voice was soothing, calm. 'We'll handle everything once this is over. We know what to do.'

Rachel bared her teeth and hunched her shoulders against the quakes that were threatening to overwhelm her. When she glanced back at me quickly, she seemed to shrink.

'Please, Mum,' Holly was repeating, over and over. 'Please, Mum. Please, Mum. Please . . .'

My whole body ached. When I swallowed, it was like swallowing glass.

'It's OK, Rachel,' I said. 'I promise you, everything is going to be OK.'

Her face collapsed then. She tried so hard to hold her aim. She whined loudly and I saw her finger curl around the trigger. She closed her eyes.

I waited for time to slow down again. For everything to

stop. But that didn't happen. Everything sped up instead. The pounding of my heart. The breath in my lungs. The rushing of the air in the room. All of it building and building, getting faster and faster, the room spinning and swirling, my head swirling with it until . . .

'I'm so sorry, Tom.'

Rachel's knees went from under her and I reached out just in time to catch her before she crashed to the ground.

62

Ryan began to rise. I snatched the gun from Rachel and swung it towards her. My finger found the trigger. My heart flipped over in my chest. Ryan showed me her glistening palms and a desperate, begging expression.

Rachel cried. I pulled her close.

'It's OK,' I told her. 'Everything is going to be OK.'

'We have to get Holly to the hospital,' she whispered.

'We will.'

My finger ached. I was terrified of pulling the trigger by mistake. One little flinch would be all it took. I wanted so badly to fix this. I didn't know how.

Lionel edged into the room behind us, the shotgun at his hip.

'Tom?'

My hearing swirled. My blood pumped thick and sluggish through my veins. I glanced back at him over my shoulder. My boss. My friend. For such a long time I'd thought I could trust Lionel with anything. But I couldn't trust him with this.

Think. Find a way out of this room. Any way out of this room.

In my peripheral vision, Ryan crouched slightly forwards

on her front leg, her hands curled into loose fists, like she wanted to rush me. Rush Lionel.

I looked between them both as Lionel's gaze darted to the pistol in my hand. His eyes darkened. I don't think he was afraid I would shoot him. Not yet. I think he knew me well enough to see that I didn't want to shoot anyone. Not Lionel or Brodie. And not Kate Ryan.

Oh, I hated what she'd done. But killing her wouldn't bring Michael back. It wouldn't ease my grief, or Rachel's, or Holly's. An eye for an eye. There was a reason civilized societies had moved on from that idea. I thought about Michael and everything I'd learned about him during the night. My heart unfurled like a flower. He'd tried to help Fiona. He'd rescued her. So, no, there was no way I would allow this grubby killing room to be my son's legacy. He was worth so much more than that.

'Why don't you pass the gun to me, Tom?' Lionel said.

Very slowly, I lowered the pistol towards my lap. Ryan tracked my move, snatching a breath. She took a nervy half-step forwards into the room, then stopped and went dead still when Lionel swung the shotgun towards her.

'You don't want to do that,' he told her. 'I don't enjoy the mess a shotgun makes in here, but don't think for one minute it would be the first time.'

She pressed her lips tight together and shook her head over and over, like she was trying to deny the inevitable.

'Tom,' Lionel said again.

I looked at him. He blinked, smiled sadly, shook his head.

'I love your family, Tom. You might not believe that right now, but I do. You can give me the gun. Take Holly to the hospital. I'm prepared to trust you here, Tom. But you need to trust me. Let me do this for you and Rachel.'

A selfless act? Maybe. Perhaps I should even have been touched. But I thought there was more to it than that. My fingerprints were on the gun now. Rachel's too. I looked up towards the camera in the corner of the room. Maybe it was still recording, but when I thought of all the equipment in the stargazing pod I began to see how easily Lionel could delete or manipulate any footage that was filmed in here. If we made it to the hospital and tried contacting the police, he could easily say I pulled the trigger. Or Rachel. His word against ours. Our prints on the gun.

'Tom, we don't have a lot of time. Holly doesn't have a lot of time. You know that.'

He beckoned to me for the pistol – a little wave with his fingers.

I looked back at Ryan, gritting my teeth. Then I turned from her, slipped a hand under Rachel's good arm and helped her to her feet. Her knees gave out. I held her up. The room began to spin.

I took one slow step forwards, feeling the air empty out of my lungs. Ryan watched us keenly. I could see she was torn. Was this her opportunity? Or had she already let it slip by?

We moved closer to Lionel. He put out his hand. I gripped the pistol for a second more, my knuckles cracking, then placed the gun in his palm. Rachel shuddered. Ice chips scattered across my shoulders. Lionel nodded to me, just once, with an expression of absolute solemnity.

'You've made the right choice, Tom.'

Had I? I glanced at Ryan one last time. Was she sorry – truly sorry – for what she'd done? Or was she just scared and prepared to say anything to get out?

The doorway was ahead of us. I steered Rachel towards it and, as we stepped through, I had a plunging sensation, like we were two skydivers jumping tandem out of a plane.

'Daddy!'

I looked up at Holly and felt the warmth spread through my chest. She was weak but she smiled through the clammy bruising on her face, lifting her arms up, ready to be carried.

I placed my foot on the first tiered step and helped Rachel up alongside me. There were four empty cinema seats to my left. Brodie was propped on his elbow against the next step up. It was hard to get a read on him because of the swelling to his eyes. He looked up at Rachel, like he was searching her for something he was afraid he'd lost.

Don't try to stop us. Don't try to stop us. Don't . . .

We advanced to the second step. Another four cinema seats to our left.

'Tom?' Lionel called. 'I think you should see this.'

No. Not now. Too soon.

I swung back – no air in my lungs – and stared wild-eyed through the one-way glass as Lionel took three swift paces into the room with the pistol at the very end of his reach and the shotgun down by his side. Ryan began to burst forwards.

Lionel pulled the trigger.

A dry *click* in the room.

Rachel jerked.

Brodie grunted and shoved himself forwards off the wall.

Lionel gasped and pulled the trigger again.

Another dry *click*.

I might not know a lot about guns but I'm a quick learner. I'd watched Brodie release and reload the magazine in the pool room. When I'd lowered the pistol to my lap, I'd pressed a button on the side and a magazine had dropped out. The magazine was stashed in my trouser pocket.

Ryan continued forwards and dived at Lionel. She knocked the gun from his hand. Then she wrenched the shotgun from him, turned it, rammed the stock into his stomach, all in one fluid, athletic motion. Lionel doubled up. He spat air from his lungs.

It all happened so fast. Too fast.

Ryan shoved Lionel aside and loped out of the room, raising the shotgun as she emerged. I heard Brodie shout something. I'm not sure what. 'Move!' maybe. I like to think so, but I could be wrong.

My instincts kicked in. I pivoted from my hips. Leaned to my left. I dived for cover between the cinema seats and pulled Rachel down with me. There was a booming flash. A mighty explosion. A hot vibration in the air.

Rachel screamed.

I heard footsteps. Yells. Another scream.

I was pinned by Rachel. It was cramped between the seats. She pushed herself off me in a frenzy. The stink of gunpowder hung in the air. There was a haze of blued smoke. My ears were ringing.

I pulled myself up to my knees, clinging to the seats. I almost fell back down again. Rachel was kneeling next to Brodie. There was blood on her hands. His chest was a cratered mess.

He was listing sideways, fading out, his breaths coming in desperate heaves. He raised a hand to her face. The hand began to slip down.

'For you,' he whispered. 'All of this. Everything for . . .'

He slumped. Rachel couldn't hold him. And I didn't know what to do.

'Tom!' Lionel clutched hold of his stomach, staggering from the room. He pointed to the top of the steps. Through the misty gunpowder haze.

I turned.

Oh no. No, no, no.

I heaved myself forwards, clambered up the steps.

A terrible emptiness opened up in my chest.

No.

Holly was gone.

I stared at her vacant seat for what felt like a long time but could only have been a fraction of a second. Then I ran.

I ran like a crazy man, bursting out through the door, crashing into the opposite wall. Buster was barking in a frenzy from the living room. I sprinted towards him, pumping my legs. The corridor tilted and jolted. My vision blurred. My heart seemed to be beating from somewhere inside my head.

I skidded into the kitchen, veered to my left.

And pulled up.

Oh no. Please, no.

Ryan had one arm wrapped around Holly's neck. She was dragging her backwards. The shotgun was pressed to her side.

'Stay back,' she yelled.

That swarm of bees again. They were in my chest now, stinging me over and over, again and again.

I stared at Holly. She stared back. I flashed on the alley. I thought of how I hadn't helped her then. I wanted so desperately to help her now.

Buster barked and snarled. Then he bounded forwards, just like he had in the woods. He opened his jaws and launched himself at Ryan.

Holly screamed. The stinging pain in my chest intensified.

Ryan lashed out with one long leg and kicked Buster hard in the side.

He yelped, hobbled away. His claws skittered on the floor-boards.

Holly howled and yanked on Ryan's arm. She bit her hand. It didn't work. Ryan just grunted and rammed the gun under Holly's jaw.

I stopped moving. Stopped breathing.

Holly's neck and chin were fully extended. I could see the veins pulsing in her throat.

Rachel stumbled into the room behind me. 'Holly!' she screamed.

Buster circled woozily. His legs gave out. He crashed to the ground.

Ryan shuffled backwards with Holly, dragging her towards the sliding glass door.

'Daddy!'

Tears prickled in my eyes. My heart pummelled my ribs.

Ryan bared her teeth and kept the shotgun to Holly's throat as she hauled her out onto the deck. I stumbled after them. Into the weak morning sunshine and the smell of the pines.

Your child's life is so precious. I'd learned that in the hardest way imaginable. I'd lost Michael to this woman already. I can't begin to explain how paralysing it was to think I might lose Holly to her too.

'Tom, do something. *Please.*'

Rachel clung to me. I heard slow footsteps behind us. Lionel emerged, cradling his side, the pistol in his hand. He offered it to me.

I fumbled in my pocket for the magazine but Ryan saw it and pushed the shotgun even harder under Holly's chin.

'Don't.'

I froze and stayed locked on Holly. I wanted her to know that I was with her right now. I wanted her to know how very badly I wanted to keep her here in this world with me.

'I'm sorry,' Rachel pleaded. 'I'm so sorry. I'm so sorry. Please.'

'Let her go!' I yelled. 'It doesn't have to be like this.'

My hand clenched around the magazine in my pocket. Lionel was so close to me. It would take less than a second to snatch the gun from him. Another second to slam the magazine in the pistol. But even supposing I somehow made it without Holly getting shot – which I wouldn't – I'd already proved myself a terrible aim. There was no way I could risk trying to shoot Ryan while she had Holly so close.

I watched, stranded, as she dragged Holly on across the deck. Wind funnelled in off the jagged sea. It picked up Holly's hair and flung it in her eyes. Holly's face crumpled. She shook her head at me. In that moment, I had the feeling she was saying goodbye and I felt something inside of me give way and collapse.

They were getting very close to the corner of the lodge now. Ryan's pupils darted side to side, trying to get her bearings.

'Please,' I said. 'She's my child.'

I couldn't think what else to do. My mind raced. Still I had nothing. Maybe we should back off entirely. Wait and hope she would let Holly go. But why would she do that? We all knew the truth now. She had so much to lose . . .

There was a sudden blur of white. A sickening crack. Ryan's head whipped sideways on a crazy angle. The breath left my lungs. Her body went slack. Then the shotgun dropped from her hand, she crashed to her knees and fell face down onto the deck.

There was a ghastly dent in the side of her skull.

Holly screamed and leaped clear, pressing her hands to her face.

My chest heaved. My lungs cramped. I couldn't move.

I was staring at the figure in the white plastic coveralls standing behind Holly.

He peeled back his hood and tugged down his mask.

Adams.

Electric shivers in my arms. I thought again about the gun Lionel was holding out to me. The magazine in my hand.

Rachel wailed as Adams lifted his right arm in the air. I saw that he was holding the bloodied wheel wrench from our Volvo. I stared at Holly. I was so very far away.

'It's over,' he said, and then he opened his fist. The wrench fell to the ground. It bounced and clattered as if in slow motion. 'Talk to me about what we do now.'

It took a few seconds for my heart to start beating again. For my lungs to start working.

'Tom,' Lionel called.

I looked at him. He offered me the pistol again.

'This is what true justice is, Tom. This is how it works.'

But not for me. Not for us.

It's over.

That was a hard thing to believe in. A hard thing to trust. We were going to have to reach a compromise with Lionel on it, somehow.

But that could come later.

I turned with the magazine in my hand and tossed it into the sea. Holly shook her head as I stepped close and slowed up. Tears smeared her face. And then everything else fell away as I wrapped her in my arms. I pulled my daughter into me. I cradled her tight. I smelled her hair. I kissed her face. I didn't ever want to let go of her again. I'm not sure which one of us slumped to our knees first or if we did it together. I know we were there for only a few seconds before Rachel joined us. We cried. We kissed. Then I heard a new sound. The slow scraping of claws on the decking. We turned and Buster limped towards us past Lionel, a forlorn look in his chestnut eyes. He lifted one paw in the air and we smiled through our tears and opened our arms to him, pulling him close, holding each other as a family for the first time in as long as I could remember.

EPILOGUE

More than three weeks have gone by. I say that and it doesn't seem possible. I have moments now where what took place in the lodge feels like something that happened to another family, in another life. And then there are other moments – spells where my pulse races, my breathing goes funny and the walls around me seem to dissolve into those woods again – and I could believe I'm still being hunted, that my life since that night is nothing more than a cruel illusion.

And maybe, in some ways, that's what it is: an illusion that Rachel, Holly and I are pretending is real.

I'm living at home again. We're a family again. And not just any family. We hug and say that we love each other all the time. We eat healthy, balanced meals together and talk without staring at our phones. We stay up late, cuddled on the sofa, watching those romcoms on Netflix that Holly loves so much. Even Buster has got in on the act. We go out as a trio now for all his walks, but when we unclip his lead in the park, he doesn't run off. He prefers to stick close.

I can live that way for now, but I worry. I worry about all the things we're not saying to each other. I worry how long we can keep the darkness at bay.

Holly is doing well, considering. We took Brodie's car and

got her to a hospital almost immediately after I left things at the lodge. We claimed she'd had an early morning accident, tripping while she was walking Buster in the woods. It turned out Holly's spleen had been punctured. She was taken into surgery right away and her spleen had to be removed. Holly will need to take antibiotics every day now for the rest of her life. Rachel tells me it could have been a lot worse – that if we'd left it any longer to get to A&E, she would have died. I nod along to that, though obviously we both know it could be a lot better. The bruising to her face is almost entirely faded. It's the emotional scars that will take longer to heal.

Holly says and does all the right things, but under that brittle facade I know she's angry with both of us. She should be. For too long she came second to her brother, even – perhaps especially – after his death. I made a vow to myself when Holly was in surgery that if she pulled through I would spend the rest of my life trying to make her feel as happy and as safe as I could. I go into her room every night and sit by her bed until she falls asleep. She always keeps a light on. That kills me. And every morning I get up and shower and remind myself of my vow. Then I see Holly and my heart swells to bursting, and I realize I would do anything to save her from more pain.

I think sometimes Rachel wonders if that's why I'm really back. Sometimes I wonder the same thing. Am I home for Holly, or because it's what I genuinely want? The truth, I think, is probably a bit of both.

I still love Rachel. Deep in my heart, I know I always will. We share a bed. We make love. We kiss and fool around like teenagers. Maybe that's a reaction to how close we came to losing each other. Or maybe it's another sign that we're trying too hard to paper over the cracks in our relationship.

There's a lot of stuff to work through. When I think of the risks she took, the danger she placed us in, the secrets she kept . . . Well, like Holly, I get angry.

But then I take a breath and remind myself of *why* she did it. Of the emotional mess she was in. Of Michael. And it gets a lot more complicated.

Rachel got involved in a scheme that was immoral and crazy, and, look, maybe I'm being naive yet again, but I still believe her when she says she did it for me. I came back home for Holly. Rachel nearly forced us apart for Michael. I guess there's a symmetry in that.

You may be wondering if it helps to know how my son died. Does it bring me comfort to know he was trying to save Fiona, and that the woman who held a gun on him and caused him to crash is now dead herself?

Would you think less of me if I told you that yes, it does? Then you should also know that my heart still aches with longing for the son I'll never get to hold again; for the young man of whom I'm so very, very proud.

Michael is gone for ever – I know that – but there is one way in which I have him back. I can think of him now without my memories being burdened by that crippling sense of shame. I have Rachel to thank for that. And I do, often. But, still, I never would have pursued this outcome in the way Rachel did, and that is something, long term, I don't know if we can get past.

Today is Saturday morning. Holly has hockey practice in less than an hour. Rachel and I are going to watch. And I am busy making a picnic for us all to take to the park afterwards – under close supervision from Buster. He's fine, by the way. He shows no long-term effects from the tranquilizer he was shot with. Like Holly, his bruises have healed.

Rachel walks into the kitchen and sees me, and when she smiles I feel that same strange mix of emotions – love and gratitude and, yes, sadness too – and from the crinkling around her eyes, the misting of her pupils, I sense she feels the same things.

'Did you see the news this morning?' she asks me, though she can't quite hold my eye.

'No,' I tell her.

'They're still running the story. I wish they'd stop.'

But they won't. Not yet. The firestorm of media interest has been too intense. Who wouldn't find the mystery of four missing police detectives tantalizing?

For now, the prevailing theory remains that the four heroic members of the Met's elite drugs task force must have fallen victim to one of the London drug gangs they'd been aiming to bring down. Kate Ryan, unsurprisingly, is the focus for most of the coverage. Since the story first broke, the police have dragged in multiple suspects for questioning but there are, as yet, no solid leads. Every hack journalist and true-crime blogger seems convinced their bodies will never be found. And, of course, they won't be.

I kept up with the stories to begin with. It seemed like a necessary precaution before the stress of it got too much. So I can tell you that Detective Sergeant Nayler, the smaller man who Brodie shot in the swimming pool, was divorced with two kids. DC Kenny, the bigger man who died in the pantry, left behind a loving mother and father who've been plastered across the tabloids clutching a photograph of their only son in uniform. DCI Ryan has been lauded as an outstanding team leader and a tragic hero by none other than Assistant Commissioner Richard Weeks. DC Adams was single. Both his parents died when he was a teenager. I sometimes wonder if that has something to do with why he stepped out of those trees and bludgeoned Ryan. Perhaps it took someone who'd lost his own family to recognize the importance of saving mine.

'I'm still worried about them finding him.'

'Me too, Rachel.'

I'm pretty sure we'll always worry about Adams being found, and that that is just one of the prices we have to pay for what happened and the agreement we all made with Lionel. Oh, he couldn't keep Adams's name out of things in the end, but he did help him to get away and hide. A private helicopter flight to Europe. A new name, a new ID and ample funds in a new bank account.

Or, possibly not.

I haven't said anything to Rachel or Holly, but it occurs to me that Lionel had a much simpler and more reliable solution available to him. He's already proven himself capable of killing people, burying their bodies in those woods and getting away with it, so what would it take for him to kill one more?

I hope I'm wrong about that, but the truth is I don't know for sure either way, and I doubt I ever will. Some nights it keeps me awake. Some nights it doesn't. That's one more burden we have to bear, I suppose.

As for Brodie, again, I don't know quite what to feel about him. He saved my life, and for that I'll always be grateful. He helped uncover the truth about Michael. But by abducting and imprisoning Kate Ryan, he set our whole nightmare at the lodge in motion. Does that make him more of a bad guy than a good guy? I don't know. And perhaps it's not that simple. Because none of us left the lodge untarnished. We all have our secrets to keep.

On the other hand, I don't think it's any great mystery why Brodie acted the way he did. Rachel tells me the two of them spent a lot of time together during the weeks and months when Brodie's investigation developed. There was a period when he was keeping Ryan and her colleagues under surveillance and reporting back to my wife late at night. Was it more than a one-way infatuation? Again, I don't know. But something pushed Brodie to act when he did. There was the mugging, sure, but sometimes I think about that weekend Rachel spent alone at the lodge with Lionel and Brodie. Did he press her to make a decision then? Did something happen between the two of them? Maybe. And maybe I haven't learned my lesson, but that is not a question I've asked Rachel. I guess there are just some secrets I'd rather not know.

There is a ring at the door. I hear Holly come rushing downstairs.

'I'll get it!' she shouts.

She must think it's the postman. It's about the right time. I hear the door open. There are many seconds of silence. The door doesn't close.

Rachel and I listen to the ambient noise from out on the

street and then, as the air tightens around us, we exchange a worried glance.

Not again. Not now.

I drop the cheese I'm grating and hurry into the hallway. Holly is there, and I feel a surge of relief to see her, but something in her eyes tells me all is not well.

'Dad? I think it's for you.'

I get as far as the doorway. There's nobody there. Then I look along the path leading away from our house. The gate is open. A black BMW is parked at the kerb. A sudden coldness seeps through me. There is a door hanging open at the rear of the car.

I know I could try to ignore it. But I also know I can't dodge this forever, no matter how many more phone calls, voicemails and text messages I block or delete.

'Tom?' Rachel sees the car and tries to pull me back. 'Don't do this.'

I almost cave. I almost tell her I won't go. But then I look at Holly. I see the fear that lives in her eyes. And I remember my vow.

'I won't be long,' I tell her, not knowing if that is true. 'We'll still have plenty of time to make practice, Holly, OK?'

And then I am walking along the pathway, up to the car, feeling like a man wading out to sea, snared by an unseen rip tide.

'Get in, Tom,' Lionel says.

He's dressed in a sharply tailored suit and tie. Freshly shaved, his hair neatly cut. There is not a single blemish on his face. It rocks me. I've known Lionel for more than six years but he is a stranger to me now.

I ease in slowly. Every instinct screams at me to stop. A driver I don't recognize sits behind the wheel, acting oblivious.

'Where are you taking me?' I ask. 'Some woods? Is this more of a one-way trip?'

It's a cheap shot, and the look Lionel gives me tells me as much. Maybe I'm projecting, but I think I see some hurt in it too.

'That's all over, Tom.'

'Is it?'

He nods sagely. I would like to tell you I believe him, but I honestly can't say. Oh, I can believe he's mothballed his Scottish lodge, but what's to stop him setting up another JFA killing room somewhere else?

'You haven't been back to work, Tom.'

'I quit. Maybe I should have written you a letter?'

This time there's no doubt about the pained look he gives me, but then he shakes off my comment and leans forwards to look along the pathway to my front door, where Rachel and Holly are watching. For the briefest second, his features soften. A smile plays about his lips. Light dances in his eyes. He begins to lift a hand to wave.

I reach out and steady his wrist.

'Don't.'

He stills and looks down then, with a slight, scolded frown, and I sense he knows what I'm going to say before I say it.

'You were my friend, Lionel.'

'Do you think I would have done what I did if you weren't?'

There is a long silence between us. It feels like one of the heaviest silences I've ever known.

'You can't come here, Lionel. I don't want you contacting

my family ever again. Not in secret. Not in any way whatsoever. Do you understand?'

It takes so long for him to look up at me again that I'm startled to see the tears in his eyes.

'I told you going to my lodge would heal your family, Tom. So answer me this. Was it really so wrong?'

I don't answer him, of course, because I can't. Because to the extent we can be fixed, we are. Oh, it might not be for the reasons Lionel thinks, but the outcome is still the same, and that troubles me almost as deeply as my memories of what happened at that lodge.

'I have something for you, Tom.'

I feel a suppressed quake building inside me and I try very hard to push it back down. Is this how Lionel got the other executive members to join the JFA board? To keep the secret? Did he coerce them with evidence of the crimes they committed? Or were they willing participants from the start? I think of all the video cameras and recording equipment at the lodge.

'Whatever it is, I don't want it.'

He lifts a brown paper package onto his lap. It's about the size of a lever arch file. I watch as he rubs his hand over the paper.

'Didn't you ever ask yourself what happened to Fiona's camera, Tom? The police found her phone. They found Michael's. But no camera. Don't you find that odd?'

Not really. To the extent I *had* thought about it, I suppose I'd just assumed it had been destroyed in the crash or returned to Fiona's parents. And her parents weren't exactly keen to communicate with us in the wake of her death.

'Do you know what happened after the crash, Tom? You never asked. We think Adams, Nayler and Kenny got there immediately after the impact. They pulled Ryan out of the rear of your car. She was badly hurt, of course, but not grievously so. They waited until the following morning and then they took her to hospital. Brodie secured a copy of her patient records. The records state that Ryan had been rock climbing as part of a team-building exercise and that she suffered a bad fall. Adams was the one who hid Fiona's camera. He guessed there was a risk she had them all on film. He didn't trust the other three. He wanted to protect himself.'

I don't say anything. And probably I can't, because there is a terrible, suffocating weight spreading through my lungs.

'Take it, Tom.'

He hands me the package, and this time I don't resist. And then, somehow, I'm standing on the pavement again, watching Lionel for the very last time as he faces forwards and his car slips away. The package is cradled in my arms. Rachel and Holly watch me approach without speaking. I pass them, trembling, like a man walking into his own home with a bomb strapped to his chest.

Without saying a word, we congregate together around the kitchen table. My hands are shaking so hard I have to sit on them to still them. It is Rachel who tears open the package.

And even as Lionel's words repeat in my mind, twisting like a knife – *I told you going to my lodge would heal your family . . . Was it really so wrong?* – for the time being, I don't care.

The photograph album is faced in pale grey leather. The pages are made from a thick cream stock. There is at least one, sometimes two, photographs mounted on every page. Most are in colour. Some are in black and white.

I see the first image and my heart breaks. It just shatters. Tears run down my face. The shot of Michael and Fiona together is so perfect – and they look so perfectly happy – that I hear Rachel choke back a sob as Holly clutches my arm.

Michael is kissing Fiona's cheek. She's pressing both hands to her mouth, her eyes wide and shining, feigning shock and surprise. Afterwards there are a handful of background shots. A high-rise apartment building. An empty shopping precinct. The top level of a multistorey car park with a damaged estate car in it.

Every other print is of Michael in motion. There are images of him leaping athletically over walls. Balancing along hand-rails. Tucked up in a somersault flip. There is so much energy in the images. So much grace and vitality. We sit together in wonder, flicking through the pages and, as my heart soars and the tears blur my eyes, I realize: seeing these photographs for the first time, after not knowing they even existed, is almost like being gifted a precious few seconds more where my son is alive.

A fortnight before the crash, Michael has a week's work experience lined up at his dad's office. He's not looking forward to it. He doesn't know what he wants to do with his life but he knows it's not this.

7 a.m. and he's standing on a packed commuter train in one of his dad's too-big-for-him suits over his school shirt and tie. The train rocks and shuffles. Everyone around him looks stressed and tired, including his dad.

Michael yawns and thinks of his mum. The way she'd kissed him and ruffled his hair as she'd handed him his lunch that morning. How she'd waved him off from the house. The smile on her face. And he thinks of Holly, watching him from her bedroom window, sticking out her tongue, acting smug and superior because she knows he'll hate this – that he'll be miserable and bored.

And he is. All morning. He sits in a corner of his dad's office, at a small table, not even reading the legal document he's supposed to be flicking through. Every now and again, he glances out at the high rises scattered throughout Canary Wharf. He thinks of all the other people in their offices. Mindless drones, surrounded by piles of paper, like his dad.

It's not the kind of future Michael wants for himself. He

wants to hang with his friends, spend time with Fiona, practise his free running, maybe go to Cornwall and surf next year, go backpacking the year after that. He has so much life ahead of him. The world is so big. Michael wants to explore it all.

His dad puts the phone down, leans back in his chair, rubs his temples. He stares at the mountain of work in front of him – like a man with so much to do, in such an impossible timeframe, he can't think where to begin.

Out of nowhere, Michael feels an urge to rescue his dad from all of this. If only for a second. And so he speaks up, asking him why he became a lawyer.

His dad blinks, surprised – almost as if he'd forgotten Michael was there – and then he begins to talk. In truth, Michael isn't really listening to what his dad has to say to him. But he is thinking. He's remembering the awful commute that morning. And he's looking around this office, thinking of how his dad had seemed to physically shrink when they'd arrived and he'd flicked on the lights.

And suddenly it hits Michael that his dad doesn't want this life any more than he does. He'd rather be out in the world exploring too. Anyone would. But the reason he's here is because of Michael and Holly. Because he wants to give them choices. A future. A life.

My dad is my hero, *he thinks, and the thought is so staggering and new that Michael almost stops him and tells him right there and then. He can feel words bubbling up in his throat and he almost blurts them out:* I love you, Dad.

But he doesn't. Because too often those are not the words that teenage sons say to their fathers, or that fathers say to their sons. And so Michael waits for his dad to finish speaking and then he tells him, 'I like your office, Dad. It's pretty cool.'

In the seconds that follow – as he holds his dad's gaze and watches a confused smile soften to something more wistful on his face – Michael can almost believe his dad gets what he's really saying to him. He hopes so, anyway, although he'll never know for sure. Because the last thing Michael thinks is how his dad isn't going anywhere. There'll be plenty of time to tell him what he means to him in the years ahead.

ACKNOWLEDGEMENTS

There's a team behind every book, but I'm incredibly lucky to have such a stellar team behind this one. I owe a massive thank you to:

Vicki Mellor, my editor, as well as Matthew Cole, Charlotte Cole, Samantha Fletcher and everyone in Sales, Marketing and Publicity at Pan Macmillan who have worked so hard on this book.

Camilla Bolton, my agent, and all at the Darley Anderson Literary Agency, including Roya Sarrafi-Gohar, Sheila David, Mary Darby, Kristina Egan and Georgia Fuller, as well as Sylvie Rabineau at WME.

Nicola Anderson, James Cavanagh, Ann Cleeves, Merilyn Davies, Clare Donoghue, Vivien Green, Lucy Hanington, Stav Sherez and Tim Weaver for their input and support.

Mum and Allie, for all you do, Jessica and Jack, for mostly (not always) letting me close the study door, and – as always – Jo, who makes everything possible.

The Interview

By C. M. Ewan

It's 5 p.m. on a Friday.

You have been called to an interview for your dream job.

In a stunning office thirteen floors above the city below, you are all alone with the man interviewing you.

Everyone else has gone home for the weekend.

The interview gets more and more disturbing.

You're feeling scared.

Your only way out is to answer a seemingly impossible question.

If you can't . . . what happens next?

Read on for an extract . . .

A fist bangs on a sheet of glass.

Bangs again.

On one side of the glass, all is still and hushed.

On the other side, the air sings with shouts and screams.

A hundred and thirty feet up, in the middle of a city of nine million people, and nobody hears or sees a thing.

CV

Kate Harding

17b Beaumont St, Balham, London

kharding@mycontact.com

I am an experienced PR Account Manager, a graduate from City, University of London with a 2:1 Honours Degree in Media, Communications and Sociology, and a former flight attendant with excellent customer care and problem-solving abilities. My career goal is to secure a Senior Account Manager role that enables me to hone my creative and business expertise and take on more responsibility at a dynamic, industry-leading PR agency with a focus on the travel sector.

EMPLOYMENT

- Account Manager with Simple PR & Communications (September 2021–present)
  At Simple, I have managed a portfolio of clients including Coachman European Travel, HomeSense Holidays and Scandinavian Getaways.
- PR Account Executive rising to PR Account Manager at MarshJet Aerospace Engineering (September 2014–March 2021)
- PR Assistant at MarshJet (September 2013–September 2014)
- Flight Attendant with Global Air (September 2009–September 2013)

EDUCATION

- 2:1 Honours Degree in Media, Communications and Sociology from City, University of London
- Diploma in Air Cabin Crew Level 2
- 9 GCSEs – 4 Grade As, 4 Grade Bs, 1 Grade C

ACTIVITIES AND ACHIEVEMENTS

- I am fluent in French and Spanish. I speak good German.
- I hold an advanced First Aid at Work qualification.
- I run regularly and I enjoy swimming.

1

Friday 5.03 p.m.

The worst thing that can happen to you in an interview is getting caught in a lie. Everybody knows that. It was one more thing for me to stress about as I waited to get inside 55 Ludgate Hill.

'Come on, come on.'

The revolving glass doors were moving too slowly. Anguish tugged at my insides. I darted forwards and back, forwards and back, then finally burst free and bolted for the front desk. There were three security personnel on duty: one woman, two men. Behind them was a back room where I could see a grid of surveillance monitors flickering against a wall.

'My name is Kate Harding.' I was panting, short of breath. 'I'm late for a 5 p.m. appointment with Edge Communications.'

'I see.' The guard nearest to me lifted a phone to his ear. He had a stiff, business-like demeanour. Early sixties, balding with a moustache, dressed in a navy blazer with shiny brass buttons. 'Let me call up for you. Sign the visitor book, please.'

I grabbed a pen, scrawled down my details. My hand was shaking. I could feel perspiration bubbling on the back of my neck despite the cool lobby air.

Had I blown it already? After waiting all day Friday, a

Tube delay had forced me to run here from Blackfriars Station. I'd had anxiety dreams where I was late for my interview. Now it was actually happening.

Then there was my CV. Why had I added that line about swimming? I suppose it wasn't a *total* lie. I used to enjoy swimming. A long time ago, I was a member of a club. It had been a much more sociable way to stay fit than the gruelling dawn jogs I'd been taking around Tooting Common for the past nine months. But if they asked about the last time I'd been swimming, I'd have no idea what to say. It was definitely before my life was upended. Everything was.

The guard set down his phone. 'They're sending someone down to collect you, but they're running a little behind themselves, so they've asked if you could take a seat for the time being.'

He pointed to an area behind me and I spun to take in the lavish atrium for the first time. The lobby was enormous. There was a lot of glass and steel. Acres of limestone flooring. Far in the distance, a group of black leather sofas were arranged near a trio of gleaming elevators.

'Go right ahead. They'll find you.'

To one side of the elevators, water cascaded down over a wall of rippled slate tiles into an infinity pool. To the other, a living wall was filled with plants in varying shades of green. In the foreground, professional men and women in office attire bustled to and fro. Some held mobile phones to their ears. Others carried briefcases or document folders. Most appeared to be hurrying for the exit and, I guessed, home for the weekend.

You used to be just like them, I told myself. But somehow it only made me feel like more of an imposter.

'And if I may, Miss – *good luck.*'

I cringed. 'Is it that obvious? How nervous do I look exactly?'

The guard's two colleagues looked up from their duties and joined him in indulging me with smiles.

'Less than some,' he said. 'You may prefer not to hear this, but they've been interviewing for most of the day. But Edge Communications? I'd say you'll fit right in.'

I wished. Once, maybe, but right now I felt daunted. The glitzy atrium wasn't simply impressive – it was imposing. And just hearing about the other candidates who'd been interviewed before me was enough for my doubts to resurface in a major way.

Not for the first time I told myself that I should have said no when Maggie, my recruitment agent, had set up this interview. Deep down, I knew I'd been too easily flattered when she'd told me that my past campaigns had impressed the team at Edge. Now I found myself wondering if Maggie had lied flat out. And . . . *Oh God.* What if the team had never actually heard of me and this was all a huge waste of time?

No, I told myself. *Focus.*

I knew I was in danger of spiralling. Knew that if I wasn't careful the swirl of negative thoughts would take hold of me and put me in a spin. In the quiet centre of my mind I conjured the calm, reassuring mantra of my counsellor, a wise and worn mother of two I meet with once a fortnight in Hackney: *Now is not the time.*

And it wasn't. It couldn't be. I was stepping out of my comfort zone here – no use pretending otherwise – but I'd lived and breathed this world before. I could do it again.

'Miss? Was there something else?'

'No, I'm fine. But thank you for your help.'

I edged away from the desk, my heels echoing into the void. June in London. There was so much sunlight streaming into the atrium I had to raise my hand to shield my eyes from the dazzle.

Ahead of me, a cleaner in grey overalls was using a noisy handheld machine to polish the floor. I could smell the cleaning fluid he was spraying – something cloying and strangely familiar that conjured up a memory I really didn't need. For a dizzying moment, I could have been striding across an airport concourse again, hurrying towards a press briefing. The stutter of flashbulbs. The clamour of questions. The choking surge of emotions at the back of my throat.

A job interview.

Why was I putting myself through this?

But in the pit of my stomach, I knew the answer to that question. I was doing it because this interview might – or might not – change everything.

2

Joel White's pulse quickened as he watched Kate cross the light-filled atrium. He'd watched her from the moment she'd entered the building. He'd watched her every second since.

He watched her now, and she didn't know it, because he was standing high up on a glass walkway that criss-crossed the lobby far below, just an anonymous employee in a shirt and tie standing alongside a second man in an expensive suit, who might have been a colleague, but wasn't.

The man standing alongside him was thin, grey-haired, grim-faced. He seemed to have shrunk a size or two since his suit was last tailored and his bunched hands were wrapped around the steel banister in front of him, wringing it so tightly the metal squeaked. A high-profile businessman who'd amassed a vast personal fortune, he was a millionaire, maybe even a billionaire on paper – rich enough, anyway, that the distinction no longer mattered a great deal.

'Do you have everything you need?' the man asked, in a voice that was wheezing and constricted, a combination of ill-health, stress and deep unease. Throat cancer, Joel speculated, though he hadn't asked and wouldn't be told if he did.

He also didn't respond to the man's question. Years of conducting interviews, years of applying his own particular skills in locations all across the globe, and still it amazed him how the big beasts of the corporate world could crumble and fall apart when their reputations and livelihoods were on the line. When that happened, often enough, they would turn to him.

'I asked you a question.' The man's voice pinched and strained. 'I was assured you wouldn't let me down.'

Again, Joel ignored him. The bank of elevators was behind them and he turned without comment to press the call button. When an elevator arrived, he paused for a second before stepping in, glancing briefly at the leather folio case the man had handed him and then staring one last time at Kate Harding. As he watched her, he could feel himself changing. A contraction of his muscles. A hardening of his resolve. A low-level burning like acid in his blood.

'Answer your phone when I call you,' he told the man as the elevator doors slid closed. 'I'll get you what you need.'

3

Friday 5.06 p.m.

I was close to the seating area when a woman stepped out from behind a tall plant to my side and took hold of my arm. 'I don't want you thinking I do this for all my clients,' she whispered in my ear.

'Maggie?'

'Sit down. Smile. Let's both just pretend you're not late and I'm not having a fit about it. You can ignore my missed calls when you finally check your phone, by the way.'

'What are you doing here?'

'My job.' Maggie tugged me down into one of the sofas, taking the seat next to me and placing her handbag on her lap. Her handbag was large and no-nonsense, much like Maggie herself. She had a mop of strawberry blonde hair, keenly intelligent green eyes. Her olive trouser suit was generous at the bosom and hips, worn over a plunging white blouse. 'It's Friday evening, Kate. I was in the neighbourhood.'

'Your office is in Dulwich.'

'So I'm protecting my investment. You do know I get a bonus if you land this job?'

I peered at her. In the Zoom calls we'd had on and off during the past fortnight, I'd placed Maggie as just a few years older than me, in her mid-to-late thirties. Now, though, the fine lines around her eyes and mouth told me she was some way past forty.

'Did you think I wouldn't show up?' I asked her.

'It's probably best I don't answer that. You look great, by the way.'

I glanced down, unconvinced, still worried my look was too formal and safe for a company like Edge. I'd gone with a black pencil skirt and matching jacket over a blush silk blouse that had cost far more than I could afford to spend on it. I'd been to my local salon first thing this morning. Nothing fancy. Just a trim and a tidy-up of my fringe. Look closely, though, and you would have seen the insomnia-bags under my eyes, the hollows in my cheeks. I suppose I was lucky that the four years I'd worked as cabin crew before switching to a career in PR had taught me all the make-up tricks anyone could care to know.

'Maggie, the security guard just told me Edge have been interviewing *all day*.'

'Why worry about it? You're the one they'll want. Trust me. They'll have applicants with general PR experience coming out of their ears, but nobody with your background in the travel industry.'

'How many candidates did you send them?'

'Just you.'

I gave her a dubious look.

'*Seriously*.' She seized my hands in her fleshy palms. 'Kate, how many times do I have to tell you this role is perfect for you and you're perfect for this role? I wouldn't have stuck with you if I didn't believe that. Not after you tried to talk us both out of it enough times.'

Her brusque show of support warmed me, even as the doubts rose up in me again. It was strange to think how someone I'd only spoken with over the phone or in online meetings before now had become such a force in my life in such a short space of time. Maggie had been tenacious when she'd first approached me just over two weeks ago, even as I'd told her (less and less convincingly) that I wasn't interested in a new job. I'm not sure whether that said more about how persistent Maggie was or how much of a loner I'd become. Secretly, I knew that if she hadn't reached out to me in the first place, told me I was wasting my talents at Simple, I could have continued in the miserable rut I'd been in for months, maybe years.

'Breathe,' Maggie said. 'Relax. Take a look around with me for a second. Didn't I tell you this place was incredible?'

Together, we looked up at the lobby as the chlorinated waterfall babbled softly behind us.

And she was right. It *was* incredible. 55 Ludgate Hill – popularly known as The Mirror – was London's most recent statement high-rise building. At thirty-eight storeys high, it dwarfed the dome of nearby St Paul's Cathedral, although its signature feature was the way the exterior above the triple-height lobby was covered entirely in silvered, reflective glass panels. From outside the building nobody could see in to the uppermost floors, but I knew from my online research that they offered breathtaking views across the Thames and beyond.

The Mirror had only been officially opened in February, but there were already rumours that the company behind the project was on the verge of going bust. Construction on the site had begun before the global Covid pandemic and now that the building was completed, the business world had changed. More and more people were working from home and that meant fewer firms were looking to rent prime office space in the City. The penthouse restaurant that had grabbed press attention because of its celebrity chef was yet to open to the public, and there was talk that multiple floors remained unlet and unoccupied. That fitted with what I was seeing in the lobby. There were people here, but nowhere near as many as the project's backers must have planned for.

I found that weird. Maybe I was in the minority, but I had zero interest in working from home, and not just because my one-bedroom flat in Balham was dingy and depressing. One of the attractions of the pitch Maggie had made to me about working at Edge was the distraction a busy office could provide. My counsellor had told me it was time to put myself out there, take risks, scare myself.

Mission accomplished, I thought now.

'I still feel bad about Simon and Rebecca,' I told Maggie. 'They've been good to me.'

'And I get that. Believe me, I'd be worried if a client of mine didn't feel *guilty* about leaving their current job. But you're not doing anything wrong here, Kate. You know you're not.'

I glanced down at my hands, not feeling so sure about that. Simon and Rebecca were the husband and wife team who owned Simple PR. I was their only outside hire. I don't think it's an exaggeration to say that they took me on more out of sympathy than need. They'd been incredibly patient as I'd built my confidence back – feeling my way into the working world again – being ready with guidance and advice. I hadn't yet had the courage to tell them I was interviewing for another position.

'Kate, listen to me. It's comfortable where you are. It's safe and I understand that. But you're a star. You know it, I know it. And Edge are the best at what they do. You belong where you belong.'

I managed a half-smile. 'Have you been practising that?'

'Little bit. Did it work?'

I hummed, the knot of guilt inside me still making it difficult to admit – even to myself – that the lure of working for Edge was the main reason I was here. Edge had fancy offices in London, New York and Sydney. They represented top-tier clients and brands across the fields of entertainment, sports and business. There were even whispers of a roster of high-end clients they never openly discussed.

Like the company name suggested, Edge were best known for high-profile campaigns that were hip and wildly inventive. The kind of noisy campaigns Simon and Rebecca would roll their eyes at, because at Simple we generally did the same things Simon and Rebecca had always done – targeting traditional media, aiming for an older demographic.

Like Maggie had said, it was safe. And by safe, I knew that what she really meant was 'dull'.

I nodded, poised to thank her for coming, to summon up a show of confidence that could make her believe her faith in me hadn't been misplaced, when my phone chimed from inside my handbag.

'One second.'

'Great.' Maggie threw up her hands in mock exasperation. '*Now* she checks her phone.'

I parted my handbag, removed my iPhone. There was a short text message at the top of my lock screen.

Go for it, Sis. You'll wow them. Guaranteed xx

'My brother,' I explained. 'Wishing me luck.'

Even as I said it, a peevish thought struck me. *It should be Mark texting me. Why can't it be Mark?* But almost as soon as the thought had surfaced, I immediately forced it back down. I couldn't afford to think that way about my husband right now. It wouldn't help. And I knew I should be grateful that my brother cared enough to send me a text in the frenzied seconds he had between patients. Luke works as a cardiac nurse at St Thomas' Hospital. He's my rock. Since we lost Mum and Dad almost a decade ago, within three cruel months of one another, he's the closest family I have.

Beneath Luke's text I could see that I also had two missed calls from Maggie's phone as well as a news notification: *MarshJet Trial Hears Evidence from Family of Deceased . . .*

Too late, I snatched my eyes away, covering up my phone with my hand. My heart contracted in my chest.

Now is not the time. Now is not the—

'Kate?'

My vision darkened, a sudden coolness sweeping in over my shoulders. I clamped down on the inside of my mouth, clenching my phone tight in my fist. Maggie squeezed my hands. Her touch felt clammy and hot.

'Stay with me, Kate. You can do this. Just remember what I told you. They're going to push you, ask you unconventional questions, get you to take part in dummy exercises, even. They're all about doing things differently and surprising you. *It's who they are.* But that's OK. You're ready for this. You're going to do brilliantly, I promise.'

I nodded, forcing a smile, knowing that I was holding back from her. Because as much as I valued Maggie's advice, there were some things I couldn't talk with her about. Things I didn't talk to anyone about except my counsellor.

'Listen, there's a pub across the road from this place, on the opposite corner.' She rose to her feet. 'Did you see it? I'm going to wait for you there. Come and find me when you're done and we can celebrate together. OK?'

I winced.

'Or commiserate, then. But no excuses. I won't keep you late. I'm driving to Devon tonight to see my parents. But I'm in this for the long haul, Kate. We'll find you your perfect role, at Edge or somewhere else if it comes to it.' Her gaze shifted briefly and she nodded in the direction of the elevators. 'Looks like this is your cue.'

I swivelled to see a smiling young blonde woman approaching me as Maggie backed off and drifted away. The woman was dressed in an on-trend jumpsuit over pristine white training shoes. The instant I saw her, I immediately worried that I was wrongly dressed, over-dressed, just too plain out of touch for Edge.

'Kate Harding?'

I stood up, tugging at my skirt.

'I'm Hayley.' She thrust out her hand. 'It's so lovely to meet you. Shall we go upstairs?'